"Let's get on[...] said. "What h[...] posed to stay [...] will *never* happen again."**

"Never, huh? That's a long time."

"I'm *serious*. I've worked too hard to get where I am to let some man screw up my life."

He pulled her into his arms and tilted her face up to his.

"I think you know I'm not just 'some man,'" he said as he brushed his lips across hers. "I'm magic."

With that, he deepened the kiss. Their tongues darted and danced and he pulled her closer, wanting more.

He was reaching for the buttons on her blouse when the sharp whistle that signalled the arrival of a text message on his phone blared.

Becky jumped back, staring at him with undisguised horror.

"I'm not sure if you're magic," she whispered. "But I *am* beginning to think you might be the devil."

"I've been called worse by my competition," he said. "But usually not until after I beat them."

Dear Reader

I've worked in the world of advertising for far longer than is healthy. It's a wild and woolly world, filled with beautiful people, strong personalities, and lots and lots of drama.

It is, in other words, the perfect place to set a romance novel.

For a really long time I was too busy living in it to find time to write about it. When inspiration finally did strike it was National Novel-Writing Month (or NaNoWriMo, as those of us insane enough to participate like to call it), and I had thirty days to pound out a fifty-thousand-word novel.

For twenty of those days the words flew through my fingers and on to my computer screen faster than I could speak them. Unfortunately on day twenty-one I discovered I was telling the wrong story. The words stopped, the story stalled, and Mark and Becky took up residence in my head.

They stayed there for almost four years. And, let me tell you, they were obnoxious house guests—always whispering in my ear, trying to get me to write the right story and set them free.

I finally did it last fall, during the *So You Think You Can Write* contest. I didn't win, but Mark and Becky caught the right editor's attention. And now, less than five months later, I'm writing you this letter.

It's been the adventure of a lifetime. A dream come true. And one heck of a relief—Mark and Becky have finally vacated my head.

If you enjoy this story one-tenth as much as I enjoyed writing it you're in for a treat. They're delightful people, living in a delightfully insane world.

Thanks for reading!

Amber

ALL'S FAIR
IN LUST & WAR

BY
AMBER PAGE

Published in Great Britain 2014
by Mills & Boon, an imprint of Harlequin (UK) Limited,
Eton House, 18-24 Paradise Road, Richmond, Surrey, TW9 1SR

© 2014 Amber Page

ISBN: 978-0-263-25024-4

Harlequin (UK) Limited's policy is to use papers that are natural, renewable and recyclable products and made from wood grown in sustainable forests. The logging and manufacturing processes conform to the legal environmental regulations of the country of origin.

Printed and bound in Spain
by Blackprint CPI, Barcelona

Amber Page has been writing stories since—well, since she could write, and still counts the pinning of her 'Bubble People' tale to the classroom bulletin board in the third grade as one of her happiest childhood memories.

She's also an avid reader, and has been addicted to romances since she first discovered them on the dusty shelves of her favourite library as a young teen. The nerdy little bookworm she was is still pinching herself to make sure that this whole 'getting published by Mills & Boon®' thing is real.

When not penning Happily-Ever-Afters, Amber works as an advertising writer in the heart of Indiana, where she lives with the love of her life, their daughter, and a menagerie of furry animals. She also blogs, gardens, and sometimes even manages to sneak in a few hours of sleep.

Don't ask her how she does it all. She's too tired to remember.

ALL'S FAIR IN LUST & WAR
is Amber Page's debut book
for Mills & Boon® Modern Tempted™
and is also available in ebook format
from www.millsandboon.co.uk

DEDICATION

To my husband, my biggest cheerleader and occasional butt-kicker. Thank you for refusing to let me give up.

To Allison, Amanda, Christina, Meagan, Rhonda and Tanya, whose speed-reading skills and smart critiques helped make this book what it is.

And to everyone else who cheered me along the way (you know who you are).

PROLOGUE

MARK AWOKE SLOWLY, his mouth fuzzy and his limbs strangely heavy. He rolled over, expecting to see...who? Certainly not the empty pillow that greeted him.

Head spinning slightly, he lifted himself up on his elbow to look around the room. He was in his hotel room, right? Seeing his laptop on the desk, he decided it was probably safe to assume he was still in Vegas and hadn't hopped on a plane to Bangladesh or something.

He kept his gaze moving, noting two wine glasses, a knocked-over bottle of red wine—damn, he hoped they didn't charge him for that stain on the carpet—and there, by the heavy hotel room door, a pair of cheetah-print stilettos.

Suddenly memory came rushing back.

Walking down to the AdWorld closing party. Seeing the pretty blonde in the tight red dress giggling into her phone. Feeling compelled to talk to her. And then—*wham!* Being hit in the gut by a lightning bolt of lust when she turned to grin up at him with her sparkling green eyes.

He would have done anything to get closer to her. To get to know her.

Which was probably why he'd found himself doing something totally out of character.

"I'm Mark," he'd said, taking her hand in his and grazing her knuckles with his lips. "May I have the honor of escorting you this evening, my lady?"

She'd swallowed loudly, and he'd seen the desire sparking in her eyes.

Nonetheless, she'd been as cool as ice when she'd answered him. "I'd love that. Shall we?"

He'd held out his arm for her to take and together they stepped through the ballroom doors into the strobe-lit party beyond.

That had been followed by copious drinking, he was sure. His mind showed him an image of her gazing at him uncertainly before raising a tequila glass.

"Let's toast," she'd said. "To one wild night."

"To one wild, scandalous night," he'd answered.

And there'd been dancing. He remembered how she'd laughed as she spun away, then melted when he drew her close again. And how sweet her lips had tasted when he'd pulled her in for a kiss...

The first of many kisses.

Eventually she'd clung to him and said, "Mark, I can't believe I'm saying this, but I *need* you. Take me back to your room?"

What had followed had been one of the most...no, *the* hottest night of his life.

She'd been so hot, so willing to do anything... And when they'd finished she'd rolled over and said, "Wanna do it again?"

His answer had been, "Hell, yes."

But what was her name again?

Just then the bathroom door opened and she stepped out, engulfed in the hotel-issue robe, her long blond hair dripping down her back. She looked at him and smiled, green eyes sparkling.

The lightning bolt hit home again.

"Becky," he said. Her name was Becky.

"Hey, gorgeous," she said.

"Hey, yourself. What are you doing up so early?"

"Oh," she said, a momentary frown crossing her small face. "My flight leaves in a few hours, and I've got some work to do this morning. I figured I should probably get a move on."

"Ah," he said, overcome with an inexplicable sense of disappointment. "I thought maybe we could go get some breakfast. Or, you know, have breakfast in bed." Which, honestly, had been the last thing on his mind until she'd emerged from the bathroom. But once he'd seen her he'd been able to think of nothing he'd rather do other than peel that giant robe off her tiny frame.

She gave him a pained smile and perched on the edge of the bed.

"I'd love to, but you know how it goes. Duty calls."

Reading her tense body language, Mark realized it was no use. He also knew he wasn't ready to let her go yet. "All right. I understand," he said slowly, seeking a conversational gambit that would keep her talking. "You know, we never even talked about our jobs. What do you do?"

"I'm a copywriter. For an agency in New York—SBD," she said slowly.

"Really? What a coincidence. I'm starting a new gig—"

Gently, she placed her hand over his mouth. "You know what? Don't tell me about you. Last night was—well, it was magical, but I'm not looking to start a relationship. Even a casual one. If you don't mind, I'd just like to think of you as Mark the Magic Man from Las Vegas...not a real person I might run into at the supermarket."

Wow. That was a first. Usually it was *him* trying to duck out while a girl tried to pry information out of him. He wasn't so sure he liked being on this end of things. But his pride wouldn't allow him to admit that to her.

"Hmm," he said. "I kind of like being a Magic Man. Maybe I should go into business."

She threw her head back and laughed, and suddenly the tension eased. Then she leaned forward and kissed him. Hard.

"Thank you for last night. Believe me when I tell you it's one I'll never forget."

He smiled. "Me neither," he said. And he meant it.

Moments later Becky finished getting dressed and, holding her heels in one hand, she blew him a kiss.

"Bye, Magic Man."

"Bye, Gorgeous Girl."

And then she was gone.

"Until tomorrow, then," he said to himself.

Reaching for his iPad, he loaded up the search engine. It was time to look up his gorgeous new coworker.

CHAPTER ONE

BECKY WAS ENGROSSED in the dreary task of sorting through her inbox, attempting to make sense of the three hundred and fifty-seven emails that had accumulated while she was in Vegas, when a cardboard coffee cup was slammed down on her desk.

"One venti dark roast with a splash of vanilla soy milk," Jessie said. "Just the way you like it."

Becky looked up and grinned at her redheaded friend.

"Aw, thanks, Jessie. You didn't have to do that."

Jessie shrugged her coat off, threw it on the visitor's chair, then collapsed at her desk.

"It's bribery. Now, *spill*."

"Spill? You want me to spill this delicious coffee?"

Jessie threw her rainbow-colored scarf at her. "Don't be an idiot. You know what I want to know. What happened after you texted me Saturday night? Were you able to prove to yourself that your libido isn't dead?"

Becky blushed. "It's alive and kicking," she said. "And very insistent."

"Woo-hoo! My girl scored! I knew you could do it!" Jessie said, grinning. "Now, tell me the juicy bits."

Becky shook her head. "A lady never kisses and tells," she said, laughing.

"Give me a break," Jessie said, rolling her eyes. "I've known you for ten years, and in all that time you've never kept a secret from me. Give it up, sister."

Becky shook her head again. While it was true that she

and Jessie had always told each other everything, this felt different. Special.

"I'm sorry, Jessie. It just doesn't feel appropriate to talk about it here. Besides, you know what they say. What happens in Vegas…"

Just then her boss's voice rumbled from the vicinity of her open office door. "Is supposed to stay in Vegas, right?"

Becky whirled, readying a snappy comeback. But what she saw stopped her in her tracks.

Her boss, David, was standing there, smiling. And with him was…Mark.

Mark? How could Mark be standing in her office? Becky stared at him, mouth open. It was not possible. Completely impossible, in fact.

Mark belonged in Vegas, not in New York City.

Heat flared in her belly as she remembered the last time they'd met. She'd been texting Jessie, trying to find the courage to walk into the closing night party by herself.

Just picture them standing in their underwear…then stalk the guy that makes you drool, Jessie had texted.

"Right. Underwear," she'd said to herself. "Must picture delicious-looking men in underwear."

And that was when she'd heard Mark's rumbling voice for the first time.

"Well, if you're looking for volunteers, I happen to be available."

"What?" she'd yelped, whirling to face the interloper. Then her heart had stopped. The man smiling at her was the living, breathing definition of delicious, from the tips of his artfully rumpled black hair to the toes of his polished leather shoes.

Brilliant white teeth flashed as he grinned down at her. "If you need help. Picturing what a man looks like in his underwear, I mean. I'm happy to serve as a model."

Becky's face flamed. "Oh, I…uh…no one was supposed

to hear that. I just…I was having trouble walking into the party by myself. My friend suggested I picture everyone in their underwear. As, you know, a motivator."

Mr. Gorgeous tilted his head back and laughed, and as he did Becky felt it. The zing. The tingle. If she'd been alone she would have done a happy dance. He'd just proved she wasn't dead inside!

Now that he was standing in her office, she kind of wished she had been.

Becky shook her head to clear it. She needed to pay attention to the conversation that was happening now if she wanted to make sense of the situation.

"Yeah, you're supposed to leave all the juicy details at the airport," Jessie said. "But I was trying to convince Becky to give me some of the gory details anyway."

"Any luck?" asked Mark, giving Becky a sidelong glance.

"None." Jessie pouted.

"Well, I was there," he said. "You didn't miss much. Although the closing night party was unexpectedly awesome."

Becky's head snapped up. Was he teasing her? And, if he was, how dared he? Mark just looked at her with a half smile on his face, his dark eyes glinting mischievously.

"That's what Becky said. Did you two meet?" Jessie asked.

"No!" Becky practically shouted.

"Yeah, you could say that," Mark said at the same time.

Becky stared at him. He said nothing, just quirked one damnably expressive eyebrow at her and leaned back against the doorframe, letting her take the lead.

"Well, what I meant was we didn't really spend much time together," she said.

Just twelve mind-blowing hours and fifty-three bone-melting minutes. Not that she'd been counting or anything.

Her traitorous mind flashed back to their first kiss. The

way he'd claimed every part of her mouth and set her whole body aflame. Within seconds she'd known she wanted more from him than a few kisses.

But it was only supposed to be for one night. If she'd known he'd turn up here she would have never…

"Mark, here, is an amazingly talented art director," her boss said, reaching up to clap him on the back. "I've brought him in on a freelance basis to work on a special project. And I want you to work with him, Becky."

"Me?" she squeaked. "But I'm busy with… I mean, I've got…"

"Whatever you currently have on your plate will be given to someone else," her boss replied. "I need you on this. Be in my office at eleven. We'll talk."

Becky snapped her mouth shut, knowing further protest was useless and foolhardy. When David told you to do something, you did it. At least you did if you wanted to keep your job.

Which she did. Unfortunately.

"Okay," she said. "I'll see you then."

"Good," he answered. "Then I won't keep you any longer. Come on, Mark."

After they were gone Becky put her head down on her desk, banging it lightly against the keyboard.

"Why, universe, *why?* Why would you do this to me?"

"Becky? What's wrong?" Jessie asked.

Becky shook her head mutely.

"Oh, come on, you can tell me. You have to."

Becky knew she was right. If she didn't, her soon-to-be-bizarre behavior wouldn't make much sense. And if there was one person she didn't want to alienate it was Jessie.

Besides, Jessie was the only one who knew what had happened…*before.* And what she had been trying to prove to herself that night in Vegas.

Becky got up to close the door before turning to face

her friend. Blowing her hair off her forehead, she said, "It was him."

"Him? Who? I'm not following," Jessie said.

"Mark. Mark was the man I met in Las Vegas. And things went a little bit further than I had planned."

"What do you mean?"

"I spent the night with him…" Becky groaned.

"Are you kidding me?" Jessie asked, falling back into her chair.

Becky shook her head.

Jessie tilted her head back and howled with laughter.

"Oh, my God. Only you… This is…it's unbelievable."

Becky glared at her. "I really don't think this is funny."

"Of course you don't. But, girl, you gotta believe me when I tell you it is."

Easy for her to say. She wasn't the one living in a nightmare.

Finally Jessie sobered.

"All right, so Mr. One-Night Stand has become Mr. Works Down the Hall. What are you going to do about it?"

"Nothing," Becky said flatly.

"Why? Was it…bad?"

Pictures from their night together flashed through Becky's brain. His lips kissing her mouth. His tongue on her breast. His hands…everywhere.

"It was amazing."

"Did you hit the big O?"

Becky blushed. "Oh, yeah. More than once."

Jessie looked thoughtful. "Then why not see if this could go somewhere? You know—like, casual relationshippy. Fate seems to be telling you it should."

Becky stood up, restless. "You know better than anyone why not. After everything that happened with Pence I'll never have a relationship with someone I work with again."

Jessie came up behind her and hugged her shoulders.

"I understand. But, Becky, that was a long time ago. You were a different person. And he was your boss, not a coworker. Besides, you can't let him ruin your whole life. If you do, he wins."

Sneaking a look at the clock on the wall, she groaned.

"We'll have to talk about this more later, Jessie. I gotta go to the Hall of Doom."

"All right, girl. Knock 'em dead."

Mark wasn't sure how much more of this small talk he could take.

He'd been sitting in David's office for what felt like hours, talking about everything except the reason he was here. He now knew where the bald man's favorite golf course was—South Carolina—what he preferred to drink—bourbon, straight up—and even how he had gotten his name—his mom had named him after Michelangelo's *David.*

But he still didn't know what his first assignment was going to be or why it had to be secret. When David had called him to see if he might be interested he'd said only that he needed help winning a giant piece of new business—one that had the potential to change the future of the agency.

That was interesting enough, but it was what David had said next that had sold him on the job.

"Mark, I've been searching everywhere for someone who can help me bring this home. When your name came up I knew you were the man for the job. I need you on this."

"How did you get my name?" Mark had asked, afraid that it was another one of his stepfather's pieces of charity.

"Mark, you've taken home gold from almost every major advertising competition there is. Your name is everywhere."

Which meant this was a job he'd gotten on his own merits—not through his damned stepfather's connections.

Even better, David had all but promised him a permanent spot in the creative leadership team once they landed the account.

It was the opportunity he'd spent the past ten years working toward. He couldn't wait to get started.

He just wished he knew what Becky had to do with it.

When he'd looked her up, he'd been amazed at how talented she seemed to be. In the five short years she'd been working as a copywriter she'd earned herself numerous awards. The whole reason she'd been in Vegas was because she was being honored with another award—this one for a social-media campaign she'd masterminded that had gone viral.

In short, she was as amazing in the boardroom as she was in the bedroom.

And what he wouldn't give to experience that again!

He remembered how hot she'd looked, standing in his room clad only in her red lace bra and panties. And how much better she'd looked out of them…

Unfortunately the look on her face when she'd found him standing in her office had been completely and utterly horrified—and, if he wasn't mistaken, more than a little bit furious. He didn't think she was having the same kinds of thoughts he was having right now.

Just then there was a soft knock on the door.

"Come in," David said.

The door opened and Becky quietly entered the room.

He wasn't sure how it was possible, but she looked even sexier in her blazer and jeans than she had wearing a cocktail dress.

She flashed a quick look at him, and flushed when he caught her eye. Man, how he'd love to see how far down that flush went.

"Thank you for coming, Becky, my girl," David boomed. Although he couldn't have been much more than forty, the man mimicked the vocal mannerisms of a *Mad Men*–style ad man. "Sit, sit, sit. We have a lot to talk about."

She glided across the thick red carpet and sat primly in the oversize club chair next to Mark.

"I trust you had a good time in Vegas, my dear?" David asked.

Becky seemed to force out a smile. "It was amazing, David. Thank you so much for letting me go."

"Of course—you deserved it. Besides, I knew you were one woman I could trust not to get too carried away in Vegas. I would have never sent that partner of yours. She's trouble with a capital *T*."

Becky's laugh sounded even more forced than her smile had been. "Yeah, you know me. Married to my job and all that."

"Oh, not to worry, Becky. Sooner or later a fine-looking girl like you is bound to get snapped up. Then you'll be too busy having babies to write brilliant campaigns for me anymore. That's how it always goes. Right, Mark?"

Mark was floored. People still talked like *that?* In an *office?* It was a miracle this guy hadn't been slapped with a multimillion-dollar lawsuit yet. Or, judging from the fury flashing in Becky's eyes, murdered.

"I don't know about that, David. I know plenty of working mothers who—"

David cut him off. "Right, right. I know. Girls can do anything men can—blah, blah, blah. None of that matters right now, because my brilliant little sparrow is as single as they come…and I'm going to be keeping you both too busy for her to change matters any."

Becky sucked in a breath and seemed about to say something, but she never got the chance.

"All right. Enough of this chitchat. Let's get down to business, shall we? You two are among the most talented creatives this business has to offer," David said. "And I'm going to need every bit of juice you've got. We've been asked to take part in the agency search for Eden. You both know what that is?"

Becky nodded. "The yogurt company?"

"You got it," David said. "They're coming out with a new line of low-fat, all-natural Greek yogurt flavors designed to get all those pretty hipster ladies hot and bothered. Our job is to figure out how to do that. And, since their advertising budget is a quarter of a billion dollars, we damn well better nail it."

Becky practically bounced up and down in her chair. "Oh, I'd love to get my hands on that one," she said.

"Oh, those pretty little hands are going to be all over it. So are yours, Mark. Just…er…hopefully not on the same spot at the same time!" he said.

Mark laughed uncomfortably. "No chance of that happening, sir." At least not that David needed to know about.

"Good. Now, the Eden people tell me they don't want any 'suits' working on their account. They want something young and fresh…something none of our existing creative directors are. That means you two have the opportunity of a lifetime."

David got up from his chair and started to pace.

"So here's what we're going to do. We're going to break the agency into two creative teams. Becky, you're going to head up one. Mark, you'll be in charge of the other. Whichever one of you comes up with the winning concept and sells it to the client will win a fifty-thousand-dollar bonus—and become the youngest creative director this agency has ever had."

Mark blinked slowly, trying to wrap his head around this new twist. David had never said anything about a competition.

"You're making me compete for the creative director position?" asked Becky, her eyes sparking angrily in an otherwise pale face. "But you told me that when I came back from AdWorld the job was as good as mine!"

"It is," David said. "All you have to do is win the Eden account."

Mark watched as Becky sprang up from her chair. There was no doubt that murder was on her mind.

"I will," she said from between clenched teeth. Then she turned to glare at Mark. "And don't you dare think for a second that you've got a shot!"

With that, she strode from the room, controlled fury in every movement. Good thing he had no problem with beating a sexy woman at her own game, because there was no way he was losing *this* job.

Turning to David, he said, "This competition's going to be quite a challenge."

"I'm counting on you to win," David said. "Don't let me down."

"I won't."

Becky slammed her office door so hard the wall shook.

"Wow. What's up *your* butt?" Jessie asked.

"David," Becky said.

"Ewww, that sounds uncomfortable!" Jessie giggled.

Becky glared at her. "It's not funny," she said. "That stupid blowhard is trying to give away my promotion again."

"The one he swore would be yours after you got back from Vegas?"

"The one and the same." Becky sighed, her heels tapping a staccato tune across the cement floor as she paced.

Jessie grabbed Becky's coat. "All right, you're going to tell me what's happened. But not here. A discussion like this calls for hot-fudge sundaes."

* * *

"You don't have to win this by yourself! You've got your whole team behind you," Jessie said between bites of hot fudge.

"I don't know who's on my team yet," Becky said, picking up her spoon, watching as the melting ice cream dripped back into her bowl. "I could get stuck with anyone."

"Did David lay out any rules when he said the creative department was going to be split in half?"

Becky shook her head.

"Then I vote we make the rules for him," Jessie said, grabbing a pen and paper out of her green velvet purse. "All right. No thinking allowed. Tell me who would be on your dream team."

"You," Becky said slowly.

"Yeah, well, obviously. Who else?"

Becky fell silent and looked out of the window at the busy street outside. Three girls walked arm in arm, laughing and talking as they went. Just then one lone man broke through their line, forcing their arms apart. They let him through, but shot up their middle fingers at him after he passed.

"I know what we need," she said, excitement zinging through her pores. "Jessie, we need girl power. Let's make this a battle of the sexes."

"Wait—what?"

"David thinks women creatives don't have it in them to be as good as men. Let's prove him wrong. Let's gather all the women in the department on our team and let Mark have the men."

"But there are more guys than girls in our department. It won't be an even match," Jessie said.

"Numbers aren't everything," Becky said. "Especially since the product in question is aimed squarely at women our age.'"

Jessie put down her spoon. "You, my dear, are brilliant."

"Well, yeah," Becky said. "Haven't you seen my awards shelf?"

"I have." Jessie snorted. "You think it's bigger than Mark's?"

"Hmm, I don't know," Becky said, her mind showing her wicked images of Mark's thick penis twitching in her palm as she kissed his muscled chest. "I honestly don't know much about him at all. Other than the fact that he's magic…"

"Magic?"

Becky started, reluctantly letting her daydream disappear.

"That's what I told him he was. Magic Man from Vegas."

Jessie stared at her, her blue eyes almost green with jealousy. "Man, that must have been one good night."

"The best," Becky said. Seeing the question in Jessie's eyes, she put her hand up in a "stop" gesture. "But it was just one night. I don't want or need a man in my life right now. What I need," she said, grinning, "is a team of Magic Women. Let's go put it together."

"I *knew* my girl was in there somewhere. And—" Jessie grinned, handing Becky the check "—since you're about to be fifty thousand dollars richer, I'll let you get this."

Becky rolled her eyes. "Fine," she said. "But only because you're about to work your ass off for me."

Mark was staring out through the window of his office at the crowds teeming past on Madison Avenue, wondering what on earth he had gotten himself into.

Usually he was brought in to save the day. Agencies never called him until they were facing a problem they couldn't solve—a challenge they couldn't meet. He got to play the part of vagabond hero. He came in, slayed the dragon, claimed a few hot nights with the delicious advertising damsels he had rescued, then left.

He didn't get to know the other players in the story. Never bothered to worry about whose toes he was stomping on, or what effect his actions had on those left behind when he rode off into the sunset.

His life, both professional and personal, was very much a case study in the "Wham, Bam, Thank You, Ma'am," approach to life. And that was the way he liked it.

After all, the one and only time he'd allowed himself to fall in love he'd found out the hard way that it had been his stepfather's name—or, more aptly, his money—that had gotten him the girl. And when she'd found out that Mark would never inherit the family fortune Sandra had turned to someone who *did* have top billing on a rich man's will.

The day he'd found Sandra in bed with his stepbrother hadn't been the first time he'd cursed his stepfamily, but it had been the last time he'd admitted to being part of it.

These days he didn't need anybody or anything. Well, nothing except for a killer job and a place among advertising's greats—a place he'd earned on his own.

So why did a certain blonde keep interrupting his thoughts?

Just then Becky strode in, fire in her eyes.

"Wow, hey—thanks for knocking," he said, trying to ignore the way his pulse quickened when she entered the room.

She stalked forward until she was standing directly in front of him. She took a long, slow look around the room and he knew she must be taking in the overly plush carpet, richly upholstered furnishings, the floor-to-ceiling windows and comparing it with her own small if brightly colored closet.

"Nice setup," she said. "What'd you do? Sleep with David to get it?"

He snorted. "I think you know that's not the way my tastes run, babe."

Her face flushed, and he would have given anything to know what she was thinking. She looked up at him and he could see the heat veiled behind her professional fury.

"Let's get one thing clear," she said. "What happened was supposed to stay in Vegas, just like David said. It will *never* happen again."

"Never, huh? That's a long time."

She looked away quickly, but not before he saw the desire flashing in her eyes.

"I'm *serious*," she said, folding her arms across her chest. "I've worked too hard to get where I am to let some man screw up my life again."

The disdain in her voice struck deep. So she thought she could just dismiss the maddening attraction that raced between them, huh? It was time to prove her wrong.

He pulled her into his arms and tilted her face up to his, giving in to the urge he'd been fighting since she'd walked into the room.

"I think you know I'm not just 'some man,'" he said, as he brushed his lips across hers. "I'm magic."

With that, he deepened the kiss. For a second she stiffened, but then something in her seemed to give. With a soft moan, she relaxed against him and opened her mouth.

He lost himself in the chocolate-flavored cavern as hunger roared to life. Their tongues darted and danced and he pulled her closer, wanting more.

He was reaching for the buttons on her blouse when the sharp whistle that signaled the arrival of a text message on his phone blared.

Becky jumped back, staring at him with undisguised horror.

"I'm not sure if you're magic," she whispered. "But I am beginning to think you might be the devil."

Mark took a breath, shaken by how fast he had lost control. Obviously the heat that had sparked between them in Vegas had been no fluke.

"I've been called worse by my competition," he said. "But usually not until after I beat them."

She briefly closed her eyes, and when she opened them again her stare was fiercely competitive.

"Right. The competition. I came to tell you that I've chosen my team. I'll take the women—you take the men."

"A battle of the sexes, huh? All right, if that's the way you want to play it," he said, still trying to get himself under control.

"No, that's the way I plan to *win* it," she said. "I never lose."

"Neither do I, Gorgeous Girl," Mark said, getting angry. "But guess what? One of us is going to. And it won't be me."

She took a deep breath and straightened her spine.

"Yes. It will. This job is mine and there's no way I'm going to let you steal it," she growled, then strode from the room.

"I'm not going to steal it. I'm going to earn it," he said to her departing back.

And he would. He just hoped he didn't have to crush her in the process.

CHAPTER TWO

BECKY LOOKED AT the team gathered around the tempered glass conference table. All eight women in the SBD creative department were looking at her expectantly.

"Raise your hand if David has ever belittled your abilities," she said.

Eight hands shot into the air.

"That's what I thought. Now, raise your hand if you'd like a chance to prove that chauvinist pig wrong."

Again hands shot into the air, this time accompanied by hoots and hollers.

Becky smiled. "Good. Today's your lucky day, ladies. We're going to win a two-hundred-and-fifty-million-dollar piece of business—and we're going to do it without the help of a single man."

Her crew burst into spontaneous applause.

"Now, let's get down to business. Cheri. What do you think of when I say delicious low-fat Greek yogurt?"

"Um…breakfast?" the brunette answered.

Becky turned to the whiteboard and wrote "BREAKFAST" in caps.

"Good. What else? Tanya?"

"Healthy."

Becky wrote it down.

"What else? Anyone?"

"A shortcut to skinny," Jessie said.

"Oh, I like that," Becky said, writing it down and underlining it. "Let's explore that."

"Not just skinny. Strong," someone else said. "Because it's got lots of protein in it."

"Popeye!" Tanya said.

Becky laughed. And then inspiration struck.

"Forget Popeye. This yogurt is for Olive Oyl. It's Olive's secret weapon for kicking Popeye's ass!" she said.

The women around the table laughed.

"Now we're on to something," Jessie said. "Here—give me the marker."

Becky handed it over and Jessie drew a ripped Olive Oyl, flexing her guns, one foot resting on top of a prone Popeye.

"Eden Yogurt. For the super-heroine in you," Jessie wrote.

Becky stepped back with a grin on her face, feeling the giddy high that always struck during a good brainstorming session.

"Ladies, we *are* on to something here. Really on to something. Something no guy would think of. So let's make sure they can't steal it. Tanya, do you know where there's any black paper?"

She nodded.

"Great. Go get it. We're going to make ourselves a good old-fashioned, women-only fort!"

A short while later all the conference windows were blocked off with thick black paper.

Jessie handed Becky the sign she'd made. It read, "Women at Work. No Boys Allowed" in pink glitter.

Becky skipped over to the door, tape in hand. She was just about to stick it up when she saw Mark approach. Opening the door, she waggled her sign at him.

"We've already come up with an idea that's going to kick the ass of anything you can come up with," she said, and grinned.

"Oh, really? Then why all the secrecy?" he asked with a raised eyebrow.

"Well, you're already in the boys' club. We thought it only fair that we create a girls' club with an equally exclusionary policy."

"I'll have you know I don't take part in any boys-only activities. I far prefer the company of women."

"Well, right now the women of this agency do not want your company. So go play with the boys. We'll let you back in after we beat you and all your testosterone-addled buddies."

He sighed. "Becky, Becky, Becky. How many times do I have to tell you? You can't beat me. I'm magic."

She sighed in return. "Mark, Mark, Mark. How many times do I have to tell you? You can't beat us. Talent beats magic every time."

"You go ahead and believe that," he said. "But soon you'll be kissing up to your new boss."

"Nope," she said. "Soon you'll be kissing this." And she slapped her denim-clad rear.

"You'd like that," he said.

"I would. Especially if you did it while I was booting your butt out of the office," she said, slamming the door.

He didn't need to know how very much she would love to kiss every inch of his magnificent body—and to have him kiss hers in return. Again.

She would beat him and then he'd be gone, taking his career-endangering sexual magnetism with him.

She had to. If she didn't she'd be lost forever.

Mark sat behind his heavy oak desk, the eerie white light of his monitor providing the only break in the darkness.

He was trying to polish an ad layout, but every time he turned his attention to the screen Becky's mocking face filled it.

Accusing him of being in the boys' club was pretty rich. Truth was, he didn't have a single close friend—in fact, he didn't have *any* male friends. Not real ones, anyway. The last time he'd had a best friend he'd been in sixth grade. His mom had still been single and they'd still been coexisting fairly peacefully, even if she'd never stopped moaning about how tough it was to be a single parent.

Then Bill had entered their lives, and everything had gone down the toilet.

Mark called up Facebook and scanned his friends list, searching for the familiar name. It didn't take long. He clicked onto Tom's profile, telling himself he was just curious. Not lonely.

Tom's page was filled with pictures of his goofy grinning kids and the short, plump brunette who had married him. He wasn't rich. Or particularly successful. But he did seem happy.

Mark leaned back in his chair and sighed. If things had been different—if he'd stayed in the working-class neighborhood where he'd been born instead of being forced to move into the frigidly upper-class world his mom had married into, where nothing mattered more than money— would he have a life like Tom's?

Would he have a wife? Kids?

Unbidden, an image of Becky holding a baby popped into his head. Feeling a sharp pang of panic, he shook his head to clear it. He didn't want a wife or kids. All he had to do was picture Sandra on the day she'd married his stepbrother to remind himself that the only kind of marriage that worked was one based on money. And he was hardly sugar daddy material.

All he needed was a distraction. Pulling out his phone, he scanned his contacts for one of his favorite sex buddies. A little sexting would straighten him right out.

* * *

Becky stood in front of the big laser printer in the central creative area, hands on hips. All her senses were on high alert. She was printing out her team's latest concepts and she didn't want anyone from the opposing side to get a glimpse.

Fortunately it was quiet in the agency. Most of the office doors were closed, and those stuck in the wall-less cube maze were plugged into their headphones. The only sounds were the click-clacking of keyboards and the occasional muffled curse word.

Finally the printer started to hum. Becky took another quick look around, but saw no movement.

She relaxed her guard, pulling out her phone to take a quick peek at her Twitter feed. She'd lost all track of what was going on outside the advertising bubble she lived in.

Suddenly she heard paper shuffling behind her. She whirled just in time to see Mark snatching her ads off the printer.

"Hey, give those back!" she snapped, reaching for the papers in his hand.

"In a minute," he said, turning his back on her. "But not before I see what you're working on."

"That's none of your business," she said, making another grab for them.

"That's what you think," he said, then strode off down the hall with her printouts.

Swearing silently to herself, she hurried after him, hoping with every fiber of her being that no one was watching them. She didn't need her team to see how easily the other side had managed to outwit her.

Once he reached his office he sat down on the front of his desk, still staring thoughtfully at her designs. She slammed the door, then launched herself at him.

"Give. Them. Back," she said, trying to snatch them from him.

He easily deflected her attack, then surprised her by pulling her against him. She went still as she registered his closeness, the heat emanating from his body putting her nerves on high alert.

Damn, he smelled good. Like grass and clean air with a hint of musk.

"Just chill out," he said, from somewhere over her left ear. "I'm not going to steal your ideas. I've got plenty of my own. I just wanted to sneak a peek."

Forcing herself out of the hormone-induced fog his presence induced, Becky pulled away. How was it possible to be so attracted to someone so infuriating?

"Fine," she said, holding her hand out. "You've had your peek. Hand 'em over."

He did, looking at her with a strangely intense expression.

"Don't you want to know what I think?"

Of course she did. "No."

"Well, I'll tell you anyway. I think they're pretty awesome."

"Oh." That wasn't what she had expected him to say. "Really?"

He nodded. "It's a really original idea. One I never would have come up with. The only thing is…"

Instantly anger sparked in her brain. Of course he couldn't let the compliment ride. Men never could. "The only thing is *what?*"

"Hey, don't get mad. I was just going to say that you might try to push the design. The copy carries it, but I think your art directors could give you more."

She looked down at the ads in her hands. He was right. She'd been thinking the same thing.

"Thank you for the advice. But I think we're doing just fine. Jessie is killing herself for me."

"Suit yourself." He shrugged.

She nodded and turned to leave.

"Don't you want to see what we've got going on?"

She stopped. "You're willing to show me?"

"Sure. Fair's fair. But you'll have to look at them on screen. I haven't printed them out yet."

Wow. A man playing fair. That was a first.

She padded across to his computer, prepared to hate whatever she saw. But when she saw what he was working on she couldn't help but smile. This guy sure seemed to know women.

"This is good," she said. "Funny. But…"

"But what?"

"It's just the headline. It's a little too much. Too smug. Tell your copywriter to dial it back a little."

He nodded. "I was thinking the same thing. Thanks."

She headed back to the door, but stopped before she turned the knob. No need to leave on too much of a friendly note.

"I'm still going to beat you," she said.

"Keep dreaming," he retorted.

"Oh, I will." She smiled. "But no matter how good my dreams are, the reality will be even better."

Becky sat staring at her blank computer screen, exhaustion beating at the backs of her eyelids with every blink of the cursor. It was eleven-thirty p.m. on Thursday, and although her team was giving her their all she still worried that it wouldn't be enough.

Three days just wasn't enough time. Not when there was a quarter of a billion dollars on the line.

As tired as she was, she couldn't keep the memories from invading. Couldn't keep from hearing the sneering voice telling her she'd never get anywhere without him. That she was a hack, and always would be. That the only way she'd ever attain any success would be if she kept warming his bed…

A gentle hand clasped her shoulder.

"Hey, space cadet? Did you hear a word I just said?" Jessie asked.

Becky blinked, shaking her head to clear it.

"No, I…"

"You were listening to the mini-Pence in your head again, weren't you?" she said, sympathy plain in her bright blue eyes.

Becky forced a halfhearted smile. "What? Of course not. How could I when I'm surrounded by such a fantastic group of talented women?"

Jessie snorted. "Liar. When was the last time you slept?"

Becky thought for a second. She honestly couldn't remember.

"I can tell by your silence that it's been too long. Go home. Rest. You need to bring your A game tomorrow. It's D-day, you know."

As if she could forget.

"I know. I'll go soon, I promise."

Jessie gave her a long look. Becky could tell she wanted to say something else.

"Really. I will. Don't worry about me."

"All right," Jessie said. "Well, I'm heading out. And I'm taking mini-Pence with me. You don't need *him* being a backseat driver."

This time Becky smiled for real.

"You're right. I don't. Get him out of here, and good riddance."

After Jessie had left Becky headed for the kitchen, and the free coffee that awaited her there. As she waited for her mug to fill with the magic brew she laid her head on the cool metal of the stainless steel countertop and closed her eyes. Just for a second…

Next thing she knew a big hand was shaking her awake. She bolted upright, trying to get her bearings.

"I'm on it, Pence. Don't worry. I just…" she blurted, her mind still in dreamland.

"Hey, it's all right. There's no Pence here. It looks like you just drifted off for a second," a familiar voice said.

Becky blinked. Sure enough, Mark was standing there, smiling gently at her. And in his hand was the cup of coffee she'd been waiting for.

"Here. It's still hot," he said, handing it to her.

She took it silently, waiting for him to comment on what he'd heard her say. He didn't disappoint her.

"Who's Pence?"

She looked at him, expecting to see ridicule in his eyes. But there was only compassion.

"He's the reason I don't do workplace relationships. Or relationships at all, for that matter."

"Ah. Why?"

Without knowing why, Becky found herself wanting to confide in him.

"He was creative director at the agency where I interned during grad school. He was my mentor, and then he became…more. Much more."

That was the understatement of the year. But Mark didn't need to know how bad things had gotten—or how far she'd run to get away from him.

She shrugged her shoulders. "The whole thing left a bad taste in my mouth. So I decided to focus on my career instead. And now here we are. Competing for the promotion that should be mine."

Mark smiled ruefully and lifted his coffee mug. "Indeed we are. Although I have to admit I'd rather be competing to see how fast we can make each other come."

Becky raised an eyebrow. "You don't want this job?"

"Of course I do," he said with a heated smile. "And I'm going to get it. But I'd also like to hear you screaming my name again. Creating killer ads makes me hot."

Becky couldn't stop the laugh that bubbled up. "Well, that's nice to know. But I'm afraid I can't help you. I've got an equally hot campaign to finish."

Mark slowly got out of his chair and walked over to where she stood. "Okay, but just so you know, I'll be thinking about you," he said, dropping a kiss on her neck.

Her blood sizzled at his touch, and she found herself hoping he'd keep going.

Instead he turned and walked away. "Sweet dreams," he called.

Grabbing her still-warm coffee cup from the counter, Becky started the trek back to her office. Sleep would have to wait. She had a campaign to perfect—and a devil of a man to vanquish.

Mark took a deep breath, straightened his black sport coat, and walked into the crowded conference room. He had timed his entrance carefully, so that he was almost late but not quite. He needed every tool in his arsenal to keep Becky off balance.

"Nice of you to show up!" David boomed.

"I was just putting the finishing touches on our concept," Mark answered. "Nothing less than perfection will do, after all."

"That's what I like to hear," David said. "Now, since you're so sure of yourself, how about you go first?"

Mark took a deep breath, then snuck a look at Becky. She was sitting quietly at one end of the giant conference table, her emerald-green dress the only bright spot in the overly industrial room.

She looked at him mockingly. "Yes, Mark, why don't you go first? We're dying to hear what you've come up with."

Mark looked at her, then looked at David.

David nodded encouragingly.

He took a deep breath as he strode to the head of the table. *This is it,* he told himself. *Time to knock their socks off.*

"I've spent a fair bit of time around women," he said. "I like to think I know what makes them tick. In fact," he said, turning to write on the whiteboard behind him, "the way I see it, women want three things… First, they want to look good. Which, for most women, means being skinny. Second, they want other women to be jealous of them. And third," he said, writing the number three with a flourish, "they want a man. Not only that, they want a man of their choosing. And they want him to drool over them. Which, if we're honest, brings us back to number one. But there are plenty of yogurts promising to make women skinny. To stand out, we need to say something different."

He turned the first board over, so the whole room could see a woman in a cocktail dress being admired by a host of attractive men. Once he was sure they'd seen it, he read them the headline.

"'Eden. The yogurt for the woman who knows what she wants.' That's our tagline. We'll use it in connection with women in all kinds of situations. At the beach," he said, flipping over boards sequentially, "in the dressing room, hailing a cab. In every scene men will be staring, open-mouthed, at the female."

When he'd finished a momentary silence filled the room. He glanced from one face to another but couldn't read what anyone was thinking. This crew would be awesome at poker.

Finally he looked at Becky and cocked an eyebrow at

her. The concept had come a long way since the last time she'd seen it.

She cleared her throat.

"So your message is pretty much: 'Eat this, be skinny, get men to lust over you'?" she asked.

He shrugged his shoulders. "In a nutshell. It's taking the bikini-clad woman in a beer commercial and turning it on its head. *Men* get to be the hangers-on."

"Huh… But what about women who aren't interested in men?"

Mark turned to look at her, expecting to see spite in her eyes. But instead he saw genuine interest. "That's a good point," he said. "But I think this idea has legs. It could cover different topics."

She walked around the room, grabbed the marker out of his hand and began to write down ideas. "Like instead of men it could be openmouthed business associates admiring her. Or cyclists left in her dust."

"Oh, I see where you're going," he said. "That could be cool."

She grinned at him, and for the first time since they'd returned to New York he got a glimpse of the happy, gorgeous girl he'd shared a night with in Vegas.

He grinned back. "So, what if—?"

David cleared his throat.

"I like where this is going—but, Becky, didn't you have a concept to present, as well? This *is* a competition," he said.

Becky blinked, and the laughter in her eyes disappeared.

"Right. Of course. Mark, can you clear your stuff out of the way? I'll grab my boards."

A few moments later Becky took center stage. And when she did she was magnetic.

"So, on my team we got to thinking about what women really want. And we think it goes deeper than just being skinny or attracting the right man. That's what our mothers wanted. But we want more. We want to be recognized as the strong, independent beings we are. We want the superhuman feats we accomplish every day to be recognized. After all, today's woman works like a dog at her corporate job, putting in twice as much effort for half the pay, then heads to the gym to ensure she stays model-thin, then goes home to run a household. Today's women are incredible. We think it's time for a marketer to sit up and acknowledge that."

Then she flipped a board over.

It showed a business-suited woman standing in a superhero pose on top of a conference table as her colleagues clapped.

"'You save your world every day before lunch. Choose the only yogurt high-powered enough to keep up with you,'" she said.

She flipped more boards. One of a soccer mom pulling a dirt-covered boy from a vat of quicksand. One of a runner flying ahead of the pack, cape billowing out behind her. And another of a lab-coated woman punching an oversize germ in the mouth so her patients could get away.

After she presented the last board she looked up and smiled. "Every woman deserves to feel like a superhero. Because she *is* one."

Her team applauded.

Mark had to stop himself from joining in.

David looked at Mark, seeming to be waiting for something. Oh. Right. He was supposed to be shooting holes in her concept.

"What about all those young hipsters who don't feel like they're accomplishing anything yet?" he asked.

"Well, we could have smaller situations. A woman stopping a cab before it can get away," she said.

"Or wowing a crowded club with her dance moves?" he suggested.

"Or saving a cat from a snarling dog?" she chimed in.

"Or what about—?"

"I hate to break this up, but we're not in a brainstorming session," David broke in. "We're supposed to be making a decision about which concept to present to the client."

Mark snapped his mouth shut. *Damn it*. He'd gone from shooting her down to making her case for her.

Thinking fast, he smirked in David's direction. "I think the choice is clear," he said. "Superheroes are great—if you're seven. I think most women would rather fantasize about a good-looking man than dress up in a Spandex suit."

The look Becky shot him was murderous. But before she could open her mouth David held up his hand.

"You have a point, Mark," he said. "But there's something in Becky's idea, too. Let me think for a minute. Everybody be quiet."

Instantly the conference room was deathly quiet.

David moved to the front of the room. "Mark, put your boards back up."

"Sure," he said, reaching for them.

"Just do it. Don't talk about it," David snapped.

Mark blinked, then did as he was told. This man could give any dictator a run for his money.

David paced back and forth, picking up boards, shuffling the order, then shuffling them again. After what seemed like an eternity, he finally spoke.

"All right. Here's what we're going to do. I want you to merge these campaigns. They both have their good points, but together they'd be stronger. So," he said, smiling broadly at Mark and Becky, "I want the two of you to work together."

Shocked, Mark stared at Becky.

She stared back, panic in her eyes.

"Together?" she blurted. "But we were competing."

"Not to worry," David said, patting her on the shoulder. "You still are. We'll just have to think of a different way to evaluate you. From now on consider yourselves partners as well as competitors."

CHAPTER THREE

DAVID'S WORDS ECHOED in the now silent room.

"Partners?" Becky squeaked.

David looked at her, a frown working its way between his piercing blue eyes. "That's what I said."

The whole idea was insane. How could they possibly get anything done when they were both focused on winning the competition? Plus, it meant spending a lot of time alone together. Too much time.

"This is a lot of work," she said. "How are Mark and I supposed to get it done without the help of our teams?"

"Well, Becky," David said, looking at her with more than a little disdain, "if you want to be a creative director at this agency you're going to have to learn to be resourceful. Figure it out."

Mark cleared his throat.

"I don't see any reason why the teams can't help us blow the campaign out after we've finalized the concept," he said.

David clapped him on the back. "Now, *that's* the way a creative director thinks. Becky, pay attention to this guy. You could learn a thing or two from him."

As Becky seethed, David gave his full attention to Mark. "You two have the weekend to get this nailed down. I expect you in my office at nine a.m. sharp on Monday morning to present it to me. Any questions?"

Mark looked over the top of the bald man's head at Becky. "You?"

She had plenty of questions. Like, why was David such

a Neanderthal? What did he see in Mark? Why the hell had she decided to be a copywriter, anyway? Surely there were better ways to make a living. Picking up the city's garbage, for example.

But neither of the men in the room could provide the answers, so instead she just shook her head.

"All right. I'll leave you to it," David said. "Jessie, would you come with me to my office, please?"

The redhead nodded and followed him from the room. Everyone else followed her lead, and soon they were alone.

Becky collapsed in one of the deliberately uncomfortable metal chairs. "Now what?"

"Now you let me take you to dinner," Mark said.

Good Lord. The man never let up.

"Dinner? No. We might be partners, but we don't have to be friends."

"Who said anything about being friends? This is just dinner. You gotta eat, right?"

He looked at her with that damn eyebrow quirked and she felt her resolve melting. She *was* hungry. And they had a lot of work ahead of them. It made sense to fuel up before they got started.

"All right. Dinner. But I'll pay. And I'll choose the place."

"You've got a deal," he said, smiling triumphantly.

"Good. Meet me downstairs in fifteen minutes," she said.

That gave her time to come up with a game plan for winning the promotion…and keeping her clothes on this weekend.

Mark paced in front of the glass doors that marked the entrance to SBD, dodging tourists with every turn.

He'd arrived at the designated spot on time. Unfortunately Becky was nowhere in sight. Just like a woman, he found himself thinking. Probably trying to figure out how big his bank account was. Then he caught himself. Where had *that* come from?

Surely David couldn't be rubbing off on him already?

Just then Becky burst through the doors. The killer green dress was gone. In its place was a pair of worn-looking jeans and a baggy rust-colored sweater. And *damn* if she didn't look just as good.

"There you are," he said. "Where are we off to, chief?"

She looked up at him and he noticed her face was scrubbed free of makeup. Without it, she looked all of nineteen.

"That's for me to know and you to find out," she said. "Come on."

He followed her as she wound her way through the congested city streets, ignoring the pressing crowds as only a seasoned New Yorker could.

"So, are you from here?" he asked.

She seemed to hesitate before answering. "No. But I like to pretend that I am."

He wasn't sure what to make of that statement, so he ignored it. "Then where *are* you from?"

"Detroit," she said shortly.

"Ah. Where the weak get killed and eaten, huh?"

"Or pushed to the end of the unemployment line," she said. Then, seeming to realize that she was being rude, she smiled up at him. "How 'bout you? Where's your magic come from?"

"Oh, here and there," he said. "I moved around a lot." From boarding school to summer camp to anywhere else his mother had been able to think of sending him that kept him far from home.

Looking around, he realized they were standing at the corner of Fifty-Third and Sixth. Tourist central.

"Hungry for some overpriced deli sandwiches?" he asked.

"Nope. Just spicy deliciousness," she said, pointing to a food cart.

"Really?"

"Don't look so surprised. It's the best halal cart in town. And it's cheap."

A few minutes later, when they were seated on a bench with their plastic containers on their laps, he had to admit that she knew what she was talking about.

"This is good," he said between bites of lamb and rice. "I wouldn't have pegged you for a street food kind of girl."

"Really? What do I seem like? A steak and champagne enthusiast?" she said with a sarcastic grin.

"No, more like a vegan foodie."

She snorted. "We don't have vegan foodies in the Midwest. Just a bunch of overweight carnivores."

"So what brought you here? To New York?"

Her expression closed. "The bright lights and big agencies, of course. Just like everybody else."

She took a big bite of lamb and rice, then abruptly steered the conversation back to him.

"So. In all your moving around you never made it to the Midwest?"

"Nope. I have an aversion to corn fields."

"Where did you live, then?"

"Well, I lived in New Jersey until I was ten," he said, hoping that would be enough to satisfy her.

"And then…?"

Man, was she persistent. He sighed.

"And then my mom married a rich man and moved to Connecticut."

"Didn't you go with her?"

He laughed bitterly.

"Well, I had a room in her house. But I wasn't really welcome there. She was too busy with her new family. I spent most of my teen years seeing how many boarding schools I could get thrown out of."

Her eyes went round. "Why?"

Thanks to the years of therapy his mom had forced him to do, he knew it was because acting out had been the only thing that got his mother's attention. But he wasn't going to tell Becky that.

Instead, he shrugged. "Why does a teenage boy do anything? But I saw a lot of the East Coast. Massachusetts, New Hampshire, Maine...everywhere fancy pants rich people live."

Becky snorted. "I would have hated you when I was a teenager—you know that?"

He looked at her, genuinely surprised. "Why do you say that?"

"I was the kid doing extra credit projects and sucking up to teachers, hoping they'd help me when it was time to apply for college. I thought kids like you were idiots."

"And what kind of kid was that?"

She looked at him, her eyes flashing with remembered anger.

"Kids who spent all their time screwing around, knowing they could buy their way into college even if their grades sucked. You would have been one of the people making my life miserable because I couldn't afford to waste my time partying with you."

He sat silently for a long minute, unsure of what to say. She was probably right. After his mom had married Bill money had lost all real value. No matter how much he'd charged to his stepfather's accounts, or how outrageous the purchase, no one had blinked an eye. Except...

"Not me. I went to all-boys schools. Girls were rare and always appreciated, no matter how geeky. Besides," he said, brushing her hair back from her face, "even if you were a nerd, I'm sure you were a gorgeous nerd. I would have been just as desperate to get in your pants then as I am now."

She rolled her eyes, looking pleased nevertheless.

"Whatever," she said, looking down at her phone screen. "Whoa. It's almost seven already. What do you say we go back and get our war room set up? That way we can start fresh in the morning."

"That's a good plan. You're just going to move your stuff into my office, right?"

Becky froze. "I...uh...thought we should set up shop someplace public. With more space, I mean. Like, you know, the conference room."

"Why? Are you afraid to be alone with me?" Mark asked, half hoping that she was. He'd love to know he had that kind of power over her.

"What? No. Of course not. I just thought we might need the whiteboards or something," she said, pointedly not looking at him.

"I've got plenty of whiteboards in my office," he said. "I don't know about you, but I like a little privacy when I'm working hard. And everybody can see into the conference room."

She picked at her fingernails. "I don't know..."

He couldn't resist the urge to tease her.

"I promise to be on my best behavior. I won't show you my underwear even if you ask me to."

Becky laughed at his reference to the first time they'd met.

"Okay. Deal. I won't show you mine if you don't show me yours," she said. "But you'll have to help me move my stuff."

By the time they'd finished moving her desk, laptop dock and giant monitors, dark had fallen and the lights from the skyscrapers that surrounded them twinkled like stars.

Becky gazed out of the window and sighed.

"I could get used to a view like this," she said.

Mark came to stand beside her. "It is pretty sweet. Definitely beats the view I had at my last office."

"Oh? Where was that?"

"Los Angeles," he said.

"Oh. Yeah… I can see how you'd get tired of looking at palm trees and bikini-clad babes," Becky teased.

"I was a contract worker. Which meant I was one small step away from sitting in the basement with a red stapler. The only thing I had to look at was fuzzy cubicle walls."

"Ah. At least I'll always have Ryan Gosling to keep me company," she said, motioning to the poster she'd tacked to the wall by her desk.

"If you get tired of looking at him I'm happy to pose for pictures," Mark said.

Becky stepped back. "Now you want to be my eye candy, huh?"

"Nope. I just want you to want me to take my shirt off."

If he only knew… But she wouldn't. She wouldn't even kiss him—at least not again. That morning in his office had been an aberration.

"Dream on, buddy. I don't sleep with the competition."

"I know, I know," he said. "But you can't blame a guy for trying. You know, if you slept with me I might not try so hard to win."

"Yeah, right. I'm pretty sure you don't give up that easily," she said, giving him a sideways smile.

Then she turned away. It was either that or give in to the temptation to rub her hands over the hard planes of his chest.

"I'm going to check my email and then head out for the night," she said. "You?"

"I think I'm just going to head out," he answered. "I

need to hit the hay so I'm ready to rock tomorrow. See ya in the morning."

Becky waved vaguely in his direction as he left and fired up her laptop. She didn't really need to check her email—that was what smartphones were for. But she did need some time to get used to her new surroundings and wrap her head around the situation.

Truth really was stranger than fiction. If she'd set out to write a book she'd never have come up with anything as screwy as this. It was almost reality-show-worthy.

She could see it now: *Flung: Where One-Night Flings Compete.*

Giggling, she peeked at her inbox. She was surprised to see it was flooded with messages of support from the whole creative team. The guy in charge of the agency might be a sleaze, but he sure did hire good people.

She was just about to close it up when she saw a name that froze her heart.

Pence.

What did *he* want?

She considered deleting the email without reading the message, but knew that was the coward's way out. Taking a deep breath, she clicked on his name, willing herself to stay calm.

Hey Babe
Saw you at AdWorld, but I knew you wouldn't want to talk to me so I didn't say hello. Couldn't stop thinking about you, though. You look good. Done good, too. I'd like to say I'm surprised, but you learned from the best—me.
Did you know my agency is pitching to Eden, too? I'd say may the best man win, but we both know who that is—me. I'm sorry I'm going to have to crush you. But, hey, there'll always be a job waiting for you here! Oh, and Chelsea hit the road, so there's a room for you, too.
Pence

Becky read it twice, unable to believe what she was see-ing. Unfortunately the message only got more infuriating the second time around.

Could the man be any more repulsive? Was he really in-viting her to take his wife's…er…his *ex*-wife's place over email?

Unable to contain her rage, Becky screamed. Her shriek echoed in the mostly empty office, carrying her pain right back to her ears.

She slammed her laptop shut and got up to pace.

There was no reason this should affect her so much. She'd outgrown him. Outstripped him. She was twice as good as that scum-sucker had ever been on his best day.

Seeking confirmation, she grabbed one of her awards off her desk, stroking the golden statue. She was good. *Damn* good. And nothing that man could say would con-vince her otherwise.

But still she heard the echoes in her brain. "No-good hack," they spat. "Bed-hopping social climber," they hissed. "As terrible on paper as you are in bed," they screamed.

Unable to help herself, Becky chucked the award across the room. It landed with a dull thud, the thick red carpet seeming to reach up to protect it from damage.

Becky caught the sob before it could escape from her throat. It was time to go home.

Becky turned the key in the faded red door that marked the entrance to her third-floor walk-up and trudged up the stairs.

This morning she had felt so confident. So alive. She'd been sure that the world was hers to conquer.

Now? Now all she wanted was a giant glass of wine and the oblivion that came with sleep.

Without bothering to flip on the light switch, Becky stepped into the kitchen and opened the tiny fridge. Wincing at the glaring light, she pulled the Pinot Grigio from the top shelf and took a swig straight from the bottle.

A cockroach scuttled across the bloodred countertop directly opposite her. Without thinking, she slammed the bottle down, reveling in the sickening crunch that sounded as it met its demise.

"There's one pest that's out of my life forever," she said, grabbing a paper towel to wipe its remains from her salvation.

She grabbed a plastic tumbler and filled it to the top before collapsing in the purple velvet chaise that was her prized possession.

Gazing out at the gently waving branches of the oak tree that graced her front window, she tried to relax.

It was no good. As soon as she let her guard down memories started to invade. And they weren't all bad. For a long while Pence had been everything she'd needed.

She remembered how patient he'd been when critiquing her first efforts at advertising copy. He'd never laughed or shown disdain, no matter how awkward the headline or script construction.

And how he'd loved to surprise her. A midweek picnic aboard a chartered sailboat here. Front row seats to the summer's hottest concert there. A private dinner prepared by the city's top chef whenever anything was seriously amiss.

All wrapped in miles and miles of seemingly sincere promises. He'd painted beautiful pictures of the life they would create together—working opposite each other all day, then playing together all night, making sweet love whenever the mood struck them. He'd even included children in their mythical future: a girl with her hair and his height, and a boy with her eyes and his strength.

She'd thought she'd been transported from her dreary hand-to-mouth existence straight into a fairytale. Unfortunately her happily-ever-after had never put in an appearance.

At least not with Pence. And not in Detroit.

But she'd spent the last five years here in New York, creating a new direction for her story. And, unless she was sadly mistaken, she was almost to the good part.

She put the tumbler of wine to her lips, only to find it empty.

It was time for bed.

She shuffled into the closet that served as her bedroom and crawled beneath the sky-blue goose down duvet that was her biggest extravagance. Her bed was her sanctuary, and normally her lavender-scented sheets relaxed her within minutes.

Not tonight.

Tonight she could only toss and turn, searching for a comfortable place to lay her head.

She was tormented by images of the flowered treasure box that lay hidden under her bed. The one that contained memories she couldn't stand to destroy—and that destroyed her to remember.

Sighing, she twisted the knob on the delicate crystal lamp on her nightstand and clambered out of bed.

With the box settled in her lap, she gently lifted the cover.

Resting there was a picture of her, snuggled against Pence's broad chest at sunset aboard a sailboat. The camera had caught him midlaugh, his blue eyes crinkling, looking happy and relaxed. She could remember the exact moment. She'd felt so safe. So loved. So incredibly sure she was right where she belonged.

The ruby promise ring he'd given her was also there, nestled in its green velvet box. As was the long gold chain he'd insisted she hang it on, so she could wear it "next to her heart." She'd loved to feel it hanging between her breasts, imagining it was him touching her every time the ring had brushed a sensitive area.

There were other pictures, including one taken at the dinner held in honor of her first award-win. He was scowling darkly at the camera, unhappiness obvious in every line of his body.

That was when things had started to go wrong. He hadn't liked it when she'd started succeeding on her own.

At the bottom of the box was the memory she was most dreading. A grainy black-and-white photo of the peanut-size blob that had been her baby at eight weeks.

The baby she had aborted a week later.

She remembered the day the picture had been taken as if it was yesterday. She'd known she was pregnant for three weeks. After the first test had come out positive she'd bought an economy-size pack of pregnancy test strips and taken a new one every morning. The little pink line indicating the baby's existence had got darker and thicker with each passing day, but it hadn't been until her doctor had shown her the blurry black-and-white ultrasound image on a video monitor that she'd allowed herself to believe it was real.

And when he'd found the heartbeat her soul had melted, reforming itself around the tiny little being growing inside her. She'd promised the little peanut that she'd take care of it. That she'd be the best mom ever.

What a joke *that* had turned out to be.

The next night she shaved every last hair from her body and perfumed every crevice before sliding into the sexy white lace lingerie Pence loved. She'd donned silky back-seamed thigh-highs and a skintight black dress that show-cased her newly voluptuous breasts.

Her one and only pair of Manolos had been the finishing touch.

When she'd arrived at the intimate French restaurant where she'd arranged to meet Pence she'd known by the slack-jawed look on the face of every man she'd passed that she'd done well.

But by the time the *maître d'* had shown her to the table and helped her settle into a chair under Pence's watchful gaze, her confidence had already been taking a nosedive. His eyes had scraped over her body, taking in the size of her breasts and the curve of her hips.

"Have you gained weight, Becky?" he'd asked.

"N-no," she'd stuttered. "It's just this dress. It forgives nothing."

"Good. You look great, but you know how important it is to stay thin if you want to make it in advertising."

Becky had nodded. "I know," she'd said quietly.

But inside her mind had been screaming. Pregnant women got fat. Would Pence love her when she was fat? It would only be temporary, but his attention span was notoriously short. By the time this baby was born and her body had returned to normal he might have forgotten all about her.

Then what would she do?

"What's wrong?" Pence had asked, reaching out to stroke her hand. "Did I say something to upset you?"

"No, not at all," she'd said with a small smile. "I've just got a lot on my mind."

"That's right." He'd groaned. "You wanted to 'talk.' What is it this time? Is your mom after you to get married again?"

She shook her head. "No, not so far this month," she'd said.

Just then their server had arrived, giving Becky a reprieve. He'd offered Pence a sample from a bottle of freshly uncorked Syrah. Pence had inhaled deeply, then swished the purple liquid around in his mouth. After a long moment he'd given a sharp nod. The waiter had smiled and filled their glasses before fading away.

Pence had looked at her over the rim of his glass. "So what is it?"

Becky had taken a deep breath and reached into her black sequined bag with a trembling hand. "I have a surprise for you," she'd said.

He looked at her suspiciously. "I don't like surprises," he'd said.

She'd pulled out the small silver-wrapped package she'd stowed in her purse and handed it to him.

"I think you'll like this one."

Lord knew he'd talked about his longing for children often enough.

"Humph," he'd muttered as he undid the bow. "We'll see about that."

He'd torn off the wrapping paper in one fell swoop. Becky had felt her heart rise into her throat as he lifted the lid of the box, unsure of what his reaction would be. He'd frowned when he saw the framed picture inside.

"What is this?" he'd demanded.

"It's a picture," she'd said. "An ultrasound."

"An ultrasound? What? Do you have a tumor?"

"N-no," she'd stuttered, taking a deep breath. "I'm pregnant. That's a picture of a baby. *Our* baby."

Pence fell back in his chair. "Pregnant? But how could that be? We take precautions."

Becky had shrugged her shoulders, knowing full well that she wasn't as religious about taking her birth control pills as he supposed she was.

"Apparently not enough," she'd said.

"So this is real? You're not joking?"

"No," she'd whispered. "I'm not."

"But this can't be. You *can't* be pregnant. I have a *wife!*"

Her heart had plummeted, smashing into the polished cement floor at their feet. "You're *married?*" she'd whispered.

"Of course I'm married. I thought you knew that? Didn't you ever wonder why I never spend the night? Or why I never invite you to my house?"

"N-no. I just thought… Well, I didn't think. You said you loved me! You talked about getting married!"

He'd taken her hand again, stroking it gently. "I do love you. And I would love to marry you. But I can't divorce my wife. Her father owns the agency. If I left her I'd lose everything."

"But what about our baby?"

"There can't *be* a baby. Don't you see? You have to get rid of it. It's the only way."

"Get rid of it?"

"Yes. Have an abortion."

"But I don't want an abortion," she'd said. "I want to keep it."

"Then you're on your own," he'd said. "I won't have anything to do with it. If you don't take care of this problem we're done."

"But you just said you love me," she'd whispered.

"Love has nothing to do with it. This is business. And I can't let a little accident like this jeopardize my position with the agency," Pence had said. "Please, just think about it?"

At a loss for words, she'd nodded.

"Good," Pence had said. "Now, if you'll excuse me, I have to attend a dinner party. With my wife."

And with that he was gone.

Becky had stared after him, mouth agape. What was she supposed to do now?

The next week had been a nightmare. She'd crunched numbers, searched the internet and racked her brain, trying to find a way through the predicament she had suddenly found herself in.

Eventually, though, she'd admitted the truth to herself.

She was twenty-three. She had seventy-five thousand dollars in student loans and only made twenty-four thousand dollars a year. There was no way she could raise this baby on her own. And there'd be no help coming from the man she had thought loved her.

Worse, if she kept the baby her career would take a nose-dive just when it was starting to get off the ground. The financially secure future she had imagined would disappear in a puff of smoke.

She'd end up like her parents, working two jobs and worrying over every penny she spent for the rest of her life. That was no way to live—or to raise a child.

There was only one choice she could make.

When she'd arrived for her appointment at the family planning clinic it was with cold anger and hot despair stomping on her heart. Rubbing her still-flat belly, she'd made her soon-to-be-aborted baby a promise.

She would never forget him—for it had become a him in her mind—and Pence would pay dearly for this betrayal if it was the last thing she did.

Hot tears leaked down her face now, as she stroked the image. She'd never forgive herself for not standing up to him. For allowing him to control her and for letting him convince her to do something that had felt so wrong.

No man would ever have that much power over her again.

Wiping her tears away with her sleeve, Becky slid the box back under the bed. She had to get to sleep. She had a competition to win—and a living nightmare to defeat.

CHAPTER FOUR

MARK ARRIVED AT the office bright and early, doughnuts and coffee in hand. After the relaxed evening they'd shared he was looking forward to working with Becky today.

Tucking the breakfast items under his chin, he opened his office door, expecting to see it empty. But Becky was already there, pounding away at her computer, punishing the keys with every clack.

"Good morning, early bird! I brought breakfast."

Becky looked up. If the dark circles under her eyes were any indication, Mark thought, she'd never left the office.

She smiled frostily. "Nice of you to make an appearance. Considering how much work we have to do, I thought it would be best to get an early start."

Whoa. Okay. Apparently they were playing a new game.

"Sorry. I thought eight-thirty on a Saturday was plenty early."

"And that's why I'm going to win and you're not," she snapped. "This job takes dedication."

"I've got news for you, princess. Neither one of us is going to win if we can't find a way to merge these two campaigns."

She waved dismissively at him.

"I'm working on it. Why don't you go over there and look for some pretty pictures or something?"

All right. Enough was enough.

"I'll tell you what I'm going to do. I'm going to go over there and come up with another, even more kick-ass idea.

And when David asks what your contribution was I'll tell him you didn't make one. How's that sound?"

She rolled her eyes. "Whatever. Just be quiet about it."

Mark stomped over to his desk and slammed the coffee down. Forget quiet. He was going to work the way he always did. With music blaring.

Seconds later, the discordant sounds of a heavy metal guitar filled the room.

She glared at him, then reached into her drawer and pulled out a pair of headphones.

He loaded up his photo editing program to look at the images he'd already created, but the glare from the overhead lights was killing him. He got up and flipped the lights off. He'd hardly even sat down before she was turning them back on.

"Do you mind?" he said. "I can't work with all that glare."

"Well, I can't write if I can't see the keys," she said,

"Come sit by the window," he said.

"Go work in a cave," she retorted.

He sighed. "Fine. Have it your way. It's not worth fighting about."

She huffed and put her headphones back on.

Mark turned to his computer to get started, but his mind refused to cooperate.

Maybe looking at the existing boards would help. He grabbed the pile from where it lay by the office door and spread the boards out on the plush red carpet, laying the two campaigns side by side.

Then he began to pace back and forth down the line, looking for common ground.

They both featured strong women. And used humor. Maybe…

Becky sighed angrily. "Really? Are you going to pace all day? Because it's really distracting."

He turned to look at her. She was standing with her

hands on her hips, completely unaware of how ridiculously her angry expression contrasted with the giant happy face emblazoned on her oversize T-shirt.

Unbidden, the image of her standing in exactly that position, laughing and naked except for a pair of cheetah-print heels, rose to the front of his brain. How could that free spirit belong to this completely aggravating woman? There had to be a way to get past her anger.

Suddenly he had an idea. Grabbing his jacket, he turned to leave.

"Where are you going?" she asked.

"Out," he said. "See you later."

"But what about—?"

"We can't work together like this. So I'm leaving," he said, shutting the door before she could see the smile on his face.

That would give her something to stew about.

Becky stared openmouthed at the shut door.

Her so-called partner had bailed on her. *Now* what was she supposed to do? True, she hadn't exactly been welcoming, but that didn't give him the right to just quit.

Of course if he didn't come back the promotion would be hers by default. At least it would if she could find the brilliant idea that would allow her to win the competition.

And she *had* to win this. She didn't even care about the promotion so much anymore. She just wanted to kick Pence's pompous ass.

Sighing, she collapsed into her chair and put her head in her hands.

If only Mark wasn't so damn hot. Just being in the same room with him made her think inappropriate thoughts. Thoughts of unbuttoning the faded blue shirt he'd been wearing and licking his chest. Of sliding her hand down the front of his jeans. Of letting him roll down her leggings and take her—right on top of the desk.

She was sorely tempted to do just that. To scratch the itch and move on. After all, she was an empowered, independent woman. Why shouldn't she take what she wanted when he obviously wanted it, too?

Because once would never be enough, that was why. And she knew better than to get involved with a coworker—even a temporary one—ever again.

If sex was out, there was only one thing to do. Work.

An hour later she was still typing indecipherable garbage when the door opened. Mark walked in, carrying a giant F.A.O. Schwartz bag. Trying hard not to feel relieved, she looked at him with a raised eyebrow.

"You went to the toy store?"

"Yep."

He waltzed over to his desk and turned his back on her. She heard a great deal of rustling, then boxes being ripped. Unable to hide her curiosity, she walked up behind him and stood on her tiptoes, trying to see what he was working on.

He turned and she quickly stepped back, nearly falling in the process.

When she caught her balance she saw that he was holding two...*plastic swords?*

Mark looked at her, a serious expression on his face.

"I would like to challenge you to a duel," he said.

"A what?"

"A duel. To settle the problems we seem to be having this morning. If I win you have to give up the attitude. If you win I'll...well, I'll do whatever you want. Leave. Stay. Draw pictures of monkeys. Whatever."

Becky wanted to laugh, but he didn't seem to think what he was proposing was funny.

"Are you serious?"

"As a heart attack."

She licked her lips. "All right."

"Good," he said, a smile quirking at the corners of his mouth. "Do you want to be red or blue?"

"Um…red."

She reached out to take it. "This is actually kind of cool," she said, taking a few test swings.

He nodded, and brought his sword up into fighting position.

"Ready?"

"Sure," she said, imitating his stance.

He started to advance and they circled each other warily.

Suddenly he struck, aiming for her stomach. She moved her sword into position just in time, batting his out of the way before striking back.

He parried her blow and the fight was on. Soon they were whirling around the room, their swords crashing and crackling. Mark kept his expression serious, but Becky felt herself grinning.

She couldn't remember the last time she'd had this much fun with a guy. Or at all.

Mark lunged forward and she backpedaled before stepping on something sharp and cold. The award she'd thrown last night. She cursed at the sudden pain, then grabbed Mark's arm to try and keep herself from falling. Instead she overbalanced, and they fell into a heap, Mark's big body pinning hers to the ground. He pulled one arm free and lightly tapped her forehead with his saber.

"You're dead," he said.

Becky gave in to the laughter frothing in her throat.

"I guess you won, fair and square," she said between giggles.

He grinned down at her.

"Yep. No more attitude from *you,* Sir knight."

"I don't think I could frown if I tried right now," she said.

"Good. I like you better when you're laughing." His

dark eyes took on a liquid sheen. "In fact, there's only one expression I'd rather see," he said.

And without warning he took her lips with his.

His lips crushed down on hers with an urgent demand that she give in to the heat that had been building between them—not just today, but every day since she'd returned from Vegas. And, God help her, but she couldn't ignore it. Couldn't say no.

She let her mouth fall open in silent surrender, giving in to the hunger his searing kisses awakened in her. His tongue plundered her mouth, claiming every inch of it for his own.

She twined her hands in his dark hair and pulled him closer, wanting all that he had to give. She gave up on thought, letting instinct drive her as she arched her body upward, wanting still more.

He took that as the invitation it was, sliding one hand down her body to cup her through her panties.

"Mmm..." he rumbled. "You're already hot for me."

Becky heard herself moan as he slid his hand back up, leaving the sensitive nub of nerves that she wanted him to touch so badly. She grabbed it and put it back, whimpering.

"Wait. Not yet," he said. "I want you naked first."

"Then help me get my clothes off," she growled, starting to squirm out of her shirt.

He pulled it quickly over her head, then whipped her leggings off.

"Yours, too," she said, and within seconds his clothes had joined hers on the floor.

Clothes gone, he lowered himself on top of her and kissed her lips again. She let him in, losing herself in the feel of the intoxicating hardness of his body. She pressed upward, moving her hips against his, almost delirious in her need to connect with him in the most primal way.

"Mark, *now,*" she begged. "I need..."

"Hold on, baby," he said. "I want to taste you first."

In seconds his mouth was on her, licking and nipping at her most sensitive parts.

"Damn, Becky, you have no idea how long I've been wanting to do this," he growled, from somewhere at her center.

She wanted to ask him how long, but the ability to form words left her as he began to suck. She could think of nothing other than the waves of pleasure he was creating. At that moment she would have given anything to keep him right where he was for as long as possible.

Seconds later she peaked, crashing into an abyss of pure sensation.

Mark kissed her as she came down, his mouth even more urgent than it had been before. Knowing what he needed, what they both needed, she wrapped her legs around his waist.

"Mark…now," she whimpered against his mouth.

"Yes, *now*," he said, and sheathed himself inside her with a quick flex of his hips.

She groaned and clenched her body around him, wanting to keep him there forever.

She let her eyes drift closed as he started moving, losing herself in the sensation.

"No, don't," he whispered. "I want you to look at me."

When she opened them he was looking at her fiercely.

"I want you to see. To know it's me that's doing this to you," he said as he thrusted, pressing against all the right spots.

"Only you," she gasped as he moved inside her. "You're the only one that's ever done this to me."

"God, Becky," he rumbled, heat flooding his gaze as his pace quickened. "You're amazing. Where have you been all my life?"

"I'm. Right. Here. Now," she said.

The heat stabbing through her from his thrusts and the

weight of his gaze melded together into a hot haze of perfection, and she felt her world beginning to splinter.

"Mark, I'm going to…"

"Come for me, Gorgeous Girl," he said, smiling down at her.

And she did, waves and waves of sensation swamping her psyche and blurring his face in front of her.

His expression turned fierce and with a guttural moan he followed her over the cliff.

Afterward they lay twined together, their hearts beating in time. Becky lost herself in the perfection of the moment, unwilling to move and let the real world in again. If she knew the sex would always be like that she'd never let this man go…

When she could put words together again, she said, "You know, until very recently I thought I was bad at that."

"Why on earth would you think that?" Mark said, genuinely shocked. "Becky, you're amazing."

He watched as she flushed, the rosiness reaching all the way down her chest.

"Oh, I…uh…shouldn't have said that out loud. My internal filter must be busted."

He pulled her into his arms. "But you did. Must've been on your mind. Why?" He was surprised at how much he wanted to know.

She looked down at her hands and picked at her fingernails. "Oh, you know. Heard from an ex. Stirred up bad memories."

Judging by the way she was closing in on herself, they must have been spectacularly awful memories. Then he remembered a snippet from the night he'd found her asleep in the kitchen.

"This wouldn't have anything to do with that Pence guy, would it?"

She looked at him sharply. "How would you know that?"

"You were talking in your sleep. That night in the kitchen."

Realization dawned on her face. "Oh. Right. Well, yeah, that's the one. But you know… Every girl's got one."

"Got one what?"

"A voice. One that points out her flaws and harps on her inadequacies. Mine sounds like him."

Mark felt a wave of anger roll across his brain. "If I ever meet this guy I'm going to have a thing or two to say to him. He sounds like a piece of work."

Becky looked at him, a wry smile on her lips.

"Well, you might get your chance."

"Chance to what?"

"Talk to Pence." Her lips twisted, the smile turning into an unconscious snarl. "His agency is pitching to Eden, too."

Mark sat up straighter, surprised.

"How long have you known?"

"Oh…" Becky said, looking up at the clock. "About fifteen hours or so. He emailed last night."

Suddenly her earlier behavior made a lot more sense. Wishing he could save her from her obvious pain, he pulled her close and kissed the top of her head.

"We'll beat him, you know," he said. "Together. That jerk doesn't stand a chance against us."

She murmured her assent, but when he looked at her he could tell her brain was busily working on another problem. Pulling her shirt over her head, she paced over to the whiteboard on the wall.

"We've been going about this all wrong," she said. "Women aren't going to buy our yogurt just because we recognize their awesomeness. That doesn't do anything for them. They're going to buy it if it solves a problem for them. So if the problem is insecurity, we need to position ourselves as a solution."

He watched as she scratched silently on the board with a red marker. Her butt jiggled ever so slightly with the movement, and he found himself wanting to feel the weight of it in his palms again.

She turned to look at him, triumph lighting her eyes.

"I've got it. Check this out. It could be something like, 'Working mom guilt weighing you down? Take an Eden moment and believe.'"

Mark's brain kicked into gear. "Maybe. Or what about, 'Eden. Your shortcut to a more perfect you.'"

Becky wrote it down.

"Good thought. But what about…?"

And they were off and running.

The next time Mark looked up, the sun was setting.

"Wow. We've been at this all day," he said. "You hungry?"

Her stomach growled loudly in response. Laughing, she said, "I guess so!"

"How about I take you out somewhere? My treat."

"I don't think so," she said, crossing her arms over her chest. "I've got laundry and stuff to do tonight."

"Oh, come on. Laundry on a Saturday night? You're not fifty. I'll take you back to my place for dessert," he said, winking suggestively.

She smiled sadly. "Mark, what happened before…it can't happen again. The situation's too complicated. Besides, I don't date people—"

"You don't date people you work with. I know. You keep saying that. But who said anything about dating?"

She flushed. "I don't do what we did this afternoon with coworkers either."

"We were enjoying each other. There's nothing wrong with that."

"You say that now. But if we keep it up before long there will be feelings, then hurt feelings, and eventually heartbreak. I don't do heartbreak," she answered.

Mark felt himself getting frustrated. "You don't do heartbreak. I don't do relationships. So we should be well matched."

"I don't think so…" she said, looking everywhere except at him.

Mark gently turned her to face him.

"Listen to me. This situation *is* complicated. We don't need to add sexual frustration to the mix. After all, we didn't get anywhere today until after we let that go. Right?"

She gave a slight nod.

"And you have to agree the sex is amazing. Probably some of the best I've ever had."

She looked up sharply. "Really?" she said.

"Really."

"I thought it was just… I mean you've been with so many… And I…um…haven't…"

"Becky?"

"What?"

"You're amazing. Period."

She smiled, her cheeks flushing pink. "Thank you."

"You're welcome. So let's just agree to enjoy each other until this—whatever this is—is over and decided. Then we'll go our separate ways. No harm, no foul."

She looked at him. "Do you really think it can be that easy?"

"I know it can," he said. "I won't let it be any other way."

She stared at him for a long moment, an unreadable expression on her face. "I'll think about it," she said.

He nodded, knowing that was probably the best answer he could hope for at the moment.

"Don't think too long," he growled.

She just smiled in response, blowing him a kiss as she walked out through the door.

He knew she'd eventually agree to his proposition. The chemistry they had was too incredible for either of them to walk away. And as long as they kept it to the physical realm no one would get hurt.

Heck, he didn't have enough cash to make her want anything more permanent anyway. She might not *seem* interested in his wallet, but he knew from experience that even the sweetest girls were ultimately moved by money.

For the first time he found himself wishing they weren't.

CHAPTER FIVE

"THIS IS GOOD. Really good," David said after Becky and Mark had pitched their concept to him. "Which one of you came up with it?"

Nice try, Becky thought. She wasn't going to let him knock one of them out of the competition that easily.

"It was pretty organic," she said out loud. "I couldn't tell you which one of us nailed the final line. Could you, Mark?"

"No, not really," he said. "We make a surprisingly great team."

"Good, good—glad to hear it," David said, leaning back in his chair, hands behind his head. "Now we just have to decide how to proceed."

"When is the presentation?" Becky asked.

"October thirtieth at ten a.m."

"Oh. Good. We've got some time, then," she said. More than three weeks, as a matter of fact.

She looked at Mark. He looked back at her, his face pinched with uncertainty. Okay, since he didn't seem to be willing to take charge they were going to do things her way.

"Here's what I think," she said. "I think we need to overwhelm the client with our awesomeness. We need to go in there with print, digital, TV—the works. Obviously we're going to need everybody's help. Mark and I will act as creative leads and work on the big concept stuff—I'm thinking we should tackle TV first—and we'll break everybody else into small teams to handle individual projects. We'll meet with the teams daily, to check their progress and keep everyone on task. When we're satisfied with a project, we'll bring it to you for final approval. Sound good?"

David leaned forward, reluctant admiration showing in every line of his face. "That's a good plan," he said. "If I didn't know better I'd think you'd been handling assignments like this for years."

Don't blush, she told herself. *Don't you dare blush.*

"Thank you," she said. "I've been waiting a long time for an opportunity like this."

"Better get to it," David said. "You have a lot to accomplish in a very short amount of time."

Becky nodded at Mark and they rose, walking silently across the office.

"Good luck," David called as they closed the door. "I'll be watching you. Remember, this is still a competition!"

It was well after eight p.m. before Becky was finally able to sit down at her desk.

It had been a long day of kick-off meetings and strategy sessions, but the teams now had their marching orders and were ready to move forward.

Groaning, she kicked off the patent leather heels that had been torturing her feet all day and massaged her toes. If this was what her life was going to be like from now on she was going to have to invest in some more practical shoes.

And some protein bars, if the tormented sounds issuing from her empty stomach were any indication.

She was seriously considering eating the wizened apple she'd found at the back of a drawer when Mark walked in, carrying a delicious-smelling pizza.

"Dinner is served, my lady," he said, presenting it to her with a flourish.

Becky tore open the box and grabbed a slice of the pepperoni-studded goodness. "It's official," she said, practically moaning as the heavenly mixture of cheese, tomato sauce and bread hit her tastebuds. "You are my hero."

"I try," he said, snagging a piece for himself. "Some days it's easier than others."

They chewed in companionable silence.

"What do you think?" he eventually said. "Can we pull this off?"

"'This' meaning…?"

"The pitch. Three weeks isn't a lot of time to finish everything you proposed."

"Oh. Well, yeah, of course we can. Especially since we've got an entire department of talented people at our disposal."

"That does help," he said between bites. "I've never experienced this level of support before. I'm usually the guy they bring in to salvage a project that's gone off the rails or save an account that's in danger. No one ever really *wants* to work with me."

She thought that sounded kind of lonely, but didn't think he'd appreciate it if she told him so. "It is a pretty unique thing you do. How on earth did you end up being a modern-day dragon slayer?"

"I'm not sure. Just luck, I guess."

"That's some luck you have. You've worked with some of the best agencies out there," she said, eyebrows raised.

"Yeah, well, I've got some connections. It's all about who you know in this business," he said, looking off into the distance.

The sour look on his face was one she'd seen only once before.

"Let me guess. The stepdad?"

"The one and only." Mark grimaced. "He'd do just about anything to keep me out of his house and away from his wife."

"What does he do, anyway?" For some reason, Becky

imagined Mark's stepdad as being some kind of modern-day nobility, living off his inheritance and not doing much of anything.

"You've heard of Kipper, Vonner and Schmidt?"

She snorted. "Of course. They're only the largest ad agency in New York."

"My stepdad's the Kipper. And he bought out Vonner."

"Oh," Becky said, trying not to be impressed. "I guess he *would* have connections."

"Yep. He's the only reason I ever got any work. At least to begin with."

Becky was willing to bet there was more to the story than that. But she wasn't in the mood to push.

"Well, connections or no, you're really good at what you do—at least according to the internet. You've got almost as many awards as I do."

"Ah, so you cared enough to look me up, huh?"

"Of course. You didn't think I'd let you back into my pants without making sure you weren't a serial killer first, did you?"

"I wasn't aware that you'd put much thought into the situation at all."

She lowered her eyes, suddenly unable to meet his penetrating gaze. "Well, I may have done it post-pants-getting-into. Last night."

"I see. And what did you decide?"

She smiled. "Well, it was quite a debate. On the one hand, you're great for stress relief."

"Sure—I'll buy that."

"But you're bad for the rep. I had an ice-queen thing going, you know."

"Well, it's too late to save her," he teased. "I distinctly remember seeing her melt Saturday afternoon."

"You might be right. But I was a little worried I might lose my competitive advantage by sleeping with you."

"A valid concern."

"But then I realized engaging in pillow talk is a great way to gather intel."

"True enough."

"There's also the brain goo problem."

"Brain goo?"

"Yeah, when I'm around you and start thinking about what we could do to each other my brain turns to goo."

"Oh," he said, looking devilishly pleased. "Well, that's a good problem to have."

"It is. Especially since the best way to fix it is to do the things I'm thinking about."

"Which means...?"

"Which means you should probably stock up on condoms. I have a very good imagination."

He grinned. "I already did."

"Good. Because you know what I'd like to do right now?"

"What?"

"Have sex in an elevator."

"Did you just...? You want to have...?"

"Sex in an elevator. Yes. It was all I could think about on the way down from David's office this morning."

He shot up from his chair, excitement and desire dancing in his eyes. "Let's go, then. I wouldn't want your brain to be clogged with goo any longer than it needs to be."

A short time later, Becky hit the lobby button so their elevator could resume its descent. Her brain was magnificently clear—and her thighs were wonderfully achy.

Elevator sex was much more acrobatic than it looked in the movies. If Mark hadn't been so wonderfully strong it wouldn't have been possible at all.

Becky peeked over at the man in question just in time to see him rubbing his biceps.

"I guess you got your workout for the day, huh?"

He smiled at her ruefully. "I think I did. Totally worth it, though."

Feeling strangely shy now that the deed was over, Becky blushed and looked up at the ceiling to avoid his eyes—only to find herself looking at a different kind of lens.

"Oh, crap," she breathed. "There's a camera up there."

Mark's jaw dropped. "What are you talking about?"

She pointed. "There's a camera. In the ceiling."

"Oh, well..." he said.

"Oh, well? I tell you we were just filmed having sex and you say, *Oh, well?"* she squeaked.

"Becky, look at me," Mark said.

Reluctantly, she did. The intensity in his gaze was almost too much to bear.

"I'm not ashamed of what we've done here. If someone wants to watch, let them," he said. "Besides, no one ever looks at those tapes unless there's a robbery or something."

Looking into the bottomless pits that were his eyes as she was, she couldn't doubt his sincerity. He meant what he was saying. Deciding there was nothing she could do about it anyway, Becky nodded.

"I guess you're right," she said, and reached up for one last kiss.

Just then the elevator bell dinged.

"Well, I guess that puts an end to the evening's festivities," Becky said as she pulled away and stepped out through the open doors into the marble lobby.

"It doesn't have to," Mark replied. "You could come home with me."

For a brief moment Becky found herself wondering what it would be like to fall asleep in his arms. Heaven, probably. Better not to think about it.

"Nah, I don't think so," she said, wrapping her arms tightly around herself. "I'll leave you to your dreams.

They're bound to be steamier than anything I can come up with."

Mark let out a bark of laughter as he held the glass door open for her. "This from the woman who just propositioned me with elevator sex? I don't think you give yourself enough credit, my dear."

"Well," she said as she breezed past him, "I guess it's up to you to top my idea, then. Better put your thinking cap on."

Blowing him a kiss, she strode off into the dark night, waiting until he was out of earshot to give in to the hysterical giggles that were bubbling at the back of her throat. Her sex-kitten act was going to need work if they kept this up very long.

Mark collapsed into the black leather massage chair in the creative conference room and closed his eyes, groaning out loud when the vibrating knobs found the tight spot between his shoulder blades.

It had been another long day spent in meetings and reviewing his team's work. He and Becky hadn't even had a chance to think about their own assignments.

This creative directing stuff was hard.

He was just starting to relax, the tension in his back mostly gone, when his phone rang. When he saw who it was he groaned again. His stepfather always had had impeccable timing.

Mentally steeling himself for a lecture, he hit the answer button.

"Hi, Bill."

There was a pause as the man on the other side of the line took a sip from a clinking glass. "Hello, son."

Mark cringed. He hated it when Bill called him that.

"What can I do for you, Bill?"

"Oh, nothing…nothing. Just checking in to see how the Eden thing is going."

"You know about that?"

His stepfather snorted. "Of course. I know everything that's going on in this industry, son. So, have you closed the deal yet?"

Mark sighed. "No, we haven't even gotten to the pitch stage yet. But it's going very well. In fact, I'm acting as creative director on the campaign…"

"That's right. You and that Becky girl. I hear she's pretty hot stuff."

"You have no idea," Mark said.

"Yeah, well, you'll keep your hands to yourself if you know what's good for you," Bill said. "It's never a good idea to mix business with pleasure."

Now it was Mark's turn to snort. "Is that what you told my mom? I seem to remember she worked for you before she married you. Unless that was a business arrangement too…"

"Just keep your hands where they belong and do this right," Bill snapped. "Our family's reputation is on the line here."

"How do you figure? I never tell anyone we're related unless I have to."

"Maybe so. But the ad world is a small place. Those who matter know you're my son."

"*Stepson,*" he snarled. "As you never failed to remind me when I was living under your roof."

"Yes, well, that was then. This is now. There's a place for you at my agency anytime you want it. Especially if you can bring—"

"I assure you, I never will," Mark broke in, and hung up.

He couldn't take any more of his stepfather's asinine advice today. Although he had deflected the question, Mark knew that love had very little to do with Bill's marriage to his mother. She had told him so herself—on their wedding day.

He had found her pinning a flower in her hair in her opulent palace of a bedroom at Bill's house. She'd looked more beautiful than he'd ever seen her.

She'd seen him in the reflection of her mirror and smiled. "Come here, handsome," she'd said. "Let me look at you."

He'd moved to hug her, then asked the question that had been driving him crazy ever since he'd heard about their engagement.

"Mom? Why are you marrying Bill?"

"Because he asked me to," she'd answered.

"But you don't love him."

"I don't have time to wait for love," she'd said as she straightened the gray-and-white striped tie of his morning suit. "I'm not getting any younger, but you *are* getting older. And more expensive. This way I'll have a partner I can count on—and you'll have a father."

"But I don't want him to be my dad," Mark had said. "He doesn't even like me."

"He does, too. He just doesn't know you very well. Be your usual charming self and everything will be fine," his mother had said.

She couldn't have been more wrong. Bill had never shown him anything other than complete and utter disdain. Mark was sure that his stepfather considered him to be nothing more than an annoyance—a piece of unwanted baggage that unfortunately could not be parted from his wife.

He would have been better off growing up poor and fatherless.

Suddenly a soft hand landed on his shoulder.

"You look lost in thought," Becky said.

Mark shook his head to clear it. "Just relaxing," he said, and pulled her down on his lap.

She put her head on his shoulder and for a moment they just sat together, the vibrations from the still-operating massage chair the only noise.

Then she sighed. "Being a creative director is way less fun than I thought it would be."

He laughed. "You know, I was just thinking that. I haven't done any actual work today, but I'm completely exhausted."

"Me, too," she said. "But I was thinking I should try to write now that it's quiet."

She shifted on his lap, preparing to get up. But when Mark caught a glimpse of a black lace stocking as her skirt crept up her thigh all thoughts of work vanished from his brain.

"What's this?" he said, running his hand up the silken material and under the lace top.

"Oh, you know… Just a little something to keep you wondering," she said, blushing.

"Oh, I'm wondering, all right," Mark growled, mentally picturing her riding him wearing only those stockings. "I'm wondering what else is under that skirt."

She shrugged. "A lady never tells. You'll have to find out for yourself."

That was all the encouragement he needed. He let his hand wander up her smooth thigh, tracing the elastic of the garter up to where it met the satiny belt. Then his hand drifted down, toward the middle, looking for the top of her panties. But nothing blocked his way, and soon he felt the soft roundness of her mound under his fingers.

"You're not wearing any underwear," he said, and a bolt of lightning struck his groin, leaving him rock hard and aching for her.

She put a mocking hand over her mouth, unable to hide her grin. "Oops, I must have forgotten. Silly me."

"You. Are. So. Hot," he said, stroking her bare center and grinning when he saw her expression liquefy.

He plunged one finger slowly into her core, enjoying teasing her. But it wasn't enough. He knew he had to have her.

He drew his finger out and nipped her ear. "Stand up for me, Gorgeous Girl."

She did, her legs shaking the tiniest of bits.

"I'm standing," she said, her voice husky with desire. "Now what?"

Mark remembered where they were and paused. "Hang on just a second," he said, and pushed a chair under the door handle. It wouldn't do to have one of the cleaning people walk in on them.

Crossing the floor in two strides, he returned to where Becky was standing, looking beautiful and unsure. "Now, where were we?" he growled.

She smiled. "I think you were trying to get a better look at my stockings."

"Oh, yeah." He grinned. Reaching behind her, he pulled her zipper down and her gray wool skirt fell to the floor, leaving her wearing only the stockings and heels on her bottom half. He paused, taking a moment to appreciate the perfection of her body. Overcome with a fierce sort of want he couldn't remember ever feeling before, he pulled her toward him.

"I want you right here, right now," he said, sitting down again.

"In the chair?"

"You better believe it," he said, freeing himself from his pants and boxers as quickly as he could. "Get over here."

Smiling, she straddled him, plunging on top of him the second he had a condom on. They both groaned, and Mark grabbed her hips, helping her to find her rhythm. He'd never met a woman who fit him so perfectly. So deliciously. If only relationships depended solely on sexual compatibility…

In no time at all she was arching backward, pushing her breasts into his face as she rocked. He kissed the tender swell of them, feeling grateful that such an amazing woman was giving herself to him.

To show her exactly how grateful he was, he slipped a finger into the place where their bodies met, searching for the nub that brought her so much pleasure.

"Oh, God, I think I'm—"

The last bit of her sentence became a wordless yell as she spasmed over him. Seconds later, he allowed himself to follow her over the edge.

She collapsed on top of him and they sat quietly, catching their breath. Just then, his stepfather's unwanted voice echoed in his head. *Keep your hands to yourself if you know what's good for you.*

Clearly the man had no idea what he was talking about. Nothing could be better for him than this. If there was a more satisfying way to relieve stress he'd yet to find it.

Kissing her neck, he said, "I want to do that again."

"Already?" She laughed. "Give a girl a moment to recover."

"Not here. I want to take you home and love you properly."

She bit her lip, clearly trying to think of an excuse not to go.

Taking her head in his hands, he looked deep into her eyes. "Don't overthink it. I just want to spread you out on a bed and do you right. Just this once."

"All right. But just this once."

CHAPTER SIX

BECKY COLLAPSED ONTO a fluffy white pillow, letting out a deep breath as her heart rate returned to normal.

"I've said it before, and I'm sure I'll say it again, but you really are Magic Man," she said. "I can't remember the last time I felt this relaxed."

Mark raised himself up on one elbow and grinned. "Glad to be of service," he said. "Think I should go into business?"

Becky giggled. "Sure—I can picture the ad now. It could read something like, 'Forget the massage. Spend an hour with the Magic Man.' And there'd be a picture of you, wearing nothing but a top hat and holding a wand."

He groaned. "Don't quit your day job, babe."

At the mention of work Becky felt some of the tension return. "Day job? Try twenty-four-seven job. I never stop thinking about the pitch. Do you?"

"Only when I'm otherwise occupied by you," Mark said, eyes smiling. "Hey, think we could work orgasmic sex into the Eden campaign?"

Becky laughed as her stomach growled. "I don't know. I'm too hungry to think. But maybe if you feed me I'll think of a way."

Pulling on his boxers, Mark said, "Message received. Let me see what I can rustle up."

As he padded the short distance over the hardwood floor to the kitchen area Becky couldn't help but admire the gorgeous contours of his muscled body. He was by far the best-looking man she'd ever slept with—not that there'd been that many.

She hadn't had time for boys in high school, and had spent her undergrad years being too afraid of making the same mistake her mother had—dropping out of college to get married—to allow herself to have any real relationships.

In fact, other than a few drunken encounters, there hadn't been anyone until Pence. And there certainly hadn't been anyone after him.

She sighed. What a waste of a decade. If Mark had taught her anything, it was that sex could be lots of fun—especially when there were no strings attached.

Mark's voice brought her out of her reverie. "What do you want? Chinese, Thai, or pizza?"

She blinked. "You have enough stuff in that tiny refrigerator to make all of that?" It didn't look big enough to house much more than a six-pack of beer.

"Nope. I've got exactly five green olives, two hunks of moldy cheese, and one gallon of expired milk. We're getting takeout."

"Oh. Thai, I guess," she answered, leaving her cozy nest on the futon to peek at the menus he was holding out. He pulled her against his chest so they could look at the menus together, but all she could think about was the delicious way he smelled: a little bit spicy, a little bit outdoorsy, and all male.

Suddenly an idea struck her. "Maybe we could work orgasms into the campaign," she said.

"What?"

"Orgasms. Eden. I bet we could do some funny videos linking them."

He blinked. "I thought you had to eat before you could have any more brilliant ideas?"

"Yeah, well, get me some of that pineapple curry and I'll be even more brilliant," she answered.

"Coming right up," he said, and punched the number into his phone.

* * *

A couple of hours later the block of granite that did double duty as a table and a kitchen counter was littered with take-out boxes and crumpled sheets of paper.

Becky yawned and stretched. "I think we've got some pretty solid scripts here, don't you?"

"I think we've got some award-winners here—that's what I think," Mark said.

"Me, too," she said, yawning again. "Which is good, because it's definitely time for me to go home."

Mark glanced up at the clock on the microwave. "It's practically morning already. Why don't you just stay?"

A small ping of alarm sounded in her brain. Coming over for a quick hookup was one thing. Staying overnight was definitely relationship territory.

"Two o'clock is hardly morning," she said. "Besides, we've got work tomorrow. I'd rather not be seen wearing the same clothes two days in a row."

"Nobody will notice," he said, his voice softly cajoling.

"No? Not any of the fifty bazillion people I have meetings with tomorrow? I think they will."

"Well, you could always stop at home in the morning. Before going to work."

"I've got an eight a.m. meeting. No time." It was just supposed to be a quick gab with Jessie at the diner. But she'd put it on her calendar, so it counted.

Mark looked at her for a long moment. She wasn't sure what he saw, but finally he sighed and looked away.

"Fine. I'll call you a cab."

"I can walk."

"No. You can't. Not at this hour."

"Really. I can!"

"Just let me do it, okay? I'll worry about you otherwise."

She shut her mouth with a snap, unsure of what to say.

No one had worried about her in a long time. It felt good to know that he cared.

But he wasn't supposed to care. And neither was she. Caring led to relationships, which led to heartbreak—and she was sure as hell never going through that again.

"Okay," she mumbled. "Call me a cab. I'll go get dressed."

Becky poured milk into her coffee and watched the cheerful chaos that was morning in the diner, waiting for Jessie to digest what she'd told her.

"So you went to his place? Big deal," Jessie said, leaning back against the red vinyl booth.

"I thought you said that was out of bounds in office affairs?" she answered.

Jessie shrugged. "I just said that to make you feel better. Think about it: most people have to have sex in their homes. We don't all have a private office to escape to when we decide we're in the mood for a booty call."

"We've only actually done it in our office once…"

Jessie covered her ears. "*Eww.* That's enough. I don't want to know where else you guys have been. I have to work there, too, you know."

"All right, all right, I won't tell you. It's just that, well, it feels safe at work. Once we venture beyond the building it all starts to feel too relationshippy," Becky said.

Just then Rachel, their favorite waitress, arrived and slammed down their pancakes. "Here you go, ladies! Two pancake short stacks, just like usual. Enjoy!"

"Thank you, Rachel," Becky said.

"No problem," the matronly woman said. "Eat up. You're getting too skinny!"

Both women were silent as they buttered the stacks and dived in. After the first bite, Jessie pointed at Becky with her fork.

"You know what your problem is?"

"What?"

"You're overthinking it. This thing with Mark is just like the stack of pancakes in front of you. They're gorgeous to behold, delicious to experience, but when you've had enough you won't be sad, will you?"

Becky shook her head.

"Exactly. You'll enjoy your post-pancake carb coma and forget about them. Until the next time you get a craving."

With that she took another giant bite and grinned. "These are really yummy."

Becky laughed. She had a point.

"I don't think he'd like being compared to pancakes."

Jessie raised an eyebrow. "You don't think he'd like you to eat him up?"

"I don't know. Maybe I'll ask him."

"Good girl. But mind if I give you a tip?"

"What?"

"Don't use maple syrup in bed. Too sticky."

Becky blushed. "I'll try to remember that."

And just like that everything was right in her world again. She wasn't having a relationship. She was just enjoying a good breakfast after a long fast.

That she could deal with.

Mark hovered at the door to their office, afraid to go in. After Becky had left his apartment he'd tossed and turned all night.

It had been a great evening. He'd enjoyed every second of it. The sex, the food, the brainstorming…he'd never experienced anything like it. He certainly hadn't wanted it to end.

But when he'd realized how much it mattered to him that Becky got home safely—and how much he'd rather she didn't leave at all—reality had crashed in. He'd never worried about any of his other bedmates like that. In fact he was usually the one rushing them out through the door.

After Mark had seen her into a cab he'd collapsed into bed, but sleep had been the furthest thing from his mind. All he'd been able to think about was Becky. He could no longer pretend this was a simple office affair. He was starting to have feelings for this woman. Big feelings. And that was no good.

He didn't do relationships. Period. And even if he did want a relationship he couldn't have one with Becky. It was just too complicated.

It had been almost time to go to work when he'd finally faced the truth. As much as he was enjoying their time together, he had to put a stop to it. If he didn't, both he and Becky were going to get hurt.

No matter how cool Becky seemed, he couldn't take a chance on her. Sandra had taught him that love wasn't worth the pain.

Besides, she deserved someone who had enough money to take care of her. Not someone who had voluntarily cut himself off from his rich family's largesse.

Taking a deep breath, he walked through the door. And stopped dead. Becky was sitting cross-legged on the floor in a patch of sunshine, laptop perched precariously on her knees. She was jamming to something on her iPhone, humming tunelessly along to whatever song was piping through her headphones.

She looked relaxed and happy, which was a far cry from the stressed-out ball of nerves he had expected to encounter this morning.

He must have made some kind of noise because she turned. When she saw him she smiled, the grin lighting up her whole face.

It took his breath away. God, she was beautiful.

"Hey, Magic Man," she shouted, clearly not realizing her headphones were in.

He laughed in spite of himself, motioning to her to take them out.

"What?" she yelled. "Oh." Giggling, she removed her headphones. "Oh. That is better," she said, unwinding herself from her spot on the floor. "Okay, let's try this again. Good morning, Magic Man."

He smiled back at her. "Good morning."

She crossed over to him and reached up for a kiss. At the last minute he turned his cheek.

She frowned. "What's with the shy act?"

He shrugged. "I just think we should cool it during office hours."

"You do, huh? That's a first. But whatever…"

She turned and went to her desk, but not before he saw the hurt that flashed across her face.

"I've got our scripts all typed up and polished. If you want, we can go present them to David now."

He took a deep breath, knowing that if he didn't tell her what he had come to say now he never would.

"Good idea. But can we talk for a minute first?"

"Okay," she said. "This sounds serious. What's up?"

"I don't think this is a good idea anymore," he blurted.

"You don't like the campaign?"

"No, I meant this," he said, motioning to the two of them. "Us. I don't think we should pursue a personal relationship anymore."

She blinked slowly. "Wow. Okay, that's a change in tune. May I ask what prompted it?"

He shrugged again. "There's just too much going on right now. We need to focus on the task at hand."

It wasn't a lie. He definitely did need to focus on his career right now. And so did she. The fact that doing so would keep all those pesky feelings at bay was just a fringe benefit.

"I thought we decided that the best way to stay focused was to give in to our personal desires," she said, in the same carefully professional voice he had used.

"I changed my mind," he said.

She shook her head as her face flushed with anger. "You're a piece of work—you know that? First you come on all hot and heavy, begging me to give this a shot, telling me how much fun we'll have, and then, just when I'm starting to enjoy myself, you pull the plug."

"I'm sorry," he said, fighting the urge to grab her in his arms and kiss her until she forgot all about this conversation.

"I should have known better than to trust you to keep your word," she snarled. "You're a selfish bastard, just like every man I've ever known."

Grabbing her computer, she headed for the door.

"Where are you going?"

"To my office. I can't stand to look at you right now."

"This *is* your office."

"Fine. I'm going to Jessie's office, then."

"What about the scripts?"

"I'll email them to you. You can present them to David by yourself."

Then she swept out, slamming the door behind her.

Mark scrubbed his face with his hands, fairly certain he'd made a gigantic mess of things. But at least he'd done it before anyone's heart had gotten involved.

That would have been even worse.

Becky sat nursing a cup of tea in the kitchen, keeping an ear cocked toward the hallway door so she could escape out the back way if necessary. So far she'd managed to avoid Mark for three days, and she had every intention of continuing the trend.

It had been easy enough to do. She'd kept herself busy managing the print and digital teams, and let him take the lead on the broadcast stuff.

It pained her to give up control of her ideas, but the only other option was to sit in a room with him and wonder what she had done to turn him off. And, worse, what it was about her that made men want to run—even when all she wanted was sex.

Her instincts had been right. She was better off without a man in her life, even if the sex was awesome. There were enough adult sites selling sex toys to keep her satisfied for decades—no emotional entanglements required.

The only thing they couldn't do was make her laugh. But as long as Jon Stewart and Stephen Colbert continued to make their nightly TV appearances she'd have plenty of funny men in her life. It would have to be enough.

She was debating whether she should make a second cup of coffee when she heard a familiar roar in the hallway.

"Becky? Becky, where are you?" David shouted. Then, only slightly more quietly, "Just like a woman. Never around when you need her."

She slammed her cup down and strode out into the hallway.

"I'm right here," she said.

He turned, a slippery smile on his face. "Oh, there you are. I've been looking everywhere for you."

"Well, I've been sitting in the kitchen for the last twenty minutes, so…"

"Never mind, never mind—you're here now. Come with me, my dear. We need you in the production studio."

"All right," she said as they hurried down the hallway. "What's going on?"

"It's these videos," he said, holding the door open for her.

"They were brilliant on paper, but they're just not coming together. I want you to have a look."

She stopped just inside the door, waiting for her eyes to adjust to the darkness of the room. When her vision returned she saw Mark frowning into one of the eight monitors, unhappiness etched into every line of his face.

He glanced in their direction, and when he caught sight of her she was pretty sure she saw a relieved expression cross his face.

"Hey," he said.

"Hey, yourself," she said. "What did you do to our videos? I hear they lost their magic."

He ignored the dig.

"I'm not sure. Take a look and tell me what you think."

He hit a button on the keyboard and the videos began to play. Becky tried to pay attention, but found herself getting distracted by the man next to her. She could feel the heat coming from him like a physical thing. It called to her, drawing her in like a moth to a flame.

What *was* it about this man? Why did the very sight of him turn her knees to jelly? It wasn't fair. Especially since he didn't seem to feel the same way.

"So what do you think?" he asked, and she realized the videos had stopped playing.

"I'm not sure. Play them again." This time she would actually watch them.

The problem became apparent almost immediately, but she let the reel play to the end before she gave her opinion.

"It's simple. The actress you hired thinks she's in a porn movie. She doesn't appear to have a funny bone in her body. And those boobs make her look like Jessica Rabbit. The women in these videos are supposed to be way more real and way funnier."

"So what do you think we should do?" Mark asked.

"Start over."

"What?" David yelled. "We can't do that. We've already spent too much. We can't hire another actress."

"We have to," Becky snapped. "These videos are what's going to make people remember Eden. We can run all the polished TV ads we want, but if we don't find a way to connect with people, to entertain them and get them talking—well, Eden's just going to end up being another yogurt in the refrigerator case. And we're going to end up fired."

"But we don't even have the business yet! I can't possibly put up the money to do a whole new shoot—the first one cost almost fifty thousand dollars!"

Mark looked at her, a silent plea in his eyes. She thought about the night they had scripted them. About how excited he'd been. And how badly she wanted to win this account. She made the only decision she could.

"Fine. I'll do it," Becky blurted.

"You'll what?"

"I'll be your actress…but only for the version we show at the pitch. It's either that or we scrap the whole idea. We certainly can't show these to the client."

David and Mark stared at her, plainly flabbergasted.

"Are you sure you want to do that?" Mark asked.

"No, but I will. Just as long as we all understand that if they like them and want to go ahead with the video campaign, we make them give us the budget to shoot them with real actresses—actresses that I choose."

"Do you think you can pull it off?" David asked.

"Oh, I'm fairly certain I can."

"How certain?"

"Very. I can fake an orgasm right now if you want me to prove it."

David blanched. "No! No, that won't be necessary. I trust you. Just get it done. Quickly."

Then he scrabbled backward out through the door as quickly as he could.

Mark looked at her. "I guess it's just you and me, kid."

"Yep. I guess so," she said, trying to ignore the way her pulse was pounding.

"I've missed you."

He'd missed her? He'd *missed* her? How dared he…? It was his fault they'd been apart in the first place.

"Good," she said. No way was she going to admit that she'd missed him, too.

He looked at her, a rueful smile on his face. "I guess I deserved that," he said.

She nodded. "Yep. You did. But never mind that. We've got a video series to film. When do you want to start?"

He sighed. "Well, unfortunately the camera crew we used the first time has moved on to another project, and I'm not sure where to get another one on such short notice."

"Camera crew? Who needs a camera crew? We're both professionals. Let's just do it ourselves."

He raised an eyebrow. "Seriously? You think we can?"

"I don't know if you've seen the agency equipment closet, but we've got some pretty sweet cameras. As long as you can push a button we'll be fine."

"Okay," he said. "You're on. I'll book a room and we can start filming tonight."

Her mind stuttered. "A room?"

"A hotel room, silly. That's how you scripted it, remember?"

Oh. Yeah. She had. But she wasn't sure she felt comfortable being alone in a hotel room with Mark now that their relationship was back to being strictly professional.

Unfortunately she had already volunteered. She couldn't back out now.

"Right," she said. "That makes sense. Okay, you set it up and email me the details. I'll meet you there at seven."

Becky decided to spend the rest of the afternoon getting herself camera-ready. While she'd told David she wanted the videos to look real, she didn't need the client to see her in her current frazzled, haven't-looked-in-a-mirror-in-four-days state.

After three hours at the salon, getting her hair blown out, eyebrows waxed, nails manicured and face professionally made up, she was feeling much better.

Especially since she had every intention of billing it all to the agency. Now all she needed was a few outfit changes and she'd be all set. The scripts she'd written called for both yoga pants and exotic lingerie.

The yoga pants she had. But the other scenes called for a visit to her favorite lingerie boutique. She hoped David had been billing their clients regularly, because this trip was going to cost him.

She wandered around the store, looking at frilly pink confections, slinky red gowns, and black lace fantasies, unable to decide which would be best. Finally she decided to just try them all on.

Once in the fitting room, she was struck by an idea that she knew was both awesome and completely evil. Since she couldn't decide what to buy, she'd snap pics and send them to Mark.

After all, he was the art director. It was only fitting that he be in charge of wardrobe. Before she could talk herself out of it Becky took a picture of herself in a slinky red gown and composed a message to send to Mark.

Can't decide what wardrobe choices to buy for the shoot, she texted. Should I get this one?

After hitting Send, she quickly changed into the next outfit and prepared to repeat the exercise. But before she could even take the picture, her phone pinged with Mark's return text.

Hell, yes.

She grinned and sent the next picture.

How about this?

Please do.

After sending the third picture, she sat back and admired her reflection. The push-up cups in the black lace chemise made her breasts look huge…making her waist look tiny by comparison. Her hair was thicker than she'd ever seen it, and her face practically glowed under the makeup.

She might not be a porn star, but she looked pretty damn good.

Finally, her phone pinged.

GET THEM ALL, his text read.

Her veins buzzed with triumph. Hopefully, he was sincerely regretting his hasty decision to end the physical side of their relationship right now. He certainly would be by the time the night was over if she had anything to say about it.

CHAPTER SEVEN

Mark drummed his fingers impatiently on the glass table-top. Everything was ready for the shoot. Now all he needed was for his talent to show up. Hopefully with her clothes on.

He'd chosen to rent a suite instead of a hotel room. He'd told himself that it was so they'd have plenty of space to set up their equipment, but if he was being honest he knew it was so he'd have somewhere to retreat if the temptation to touch her got to be too much.

Lord knew the pictures she'd sent this afternoon had been enough to get him rock hard. She looked like something out of his fantasies, her innocently mischievous expression contrasting wildly with the siren's body underneath. He was certain better men than him would fall victim to the silent promise in every pixel of those images.

But he wouldn't. Couldn't.

If he touched her again he wouldn't be able to stop. And if he didn't stop touching her, their hearts would get involved. And then, if he wasn't careful, he'd find himself with a life full of... His mind showed him pictures of weddings and babies and laughing families. But he shook his head, rejecting the images.

It would all end in heartbreak. Even if they made it to the altar, love never lasted. She'd get bored, find someone better and wealthier, and he'd end up crushed. It was better not to go there in the first place.

He jumped at the sudden knock on the door.

Becky had arrived. After taking a moment to push all

his inappropriate emotions back into the box where they belonged, Mark opened the door.

And felt lust roaring to life all over again.

Gone was the fresh-faced woman he worked with. In her place was a primped and polished beauty who looked as if she'd just stepped out of a magazine cover.

"Wow," was all he could say.

She raised her eyebrow. "Is that your new version of hello?"

"No. Sorry. Come in. It's just…you look fantastic."

"Well, it's not every day I find myself starring in an advert," she said as she breezed past him. "I thought I should look the part."

Once inside the door, she stopped dead and whistled.

"Whoa! When you do something, you don't believe in going halfway, do you?"

The suite *was* pretty spectacular. Dark mahogany wood covered the floor and supported the sky-high ceiling. The bed was king-size and ultraplush, with what seemed to be a mountain of fluffy blankets and pillows piled on top. Through a door to the right there was a kitchen area that gleamed with stainless steel appliances and sparkling granite counters. At the back, just in front of the two-story-tall windows, was a living area outfitted with a white leather couch and vivid red club chairs. And, although Becky couldn't see it, Mark knew she'd die when she saw the bathroom. It had a tub big enough to swim in, a two-person shower, and more complimentary beauty products than he'd ever seen.

"Well, you know… This is on the company. I figured why settle for anything less than the best?" he said, grinning.

She laughed. "We're on the same wavelength, then. I don't even want to tell you how much I spent in the lingerie store."

A strange kind of hunger growled to life in the pit of his stomach. "Well, if the pictures you sent were any indication, I'd say whatever you spent was well worth the cost."

"Well," she said with a wicked smile, "you'll be seeing them in the flesh in just a few minutes. Where do you think we should start?"

The bed. That was where he wanted to start…and finish. But only if he was in it with her. Unfortunately, that was the one place he couldn't go.

"Maybe we should tackle the 'before' parts of the skits first, then tackle the 'after.' That way you don't have to keep changing back and forth."

Plus, that way, he wouldn't have to see her in that sexy lingerie for a while.

"Okay," she said. "Why don't you get set up? I'll get changed."

He nodded, wondering if he should take a cold shower or slam his hand in a drawer or something while she was gone. He needed to do something drastic or there would be no way to keep his libido under control.

Three hours later they were done with every yoga-panted scenario the scripts called for, plus a few more Mark had thrown in just for good measure. It was time to move on to the sexy stuff.

God help him.

He busied himself setting up lights in the bedroom area, telling himself that it was no big deal. After all, the woman who'd been their lead actress in the first version of these videos had been a bona fide porn star.

He'd made it through *that* shoot with barely more than a tingle in his nether regions. Surely he could do the same now? It might be Becky playing the part, but it was still business. Sex had no place here.

None.

"All right, I'm ready," Becky called from somewhere behind him. "Where do you want me?"

Mark turned, his most professional smile on his face. "Did you remember to bring the yogurt con...?"

The sentence trailed off as his mind registered what Becky was wearing. She looked like sin made flesh. Her blond curls tumbled over shoulders covered only by a pair of spaghetti-thin red satin straps.

His eyes traveled farther down, noticing that the straps led to a slinky red gown that made the most of Becky's perfectly mounded breasts, begging him to touch them. Then it followed the contours of her itty-bitty waist before splitting into a thigh-high slit.

The leg that peeked through was wrapped in a matching red fishnet stocking, and was made to look all the longer by the spiky cheetah-print stilettos.

"Hey, I remember those shoes," he said, cursing himself for his stupidity the moment the words were out of his mouth.

She laughed. "Yeah, I figured I was spending enough of David's money without going shoe shopping, too. And these babies certainly had the desired effect the first time around."

Inwardly he groaned, remembering that first night. He hadn't thought she could possibly look any hotter than she had when he'd met her in Vegas. He'd been wrong.

"You look amazing," he said. There. That was innocent enough. He was just giving the lady her due. She didn't need to know how very close he was to ripping those amazing clothes off her body and throwing her on the bed.

She grinned happily and did a pirouette.

"I know. I really should buy things like this more often. It does wonderful things for a girl's self-confidence."

Then she swished over to the bed, crossing her legs seductively after she dropped onto its surface.

"In answer to your earlier unasked question—yes, I did bring the yogurt container. And now I am prepared to do nasty things with this spoon," she said, holding out her intended weapon.

Mark watched helplessly as she brought it to her lips and licked it seductively, then plunged it deep into her mouth. Throwing her head back, she pulled it slowly out, then traced it down her neck to linger at the top of her breasts.

Mark groaned involuntarily, every muscle in his body aching with the need to kiss her everywhere the spoon had touched—and in many places it hadn't.

Her head popped up and she grinned.

"Guess I'm doing that right, huh?"

"I'd say. You may have missed your calling as a porn star."

Her nose wrinkled. "Nah. Too many scary dudes. But maybe I could moonlight as a pinup girl. At, like, an ice cream parlor or something. Ice cream really does make me hot."

He laughed. It was good to know that the Becky he knew was still in there somewhere.

"All right, let's not get ahead of ourselves," he said. "First we've got to make you a video star."

She nodded. "Okay, let's do it."

"So, in one script you have yourself taking a bite while in bed, then having a screaming orgasm. Want to start there?"

She blushed. "Um…let's start with something tamer, shall we? I think I need to work up to that."

"Okay," he said, flipping through script pages. "Well, that thing you were just doing there was pretty close to what you've got here. But at the end you've got to call to your husband and tell him to—and I quote—'Get in here and take care of business.'"

"Right," she said, a worried look on her face. "That seemed like a much better idea when someone else was doing it, but what the hell? I said I wanted this to seem sexy and real and kind of funny, right? I can do funny sexy stuff. I'm almost sure of it."

"Based on what I just saw, I have absolute faith in you," he said. "Let's give it a try. Ready?"

"Just a minute," she said, and paused to plump her hair and her breasts. "How's my lipstick?"

"It's…fine," he said, although it took everything he had to tear his eyes from her chest.

"Good. Let's do it."

He nodded and began the countdown. "Three, two, one…action!"

At his signal she began her routine with the spoon again. But this time she added in strategic little whimpers and moans.

Mark felt himself growing hotter and harder as the seconds ticked by. Just when he thought he couldn't take it anymore, she sat straight up in bed.

"David!" she shouted. "Turn off the TV and get in here. I need you to take care of some business!"

The last part was said with a comically suggestive waggle of her eyebrows and Mark just barely managed to shut the camera off before giving in to the gut-deep laughter that was begging for release. "Oh. My. God," he said between laughs. "Did you have to use David's name?"

"You're darn right I did," she said. "Revenge is sweet." But she was smiling as she said it, and soon she was laughing, too.

Mark collapsed on the bed next to her and she let herself sag against him, still giggling. They sat like that for what felt like forever. As soon as one stopped laughing, the other would erupt in a contagious peal and they'd both be off again.

At long last the laughing fit ended and they sat, gasping, trying to catch their breath.

Mark looked in her sparkling green eyes and felt something shift way down deep in his stomach. He'd never met a woman he could laugh like that with before.

Refusing to put a name to the emotion that threatened to make itself known, he kissed her forehead. "I really did miss you, Gorgeous Girl. You're one funny lady."

She jerked back, anger suddenly sparking in her eyes. "Well, I'm glad I can make you laugh, if nothing else," she said.

Whoa. He wasn't sure what he had said that was so wrong, but he definitely wished he hadn't said it. Time to get back to business.

"All righty, then. I guess we should move on, huh?"

"Give me just a minute to change into the next outfit," she said, and clacked angrily out of the room.

Mark took a deep breath. One sexy scene down, three to go. It was going to be a hell of a long night.

Becky slathered on one last coat of crimson lipstick. They were down to the last scene. The faked orgasm scene. The one she was least sure she could pull off.

But the rest of the shoot had gone much better than she'd ever dreamed it would, so there was hope. She looked at her artificially rumpled reflection and took a deep breath. So far she'd done well, both in front of the camera and in the psyche of the man who was trying to resist her. Now all she had to do was bring it home.

This black lace get-up could only help.

She stalked out to the bedroom area, trying to remember exactly how the orgasm scene had gone in *When Harry Met Sally*. Surely it couldn't be that hard?

A low whistle brought her back to the present.

"Damn, Becky, what are you trying to do? Kill me?" Mark asked in a strained voice.

Becky raised her eyebrow. "You're the one who decided

you didn't want to touch me anymore," she said. "So, if you die from what you're seeing here tonight, I'm thinking they'd have to rule it a suicide."

He sighed and waved her over to the bed. "*Touché.* Let's just get this over with, okay?"

As Becky crossed to the bed she swished her hips as much as she was able. Then she spread her golden hair out on the pillows and prepared to play her part.

"Ready?" she called to her reluctant cameraman.

He shook his head. "No. You still look too controlled. Let your limbs go a little."

She tried to let her arms and legs relax, but felt strangely tense under Mark's dark-eyed gaze. "How's this?"

He moved forward. "No. That's not how you look when you're…in the moment. May I touch you?"

She could only nod, her mouth suddenly dry.

Gently he cupped her knees, splaying them apart slightly. The fabric of the black lace chemise fell to the side, revealing the matching panties underneath. Mark's eyes flashed, dark with desire.

"There. That's better. Now, channel your inner porn star."

Feeling too exposed, she moved the chemise so it again covered her fully. Then she looked at Mark from under her eyelashes and smiled as she lifted her hands to cup her breasts.

He hissed in response, then disappeared behind the camera.

"That's the spirit," he said. "I'm going to start the countdown now."

By the time Mark said "action" she was already turned on. She let her eyes flutter closed and sank deep into the alternative reality she wished she was living in right now. The one where Mark abandoned his camera and came to kneel at her side, gently caressing her breasts and stomach before finding his way lower, to the heated mound that hid beneath the black lace of her panties.

She moaned loudly for Mark's benefit and grabbed the yogurt container from the bedside table. Running her hands up and down its smooth surface, she tried to imagine it was Mark's penis she was stroking.

She let her moans come faster as she pictured Mark putting his mouth to work in her hot wet folds, flicking and sucking and bringing her right to the brink…

"Oh, yes," she groaned. "Oh, please. Oh, God…"

She was wondering how much longer she should continue when she felt a rough, masculine hand fumbling with her undies.

Opening her eyes, she saw Mark hovering over her, desire blazing out of his eyes.

"Oh, Mark," she breathed, seeing that victory was within her grasp. "Oh, please. Please make me come."

A primal growl rumbled in his chest as Mark tore the black lace panties off her body. Seconds later he was plunging a finger deep into her core, a ferocious look on his face. Although he was only touching her in that one sensitive place his gaze pinned her down, making her feel strangely, wonderfully helpless. This wasn't a man giving a woman what she wanted. It was a man taking what he needed— and she was happy to give it to him. Feeling the delicious pressure mount inside, she let her knees slide out to the side, giving him even better access.

"Come for me," he said gruffly. "I want to see you do it."

As soon as the words were out of his mouth she felt herself doing exactly that, her body clenching around his hand in an orgasm so intense that it left her shivering and shaking.

Quickly Mark shrugged out of his own clothes and fumbled with a condom, hands shaking as he rolled it on.

Desperate to feel him inside her, she scooted to the edge

of the bed and tried to wrap her legs around him, but he shook his head.

"No. Not that way. Flip," he said, still using that strangely authoritative tone.

She just looked at him, confused.

"Like this," he commanded, rolling her on to her stomach and propping her up on her hands and knees. Becky found herself looking down at the bed, unable to see what was going on behind her. The suspense thrilled in her blood as she waited, her whole body crying out for his touch.

Suddenly she felt his hands on her hips, grabbing the tender skin possessively.

"I want you to feel how deep I can go," he growled from somewhere behind and above her, his manhood nudging at her sensitive folds. "I want you to know that it's me, reaching into the center of you, making you mine."

He slid deep inside her core, burying himself to the hilt. She gasped, loving the feeling of complete possession, wanting him to take even more. He was claiming her, and every cell of her body celebrated, wanting to feel his imprint on her.

She rocked back against him, signaling her silent acceptance. He slammed into her, filling her to capacity, his hard thick length rubbing against all her most sensitive spots, and as he did something primal roared to life inside her. This man was hers, and she was his, in every way that mattered.

He reached down and grabbed her hair in his hands, pulling her head back. "You. Are. Mine," he said, thrusting even harder, and she shattered into a million tiny pieces, her orgasm hitting her more strongly than any ever had.

With a tortured-sounding moan he let himself go, shuddering as he came apart inside her. Then he collapsed sideways on to the bed, their bodies still connected.

She followed him down, breathing hard, trying to wrap

her head around what had just happened. She had intended to get through his defenses and get him to touch her. And, boy, had she succeeded. If only he hadn't managed to get through so many of hers, as well…

Something monumental had happened here tonight. She only hoped she had the strength to cope with whatever came next.

Suddenly exhausted, she closed her eyes and started to drift into sleep.

"I don't think we're going to be able to use that take," a sleepy voice said behind her.

Alarm bells rang in her head. "You filmed that?"

He laughed. "No. Of course not. That would get us both fired."

"Oh. Good," she said and yawned.

"Close your eyes, Sleeping Beauty," he said. "It's time to rest. It'll all still be here in the morning."

That sounded like the best idea she had ever heard.

The next thing she knew it was morning. She yawned and stretched, reaching for the warm male body she knew must still be beside her. Except…it wasn't. His side of the bed was empty and cold.

She sat up, alarmed. "M-Mark?"

Surely he hadn't run again. Not after what had happened last night. "Mark? Are you here?"

For a long moment there was silence and she began to panic. He couldn't be gone. They needed to talk. She needed to make sure none of those last scenes had been captured on film.

"Mark?" she yelled. "Where are you?"

Still nothing.

She was fumbling for her flimsy excuse for a nightgown, swearing quietly to herself, when she heard the suite's door open. "Mark?"

"Yeah, babe. I'm here," he said, coming to stand in the bedroom door. "I just went to get you some coffee. Venti soy, right?"

Relief flooded through her system. "Yep. I'm impressed that you remembered," she said, padding over to where he stood.

He handed her cup to her, then swooped down to give her a tender kiss. "I try to remember everything about the people who are important to me," he said.

Important? She was important to him? That was a switch. Suddenly she felt vaguely ashamed of her behavior the night before.

"Look, I know you didn't want to be physical anymore," she said, looking down. "So if you want to forget what happened last night I understand."

He sighed.

"I couldn't forget it if I wanted to," he said. "Becky, look at me."

Reluctantly, she looked up, expecting to see derision in his eyes. Instead there was only happiness.

"Look, I know I've been an ass. And I don't blame you if you want to forget *me*," he said. "But that's not what I want."

"It's not?" she asked.

"No. Truth is, I did nothing for those three days other than wish I could be with you, and laugh with you, and touch you. I was useless. You had it right all along."

"Well, of course I did," she said, trying to catch up to him. "What was I right about, exactly?"

"There's no harm in what we're doing. We're just making the best of a crazy situation and enjoying ourselves along the way."

"So you want…?"

"I want you. For as long as we're both into it. No strings, like you said. Just fun."

Just fun. That was definitely what she had wanted. But,

remembering the way her heart had flipped the night before, Becky was pretty sure she was getting into deeper waters.

But he didn't need to know that.

"Okay, you're on," she said, injecting a smile into her voice. "But if you freak out on me again, I reserve the right to do serious damage."

He raised an eyebrow. "What kind of damage?"

She gently caressed his penis through his pants, bringing it roaring back to life.

"I'm not going to tell you. Where's the fun in that? But it would be in an area that's precious to you."

She waited for the shocked expression to cross his face, then turned her back.

"Last one in the shower's a rotten egg," she called as she pulled the gown free of her body and headed for the bathroom.

Seconds later, Mark sprinted by. "Nope, last one in the shower's the first to get taken advantage of," he said, laughing.

At that, Becky slowed. She'd never heard a better reason to take her time.

Becky plopped down on to the red vinyl seat across from Jessie, unable to keep the smile from her face.

"Wow, you look happy," Jessie said. "Did Mark suddenly drop out of the competition?"

Becky laughed. "Of course not!"

"Did David finally come to his senses, realize you're the most amazing copywriter who ever lived, and promote you?"

Becky could only snort. "As if."

"Did he have a heart attack and die and leave the agency to you?"

"Who?"

"David, of course," Jessie said. "Who else?"

"Oh," Becky said. "No. Which is good. I wouldn't want someone's death on my conscience. Besides, I want David to have to admit that I'm talented and worthy of promotion before he kicks the bucket. If he doesn't, I may have to chase him into the afterlife."

"All right, then, I give up. Why are you so smiley? Did you forget you have the biggest pitch of your life in less than two weeks?"

"I wish I could," Becky said, scooting to the window side of the booth and stretching her legs out on the seat. "But there's not a chance of that."

Their favorite waitress bustled over with a gap-toothed smile. "Well, if it isn't my two favorite advertising ladies," she said. "You're looking good today."

Becky giggled up at the matronly woman. "Thank you, Rachel. Your uniform looks pretty fetching today, too!"

Rachel cocked an eyebrow at Becky. "You look different," she said. "All glowy and stuff. Are you in love? Are you finally going to bring me some eye candy? We could use some good-looking man flesh to pretty up the place around here."

Becky felt herself pale. "In love? N-no. Farthest thing from it. I haven't got time for anything like that," she sputtered.

"Mmm-hmm," Rachel said. "Whatever you say. Should I bring you two the usual?"

Becky felt her stomach flip uncomfortably at the idea of pancakes.

"I'll just have a piece of dry toast, if you don't mind. And maybe some tea?"

Rachel gave her another piercing look, but just nodded and turned to Jessie. "How 'bout you? Are you going all rabbitlike on me, too?"

Jessie shook her head. "Nope. In fact, you can bring me

her stack of pancakes, if you want. Working all these hours has made me hungry!"

"You got it," Rachel said, and walked away.

"So what did you do this weekend?" Becky asked, desperately trying to deflect the question she knew was coming.

"Doesn't matter. Right now, I'm interrogating my best friend. *Are* you? In love?"

"No," Becky said, "I most definitely am not. I'm making plenty of love, but not falling into it."

"Ah. So you and Mark are at it again, huh? That didn't take long."

"No," Becky said, "It didn't." Even though it had felt like an eternity.

"And how is it? The sex? Still good?"

"It's…amazing."

Truth was, since the night of the videos they'd spent almost every nonworking hour together—and some working ones. On Friday she'd cooked him dinner in her tiny apartment and fed him dessert in bed.

Then, on Saturday, he'd taken her to his favorite Vietnamese restaurant, fed her drinks in his favorite dive bar and introduced her to the dirty high that was sex in a public bathroom.

And they'd spent yesterday in the production studio, editing videos and teasing each other. It had been the most amazing weekend she could remember having in a very long time.

"Hey, space cadet?"

Becky blinked, bringing herself back to the present. "Yeah?"

"You sure this is just a fling?"

"Yes. Positive," Becky said, trying to convince herself it was true. "We both know the rules. We're having a lot of fun."

"Hmm," Jessie said. "It's just I haven't seen you look this happy…well, ever. Maybe you should rethink where you're headed with this thing. This guy's good for you."

Becky glared at her friend. "No. When this pitch is over, this thing with Mark and me ends, too. I'll be too busy after I get promoted to bother with a man."

"All right, you know I support you, girl. But there's more to life than work."

Unfortunately that was something Becky was becoming all too aware of. Good thing she knew that Mark had no intention of starting a "real" relationship…

Otherwise she might find herself tempted to take Jessie's words to heart.

Mark hit Stop on the remote and flipped the lights back on, pride snaking through his belly. The videos had turned out well. Really well. If David didn't like them—well, he was an ass.

"So what do you think?" he asked.

David blinked slowly for a moment, silent. Then he smiled.

"I think you two deserve congratulations. If Eden doesn't sign on the dotted line after seeing these, then nothing will convince them. These are deal-closers," David said.

Mark looked at Becky and grinned. "I'm glad you like them. We worked hard to put these together."

David looked at Becky.

"I had no idea you had it in you to act like that, my dear," he said, leering slightly. "If you didn't work for me, I'd be tempted to ask you out for dinner."

Mark felt his hackles go up. Instinctively he moved closer to Becky, even though he knew she didn't need protecting.

"Wow, David, that's quite the compliment," she said. "But if you asked me I'd say no. I don't date married men."

David flushed. "Well, uh, I was just speaking hypothetically," he stuttered.

Mark decided it was time to step in.

"I'm glad you liked the videos," he said. "But we've got a lot more work to do. Far too much to think about even hypothetical dates."

David took the out he'd been offered.

"I'm sure you do," he said as he headed for the door. "So, uh, I'll leave you to it! Keep up the good work."

After the door closed Becky kissed him on the cheek.

"Thank you, Magic Man."

"No need to thank me. You were doing a fine job of putting him in his place."

"Yeah, but if you hadn't spoken up it may have come to blows," she said. "And I don't feel like going to jail today." She stretched and yawned. "But you know what? I *do* feel like I need a break."

"One that involves taking your clothes off?" he asked, waggling his eyebrows suggestively. He hadn't had her in his arms in…almost eighteen hours. They were overdue.

Becky laughed. "Nice try. Actually, I'd like to go on a picnic."

"A picnic?" That was definitely not what he'd had in mind.

"Yeah. Have you been outside today? It's beautiful," she said, opening up the window shades.

He turned to look outside. Sure enough, the sun was shining, and if he looked down he could see that the people below seemed to be wearing warm weather gear.

"Well," he said slowly, "it has been several days since I've seen the sun. But I have to admit I've never been on an actual picnic. How does this work?"

"You're a picnic virgin? At your age? Huh! Leave it to me, big boy. I'll take good care of you," she said, smiling.

* * *

A short time later they were outside in the warm October sunshine.

"First we need to get some eats," Becky said, pulling him into an upscale bodega. Grabbing a shopping basket, she headed for the dairy section. "Cheese," she said. "We need cheese."

"How 'bout this?" Mark asked, holding up a package of precut artisan cheeses.

"Perfect," she said.

"Next up, bread," she added, placing a warm baguette in the basket. "And these strawberries will do nicely." Then she headed to the deli case. "Are you hungry? Because I could really go for some meat."

She motioned to the butcher, and soon a hefty packet of sliced deli meats joined the treats in their basket.

"Oh, and wine! But I'll let you choose."

Mark grabbed a bottle of Chardonnay, adding a bar of dark chocolate for good measure. He felt himself getting absurdly excited about their upcoming picnic. It was the kind of thing he'd always wanted to do with his mother. But she'd never had the time or the inclination.

Becky found him and he snapped out of his reverie.

"Ready?"

He nodded.

They paid and rejoined the happy throng outside, everyone seemingly intent on getting the most out of what could be the season's last warm day.

"We've got our food. Now where to?" he asked.

"That's for me to know…"

"And me to find out?" he finished.

"Yep." She grabbed his hand and tugged. "This way."

They walked in companionable silence, enjoying the warm breeze and rambunctious crowd. A toddler raced by, giggling gleefully.

"Josh! Josh, get back here, or so help me God…" a frantic voice yelled from somewhere behind them.

Mark jogged forward and grabbed the hood of the child's sweatshirt.

"Hey, little man, I think you're forgetting someone," he said, smiling.

Scooping him up, he carried the boy back to his petrified mother.

"I take it this is Josh?"

She took the boy from his arms, relief flooding her face.

"Yes. Oh, thank you. He was right there and then…I thought I'd lost him!"

"Hey, no problem," Mark said, squeezing her shoulder. Tapping Josh's nose with his finger, he admonished him. "No more running for you, young man. Don't you know that there are alligators in the sewers, just waiting for a tasty morsel like you to run by?"

The boy's eyes grew wide.

"Really?"

"Really. Your mom will tell you all about it," he said, and jogged back to Becky.

"That was really nice of you," she said, a thoughtful look on her face.

"I am the child of a single mom—or at least I was when I was young. I remember doing things like that to her. This was my penance."

"That's right. You said your mom didn't remarry until you were a little older?"

"Marry. Not remarry. I was born a bastard."

Becky winced. "That's pretty strong language. I'm sure she never thought of you that way."

Mark smiled bitterly. "Oh, I'm sure she did. Her pet name for me was Mr. Mistake. I pretty much ruined her life."

Lord knew, he had enough memories of his mother looking tired and worried, massaging her temples at the kitchen table.

Whatever you do, Mark, she'd say, bending over her calculator, *don't have kids. Life's hard enough as it is.*

He certainly never intended to. Especially since he had no desire to get involved enough with a woman to make a child. No relationships, no children, he chanted to himself. No relationships, no…

Becky squeezed his hand, bringing him out of his daydream.

"I'll bet you were her favorite mistake," she said. "You're definitely mine."

He smiled, which he was sure was the effect she had intended. "Oh, so I'm a mistake, am I?" he asked, one eyebrow raised.

"Oh, most definitely. One I enjoy making over and over again," she answered, her hand sliding into his front pocket and caressing his suddenly hard penis. "In fact, I'd like to do it again this afternoon."

"Mmm," he growled. "Keep doing that and you'll be making it in the next alley I can find."

"Now, now," she said. "Have a little patience. We're almost there."

"I guess we are," he said, suddenly realizing they'd arrived at Central Park.

A short while later she tugged at his hand again, urging him off the blacktopped path they'd been following and onto a carpet of green grass.

They were standing on a gentle slope. At the bottom was a peaceful lake, its waters reflecting the blazing reds, golds and oranges of the trees that surrounded it.

"This is amazing," he said.

"Isn't it? It's just about my favorite spot in the whole park."

She sat down under a fiery red maple tree and started unloading their picnic.

"What do you want to try first?" she asked, looking up at him.

Mark sat down next to her and gathered her up in his arms. "You," he said, and kissed her.

As always, the gentle kiss he'd intended to give her quickly morphed into something more. Her mouth opened under his and he moaned.

"Becky," he said, nibbling at her neck, "you make me crazy."

"Mmm," she murmured, tilting her head to give him better access to the sensitive pulse point, "I could say the same thing about you."

Mark glanced up. For the moment, at least, they were alone. He pushed his hand underneath her brown corduroy skirt, his fingers seeking the place his mouth wanted to go.

He stroked the edges of her cotton panties and said, "I want to make you come."

"Do you think it's safe?"

"Don't worry. Nobody will see."

Panting slightly, she nodded. "All right. If you're sure."

"I am," he said, scooping her up into his lap.

He stroked her silken folds through her underpants, smiling when she moaned. He loved that it was so easy to get her going. Slowly he increased the pace, his heart rate increasing as her breath sped up. Finally, when he couldn't take it anymore, he reached underneath to caress the tiny knob of pleasure at her core. In seconds she began writhing silently on his lap as she climaxed, then collapsed against his chest. He smiled with satisfaction, knowing she'd never trust anyone else enough to let go like that in public.

"You are amazing," she sighed.

"I thought the word was *magic?*"

"That, too."

He lay back on the grass, keeping her snuggled securely against his chest.

Looking up at the scarlet leaves above them, he sighed contentedly. "You were right," he said. "This was a fantastic idea."

"I usually am." She grinned.

"True enough."

He closed his eyes and relaxed, letting the sound of the wind in the trees lull him to sleep.

He woke up with a start when his phone burst into life.

Groggily, he reached into his pocket and grabbed it, hitting the Talk button without even looking to see who it was.

"Hello?" he said sleepily.

"Forget hello. Where the hell *are* you?" David said.

He sounded furious.

"Becky and I decided to take advantage of the nice weather and do a little brainstorming off-site," he said.

"Well, get your asses back here. The client has decided to move up the presentation by an entire week. That means we have three days."

Crap.

"We're on our way," he said, and hung up.

"What was that about?" Becky asked, blinking sleepily.

"Eden has moved the presentation up. We've got three days."

"What?" she said, rubbing her face sleepily. "Okay… okay, we can do this. We just need to get our asses in gear."

She stood and gathered up their food.

"We never got to eat," he said sadly.

"No worries. I have a feeling the food's going to come in handy. Sounds like we're not going to be leaving the office much for the next little while."

"You're right about that," he said, leaning down to give her one last kiss.

"What was that for?"

"I don't think we're going to have much time for fun and games," he said. "That's to tide you over."

The next three days passed in a caffeine-fueled blur. Mark and Becky worked nonstop, pausing only to sleep when it became absolutely necessary.

Their teams toiled beside them, and against all odds they created a stunningly good campaign. When it was over, Mark was proud of the work they had done—and even more proud of the woman who had worked at his side.

She was the heart and soul of the team, doling out encouragement when needed, praise when deserved, and tissues whenever the occasion seemed to call for it.

It was obvious that everyone loved and respected her, and Mark realized that if there was any justice in the world he'd have no shot at the creative director title. She deserved it far more than he did.

Mark had sent her to get some rest and was just packing the last of the boards away when David found him.

"You've done great work here, Mark," he said.

"Thank you, but it was a team effort. I couldn't have done it alone."

"Still, I've been watching you and I've been impressed by what I've seen. You have the makings of an outstanding creative director."

Mark couldn't help but be pleased by the praise.

"Thank you. I hope to be when my time comes."

"I have a feeling your time will come tomorrow," David said. "There's still a promotion up for grabs, remember?"

"I do, but I don't know how you're going to decide who gets it. Becky has worked just as hard as I have."

"She has," David agreed. "But I'm just not sure I sense the same potential for leadership in her."

Obviously the man was blind.

"Are you kidding? The team would follow her right up to the gates of hell—and even beyond—if she asked them to."

"You're right. The power of a pretty face can't be underestimated," David said. "Don't sweat it. I'll find the right place for her."

Mark stared hard at David's retreating back. How could the man be so willfully obtuse? He had one of the industry's most talented women working for him and he didn't appreciate her at all.

One thing was for sure. When he was in charge things would be different.

CHAPTER EIGHT

As THEY RODE the elevator to the twenty-sixth floor of
Eden's headquarters Becky checked her reflection in the
shiny metal door, nervously tucking a stray hair behind
her ear and checking her teeth for lipstick for the hun-
dredth time.

"Babe, don't worry," Mark said. "You look great."

She knew she did. Her hair shone like gold against the
navy blue of her suit jacket. The A-line skirt flattered her
curves, and her heels were a to-die-for shade of ruby-red—
not to mention dangerously high.

"We're a pretty good-looking team, if I do say so myself." She grinned, enjoying the sudden rush of adrenaline
that flooded through her veins.

"You better believe it. Flash those pearly whites at them
and they'll be ours before we even say a word."

"I hope you're right," Becky said.

"I know I am," Mark answered, bending down to give
her a quick peck on the mouth.

Just then the elevator doors dinged open and Mark
straightened.

"You ready?"

"As ready as I'll ever be," she replied.

They made their way through an empty oak-paneled
lobby and headed for the conference room labeled Agency
Pitch.

They hesitated outside and Mark squeezed her hand, a
question on his face. She winked up at him and whispered,
"Let's do this thing."

He nodded and stepped inside. Becky followed.

There were twelve business-suited men and women sitting around a long oak table. They were making polite conversation while noshing on coffee and doughnuts, but all chatter ceased when they noticed Becky and Mark standing there.

"Ah, there you are," David said, rising from his chair. "Ladies and gentlemen, this is Becky Logan and Mark Powers, the creative masterminds behind today's presentation. Between the two of them they've won more than a dozen major advertising awards and worked for some of the hottest brands around. I selected them for this project specifically because I knew they had the fresh attitude and unexpected creative flair you need. I know normally we'd do a round of introductions, but we have a lot to cover, so if it's okay with you I'd like to just let them dive in."

There was murmured assent from around the table.

"Great," David said. "Mark, Becky—take it away."

Mark looked at Becky and she nodded. They'd already agreed that he would start the presentation.

He took a deep breath and strode to the head of the table.

"Good morning, ladies and gentlemen," Mark boomed, smiling at the multitude of gray suits in the room. "I hope you brought an extra pair of socks, because we're about to blow the ones you're wearing right off."

"That's right," Becky chimed in. "The campaign we're about to present to you is like nothing you have ever seen. It will change the way business is done in your industry— and make your competition green with jealousy."

"She's not kidding, folks. Tell them how you came up with the idea."

"Well, I was sitting at my desk late one night, thinking, *Now, why would a woman buy our yogurt? What does it do for her?* What do you guys think? Why does a woman buy yogurt?"

A tall redhead raised her hand.

"Yes?" Becky said, waving in her direction.

"Well, because it tastes good," the woman answered.

"Yeah, it does—but so does ice cream. Anyone else?"

"Well, she buys *our* yogurt because it's all natural, high in protein and low in fat," a gray-haired man said.

"Ah-ha, now we're getting closer to the truth. Women buy yogurt because it makes them feel good about themselves. Not only are they making a healthy choice, but they're making a decision even the most critical part of them can appreciate."

"So you're saying we should market our yogurt as a diet aid? That's already been done," the redhead said.

"No, not as a diet aid," Mark said. "As a portal to another world—one where every woman achieves her version of perfection. Show them the concept, Becky."

Becky uncovered the first board.

A woman sat in a classic yogini pose, looking calm and Zen, while surrounded by screaming kids and spilled milk.

"Eden. The snack for the perfect you."

Over the next hour the two of them bantered back and forth effortlessly, trapping the client in a silken web. When the presentation was over, everyone at the table clapped.

The graying middle-aged man who had chimed in at the beginning stood up.

"I'm sold. David, get your team moving, because I want to get this campaign in market by January one."

"You've got it, Larry," David said, clapping the paunchy man on his back. "We look forward to it."

"Great. And, just to be clear, I want these two in charge," he said, pointing at Becky and Mark. "No one else. Don't foist me off on your B team—you hear me?"

David smiled his sleazy salesman grin. "Not to worry, my man. After all the work this team has put in, we wouldn't dream of giving it to anyone else."

The man nodded his satisfaction. Turning his attention to Becky and Mark, he said, "I look forward to getting to know you two better. I know we're going to do wonderful things together."

Becky gave him her brightest smile, her heart soaring. "We certainly will. Thank you for your confidence in us."

"Yes, thanks," Mark chimed in. "We'll try to knock your socks off every time we meet."

"I'm counting on it," said Larry. "Now, if you'll excuse me, I have some business to take care of. Where's Mary?"

A tall woman rushed to his side. "Yes, sir?"

"Is that other creative team still waiting downstairs?"

"Yes, they are. They're scheduled to begin presenting in fifteen minutes."

"Send them home. I have no use for them now. Can't stand their creative director anyway."

"Right away, sir," she said. Then she turned her attention to David. "Can you see yourselves out? I really need to take care of this."

David nodded. "Of course. We'll get everything cleared up and be on our way."

"Great," she said, and hurried out.

Becky busied herself with the boards so no one would see her triumphant smile. Inside, though, she was jumping up and down with glee.

Take that, Pence, she thought. *You've just been schooled by your former student. Booyah!*

When the last bigwig had left the room, David came over and clapped them both on the back.

"Well, team, I believe congratulations are in order. You pulled it off!" He looked down at the gold Rolex on his wrist. "Let's see. It's noon now. Meet me in the large conference room at four and we'll make it official."

"Make what official?" Becky blurted.

David gave her a sly smile. "I guess you'll have to show up to find out."

He waved goodbye and left, leaving them alone in the conference room.

Mark held up his hand. "High five," he said, grinning. "We did it."

She slapped it enthusiastically.

"What do you think David will do? Larry specifically said he wants both of us on the team."

"I have no idea," Mark said. "And I'm not really in the mood to worry about it. Let's go have us a Midwestern carnivore kind of lunch—and charge it to the company."

"That sounds fantastic," she said. "But let's go see if we can find Pence's team and gloat first."

The moment they stepped off the elevator Becky heard the sound of raised voices. One definitely belonged to Pence.

Becky grabbed Mark's hand and followed the squawks into the central reception area.

"What do you mean, he won't see us? I flew my entire team from Detroit for this meeting!" Pence sputtered, his face flushing beet-red as he gesticulated wildly. "I demand that he make good on his promise to meet with us!"

Mary was doing her best to calm him. "I'm sorry, Mr. Britton, but there's nothing I can do. Mr. Richards has left for the day."

"Left for the day? How can that be? I—we…"

Becky knew she'd never have a better chance to exact her revenge. Stepping forward, she said, "Mary? I'm sorry to interrupt, but can I steal you for a second?"

Relief flooded the other woman's face. "Yes, Becky? What can I do for you?"

"David had to leave, but he wanted me to make sure to tell you that he'll be emailing over some contracts later this afternoon. In order to stick to the timeline Mr. Richards has requested we're going to need to move fast."

"Of course. I'll be on the lookout for them. Tell David he'll have the signed contracts by the end of the week."

"Wait. What?" Pence squawked, his blue eyes flashing with anger as he moved to stand in front of Becky. "Are you telling me *your* team won the business?"

"As a matter of fact I'm not telling you anything at all. You can read all about it in the next issue of AdWorld."

"You little…" Pence said, rage suffusing his face.

Before he could finish the thought, Mark stepped forward.

"Is this your old boss, Becky?"

She nodded. "The one and only."

"I've heard a lot about you," he said, extending his hand. "None of it good."

Pence reluctantly shook it. "And you are…?"

"Mark Powers. Becky's teammate. You have no idea what you missed out on when you let her go, buddy. This woman is brilliant."

Pence's already scarlet face turned even redder.

"I don't know what she's told you, but it's almost certainly not what actually happened," he said.

"I'm not interested in your opinion," Mark said. "Come on, Becky, let's get out of here."

But Becky wasn't done yet.

Turning back to Pence, she smiled sweetly. "If you get canned, give me a call. We might be able to find a job for you. In our mail room."

Then she turned on her heel and swaggered out, leaving Mark to follow.

When they were clear of the building he pulled her to him and kissed her soundly.

"That," he said between kisses, "was amazing."

"I know," she said smugly. "You have no idea how good

that felt. It's like a million-pound weight has been lifted off my back."

"Wanna celebrate...in bed?"

"I do. But not until we know for sure what we're celebrating," she said, stepping backward out of his arms. If David announced he was giving the promotion to Mark, she didn't want to hear the news while still tingling from his touch.

"Okay, then. Still up for lunch?"

She shook her head. "I'd like to be alone for a little while. It's been a big morning. I need some time to process it, you know?"

He nodded, a sad smile on his face. "I get it. See you back at the office, then?"

"Yep," she said, then reached up to give him one last melting kiss.

"What was that for?"

"Just a little something to tide you over," she said. Silently she added, *And something for me to remember you by.*

Mark jogged around the corner, his dress shoes slipping on the polished cement floor. If there was one meeting he didn't want to be late for it was this one.

Once the frosted glass doors were in sight he stopped for a second to catch his breath and straighten his tie.

This was it. If he got this promotion he could finally feel as if he'd made it. That he'd gotten where he had in his career because he was talented—not because his stepfather had greased the wheels. His mother might even be a little bit proud of him. Maybe she'd stop thinking of him as a mistake.

Taking a deep breath, he stepped through the conference room doors.

It was crowded. And hot. Everyone in the whole agency

seemed to be there, and the air was quickly growing stale. David stood at the head of the big table, with Becky on his right.

"There you are, Mark. We were beginning to wonder if you'd gone off somewhere to celebrate without us."

"Just staying true to form. You know how I like to make an entrance," he joked.

Becky rolled her eyes at him.

"Yep," she said. "He's the diva on this team. I'm the brains and the brawn."

The assembled crowd laughed appreciatively.

"All right, enough monkey business," David said. "Come on up here and we'll get this show on the road."

Mark made his way to the front of the room, taking his place at David's left.

Once the audience had stilled, David launched into his speech.

"As you all know, we delivered our pitch to Eden this morning. Mark and Becky led the presentation, and I must admit they did a fantastic job. They had the client eating out of their hands. They even got a standing ovation."

There was a smattering of applause in the room.

"In fact," David said, "the client bought into the campaign on the spot. We're the new marketing partner for Eden Yogurt—and about to be two hundred and fifty million dollars richer as an agency!"

The room broke out into riotous applause as their colleagues cheered their victory.

"That's not all," David continued. "As you may remember, Becky and Mark have been involved in a competition of sorts. The prize was a creative director title and a hefty bonus."

The room stilled as everyone waited for the next part of the announcement.

"But choosing one over the other has proved to be surprisingly difficult. They're both incredibly skilled creative geniuses. They both worked on the winning concept from beginning to end. And they both gained the respect and admiration of the client."

Mark drew in a breath and held it.

"So in the end I decided to create a new type of position. One that gives them each their due. Mark and Becky, you're now creative codirectors. You'll function as a creative director team, splitting the responsibilities for the Eden account according to your skillsets."

Mark blinked, trying to connect the dots.

Next to him, Becky said, "So there's no winner or loser? We're both getting promoted?"

"That's right," David said. "Eden is a new kind of account for us. It's only right that a new type of team heads it up."

The room exploded with cheers.

Becky shrieked happily and threw her arms around David. "Thank you," she said. "Thank you so much!"

He chuckled and patted her back uncomfortably.

"I'm the one who should be thanking you, my dear. You've just secured my retirement. Which brings me to my last announcement… If this were a television show I'd have a giant check sitting here. But, since it's not, you'll just have to make do with these regular-size ones."

He turned to Mark.

"One fifty-thousand-dollar check for you," he said, and, to Becky, "One fifty-thousand-dollar check for you."

Stunned, Mark looked down at the check in his hand. This was really happening. The check was his. The job was his. And, he thought, looking at Becky's laughing countenance as she accepted congratulations from her friends, at least for now the girl was his.

He was surprised to discover that it was that last ingredient that made him the happiest.

Maybe it was time to rethink the no-relationship clause.

* * *

By the time Becky managed to break free from her excited colleagues and escape to their office, darkness was falling over the city.

She closed the door and leaned against it, reveling in the blessed quiet.

She jumped when Mark's voice rang out in the darkness.

"Congratulations, creative codirector," he said. "You did good today."

"Mark? Where are you?"

"Just admiring the view," he said, clicking on a lamp by the windows. "And enjoying the fact that I'll get to look at it every day from now on."

Becky crossed over to where he was standing. Time to reintroduce reality.

"What if I want this office?"

He blinked. "What?"

"Now that we're both creative directors, or at least co-directors, David will probably give us each our own office. What if I decide I want to keep this one?"

"I guess I assumed we'd continue to share," Mark said. "Since we're heading up the same account and all."

"I doubt it," she said. In fact she hoped not. It would be almost impossible to keep her distance from him—something she knew she had to start doing—if they were in each other's physical space all day.

"Do you want your own office?" Mark asked, a dark look on his face.

She sighed. "Yes and no. Mark, these last few weeks have been fun, but we've known from the beginning that this couldn't last. Remember what you said?"

"I said that we could both go our own ways after this thing between us had run its course."

"Right," she said. "No harm, no foul."

"But, Becky," he said, looking deep into her eyes, "I

don't think it *has* run its course. I'm having a lot of fun with you—even when our clothes are on. Let's not give up yet."

Uh-oh. Unless she was very mistaken, he was talking about more than the occasional sexual romp.

"That was never the deal, Mark. You don't do relationships, remember?"

He sighed and ran his fingers through his dark hair. "No, Becky, I don't. Or at least I never have. But this… It's different somehow."

She knew exactly what he was talking about. Somewhere along the way they had crossed the line from being sex buddies to…something more. Something that scared her even to think about.

"I know," she said. "But we can't keep going on as we are—hooking up in the office on the sly and slipping out of the building when no one's looking. We're in charge now. Role models. We're going to have to try to act like we realize that."

He wrapped his arms around her and pulled her close. "Well, what if we try something different? Something normal and grown-up-ish. Like, you know, going out on actual dates. And spending the night together whenever we want, rather than heading home after a hookup. That could be fun."

"Mark…" she whispered. "What you're talking about sounds an awful lot like a relationship."

"I know," he said. "But I bet we can make it work."

"You and your bets," she said, smiling. "Nothing is worth doing unless you can bet on it."

He grinned and lowered his lips to hers.

"So what do you think?" he said. "Are you in?"

"I don't know. I'll think about it."

Then he claimed her with his mouth and she stopped thinking at all.

The next thing she knew someone was knocking. She

jumped backward—but not before the door opened, admitting David.

His eyes darted back and forth between her and Mark, taking in their slightly disheveled clothing and flushed faces.

"David," she said. "We were just, uh, I mean, we were—"

"We were just cementing the official end of our feud slash competitive relationship with a hug," Mark broke in.

"Oh. I see," David said, twitching his tie. "Well, that makes sense. Especially since you're going to be working together every day. It's important to present a united front."

"Exactly," Becky said, glancing at Mark.

"Well, I was just coming in to congratulate you one more time," David replied. "Make sure you get some rest this weekend. We're going to hit it hard on Monday. Becky, you'll be moving into the office next door to this one—Fred Sutherland's old digs."

She nodded, relieved that he seemed to be buying their story.

"Sounds good," she said.

"See you Monday," Mark chimed in.

"Right you are," David said, giving them one last suspicious glance. "Have a good one."

When the door was once again closed Becky whirled on Mark. "That," she hissed, "is why an 'us' is not a good idea. I just got promoted. I don't want to get fired."

"I don't remember signing anything that said we couldn't date coworkers."

"Maybe not, but I'm sure David wouldn't approve of the two of us getting together. And you know how tough it is for him to treat me like a creative professional. He'd find a way to use our relationship as a way to discredit me."

"I think you're being a little tough on the guy. All he cares about is the bottom line. And you just tripled his income. I don't think he's going to give you a hard time about anything."

Becky shook her head. It was no use. Mark would never understand how tough this business was for women. Or how biased David was against female employees.

"Well, whatever. Only time will tell," she said. "But I just don't think he could handle the thought of us as both a couple and a working team."

If she was being honest, she wasn't sure if she could, either.

"Just promise me you'll think about it," Mark said.

She sighed and stood on her tiptoes to kiss him good-bye. What she wouldn't give to be able to throw caution to the winds and just say yes. But she had to start focusing on her career again.

"I will," she agreed. "But don't expect me to change my mind."

CHAPTER NINE

BECKY WAS JUST sitting down with a steaming pot pie and a glass of her favorite Pinot Grigio when her cell phone began to whistle cheerfully.

It was her mother.

Becky stared at the screen. Should she answer it? Probably. If she didn't, she'd just keep calling back.

"Hi, Mom."

"Well, there you are. I was beginning to wonder if you were lying dead in an alley somewhere."

"Don't be so dramatic, Mom. It hasn't been that long since we talked."

"I haven't heard from you since you called to tell me you got home safely from the conference! That was almost a month ago."

Surely it hadn't been that long? But, now that she thought about it, maybe it had. She had considered picking up the phone on countless occasions, but when she'd thought about everything that was going on, and how impossible it would be to explain to her mom, she never had.

"I'm sorry, Mom. Things have been really busy at work."

"Work, work, work. That's all you ever talk about. When are you going to give me something to brag about to the ladies in my book club?"

"Well, actually, something pretty huge happened today," Becky said, suddenly eager to tell her mom. "I got promoted. To creative director."

There was a brief silence.

"That's nice, dear. Does that mean you'll be able to afford to come home more often?"

"I don't know. We haven't discussed salary yet. But I did get a really big bonus."

"Maybe you should use it to buy a place in a better neighborhood. I worry about you, you know. It doesn't seem safe, especially with those tattooed hippies wandering around at all hours of the day and night."

"Mom. I live in Greenwich Village, not Hell's Kitchen. This is a great neighborhood."

"I'm sure it is, but I'd feel much better if you didn't live right in the city like that. There's so much crime."

Becky smacked her forehead with her palm.

"We've been over this a hundred times. I moved to New York because I wanted to live in the city. Not in some cookie-cutter house in the suburbs."

Now it was her mother's turn to sigh. "I know, dear. I know. I just wish you'd move past this wild phase of yours and settle down with someone nice."

Becky snorted. Wild phase, indeed. "I'm only twenty-nine. There's no rush."

"That's what you think, dear. But once you hit thirty, your best baby-making years are behind you. I don't want you to end up in some infertility clinic, trying to get your tired eggs to work."

"I know. I've read every article you've ever emailed me on the subject."

Her mother continued as if she hadn't heard.

"You know, your cousin is pregnant again."

"Which one?"

"Tiffany. This will be her third."

"Well, tell her I said congratulations."

"You could come for the baby shower and tell her yourself."

"I'd rather stick needles in my eye," she muttered.

"I heard that," her mother said, sighing loudly. "Well, I'll let you go. I'm sure you have far better things to do than talk to your mother on a Friday night."

If only, Becky thought. Out loud, she said, "All right. Well, I'll talk to you soon, Mom. Love you."

"Love you, too. Remember to take the pepper spray I bought you if you go out."

"I will."

"And never leave your drink unattended."

"Okay."

"And…"

At long last her mother hung up. Becky flung herself backward on the chaise. Any other parent would be thrilled to hear their child had just gotten promoted. But not her mom. The only promotion she wanted to hear about was one that involved putting a "Mrs." in front of her name. Or the title "Mother of" after it.

Infertility clinic, my foot, she thought, taking a giant swig of wine. She already knew her ovaries worked. The proof was in the box under her bed.

Speaking of ovaries…shouldn't she be getting her period about now? Becky reached for her phone and fired up her period-tracking app. Yep. Her last one had been the week before AdWorld. That meant Aunt Flow should show up…

Damn. It should have come a week and a half ago.

Becky's mind froze.

There were all kinds of reasons why she could be late. She'd been under a huge amount of stress. Not sleeping well. Eating too much fast food and drinking too much wine.

But being stressed out was a way of life for her. And she didn't eat all that well on even the best of days.

And she had been having lots of sex. But they'd been safe about it, right? She thought hard, trying to remember

all the moments they'd stopped to put a condom on. Yep.
They had. Every single time. Except…

The afternoon of the sword fight.

Neither of them had even thought about a condom. She
hadn't even realized they'd forgotten until she'd seen the
undeniable evidence in her underwear while getting into
her pajamas that evening.

She raced to the bathroom and tore off her shirt and
bra. If she wasn't mistaken her boobs did look bigger than
usual. She squeezed one, just to see.

"Ow!"

Yep. They were tender.

Time to call in the troops.

She pulled out her phone and texted Jessie.

We have a 911 situation over here.

Seconds later, the phone rang.

"Becky, what's wrong? Are you hurt? Is someone dead?"
Jessie asked, sounding breathless and shaken.

"No. Sorry. I didn't mean to scare you."

"Then what was the 911 about?"

"I think I might be pregnant," she said quietly.

"What? How? I mean I know how, but…"

"I'll explain later. Could you come over, please?" Becky
asked, hating the tremor in her voice.

Jessie sighed. "I'm kind of on a date."

"Oh. Okay. Never mind. I'll just run out and get a test."

"Keep me posted, okay?"

"I will," she whispered, and hung up.

Knowing she should head right to the drugstore, she instead found herself on her knees in front of her bed, gazing
at the old sonogram picture.

How many times had she sworn she'd never put herself
in this position again? That she'd protect herself at all costs?

Too many to count.

The first time had been in Pence's office, right after she'd told him she was quitting.

"What do you mean, you quit?" he'd said. "You can't quit."

"Yes, I can. I am. And I'm using my vacation time as my notice. I've got two weeks coming to me," she'd said, hoping beyond hope he couldn't see her knees trembling.

"What will you do?" he'd asked, his voice suddenly cold. "You know as well as I do that I'm the only reason you've made it as far as you have."

"That's not true," she'd said quietly.

"Sure it is. I could've gotten rid of you after your internship was over. But I kept you around. Made sure you got put on the best assignments," he'd said, walking over to his awards shelf. "The only reason you got your award was because I convinced the client to go with your idea."

"They would have chosen it even if you hadn't pushed it," she'd said, anger sparking in her veins. "But you had to feel like you were in control of every part of my life. You never let me do things on my own!"

"That's because you would have failed," he'd said, stalking silently across the plush green carpet toward her. "You screw everything up. Heck, you can't even manage to take your birth control pills the right way."

She'd gasped, his barbed comment tearing open the thin scab on her heart. "Oh, my God, you're unbelievable."

He'd smiled coldly as he came to stand in front of her. "I deserved that, so I won't hold it against you." Then, taking a deep breath, he'd said, "Let's start over. Becky, please don't leave. We've got a good thing going here. Stick with me and you'll be a star."

"I already am a star, Pence. And I don't need you to continue being one."

"No one will hire you," he'd said softly.

"I already have a job," she'd said defiantly.

"Where? Ads R Us?"

"At an agency with more awards than you can count. In a place where they've never heard of you."

"You'll fail," he'd said, turning his back on her.

"No. I won't. I'll knock their socks off," she'd said with more confidence than she'd felt. "But I do have you to thank for one thing."

"What?" he'd said over his shoulder.

"Now I know better than to let some egotistical man get in my head. Or my bed. No one will ever be able to mess up my life the way you have, Pence."

He'd snorted.

"You'll be knocked up and out of the game before the year is up."

"I doubt it. But you'll definitely still be a bitter asshole stuck in a loveless marriage. If she doesn't wise up and leave you."

His answer had been a wordless roar. One she still occasionally heard in her dreams.

Her reverie was broken by a loud buzzing sound. Someone was at the front door.

She got up and shuffled to the intercom. "Hello?"

"Let me in, girl. It's cold out here," Jessie's voice called.

'What happened to your date?"

"You're more important. Now, hit the dang buzzer!"

Becky did, and went to hold the door open for her friend. Jessie bounded up the stairs, plastic bag in hand.

"I come bearing gifts," she said. "Five flavors of pee sticks and two flavors of ice cream."

"I told you I was going to take care of it," Becky protested.

"And did you?"

Becky shook her head.

"Right, then. Pick your poison. Pink, purple, blue, red or generic?" Jessie said, holding the bag out in front of her.

Becky closed her eyes and reached inside.

"Looks like we're going with pink," she said.

Becky sat on the closed toilet lid, eyes squeezed tightly shut. In three minutes she'd have her answer.

There was a soft knock and Jessie came in, her sequined skirt sparkling in the harsh fluorescent light.

"How are you doing?" she asked.

"Well, I won a two-hundred-and-fifty-million-dollar piece of business, told off my ex, got promoted and found out I might be pregnant. All in one day. How could I be anything less than fabulous?" she said.

Jessie squeezed her hand. "It'll be okay," she said.

Her phone alarm shrilled loudly. Becky blew out a big breath of air.

"Do you want to look or do you want me to?" Jessie asked.

"I'll do it," Becky said.

Reaching out with one shaking hand, she grabbed the pink-capped stick from where it sat on the edge of her ugly green tub and looked down.

"Well?" Jessie asked, her voice shaking.

Mutely, Becky held it out for her to see, stomach roiling.

"Oh, no," she breathed. "Becky, I'm sorry."

She was pregnant.

Becky slammed the toilet lid open seconds before her dinner made a reappearance.

"Well," Jessie said, when the heaving had stopped. "That's not the reaction you see on TV."

Becky tried to smile. "Yep, but—as we well know— advertising tells only a selective version of the truth."

Jessie helped her up. "You took the words right out of

my mouth. Now, come on, let's get you out of here. Nothing good comes of extended visits to the bathroom."

A short while later Becky was again stretched out on her purple chaise, a bottle of hastily purchased ginger ale fizzing on the table beside her. Jessie was curled up on her only other piece of furniture—a very faded red couch.

Jessie looked at Becky over the rim of her wine glass. "So, I'm assuming this is Mark's kid, right?"

Becky raised an eyebrow at her. "While I admit my behavior has been a little more reckless than usual, I assure you I haven't been having sex with random men I meet on the street."

"No. I know, I didn't mean... I'm sorry, Becky."

She waved her comment away. "No worries. I understand."

"You know, there's a clinic in my neighborhood. They have a reputation for being very discreet..."

Becky shook her head. "I don't need a clinic. I'm keeping it."

Jessie's jaw dropped.

"Are you sure that's a good idea? I mean, you just got the world's biggest promotion today."

"Positive. I'll figure out how to make it work." She'd made her decision the second she'd seen the plus sign on the pregnancy test. It was the only thing she could do.

Jessie looked unconvinced. "Well, if you change your mind, just let me know. I'd be happy to go with you."

Suddenly angry, Becky glared at her friend. "How could you say that to me? You know what happened...before. Having that abortion almost destroyed me. Do you want me to have to go through that again?"

Jessie paled. "I'm sorry. I...I wasn't thinking. I just don't want you to rush into anything. It's a big decision."

Becky immediately regretted her outburst. Her friend

had never been anything but supportive. And there was no way she could know how concrete her decision was.

"I'm sorry, Jessie. You didn't deserve that. But I'm keeping this baby. I couldn't live with any other choice."

Jessie nodded. "All right. Well, I'll support you, then."

Becky smiled her thanks and the two women sat silently for a while. Becky thanked her lucky stars she'd gotten that bonus check today. She'd be able to buy the baby everything it needed. And, she thought, looking around her shoebox-size apartment, she might even be able to afford a bigger place.

"What are you going to do about Mark?" Jessie asked suddenly.

Her brain stuttered. "Do?"

"Well, you're going to have to tell him. It's not like he won't notice. Besides, he deserves to know."

Unbelievably, she'd forgotten about that small detail. She'd been thinking about the baby as hers, not theirs.

"You're right," she said. "I don't think he's going to be very happy though. He's pretty anti-kids."

"Well," Jessie said, "whatever happens, you know I'll be there for you. I'll even be your labor coach, if you want."

Becky laughed. "I'm not quite ready to think about that yet."

Jessie looked at her watch, then heaved herself off of the couch. "Man, it's getting late. I better get going so you can get some rest. Are you going to be okay?"

Becky nodded.

"Okay," she said, wrapping her rainbow scarf around her neck. "Take care of yourself."

"I will."

After one final hug Jessie was gone.

Becky sank to the floor and hugged her knees, allowing herself to hope for a minute. Mark had been ready to start a relationship this afternoon. Maybe it would all be okay.

Her mind flashed back to the way he'd behaved with that little boy on the way to the park. He was a natural. Maybe he'd jump at the chance to be a dad.

And maybe pigs were getting ready to fly.

Oh, well. No time like the present to get the ball rolling. Pulling out her phone, she texted Mark.

We need to talk.

Almost instantly her phone pinged with his reply.

I'm listening, Gorgeous Girl.

Not over text. In person. Dinner tomorrow?

Sure. Where?

Come over. I'll cook.

This was a conversation that needed to be held in private.

See you at seven?

Can't wait.

A bald-faced lie.

Hopefully tomorrow night would go better than it had the last time she'd had this conversation with a man.

It could hardly be worse.

CHAPTER TEN

MARK WOKE UP on Saturday morning feeling happier than he could remember ever being. For once, all was right with his world.

He swung his legs over the edge of the bed and padded across the hardwood floor of his studio apartment to the granite kitchen island where the fifty-thousand-dollar check was sitting. He ran his finger across the dollar amount. All those zeroes belonged to him. And he hadn't had to beg his stepfather for a penny of it.

On impulse, he snapped a picture of the check and texted his mother.

Your boy done good. Got promoted to creative director yesterday. With this as a bonus.

He hit Send and waited for a response. None came.

Not that he had really expected anything else. His mother had made it quite clear over the years that she'd really rather her son disappeared so she could focus on the family she *did* want.

Shake it off, he told himself. Much better to focus on the things he had a chance of fixing—like his relationship with Becky.

And, although it scared him to admit it, he did want a relationship. He wanted to wander the city with her. He wanted to walk in Little Italy at night and explore Central Park during the day. He wanted to eat with her in her tiny apartment and see her golden hair spread out on his pillows after a night of love.

Not even the fact that they worked together deterred him. They made a crazy good team—both in and out of the office.

All he had to do was convince her to give it a try.

Night had already descended when Mark arrived on Becky's doorstep, bearing a bottle of wine and a bunch of daisies tied with a ribbon that matched her eyes.

Taking a deep breath, he pushed the buzzer.

Seconds later, the door clicked open.

Becky was waiting for him at the top of the dark staircase. "Hey, Magic Man," she said with a smile.

"Hey, yourself," he said, taking the time to appreciate the plunging blue V-neck top and tight black leather skirt she was wearing. "You're looking even more gorgeous than usual, Gorgeous Girl."

"Thank you," she said shyly, turning her cheek when he reached down to kiss her.

Hmm. That was a new one.

He handed her the wine and flowers. "For my beautiful hostess," he said.

"How did you know daisies were my favorite?" she asked.

"Lucky guess," he said.

She ushered him inside, then busied herself in the kitchen, putting the flowers in water. "Make yourself at home," she called.

While small, her apartment felt cozy and warm. The walls were painted a cheerful yellow and decorated with pictures of brightly colored flowers and tropical beaches. Although a tiny dining table was tucked away in one corner, a giant purple chaise dominated the room. It shared the space with a comfortable-looking couch and a plethora of rainbow-hued pillows.

"I don't think I mentioned it the last time I was here, but I really love your place."

"Thank you," she said, rounding the corner from the kitchen. "It's tiny, but I kind of love it."

"From what I can tell, every apartment in New York is tiny—even the ones you pay millions of dollars for."

"That's true," she said. "Although I hear the roaches in the expensive ones wear diamond-plated shells."

"That figures. Roaches are excellent at adapting to their surroundings."

She laughed and reached up to kiss him. "Thank you for coming," she whispered.

When he sensed her backing away, he reached out to pull her closer.

"I wouldn't have missed this for the world," he said. "Maybe later we can have dessert in bed again. This time I'll be the plate."

"Mmm," she said with an enigmatic smile. "We'll see how the evening goes. Are you hungry?"

"Starving."

"Good. I've got lasagna. It'll be ready in just a sec."

"Can I help?"

"No need. Unless you want to open the wine?"

He followed her into the kitchen and took the bottle she handed him.

"Glasses are on the table," she said. "But just pour me a drop."

"Are you sure? The guy at the wine shop told me this was an excellent vintage—whatever that means."

"I'm sure," she said.

She was definitely acting a little odd. He hoped it was because she was trying to get used to the idea of them being a couple and not because she had something bad to tell him.

Mentally he shook his head. No use borrowing trouble before he had it.

Soon Becky brought out plates of lasagna and garlic bread.

"It looks awesome," he said.

"I hope so," she said. "Dig in!"

He picked up his wine glass. "I'd like to propose a toast," he said.

Becky smiled and raised her glass. "Okay, let's hear it."

"To the kick-ass team that is us. Here's hoping this is the beginning of a long and beautiful relationship."

She seemed to wince a little at his words, but gamely clinked her glass with his. "To us," she murmured.

An awkward silence fell, and Mark watched as Becky picked at her food.

He let the quiet go on, hoping she'd be the one to break it. She didn't.

"Becky, what's wrong?"

She looked up, her eyes bright with unshed tears.

"I have something to tell you," she said. "Something I'm pretty sure you're not going to like."

Trying not to be alarmed, he said, "Try me."

She took a deep breath. "There's no easy way to say this," she said. "So I'm just going to blurt it out."

"Okay. You're not dying or married or something, are you?"

"No. Nothing like that. I'm just pregnant."

He heard a distant clatter as his fork dropped from his suddenly nerveless fingers.

"I'm sorry. I think I misheard you. You're what?"

"Pregnant." She made herself say it again. "I'm pregnant. With your baby."

"What? How can that be?" he spluttered.

"Well, you see, there's this stork," she said, trying for

humor. "Last night he flew by my window and told me he'd be delivering a baby to us in about eight months. I told him he was mistaken, but he showed me the paperwork. It was all in order."

"This is no time for jokes," Mark snapped. "I don't understand. We used protection."

"We did. All except for one time."

She could see his mind working busily, trying to connect the dots.

"What? When?"

"Remember the afternoon of the sword fight?"

He paled as she watched.

"Son of a…" Mark swore. "I can't believe we were so stupid. *Damn it!*"

He put his head in his hands. After a moment, he took a deep breath.

"Okay. You're pregnant. It happens. Unplanned pregnancies happen all the time. But we can fix this."

He got up and started to pace.

"How far along are you?"

"Just five or six weeks."

"Oh. Good. That's not very far at all. You can probably even still get that pill from your doctor. The one that causes a miscarriage or whatever."

"Mark?"

He stopped and looked at her. "What?"

"I don't want to do that."

"Okay, well, there's bound to be a good clinic around here somewhere. It is New York, after all."

"No," she said. "I don't want an abortion."

He looked sick—as if she had just punched her in the stomach.

"What are you saying?"

"I want to keep it," she said quietly. Then, with more determination, "I'm *going* to keep it. I want this baby, Mark."

"No. You don't."

"Yes," she said, getting annoyed, "I do. I'm a grown woman, Mark. I know what I'm doing."

"No, you don't!" he said, his face turning red. "You only think you do. But once he's born he'll get in the way. There will be sick days and doctor visits and daycare issues. You'll be exhausted all the time, and frazzled, and run down. Before you know it your career will be in the tank. Soon, you'll start to resent him for being born. You'll wish you'd gotten rid of him while you still could. No kid deserves to go through life like that, Becky. No kid should be stuck with a mother who doesn't want him around."

He gazed down at her, shoulders hunched, and she could see a lifetime of hurt reflected in his eyes.

"Please don't do this, Becky."

Becky's heart broke for the man in front of her, and for the mother who obviously hadn't been able to give him what he needed.

She went to him, cupping his cheek gently with her hand.

"It won't be like that, Mark. I've only known about this baby for twenty-four hours and I already love him with all my heart. I always will."

"You can't promise that, Becky," he said miserably. "You don't know what it's like. How hard it is."

"I won't be alone. I'll be surrounded by people who love me—and him. Heck, my mother will probably try to move in with me. The only question is whether you're going to be one of those people."

"What are you asking me, Becky?"

She pulled him down on the couch next to her. "Yesterday you were begging me to give this relationship a chance. To give us a shot. Now I'm asking you the same thing."

Grabbing his hand, she placed it over her stomach.

"Are you willing to see if we can make this work? To

give this family a shot? The stakes are a lot higher now, but I'm willing to go all-in if you are."

He looked at her with horror on his face.

"Are you asking me to *marry* you?"

She snorted. "As if. No. I'm just asking you not to slam the door shut. To be a part of our lives. To see if you can make room for this baby in your heart."

His face grew cold and he stood.

"No, Becky. I'm sorry, but I can't. If you want this baby it's all on you. I won't be a part of it."

She nodded and swallowed, looking down at her hands so he wouldn't see the tears in her eyes.

"Okay. I understand."

A moment later she heard the door open and shut. She was alone.

She rubbed her stomach absently. "Looks like it's just you and me, kid," she whispered, tears running down her face.

Funny. Yesterday she hadn't been sure she wanted to let Mark into her heart. It was only now that he was gone that she realized she already had. And that when he'd left he'd taken half of it with him.

Mark stomped down the cold dark streets, glaring at any-one who dared to meet his eye.

How could she have let this happen? He had assumed she was on some kind of birth control. That she was be-having like a responsible adult.

It wasn't fair. Just when he'd thought he'd finally found a place where he could make a career he was stuck work-ing with a woman who wanted more from him than he could give. A woman who was pregnant with his baby, for God's sake.

The sound of his phone ringing yanked Mark into the

present. Fishing it out of his pocket, he looked at his screen. It was his mother. Impeccable timing, as always.

He considered flinging his phone into the street, but decided talking to her would probably give him all the confirmation he needed that he was making the right decision.

"Hello, Mother."

"Mark, darling, I got your text. How wonderful!"

"I sent that twelve hours ago," he snarled.

"Yes, I know. But we had a tennis tournament today at the club. And then the Petersons came over for dinner. They send their love, by the way."

"Do the Petersons even know who I am?"

"Of course they do, Mark. They've been coming to the house since you were in the seventh grade."

"Yes, but I was never there," he said.

"Oh, don't be so dramatic. You were home for nearly every school vacation. For months at a time in the summer, in fact."

"Only if you couldn't find somewhere else to send me," he said.

There was a beat of silence. "What is this all about, Mark? I made sure you had the best education money could buy. Was that wrong?"

"Oh, come on, Mom. I know the only reason you sent me to boarding school was because you couldn't stand to have me around. Didn't want to be reminded of your mistakes after you married into money. I didn't belong in your fancy new family."

"Is that what you thought?" his mother said, her voice a horrified whisper. "Mark, you couldn't be more wrong. Why, I—"

"Save it for someone who cares, Mom. I gave up a long time ago."

It wasn't until he hung up that he realized he'd been

shouting. Good thing he was in New York. Nothing fazed the people here.

God, he needed a drink. A stiff one. Looking up, he realized he was standing right across the street from a bar.

He'd get drunk tonight. Then decide what to do about the train wreck that was his life in the morning.

CHAPTER ELEVEN

By the time Monday morning dawned Becky had bottled up her heartbreak and shoved it into the darkest recesses of her brain. She couldn't afford to be weak.

She was starting a new job: working with a man who would prefer never to see her again and for a man who still had a hard time believing she was anything but a pretty face.

She was going to have to be on her A-game every day from here on out. She'd have to prove she was worth every dime they were paying her and, pregnant or not, could kick the ass of every male creative in the city.

That was the only way she'd be able to get through this with both her pride and career intact.

She spent the entire train ride pumping herself up. By the time she strode through SBD's doors she had convinced herself that she could handle absolutely anything the world cared to throw at her. Even a lifetime of working with Mark.

But she couldn't bite back the sigh of relief that came when she realized she had beaten him to the office. With luck, she could have her stuff packed up and moved into her new space before he arrived.

Becky grabbed a box and got to work. She hadn't gotten very far, though, when there was a knock on the door.

"Come in," she called.

David's executive assistant glided through the door.

"Hi, Pam, what can I do for you?"

"I take it you didn't see the email I sent you?" the elegant woman asked.

"No," she answered slowly. "Is something wrong?"

"I don't think so," she said, looking everywhere but at Becky. "But David did say he wanted to see you as soon as you got in."

"All right," Becky said. "Then I guess I'll head up there with you now."

The two women spent the elevator ride in an increasingly heavy silence. Becky was practically squirming by the time they arrived on the forty-third floor.

"I'll let him know you're here," Pam said. "Why don't you have a seat?"

Sensing it was more of a command than a request, Becky sat down in one of the black leather chairs.

She wished she had some idea of what this was all about. Mark wouldn't have told David about her pregnancy… would he?

Thankfully Pam returned before that train of thought could go any further.

"You can go in now," she said.

Becky thanked her and squared her shoulders before stepping through the heavy oak door.

David was ensconced behind his giant mahogany desk, his chair arranged on a riser so he could tower over the people sitting in front of him. But he wasn't alone.

Mark sat in one of the chestnut-colored club chairs while Cindy, the head of HR, perched on the couch.

No one looked happy.

"Ah, there you are, Becky," David boomed. "I was beginning to think we were going to have to send a search party after you."

"Sorry," she said. "I was downstairs. I just hadn't opened my email yet."

'Not to worry," he said. "We've been having a nice little chat while we waited—haven't we, Mark?"

Mark nodded, his face looking pale and strained.

"Good, I'm glad I haven't inconvenienced anyone. May I ask why we're all here?"

David nodded. "I'm going to cut right to the chase, Becky. It's come to my attention that you and Mark are involved in a relationship."

"Excuse me? We most definitely are *not*," she said sharply.

"Don't try to deny it, dear. I have security camera footage of the two of you engaged in rather passionate embraces in several places throughout the building."

Oh, no.

"Yes, well, that may be true, but I can assure you that any relationship we may have had has already come to an end. Tell him, Mark!"

Mark glowered at her. "I already tried."

"Be that as it may, I am afraid you two are in blatant violation of your contracts with us. Cindy, could you read the relevant clause to them?"

The woman nodded. "It's in section twenty-seven A on page seventeen," she said. "'The employee agrees to refrain from establishing relationships of a romantic or sexual nature with any SBD employee, vendor, client, or contractor. If conduct of this nature is discovered the employee understands that he or she will be considered to have violated his or her contract, and will be subject to punitive action up to and including termination of employment.'"

Becky paled. "I honestly don't remember seeing that in my contract," she said.

"It was there," Cindy said. "I have your initialed copy right here. I suggest you pay closer attention to what you're signing in the future."

She nodded, furiously trying to process the predicament she now found herself in. "Obviously. So where does that leave us, David?"

He took a deep breath and smiled a nasty smile.

"If this was an ordinary situation I would dismiss both of you and wash my hands of the whole thing. But it isn't. As you know, Eden has specifically requested that you both be on their team. Which was why I promoted the two of you to the codirector positions. However, in light of this new information, I cannot, in good conscience, allow that arrangement to stand. Therefore I am going to allow one of you to stay and continue on in a creative director capacity. The other person will be allowed to resign, with the bonus received on Friday serving as a severance package. I'm leaving it to you to decide who will go and who will stay. You have until the end of the day."

Becky blinked. *They* had to decide who got fired? Who *did* that?

"But what about Eden? They want both of us on their team," she blurted.

"I'll tell Eden that whichever one of you resigns has had a family emergency and will be on leave indefinitely, and that you'll return to work on their account when things are squared away. You won't, of course, but by the time they figure that out they'll have forgotten why they thought they needed you both anyway. That's it. You're dismissed," David finished. "Now, get out of my sight."

She didn't have to be told twice. She was punching the elevator button before Mark had even risen from his chair.

Unfortunately the elevator was its usual poky self. By the time the door dinged open Mark was approaching. She stepped in and held the door, unable to abandon her innate Midwestern politeness even in a time of crisis.

"Thanks," Mark muttered.

She nodded.

"Look," he said, "I know we need to talk about this, but—"

"I can't right now," Becky cut in. "I need time to wrap my brain around everything we just heard."

There was an awkward pause as Mark stared at the ceiling.

"I guess I was wrong. Someone did watch that footage of us in the elevator," he said.

"Whoever it was certainly got an eyeful."

"You don't think David saw it, do you?" Becky asked with a dawning sense of horror.

"Oh, I'm sure he did. The man is a horndog, you know."

The elevator dinged again and they arrived at their floor.

"Look, I'm going to go for a walk and try to sort things out," Mark said. "How about we meet for a late lunch?"

"Sure. The halal cart at one-thirty?"

"You got it," he said, and headed off.

Becky knocked on Jessie's office door.

"Come in," she called.

"It still feels weird not to be sitting here anymore," Becky said as she entered.

"You're welcome in my closet anytime," Jessie said. "Your chair is still here and everything."

"Thanks," Becky said. "But I don't think I'm going to be working here very much longer."

"What are you talking about? You're my new boss, aren't you?"

"It's a long story. Let's go get some coffee."

Once they were settled in their favorite booth, with steaming cups of coffee, Becky launched into the story.

"So one of you has to quit?"

"That's the long and the short of it."

"Well, obviously it should be Mark. You're the one who belongs here. He just got hired!"

Becky sighed. "That would make the most sense, I know."

"But…"

"But I think I'm just going to do it. David will never

respect me now that he's seen me in such a compromised position, and I'm tired of fighting to prove myself to him."

"What about your promotion?"

"I don't know. It doesn't seem so important anymore." As soon as she said the words Becky realized she meant them. Although she'd been prepared to fight to keep her job, her heart wasn't in it. It was still lying in pieces on the floor of her apartment.

"It sounds like you've already made up your mind," Jessie said.

Becky sipped her decaffeinated coffee in silence for a moment. Truth was, she'd known in her gut what she needed to do almost before the words had come out of David's mouth.

"Yes," she said finally. "I guess I have."

"I sure am going to miss you," Jessie said sadly.

Becky reached across the table to squeeze her hand. "Don't worry. You're still going to see me. You volunteered to be my birth coach, remember?"

"Oh, yeah. I forgot about that. Cool!"

Taking a deep breath, Becky prepared to launch into the real reason she'd asked Jessie to have coffee with her. "So, listen, I need you to do me a favor."

"Anything."

Mark sat on a bench in front of the halal cart, waiting for Becky.

He'd racked his brain for a good solution all morning, but still didn't know what to do.

Common sense dictated that he be the one to go. After all, Becky had been working for years to get the promotion they'd just been granted. He'd just stepped in.

But he wanted to stay. He wanted to launch the Eden campaign into the stratosphere and make a name for himself. He wanted to earn a steady paycheck, get to know his colleagues, just live like a normal human being for a while.

But Becky was pregnant. She needed this job and the medical insurance that came with it. He might not want the baby, but that didn't mean he wanted the child to be denied basic medical care.

He sighed, hating the fact that at his core he still seemed to be a decent human being. Life would be easier if he could stop caring about other people.

He knew he had to be the one to walk away. He couldn't live with himself otherwise.

"Hi, handsome," a voice said from beside him.

He jumped. "Where did you come from, Jessie?" he said to the woman who had suddenly appeared next to him.

"I've been sitting here for five minutes. You've just been on another planet," she said.

"All right, then, here's a better question. What are you doing here?"

"Becky sent me," she said. "She asked me to give you this."

In her hand was a bright blue envelope. It looked like a greeting card.

"You're to read it, then ask me your questions."

"Okay," he said, hoping he sounded calmer than he felt. What could this be about?

Taking a deep breath, he opened the envelope and pulled out the card. The outside featured a black-and-white image of a magician. The inside was cramped with Becky's writing.

Dear Magic Man,
By the time you read this I will have already submitted my resignation. The job is yours. Enjoy it. Rest assured, though, that I will be watching you. If you don't turn our concept into a showstopping,

award-eating monster, I'm going to come back and kick your ass.

Please don't try to get in touch. Don't call. Don't email. Don't stop by. I don't want to ever see you again. At least not until you're ready to step up and be a dad. Which, let's be honest, will probably never happen.

So this is goodbye. Have a nice life, Mark. You deserve to be happy.

Your Gorgeous Girl

XOXO

P.S. Jessie will know how to find me. Just in case you ever want to know.

Mark read the note three times. Finally, he looked up. "So, she's gone?"

"Well, not yet. But she's leaving."

"Where is she going?"

"Come on, Mark. You know I can't tell you that."

"Do you know why she's leaving?"

"I'm going to guess it's got something to do with the little seed you planted in her belly," Jessie said, rolling her eyes.

"Hey, that wasn't my fault," he said.

"Whatever, dude. It takes two to tango."

She had him there.

"Right. Well, I'll see you back at the office," she said, hopping up off the bench. "Enjoy your lunch."

After she left Mark waited for the relief to set in. After all, Becky had given him what he wanted. He'd be able to keep his dream job for as long as he wanted.

He should be happy. Instead he was miserable.

She hadn't even left yet, and he already missed her.

That couldn't be a good sign.

CHAPTER TWELVE

BECKY SAT ON the bed in her childhood room, trying to find the energy to unpack. It had been an exhausting week. She'd whirled into action the very same day that she'd quit, burying her pain in activity.

Finding a renter to sublet her apartment and getting her things packed had been the easy part. Making peace with leaving New York had been a good deal harder. She'd always thought she'd spend the rest of her life there. She'd dreamed of having a wedding in Central Park and of raising a family in a brownstone on the Upper West Side. And as for her career—well, she'd assumed she'd spend it in the ad agencies on Madison Avenue.

Returning home to Michigan had never been part of the plan.

But without a job she didn't have a lot of choices. Her fifty thousand dollars wouldn't last very long in New York. And raising a baby alone in the city was a challenge she wasn't sure she was up for.

So here she was, back where she'd started. She sniffed, quiet tears falling down her face. So much for her big plans.

There was a soft knock on the door.

"Come in," she said, hastily wiping the evidence away.

Her mother entered, carrying a laundry basket.

"I brought you some clean sheets."

"Th-thanks, Mom."

"Are you crying?"

"No. Yes. Maybe?"

"Oh, honey," her mother said, perching on the bed beside her. "I know things look bad right now. But it'll get better. Before you know it you'll have a job, and a place of your own, and a baby to love."

"I never meant for this to happen, Mom," she said, leaning her head on her mother's shoulder. "I'm sorry if I've disappointed you."

"You could never disappoint me," she said. "Especially not when you're carrying my grandchild! It would have been better if you'd gotten yourself a husband first, of course. But you're young. It will happen in its own good time."

Becky looked at her mom, flabbergasted. That didn't sound like the conservative Catholic she knew her to be. "I didn't expect you to be so calm about all of this," she said.

"We've been watching a lot of reality TV these last few years," she said. "I know the world has changed."

Becky just barely managed to stop herself from laughing. She could tell her mother was completely serious.

"Well, I appreciate it. You don't know how much."

"Not to worry. It's all part of the job. You'll find out soon enough."

Becky put her hand on her still-flat belly.

"I guess I will at that." The thought filled her with fear. "Mom?"

"What, honey?"

"Do you think I'll be any good at it? At being a mother?"

"Of course you will. You'll be an amazing mother."

"But I don't even like kids."

Her mother laughed out loud. "You probably never will like other people's children. But you'll always love your own. Trust me."

Since she didn't have many choices, Becky decided to try.

Mark scowled as he examined the printout Jessie had brought him.

"Jessie, this is nothing like we discussed," he said.

"I know, but I thought this was better," she said. "No offense, but your idea kind of sucked."

"Jessie, I'm your boss. You can't talk to me like that," he snapped.

"Just look at it," she said. "Please?"

"No. I need you to do what I asked you to do. *Now.*"

She glared at him and stomped out.

Sighing, he sat down in his chair and glanced at the printout. He hated to admit it, but she was right. It *was* better.

He called to his assistant. "Susan?"

She poked her head in the door, looking tense. "Yes, Mark?"

"Can you ask Jessie to come back to my office, please?"

She nodded and left.

A few minutes later Jessie returned, looking even more furious than she had when she'd left.

"You wanted to see me?"

"Yes. Sit."

She did—reluctantly.

"Look, I'm sorry," he said. "This *is* better. I don't know what the hell is wrong with me lately."

Jessie snorted. "I do. Its name is Becky."

"This has nothing to do with Becky," he said, feeling the weight of the lie in his heart.

"Whatever you say, dude. Have you told the client she's gone yet?"

"We've told them she's taking a leave of absence. We didn't clue them in to the fact that it's a permanent one." And if he had his way they wouldn't. At least not until they were happy with what he and his team had put together without her. He owed it to Becky to keep them on board and in love.

"I could dress up in a blond wig and pretend to be her at your next meeting if you want."

He laughed. "Thanks for the offer, but I don't think that would go over very well."

"Okay, but if you get desperate you know where to find me," she said, turning to go.

"Hey, Jessie?" he asked, hating himself for what he was about to say.

"Yeah?"

"Have you heard from her?"

"Her who?"

"You know who. Becky."

"Oh, her. Yeah. She's okay…considering."

His blood ran cold. He'd never forgive himself if something bad had happened to her… "Considering what? Is something wrong?"

"She's pregnant. Unemployed. And the father's being a dumbass. So, yeah. There are some things that are wrong."

He had asked for that, he guessed. Sighing, he motioned for her to go, but she was already gone.

He'd thought it would be easy to forget about Becky. After all, their—well, whatever it was they'd shared had only lasted a few weeks. Just the blink of an eye, all things considered.

But he missed her right down to his core. He'd thought about asking Jessie to give him her contact information on a hundred different occasions, but stopped himself every time. No matter how much he wanted Becky, he did not want to be a father to their child. Which meant he had to respect her wishes and stay away.

Just as he was about to sink into a vat of self pity there was a knock on his door.

"Yeah—come in," he said.

"That's how you greet your guests?" a familiar voice asked. "I thought I had taught you better than that."

Mark looked up and was shocked to see his mother

standing there, looking out of place in her conservative pantsuit and sensible shoes.

"Mom? What are you doing here?" he said, trying not to let the shock show as he rounded his desk to give her a hug.

"Oh, you know. I was in the neighborhood and thought I'd stop by."

"Mom, you live in Connecticut."

"I just came into the city to do some shopping," she said, picking nonexistent dust off her navy jacket.

"You hate shopping in New York," he said, flabbergasted.

"All right," she said. "I came specifically to see you, if you must know."

"Why?" She'd never done that. *Ever.*

"Because I haven't heard from you since that night you yelled at me over the phone. I was worried."

Worried? His mom was worried about him? That was news to him. He couldn't stop the sudden warming of his heart.

"You could have called."

"I did. Repeatedly. You never answered."

Damn it. She had him there. He was behaving more like a spoiled teenager than the adult he was.

"Look, Mom, I'm sorry. Let's start over, okay? It's lovely to see you."

"Thank you, Mark. It's wonderful to see you, too. Do you have time for lunch?"

He really didn't, but he'd have to be a total ass to tell her so.

"Sure. Where would you like to go?"

"I've already booked a table, darling. The car's waiting downstairs."

She had chosen a kitschy bistro in Little Italy, complete with red-checkered tablecloths and traditional Italian music playing in the background.

"This has always been one of my favorites, but your step-father won't come here," she told him as she settled herself into her seat. "The lasagna is to die for, but he can't appreciate it. Too many carbs, he says. As if that's possible."

"He does seem to have a hard time appreciating anything enjoyable," Mark said blandly.

"He means well—you know that. But he takes his responsibilities very seriously. He has a hard time letting go."

"That's the understatement of the year."

"Be nice, Mark," his mother said sharply.

"Sorry," he said. But he wasn't. Not really.

A smiling waiter came to greet them. "Lucille," he said. "How lovely to see you. The usual?"

"Yes, please." She smiled.

Turning to Mark, he said, "And you, sir?"

"I'm told the lasagna is to die for. So I guess I'll try that. In fact, bring me whatever she's having."

"Very well. Two usuals. I took the liberty of bringing your favorite wine with me, Lucille. Would you like me to pour?"

"Certainly. Mark, can you have a glass during working hours?"

"Sure, why not?" He'd probably need it to get through this conversation.

Once the waiter had retreated his mother looked at him with a serious expression on her face.

"I want to talk about our last conversation," she said.

"Look, Mom, I was out of line. I'm sorry. We don't need to talk about it."

"Yes. We do," she said, a hint of steel in her voice. "We need to clear the air. Or at least I do. Now, listen very closely. I love you very much. I always have. I sent you away to school because your stepfather insisted it was necessary to ensure you had the best possible foundation for college. Every family we know did the same thing. It's what people with money do."

Mark squirmed uncomfortably. He so didn't want to have this conversation.

"It felt like he was just trying to get me out of the way. Why would he want to look at his wife's illegitimate child every day if he didn't have to? Especially since everyone knew I was a mistake."

"You probably won't believe me when I tell you this, but he's very proud of you."

"That's not what you said when I was a kid. You told me I was an embarrassment to you both almost every time you saw me," he said, unable to keep the whine from his voice.

"I admit when you got yourself thrown out of three boarding schools in the space of one term I was a bit frustrated with you. Anyone would have been. I probably said some things I didn't mean. But, Mark, I never meant to make you feel unwanted. You're one of the best things that ever happened to me—even if you were, ahem, unexpected."

"Did you ever regret having me?" he blurted, unable to stop himself from asking.

"Never. Not even for a minute. How could I? You're my son. I can't imagine life without you," she said, practically glowing with sincerity.

Mark smiled, surprised to realize how much her answer mattered.

"Thank you," he said. "Thank you for telling me that."

Their food arrived and they applied themselves to the delicious baked concoction, watching the traffic go by on the street outside. A mother passed by with a gorgeous little blonde girl in tow. The child saw them looking and waved, her whole face lighting up as she smiled. Mark laughed and waved back.

"I hope you have children of your own someday," his

mother said, a certain wistfulness playing across her face. "A family makes life worth living."

"Maybe someday," Mark said, trying not to think about the baby currently growing in Becky's womb. "When I'm ready."

His mother snorted. "You'll never be ready. No one ever is. You just figure it out as you go along and hope you don't make too many mistakes."

He nodded. He was pretty sure if he told his mom what had happened she'd tell him he'd already made a giant one.

Becky slammed her car door and hit her fist on the steering wheel. This had been the week's third job interview and it had been just as big of a bust as the last two.

Although her interviewer probably didn't think so. Judging from the light in his eyes when they'd said goodbye, he thought he had found his next senior copywriter. If only the job hadn't sounded so boring.

Her phone blared in the silence. She looked down at the number. It was the recruiter she'd been working with.

"Hi, Amy," she said, sighing into the phone.

"Hey, girl, you rocked another one," an excited voice said. "I just talked to Jim and he said he'll have an offer put together by the end of the week. That means you'll have three opportunities to choose from."

"That's nice," Becky said.

"Really? I tell you you're about to have three offers thrown at you and all you can say is 'That's nice'?"

"It's just—well, I don't want to work on cars," she said.

There was a beat of silence. "Becky. You *do* realize you're in Detroit, right? Cars are what we do here."

"I know, I know. And I'll do it. It just doesn't thrill me."

"Well, I'll bet you'll feel differently when the offers come in. They're going to throw buckets of money at you, honey."

"All right. Call me if you hear anything," she said, and hung up the phone.

She turned the key in the ignition and drove out of the soulless office park. Everything here seemed so sterile. Although cars jammed the streets, there was not a single person on the sidewalk. There was no music. No street vendors. Not even any taxis leaning on their horns. It was as if somebody had hit the mute button on the world.

The leaden skies didn't help, either. The only thing worse than early December in Detroit was late February in Detroit. It was cold. Wet. And eternally cloudy. Only the twinkling Christmas lights that winked into life after the sun went down relieved the monotony.

But that didn't help during the day.

God, but she missed Mark…er…New York.

She put her hand on her belly and sighed. "I hope you appreciate what I'm trying to do here, kiddo. Because I gotta tell you, it kind of sucks."

Mark stepped into the dimly lit bar, hoping a night out with his college roommate would snap him out of the funk he'd found himself in. Quickly he scanned the room, looking for the former football player.

It didn't take long to find him. Although John had blown his knee out the season before, he was still the guy who'd kicked the winning field goal in the Super Bowl a couple of years back. He attracted a crowd wherever he went.

Tonight he was surrounded by a gaggle of beautiful women, as usual.

He strode up to the booth and slapped him on the shoulder.

"Hey, Casanova," he said.

Immediately John turned and grinned. "Mark, you made it! Sit down, buddy. It's been too long."

"It has, hasn't it? We'll have to make up for lost time. What are you drinking? I'll get the next round."

John waved his arm dismissively. "Don't worry about it. Unless you've cozied up to that rich stepdad of yours I've got more money than you do. Still like tequila?"

He nodded.

"All right." He motioned to the bartender. "Jake, I'm going to need a double of Patrón. Fast."

Within moments a large glass of tequila landed in front of Mark.

He downed it, trying hard not to think of the last time he'd done shots of tequila—or who he'd done them with.

Unfortunately his brain insisted on showing him Becky's eyes glittering at him from behind an empty shot glass.

Her voice echoed in his ears. *All right. Let's toast,* she'd said, raising her glass. *To one wild night.*

He'd clinked his glass and locked eyes with hers. *To one wild, scandalous night.*

If he'd known how much that one night would change his life he probably would have walked away after that toast. Although he was really glad he hadn't. Even if what they'd had wasn't meant to last, he was glad he'd gotten the chance to experience it. To experience *her.*

"Hey, dude. You still with us?" John asked.

Mark shook his head to clear it. "Yeah, man. Sorry. Just lost in my thoughts."

"Ri—ight. Dude, the last time I saw you looking this pathetic you'd just found out about Sandra… Oh. This is about a chick, isn't it?"

Mark just looked at him. "I don't want to talk about it. Especially not while you're covered in women."

"Say no more," John said. "Okay, ladies, it's time to shove off. I'll see you later, okay?"

Although they pouted and whined they slowly left the booth. Once they were alone, John turned back to him.

"Okay, out with it. What's wrong?"

"Nothing," said Mark, looking down at his newly refilled shot glass. "I'm just a little off my game tonight."

"Right," he said. "And I'm Robert DeNiro. Try again."

He looked at him and sighed. "All right, but you're going to think I'm a jerk."

John just looked him, one eyebrow raised. "I'll be the judge of that."

By the time the story was done the tequila was long gone. John took one last swig of his beer, then shook his head.

"You were right," he said.

"About what?"

"I do think you're a jerk. How could you abandon her like that?"

Immediately he felt his hackles rise. "I didn't abandon her. It was her choice to go. She left without even telling me."

John stood. "Only after you proved yourself to be an immature cad who runs the second the going gets tough. She did the right thing."

"Where are you going?"

"Nowhere. But you're leaving. You've got no business being here, Mark. Man up and go get your woman. You're too old to sulk because things got too real."

Unable to think of anything to say, Mark got up and left. He didn't want to drink with someone who was lecturing him, anyway.

He wasn't sulking. And he certainly wasn't immature. He'd done Becky a favor by refusing to get involved— better that the child never have a father than have one who didn't really love his mom. He knew from experience how much that sucked.

And he didn't love Becky. He was infatuated, maybe, but not in love.

It never would have lasted.

Even if he did love her she wouldn't have stuck around. A woman like that could have any man she wanted. She'd never be happy settling for a schmuck like him.

Logically, he knew he had done the right thing.

Maybe in a couple more years his heart would believe it, too.

Becky lay back on the paper-covered pillow and breathed out, trying to relax. As the technician moved the gel-covered wand around, trying to get a clearer picture, she did her best to avoid thinking about the last time she'd been in this position, or about the baby that first sonogram had shown her.

"There you are, little bean," the technician said. "It's time to check you out."

Becky looked up at the video screen, trying to identify which of the grainy black-and-white blobs was her baby.

"Mmm-hmm," the technician muttered. "That's good. And there's that…perfect." Then, louder, she said, "Ms. Logan, your bean is in good shape. So far everything looks just the way it should."

Becky still wasn't sure where to look. "Good, but can you show me? I'm embarrassed to say I'm not exactly sure what I'm looking at."

"Oh. Of course. Silly me."

She punched a few keys on the computer and in seconds a peanut-shaped fetus zoomed into focus.

"There's your baby," the technician said. "All curled up and ready to grow. Want to hear the heartbeat?"

Becky nodded.

"All right, here it comes!"

Soon a soft, rapid-fire whooshing beat filled the room.

"That…that's my baby?" Becky asked.

She nodded.

"Oh. Oh. wow." She lay silently for a moment, struggling against tears as a flood of emotions washed over her. Joy. Fear. And a fierce, all-consuming wave of love.

She was going to be a mommy. In fact she already was. And this time nothing would stop her from loving her baby with everything she had.

Eventually the technician cleared her throat. "Sorry to rush you, Ms. Logan, but I have another appointment in just a few minutes. I'm going to have to shut this down. How many pictures would you like?"

For a moment she thought about asking for three. One for her, one for her mom, and one to send to Mark. Maybe seeing the baby would bring him around.

But. No. That was just the hormones talking. Mark didn't want to be involved in the baby's life. And she didn't need him to be.

"Just two, please."

Mark was reviewing the latest round of Eden coupon designs when David let himself into his office.

"We're going to the bar. Come with us."

"Oh, I don't know, David. I have a lot of work to do," he said. Truth was, he had no desire to spend a second longer in the older man's company than he had to.

"Come on. I'm tired of seeing you moping around here. It's time to go out and have some fun."

Fun? With David? Somehow, Mark didn't think that was going to happen. But he knew it was important to appear to be a team player.

"All right," he said. "Just let me get my coat."

A short time later he found himself sitting on a stool in David's favorite dive bar.

"Two whiskeys on the rocks," David said to the bartender.

"Actually, I don't—"

"Every ad man drinks whiskey, son. Buck up."

Mark nodded and fell silent. *Think about the money,* he told himself. *And the job. Thanks to this man, you've finally made it. You can drink a little whiskey if it makes him happy.*

When their drinks came David took a deep swallow. Mark copied him, feeling the burn all the way down into his intestines.

"Listen, Mark, I asked you to come for a drink so I could set you straight on a few things," David said.

"Oh?" Why was it everyone wanted to talk to him all of a sudden?

"I know you think what happened to Becky was unfair. That it was none of my business what you two were getting up to once work was done."

"Well, sort of." The man was a master of understatement.

David continued as if he hadn't heard. "Here's the thing, though. It had to be done. If it hadn't been because of you I would have found another reason to get rid of her."

"But she got rid of herself," Mark protested.

"Oh, please. I knew what she would do when I called the two of you in there. I'd even warned the Eden people that she would probably be taking a leave of absence. Becky's got too big of a heart to let someone else take the fall for her. And you have too much common sense to let go of a golden opportunity like this one."

"I'm not sure I follow you," Mark said slowly, his stomach churning.

"Women don't belong in advertising," David said. "Not in the upper ranks, anyway. They're too emotional. Too distracted. Becky is a damn fine copywriter, but she's incapable of achieving the single-minded focus men like you bring to the table. Eventually she would've found a man. Started a family. And just like that her career would have fallen to third place in her priorities. This agency is too important to me to allow it to take anything less than top priority in the lives of my management team. Advertising isn't a business. It's a lifestyle. I have yet to meet a woman who gets that."

He took a sip of his drink and chuckled.

"Sometimes you have to get creative to persuade them to make the right choice. Like, say, with a 'no relationship' clause."

Mark slammed his glass down on the counter, barely containing his sudden fury.

"Wait a minute. Are you're telling me there's *not* a no-relationship clause in our contracts?" he asked.

"There is now," David said with a smug smile.

It was all Mark could do not to punch him.

"Did you actually have proof that Becky and I were involved?"

"Well, I saw you hugging in your office that day. I didn't need any more proof than that. It was written all over your faces."

Mark's jaw dropped. This man was the biggest ass he'd ever met. And he'd chosen him over the woman he loved.

Loved? Yes, *loved.* As soon as the thought ran through his consciousness he could no longer deny the truth. He loved her with every fiber of his being. No job, no matter how awesome, would ever fill the hole her absence had left in his heart.

Suddenly he knew what he had to do. And it didn't involve wasting any more time with the man sitting next to him.

"David, do you have a pen?"

"Sure," he said, reaching into the pocket of his suit coat. "Here you go."

"Thanks," Mark said. Then he grabbed a fresh cocktail napkin from the pile on the bar. Uncapping the pen, he wrote "I QUIT," in all caps, and signed his name.

"Here," he said, handing it to David.

"What's this?"

"My resignation letter. It's effective immediately. Good luck with Eden," he said and strode out through the door, already punching a number into his phone. "Jessie? I'm going to need Becky's address. I have a mistake to fix."

CHAPTER THIRTEEN

BECKY STEPPED BACK to admire the Christmas tree. Twinkling lights sparkled from its branches, highlighting the perfectly coordinated red and gold ornaments.

"It looks like something out of a store catalog," her mother said, a note of wistfulness in her voice.

"A little too perfect, huh?"

"No, I just wish you'd saved a little room for our family ornaments. I really love that snowman you made when you were five."

Her shoulders slumped. "I'm sorry, Mom, I was just trying to do something useful. I feel like such a mooch."

Her mom hadn't let her do anything since she'd arrived home. She didn't want any help cleaning. Wouldn't allow her to touch a pot or pan. And she refused to accept any money for her room and board—money Becky knew her parents could use.

The forced idleness was driving her batty.

"You're not a mooch. You're my daughter, recovering from a very recent heartbreak and trying to build a whole new life—while making a new life. Cut yourself some slack."

She sighed. "I'll try. It's just that I'm feeling itchy. I need to go back to work. I haven't had this long of a break between jobs since I was sixteen."

"I know. Give it time, Becky. The right opportunity will come along."

"I hope so. Can you bring me the other box of ornaments? I'll fix the tree."

As her mother disappeared into the basement Becky heard the muffled sound of her phone trilling from somewhere in the room.

"Oh, great. Where'd I put the damn thing now?" she muttered, lifting boxes and tossing pillows.

She finally found it, mushed between two couch cushions.

"Hello?" she said a little breathlessly.

"There you are. I was just getting ready to leave you a message."

"Oh, hey, Amy. What's up? Another car agency sniffing around?"

"Nope, I promised not to bother you with any more of those. This one's different."

"All right, I'm listening," Becky said.

"Well, it's a new agency. Pretty much brand-new."

"Uh-oh…"

"Now, hang on. They have some pretty big accounts. And not automotive, either."

"Which ones?"

"I'm not allowed to tell you. You have to sign a nondisclosure agreement first. But they said you're first on their list of candidates. Said they'd pay a premium if I could snag you."

"Hmm. That's flattering."

"It is. *Very*. Why don't you just go and see what they have to say? It could be just what you're looking for."

She looked over at her OCD tree and nodded. "All right. At the very least it will give me something to do."

Becky parked in front of a bright yellow Victorian house, checking the address one more time. Yep, this was where Amy had directed her to go.

Huh? It didn't look like any ad agency she'd ever seen. She had to admit that the surroundings were charming, though. It had the same vibe that all her favorite New York neighborhoods had—young and hip and full of life.

She shouldered her laptop bag and clacked up the carefully manicured walk. As she crossed the covered porch she noticed a small woodcut sign that read 'Trio' hanging from the wreath hook.

Definitely the right place, then.

She was about to ring the bell when a gawky pink-haired girl opened the door.

"You must be Becky," she said, blue eyes sparkling.

"I am. And you are…?"

"Izzie. I'm just a temp, but I'm hoping to convince the owner to keep me on," she said conspiratorially.

"Ah," Becky said, at a loss for words.

"Come on in," she said. "He's expecting you."

She stepped inside and handed Izzie her coat, taking a moment to check out her surroundings. The house looked fabulous—contemporary furnishings contrasting nicely with ornate woodwork and jewel-toned walls.

"It's this way," Izzie said, leading Becky into what must have once been the dining area but what was now a fully kitted-out conference room.

"Have a seat anywhere you like. He'll be right in."

Becky pulled out one of the cushy wood chairs and sat down, realizing she had no idea who she was about to interview with. No one had ever given her a name.

Oh, well. The mystery would be solved soon enough.

She fired up her laptop and was opening her online portfolio when she heard a familiar rumble.

"There you are. Detroit's hottest copywriter, in the flesh. Thank you for agreeing to meet with me."

Her head snapped up. *It couldn't be.*

It was.

Mark stood in the doorway, wearing a tailored black suit, looking even more delicious than she remembered.

Her emotions spun, unsure whether to settle on absolute fury or melting delight. She stood, fighting the urge to either hug or throttle him.

"M-Mark? What are you doing here?"

"This is my agency."

"Wait. What? No. You belong at SBD."

"Not anymore. I quit."

"You quit?" she asked, fury winning. "After I gave up everything for you? What the hell did you do that for?"

"I had to."

"Why? Did you lose the account?" Surely he couldn't have screwed up that badly that fast.

"No. I brought it with me."

She sank back down in her chair. "Okay, I am completely lost."

Mark stepped into the room and pulled down a white screen.

"Let me do this right," he said. "I put together a presentation to explain everything to you. Will you listen?"

Unable to speak, Becky nodded.

"Okay," he said, clicking a few buttons on his Mac. A picture of a sullen teenage boy filled the screen.

"Once upon a time there was a boy with a nasty attitude. He lived in a big house, and attended the most exclusive schools, but had the world's biggest stick up his ass. He had long ago decided his mother didn't love him, her illegitimate son, and nothing she did could change his mind."

He clicked forward to an image of a grinning Mark in a graduation cap and gown.

"He managed to graduate from college in spite of himself, and soon embarked on a career in the soulless world of advertising. He was quite good. Racked up lots of awards. And he managed to get through his twenties without ever having a real relationship."

He clicked forward to a shot of the famous Vegas sign.

"Then he went on a business trip and met a woman who would change his life forever. They spent only one night together, but by the time she left he was already falling in love. Not that he was capable of admitting it."

He flipped forward again to show the SBD sign.

"Then he got hired to work with and compete against the same phenomenal woman. Although he told himself not to get involved, he quickly did. They worked together, played together and won the account together. Somewhere along the way he fell head over heels, but still couldn't admit it to himself."

He clicked forward to a shot of a pregnant tummy.

"When she told him she was pregnant he reverted back to that sullen little boy and ran for the hills."

He clicked forward to David's headshot.

"Then the evil agency owner cooked up a plan to get rid of the girl. Both the girl and the boy fell for it, and before he knew it she was gone."

He clicked forward to a gray sky.

"Without her, his world fell apart. But it wasn't until he discovered the evil agency owner's dastardly plan that he managed to get rid of the stick still up his ass."

Another click and one of their Eden ad designs filled the screen.

"He submitted his resignation on a cocktail napkin and headed to the Eden company to tell them what he knew. Being decent people, they fired SBD and signed on the dotted line with the boy's as yet unnamed agency—on the condition that he find his better half."

He clicked forward to the yellow house.

"So here he is. Starting over. In Detroit. Betting that the woman he doesn't deserve will give him another chance with her heart and let him be her partner and her baby's daddy."

"Are you serious?" she whispered.

"Do I ever bet when I think I might lose?"

"I don't know," she said, her mind whirling. "This is all so sudden…"

"I have one more thing to show you," he said. "Will you come?"

She nodded and he led her up the ornate wooden staircase. He opened a door and stepped through to the sunny yellow room beyond.

"This is your office," he said. "And this," he went on, opening a door with a placard reading CEO, "is our baby's office."

It was a nursery, done in shades of green and yellow, complete with crib, rocking chair and changing table.

"My office is just over there," he said, pointing to a door on the far side of the room. He turned to her and smiled. "What do you think?"

She opened and closed her mouth, spinning in a slow circle in the middle of the room. "It's amazing," she breathed.

Mark crossed the room in two steps and got down on one knee, producing a diamond ring from his suit pocket.

"Becky, I'm ready to go all-in. I want us to be a family. Will you do me the honor of becoming my wife, partner and best friend?"

Becky thought her heart might explode with joy.

"Yes," she said. "Oh, yes."

Mark solemnly placed the ring on her left hand, then grinned up at her.

"I bet I know what you want me to do now."

"What?" she asked, smiling through the tears streaming down her face.

"This," he said, rising to take her in his arms and claim her lips.

Becky looped her arms around his neck and kissed him back with everything she had.

"You win again, Magic Man," she murmured. "But do you know what I want more than anything right now?"

"No. What?"

"For you to take me to bed."

"I don't have any beds here yet. Will a desk do?"

"Splendidly." She grinned.

He swooped her up into his arms and carried her over the threshold into his office.

"God, I missed you, Gorgeous Girl."

"Prove it," she said.

And so he did.

EPILOGUE

BECKY WAS JUST clicking through to her final PowerPoint slide when a baby's cry echoed through the monitor placed discreetly under the conference room table.

She grinned and nudged the power switch to the Off position with her toe.

"And that's how we'll make the Eden campaign the advertising darling of the new year, fueling New Year's Resolutions across the country."

As applause broke out around the crowded conference table Izzie poked her head through the white-paneled door.

"He needs to be fed," Izzie said in a stage whisper.

Becky motioned for her to come in and gathered the baby into her arms.

"If you have any questions, Mark can field them," she said, moving to the comfy rocker tucked behind a folding screen in the corner.

She listened, baby nestled at her breast, as Mark swung into action. In no time he had sweet talked the Eden people into spending even more money with their tiny agency in the next year.

Trio's future was secured.

When they were finally gone, Mark plopped down on the rocker's ottoman and stroked the baby's cheek.

"Well, I'm glad that's over," he said.

"Were you worried they wouldn't sign?" she asked.

"No, not really. I just want to move on to the day's big event."

"Big event? I know I've been preoccupied," she said, indicating the baby nestled on her chest, "but I thought that meeting was our last piece of client business until after the holidays."

"It was. This has nothing to do with business."

"Then what is it?"

Mark grinned. "It's a surprise. Do you trust me?"

"You know I do," Becky said.

"Good. Then I need you to head up the back staircase into your office and do whatever Izzie tells you to do. Okay?"

"Okaaayyy… I guess," Becky said. "Now?"

"Yep. Now," he said, pulling her to her feet.

"What about Alex?"

"I'll take care of Alex. Hand him over," Mark said, holding his arms out for the baby.

Becky kissed his soft head, then reluctantly gave him to Mark. Even after five months of life as a mom it still amazed her how in love she was with her baby.

"He just ate, so he's going to need a diaper—"

"I know," said Mark.

"And he needs to do some tummy time…"

"Got it. Just go."

"Okay. If you're sure…?"

Mark sighed. "Becky. You're just going to be upstairs. I've got this."

She realized she was being a bit ridiculous. "All right, I'm going," she grumbled, and headed for the kitchen door.

When she opened her office door, she was shocked to see four different people rushing about, setting up mirrors and plugging in hair appliances.

"What on earth is going on here?" she asked.

Izzie's pink-haired head popped up from behind her desk, plug in hand.

"Oh, there you are! We're on a mission to doll you up. Now, hurry up and get in here. There's not much time!"

"Time before what? I'm so confused," Becky moaned.

Izzie grabbed her by the hand and pulled her behind a screen that had been set up in the corner.

"Don't worry about it, boss lady." Izzie grinned. "You're going to love it. Now, just relax and go with the flow."

Realizing she had no real choice in the matter, Becky nodded. "All right, I'll try."

"Good," Izzie said, unzipping a dress bag. "You can start by stripping down to your skivvies. We need to make sure this fits you."

Becky gasped when she saw the confection Izzie was holding. It was a full-length evening gown made of red velvet. Gold and red beaded embroidery sparkled at the bodice and traced a delicate path down to the hip of the A-line skirt, then flowed along the hem. Cap sleeves finished it off.

"It's beautiful," she breathed.

"It'll look even better on you," Izzie said. "Now. come on—off with your clothes."

Two hours later Becky was staring at her reflection in a full-length mirror, not recognizing the gorgeous woman staring back at her, when there was a knock on the door.

"Come in," she called, not bothering to turn around.

"Wow. If that's what having a baby does for your body, sign me up," a familiar voice said.

Becky whirled, unable to believe her ears. "Jessie!" she shrieked when she saw her beloved redheaded friend grinning at her from the doorway. "Jessie, what are you doing here?"

"Oh, you know," she said. "I was just in the neighborhood, so I thought I'd stop by…"

"You are such a liar." Becky laughed, throwing her arms

around her friend. "But I don't care. I'm just so glad to see you!"

Jessie squeezed her back. "Me, too, lady. Me, too. But, hey, we better be careful. I don't want to muss that gorgeous gown you're wearing."

Becky disentangled herself and did a little twirl.

"I know. Isn't it amazing? But I have no idea why I'm wearing it."

"I do. And so will you in a few minutes," Jessie said. "But first I need to freshen up. Izzie? What have you got for me?"

Izzie dragged her behind the screen and Becky went back to gawking at herself in the mirror. Her blond hair was swept up with an elegant mass of sequined hairpins, artfully crafted curls framing her face. The makeup artist had made her emerald eyes look huge, and she was sure her lips were nowhere near that plump.

The dress emphasized her newfound curves, and for the first time since Alex was born she felt beautiful.

Tears welled in her eyes. She had no idea what Mark was planning, but she owed him big for helping her feel like a woman again.

Just then Jessie's faced popped up behind her shoulder. "Hey, hey, hey—no crying allowed! You're wearing way too much mascara for that."

Becky smiled, wiping at the corner of her eye as she turned. Jessie had changed into an elegant green cocktail dress, with the same gold embroidery flashing around the knee-length hem.

"Wow. You clean up good. Wait a minute…" she said, realization dawning. "That looks like a bridesmaid's dress. But we haven't even begun planning the wedding. It's supposed to be in June!"

Just then the lilting sound of a harp playing her favorite hymn floated up to her ears.

"Isn't it?"

Jessie just winked and peeked her head out through the door.

"Mark? We're ready for you!"

Seconds later Mark stood in the doorway, wearing a tuxedo. "Hey, babe." He grinned. "You ready to get married?"

Becky sat down heavily in her chair. "But I thought— I mean, we'd always talked about June!" Not that she'd done anything to put plans in motion.

Mark crossed the room and kneeled down in front of her. "I know, Becky, I know. But it was a year ago today, right here in this house, when we became a family. I thought it only fitting that we make it legal in the same place. Besides," he said, kissing her fingers, "I don't want to wait another six months. I want the whole world to know you're mine *now*. Becky Logan, will you do me the honor of becoming my wife today?"

Becky dabbed at her eyes again, holding back the tears by force of will alone. "Of course I will," she said, joy fizzing in her veins.

"Good," he said. "Then let's do this thing."

From the hallway, Izzie called, "Hit it, guys!" and a string quartet launched into the "Wedding March."

Becky put her hand in the crook of Mark's arm. "Let's do it."

Mark stood in front of Becky's childhood priest, listening to the sermon with half an ear as he gazed at the beautiful woman who had agreed to be his wife. Even the glow of the twinkling white Christmas lights that sparkled around them paled in comparison to the joy emanating from her.

To think he had almost missed out on all of this. Now that their baby had arrived he couldn't imagine life without him. Not to mention his mother.

Becky caught him staring and smiled, love shining from her eyes. "I love you," she mouthed silently.

"I love you, too," he mouthed back.

"If I can get these lovebirds to stop mooning over each other for a minute, we'll get to the real reason you're all here," the priest said, breaking into their silent communion. "But first let me ask all who are gathered here an important question. Is there anyone here who objects to this marriage? If so, speak now or forever hold your peace."

Silence fell, making the sudden outraged shriek from their baby's miniature lungs echo all the louder.

"We'll assume that's his way of objecting to his place on the sidelines and not to his parents' matrimony," the priest joked as the room erupted with laughter.

"Well, let's fix that." Becky giggled, and motioned for her mother to bring the baby forward. "After all, he's part of this family, too."

Once he was settled on her hip, the angry cries turned into contented coos.

"All right. Now that we're all settled," the priest said, "do you, Becky, take this man to be your lawfully wedded husband, to care for him and keep him, in sickness and in health, in good times and in bad, all the days of your life?"

"I do," she said softly, and Mark's heart swelled.

"And do you, Mark, take this woman to be your lawfully wedded wife, to care for her and keep her, in sickness and in health, in good times and in bad, all the days of your life?"

"You bet I do," he said, putting his whole heart into every word.

"Then it is my honor to proclaim you husband and wife. Mark, you may kiss the bride."

Mark gathered her to him, careful not to dislodge the baby from her hip. "Now you're mine," he whispered, and pressed his lips to hers, silently communicating his joy.

"I always was," she whispered against his mouth.

Alex chortled happily as they broke apart, and, laughing, Mark bent to kiss his cheek.

"Ladies and gentlemen, I am overjoyed to present to you Mr. and Mrs. Powers!"

The small crowd rose to its feet and applauded.

Looking around at the sea of happy faces, Mark felt at peace. Love might be a gamble, but he was pretty sure he'd hit the jackpot.

* * * * *

'I bet we could find at least one thing we both enjoy.'

'What did you have in mind?'

'It's way too early in the night for me to tie myself down to anything specific.'

'You've got an answer for everything, Ms Devine. Sadly it's too late in the night for me to stay on and find out what you'll tie yourself down to. Or tie yourself up with. It's been…interesting.'

He leant a hand on her shoulder and leaned down for the obligatory goodbye cheek-kiss. He smelled product—perfume, hairspray, cosmetics. He touched smooth skin. He let his lips linger for a second too long to be strictly platonic. He curled his other arm round her waist, drawing her closer into him. Her body was soft and nestled perfectly, and he moved his lips to her other cheek. But her lips were in the way, so he placed his kiss there. Just one.

She. Was. So. Hot.

Dear Reader

When Tara Devine first burst onto the page even *I* was taken aback by her sass! Every time she met a challenge she climbed right over it—in her highest, most inappropriate heels. Sometimes I had no idea how she badly she would behave, but one thing was for sure: when she met her match, the feral cat would turn into a kitten. Getting to that stage was never going to be easy, and only a very tough guy showing her very tough love would cut it.

Enter one super-sure, super-hot Michael Cruz. He's seen more than enough of life to see right through Tara. But what he does see hooks him. And even though she pushes him to his very limits, and brings out every chest-thumping, testosterone-pumping part of him, he's her guy and he's prepared to hold on until all the champagne's been drunk and the party's over.

I truly loved these characters. I loved their hot sex and their love story. And I so admired Michael for the patience he was prepared to show. Falling in love with love is easy. But playing the long game and putting yourself second is what really counts.

I hope my very first Modern Tempted™ rocks you the way it rocked me. To be part of this wonderful world of writers and readers sharing the eternal quest for eternal love is the best feeling ever!

With my warmest wishes

Bella x

DRESSED
TO THRILL

BY
BELLA FRANCES

Unable to sit still without reading, **Bella Frances** first found romantic fiction at the age of twelve, in between deadly dull knitting patterns and recipes in the pages of her grandmother's magazines. An obsession was born! But it wasn't until one long, hot summer, after completing her first degree in English Literature, that she fell upon the legends that are Mills & Boon® books. She has occasionally lifted her head out of them since to do a range of jobs, including barmaid, financial advisor and teacher, as well as to practise (but never perfect) the art of motherhood to two (almost grown-up) cherubs.

Her eclectic collection of wonderful friends have provided more than their fair share of inspiration for heroes, heroines and glamorous locations, and it was while waiting to board a flight home after a particularly lively holiday that the characters for her first competition success in *So You Think You Can Write*, were born.

Bella lives a very energetic life in the UK, but tries desperately to travel for pleasure at least once a month—strictly in the interests of research!

Catch up with her on her website at www.bellafrances.co.uk

**DRESSED TO THRILL is Bella Frances' debut book
for Mills & Boon® Modern Tempted™
and is also available in eBook format
from www.millsandboon.co.uk**

DEDICATION

For Margaret Isabella Mustard, who loved literature and life.
Governess, teacher, farmer's wife, mother and grandmother.
Thank you.

CHAPTER ONE

TARA MARIE FITZPATRICK DEVINE knew how to behave badly. Very badly. She made it her business to work hard, play hard and then read the hard online copy of her triumphs. It was quite simply the most delicious way to promote herself in the dog-eat-dog world of international fashion. And tonight—the culmination of a whole season of glamorous graft—tonight, her wild streak was shining like neon body paint in a nightclub-dark room.

'But what am I going to do?'

Barely aware of the feet that drummed beside hers under the table in the shady booth, Tara dipped into her clutch and pulled out her compact. Another streak of siren-red over her pout while she was still sober enough to care.

'You'll be fine,' she managed to say, looking at her reflection in the tiny mirror.

The thick slicks of liquid eyeliner were almost perfect—crazy that she had never rocked this look before—it was so, *so* burlesque!

'But I'm sure he'll be on his way here next! And if he catches me here…after I told him I was going straight home…'

Tara replaced the lipstick in its little case. Honestly, there was no getting through to this girl.

'Fernanda.'

She swept a glance from the now resting silver platforms to the mouthwateringly beautiful face of Fernanda Cruz—the sexiest Spanish teenager to grace the runways and the tabloids in a decade. Her brown mane hung sexily over one eye and her fuchsia silk mini-dress rode high on endless thighs. The girl looked as if she had never even heard of the word carbohydrate.

'What?'

Tara pointed her lipstick at her.

'You need to stop this. First of all, you're not even sure if he'll definitely turn up. Secondly, if he does… and—let's face it—it is quite likely, then you need to stand up to him. Tell him to get out of your life and stop acting like the overbearing, macho pain in the ass that he is.' She flipped open the compact again and checked her slightly wonky teeth for lipstick, rubbing at them until they squeaked. 'It's not as if you've done anything wrong, Fernanda. It's only an after-party! '

'But you don't understand. My brother Michael rules the family. If he *is* here, I'm…' She mimed being garrotted.

'And *he* has to realise that a life in fashion these days means you have to promote yourself—be seen, get papped, kiss Harry…'

'But I'm his baby sister, Tara! And he hates it. Hates all of it. He wants me to study to be an accountant or something. He thinks models are airheads and designers are fakes.'

Tara's snapped her clutch closed with a little more attitude than was necessary. She knew all about the über-dominant Michael Cruz, Fern's brother and legendary King Machismo. Ten hours earlier, as Fernanda had sublimely showcased Tara's funkiest spring/summer dresses on the runway of her London show, her sickeningly handsome brother had sat in the front row, looking as bored as if he were watching paint dry—the dull shades.

And, though no one had dared tell Tara at the time, the press had been all over it. Photos of him in his immaculately tailored suit, with his perfectly masculine jaw and utterly uninterested expression had hit every online fashion site within moments. Thank heavens his other sister Angelica had shown enough enthusiasm for the whole row. And had been kind enough to drop that she was 'considering' commissioning Tara to design her wedding dress. That just about made up for the arrogance of the man!

'Fern, honey, we've worked hard. Our careers are just taking off. For me, this party is as important as the show. And for you it's what you've been looking forward to for the last month. And we've got it all to do again in two weeks' time in Paris! *Cha-ching!* So if he is here we'll tell him to...to go and count his own beans—and we'll mingle and dance and see what column inches we can capture. Come on!'

She grasped Fern's hand and pulled her to her feet. All six feet of her size zero frame only served to highlight Tara's own whipped cream curves. *Fattest woman in fashion. Overeater von Tease.* Yep, she'd heard them all. And sometimes it hurt—of course it did. But she'd learned long ago that even if she ate air and drank dew she was only ever going to be voluptuous. So she'd put her voluptuousness to good use—she knew how to en-

hance a cleavage and minimise a belly better than any
bra or pair of magic pants.

And, now that the fashion elite had begun to show
interest, getting some mainstream press was her next
mission. Hence the headline-grabbing dress from her
show—she'd styled it *The Seven-Year Bitch: Marilyn
meets Madonna*. Though maybe it *hadn't* been the best
idea to go this short when there was nothing surer than a
cringe-worthy 'getting into the limo badly' photograph
appearing in the morning's news feed. More column
inches, and even more reasons for Team Devine back
home to decry her. Devine girls were supposed to put
up and shut up—two of her weakest skills...

The DJ changed and the music turned darker. Tara
saw Fern head onto the dance floor with some up-and-
coming young cutie and wandered off herself into the
throng, smiling and air-kissing the other bottom-of-the-
food-chain celebrities. She snagged a glass of champagne from a passing tray and moved back out to the
foyer—keen to avoid having to chat with her Dutch fi-
nancier, easily the most boring man on earth. But when
her breath seemed to catch as a gulp of fizz hit the back
of her throat, and the faces of the crowd all turned, she
realised that someone *very* A-list had just arrived.

Everything in Tara Devine's life happened at a million miles an hour. Her brain processed thoughts that
her mouth duly delivered. Which sometimes led to problems. Like when she didn't actually *know* what she'd
just said or done until two seconds too late. But here—
now—she felt as if she had slipped into slow-mo. She
watched, transfixed, as the foyer seemed almost to fade
and there, stalking along the red carpet, was the arrogant alpha himself. Michael Cruz. Incorporated.

As the camera flashes whited out the space he turned his head slightly, as if a mildly irritating noise had sounded. Now that she could see him clearly, she saw he was as tall as she had imagined, his physique as perfect. And, though she rarely dressed men, she just knew what lay under the cut of cloth on his back. The ripple of muscle over the perfect masculine ratio of shoulders to waist was flawless.

One hand was at his hip, pushing back his jacket, and the perfect illumination of a white silk-linen shirt gleamed. He turned, paced, and took something handed to him by one of his security team. He slipped it into his pocket, seemed to search out the faces closest to him, and then...

And then a flash of intensely dark eyes landed on her. He scanned her, and her heart raced the moment his gaze probed and zoned over her. His eyes narrowed as they landed on her chest and she instinctively lifted her arms to shield herself. He turned full body to face her as he continued to stare, his eyes sliding down, over and up her legs.

The cameras whirred and flashed, people were talking, calling out to him, capturing his appraisal of her. And then, with what seemed infuriatingly like a condescending smirk, he turned away, dismissing her.

Tara felt colour rush up her chest and burn her cheeks—the stab of childhood sensitivities all over again. It had been a long time since anyone had pierced her armour. And that made her even angrier—how *dared* he? She made to step forward, to tell him what she thought of him—him and his dull, dark, bespoke suit. He was here in the hub of one of the most creative cities in the world, at one of the most exciting times—

when the eyes of the fashion media were trained upon young talent—and he was being openly dismissive of anything other than twenty-four-carat conservatives just like himself.

She had checked him out—the media darling, yet another poacher turned gamekeeper whose definition of art was as narrow as his totally on-trend, no-risk tie. There was no way anyone other than the beautiful people would get a foothold in *his* world. Old money and limb length spoke more than any genuine talent. As far as she could see.

As if to prove her point, a little posse of coltish runway girls circled him, giggling and preening and flashing their thigh-gaps like currency. He brightened and slung arms round two who snuck right under his 'Daddy's home' embrace. Their coquettish display was vile. Sometimes the sisterhood let itself down *so* badly.

'Tara, *querida*! How lovely to see you again.'

Tara turned to see the third member of Club Cruz glide her way towards her. The outrageously elegant Angelica: dream customer and media-savvy goddess of style. Oh, yes. Let the Lord be thanked for the double X chromosomes in the procreation of generation Cruz.

'Angelica!'

Air-kiss, air-kiss and smug glare right over to the arrogant alpha himself. He caught her look and made no effort to hide his calm assessment of the scene. Stood with his adoring troupe, relaxed and controlled. And who could blame him—the way they were practically licking the air around him?

'Angelica, you look beautiful—as ever. Let me see.' Tara stepped back to scan the perfect ensemble, 'You wear couture so well. It's a shame your brother is rocking the boring businessman look, though.'

Angelica laughed lightly and preened politely, linking her arm in Tara's and stepping into the party. 'Michael is putting up with this for me. He doesn't really like the scene any more. But he does enjoy some of the benefits.'

She flicked her eyes to where he stood, acknowledging his current difficulties with amused acceptance.

'This is the third party we've been to and his ego must be bigger than the bar bills. All these beautiful young girls and so few men for them to flirt with. Well, men who like women, that is.'

Tara scanned her fellow partygoers, nodding her agreement. There was more oestrogen in the room than you could shake a fluffy pink wand at. The legions of gay best friends didn't quite boost the already depleted testosterone levels. Even the men in the celebrity underclass were over-preened, with their shaped, tinted brows and oily orange complexions. Really, *really* not a turn-on.

Tara's men were edgy, dark, beta. And invariably in her past. The last real relationship she'd had, with a sensitive, eyeliner-wearing musician, had been during college. The relationships she had now were with champagne and investors. Oh, and the media. Her biggest flirt of all.

'I was wondering if you had seen Fernanda, actually.'

Angelica's tone still had its feather-lightness but Tara could sense a little edge of concern.

'I thought she was staying home, but maybe she has come here with you?'

Tara looked around. Fern hadn't been with her for

quite some time now. 'She *is* here—she went to dance. But if she knows Michael's here she'll be hiding out in the toilets. She had a major meltdown earlier. He must have some hold over her.'

Angelica steered them through to the dance floor, smiling as she passed the partygoers and securing them two glasses of champagne from a conveniently placed table.

'He means well—just worries about her because he is responsible for her. It was never easy for him, being guardian to two orphaned girls.'

She patted her arm as Tara vaguely recalled their back story. Something about him halting his own highly successful model/actor/presenter career when his mum and stepdad were killed in a car crash. Overnight he'd gone from number one Euro party boy to serious, silent and sober. What was it her Irish granny used to say? 'A young tart an old nun makes.' Or something like that. Yes, there was no doubt that his condescending aura was just reformist hot air.

'He thinks everyone in fashion is self-serving and nasty or stupid—because he had such a bad experience when he was younger. You should meet him. Help him put his mind at rest. Oh, and we must have that chat about my dress.'

The very words Tara had been longing to hear. She swallowed her gushing mouthful of thank-yous and smiled coolly. 'Of course. Any time you like. I won't be heading to Paris for a week.'

'Lovely…' Angelica sounded distracted. She unlinked her arm and squeezed her hand. 'I think we should go and find Michael. Maybe you can convince him to stay on here while I take Fernanda home. Discreetly.'

She nodded to where Fern, locking lips with her cutie, was swaying in time to some bassy, carnal music. The fact that she didn't seem to care who saw her grind her hips and lose herself in his mouth kind of screamed that she had kissed goodbye her inhibitions along with several glasses of booze.

Angelica rolled her eyes ever so slightly. 'He won't like it if she's been drinking. He's so protective of her, and it would save a load of heartache if he never had to know.'

Actually, Tara thought that a hell of a lot more heartache would be saved by telling him where to get off—but each to their own.

She squeezed Angelica's hand back. 'I'm on it.'

Helping her friend and getting more into Angelica's good books made a whole lot of sense, too. The only downside was that it was going to mean actually communicating with the grade A-is-for-ass, macho man. What on earth did they have in common? Spain's one-time boy idol, all grown-up and gone cerebral. Who only spoke in words of five syllables in the language of the super-successful.

Maybe it would be simpler if she dropped her clutch and twerked for him. It was rumoured that he still spoke *that* particular language, and maybe then she'd be able to hold his attention long enough for his sisters to get out and away from his overbearing presence.

She had. She'd escaped—or rather, she'd plotted and executed her plan. Walked away when the time was right. And if she could do it any woman could. It was the best thing that had happened to her. *Ever*. Hon-

estly. When she ruled the world she'd arrange for all
the arrogant bullies to be herded together and thrown
in a pit. And Michael Cruz would be the perfect trophy for the top.

She stomped along, in the wake of Angelica's smooth
glide, back to where Michael and his guardette of hon-
our were still lending their eye-blinding beauty to the
club photographer. She watched a couple of the better-
known runway girls strike poses and got the feeling
he wasn't really keen to play any more. But his smile,
when he used it, was as dazzling as his sisters'—and,
heaven help her, for a moment she could only stare at
the masculine beauty of it all.

And then he turned it on Angelica, and warmth crept
over his face. So he had a heart?

He eased himself away from one photo op right into
another as he greeted his sister. Then he distanced himself from all the white noise as he guided her—only
her—with a proprietorial hand on the small of her back,
to the bar. Was he being a deliberate jerk or did he truly
not know that Tara was behind them?

She could really take it or leave it. This whole, keeping up with the Cruzes, thing. It was taking her well
away from where she wanted to be. There were some
very interesting new faces and Mr Arrogant had diss'd
her twice already—three times if you counted the show
today.

She was just about to let them all get on with it when
she saw him turn round. Not fully round, but grudg-
ingly, and then, as if he was giving alms to the poor, he
gestured that she should catch up with them.

If there was a DEFCON higher than one she might
just have reached it. Who the hell did he think he was?

Did every female he met just fall at his feet, or—worse—into line? Not this one. He might look like the man of everyone else's dreams, but he was her personal idea of a nightmare come to life.

'Tara. I don't think we've properly met.'

He didn't think they'd properly met? Really?

She could just see Angelica's dazzling smile through the haze of red that had fallen around her. *Play it cool, play it cool. Don't give him the control. Don't make a fool of yourself.*

She lifted the glass she was almost crushing in her hand and took a long sip.

He gave a little indulgent, half-cocked smile and then walked towards her slowly, hand extended. 'I'm Michael—Angelica's brother. And Fernanda's. Pleased to meet you.'

Oh, he was good. But she was better. She paused, set her drink with very deliberate care on little elbow-height table closest to her, and turned back to face him.

'Yes, I'm sure you are. You were at my show today.' Just in case he thought he would try to gloss over his rudeness. 'You didn't really seem to get it. Fashion not your thing?'

Well, he probably didn't have a lot of women launching conversations with insults, so that might explain his slight double-take. But he covered it well and took her hand. A very warm, very appropriate handshake. No crushing, just firm and male. Very, *very* male.

His eyes bored right into hers. Combative. He let go of her hand. 'Yes, you're absolutely right. I've sat through quite a number of runway shows this week. Wouldn't say it's been the best use of my time, but…it filled a few hours.'

'And created a few million for our economy,' Tara added, sweet as the pie she'd like to throw in his face.

And it was such a yawningly attractive face. Some might even get swept up in the masculine brilliance of the angled cheekbones and defined jaw. Eyes that were slightly almond-shaped and as fathomless as his mood. Lips that were full and dark red, but too hard to be feminine. Lips that she suddenly imagined could give a whole load of pleasure.

Dangerous. Oh. Yes.

She swallowed and forced her thoughts back on track. 'I often think some people forget just how much is involved in the creation of one dress.' She fingered the skirt of her own, unintentionally inviting his appraisal.

Damn, but he didn't think twice about giving it. Was there no end to the gall of the man?

'We were both thrilled to be at your show, Tara. Your designs really are beautiful. And you have the perfect body to show them off.'

Angelica's sparkling tones cut through the heavy air that was swirling between them. 'You are so wonderfully hourglass. You know, I was reading the other day that we are all turning into rectangles. Can you imagine? Straight up and down. No waists to speak of. No wonder you are the toast of the week, sweetie. All us skinnies want to look as feminine as you. Isn't she just adorable, Michael? Oh, look, there's the photographer. We must give him a snap. Michael—you there, arm round Tara. Perfect.'

Angelica buzzed and fluttered and placed herself on Tara's other side as the cameras flashed. And even though she was still fizzing at the easy way he was glossing over his arrogance Tara knew that now wasn't the time to challenge.

Because now he was moving right into her space, extending his arm. Even as her eyes fell on the mouth that twisted into that slight smirk she had just seen. Even if this time the smirk was eclipsed by the pure male sensuality of his lips. And, though she hated that predictable shadowy stubble, defined jaw look, her eyes widened as the up close and personal space of Michael Cruz became shared with her.

She felt his arm circle her waist and draw her to his right side. Firmly. He held her firmly—as if he had every right to wrap his big arm around her and pose her in the camera glare. As if it was totally fine for him to pull her so close to his body and cause fireworks in her nerve-endings. Could everybody see what she was feeling? How embarrassing! Since when was Tara Devine reduced to a puppet by anybody?

She really didn't want to run with that particular thought…

His grip on her waist was tight and unequivocal. She was just a full-fat version of the calorie-free hors d'oeuvres he'd sampled five minutes earlier. And she hate, hate, *hated* that he could do that to her.

Michael felt sure the muscles in his face would spasm any moment now. After the day he'd had, these brutal after-parties were the last thing he needed. But what the hell? He saw Angelica so little that he could stomach hanging out here, since it seemed to be such a big deal to her. Though he hadn't figured on winding up next to this pocket Miss Whiplash: Tara Devine, wildest little firecracker in the box, renowned for her partying, her comic book curves and her utter lack of self-control.

But more to the point—he scanned the room—thankfully Fernanda had been smart enough to leave all this well enough alone. At least she'd been as good as her word and stayed home. And, despite begging him to let her model this week, she seemed to have retained some of the self-control he'd spent the last sixteen years drilling into her. She was young, she was naïve. And she was allying herself to the vacuous people in this awful industry.

He'd be damned if the sense and intelligence she was blessed with would be wasted on all of this. The place was awash with drugs and drink—these parties always were. He'd had more than his fair share back in the day. And he'd be a fool to think there wouldn't be predators trying to get his sister hooked up in it.

He glanced down at the mini sex bomb tucked beneath his arm. She seemed to have burst onto this scene overnight—and wasn't it just typical that his two sisters found her so 'engaging'. This woman had her own look, all right—strawberry blonde hair with strange streaks of platinum and gold, combed and pinned in a kind of soft beehive—not his thing at all. He could see the curve of her throat as it met the creamiest, most flawless skin of her décolletage. The swathe of ivory satin that skimmed the most talked-about society breasts just enhanced them even further, and he dropped his eyes to take them in again.

What the hell? He was a man.

Angelica was right. Tara's waist, now that his hand had relaxed and splayed out against her hip, was actually much smaller than he'd thought when he'd ever thought about it—which was never. And her hips in that skirt—what little there was of it—were soft and round. The whole look reminded him of someone. Someone very feminine. Very sexy. She'd turned, was looking up at him, and her eyes were so blue, outlined in thick black make-up that she just didn't need. Her lips… The reddest, fullest most swollen pout of a mouth he could remember seeing. She was saying something.

'Yes, Fernanda is an amazing model. She has potential to be world-class—a real supermodel. I've booked her for another week. For Paris.'

The fog in his head suddenly cleared. If Fernanda thought he was letting her loose into this circus again she was out of her mind. He'd indulged her notions this once—let her get it out of her system. But no way was she making a career out of this—not when she had the potential to do something worthwhile with her life.

Time for a little distance.

He leaned in to whisper in Tara Devine's ear. 'You'd better *un*book her, then. No way will my sister be working for you, next week or any other.' He smiled as he spoke his words right into her ear, felt her stiffen. He lingered a little longer, and could have sworn she shivered. 'I don't know what she told you, but she has more important things to do than walk up and down wearing a bunch of crazy clothes.'

'Wow, you really *are* a control freak!' Tara hissed at him out of the corner of her mouth, even while she pouted and posed.

She was playing her coy little games for the snappers. The men in the room—the men who weren't caught up in this fashion nonsense—were all posturing, their eyes trained right at her and her frankly ridiculous curves.

She smiled at them, turned in his grasp and cupped his cheek. 'What are you so afraid of? That she'll actually enjoy herself?'

She leaned right into his ear as she spoke and he felt her lips brush his skin and the press of her breast on his arm. So she wanted to play? He could live with another minute of her company if it taught her a lesson.

He caught her wrist, brought her insolent hand down sharply behind her, so that her back arched into him and the spill of those creamy breasts was even more obvious. She let out a little gasp and he trailed his eyes superslowly right over her smooth silky skin. The bodice of her satin dress was *so* low and his view was *so* good. And damn it if the slow smirk he was feeling didn't warm him all the way to his groin before he could turn back to the cameras.

He could feel the air in the room shift. He could feel the interest in the scene sharpen.

Your move, honey.

And, boy, did she move. Just as a TV crew arrived. *Brilliant.*

'Well, guys, I think it's safe to say that Señor Cruz has just shown us, in the most obvious way imaginable, that he's a big fan of Devine Design. You all know that I had the best of times this week—my clothes are for *real* women, with *real* bodies. I design beautiful, feminine clothes for beautiful, feminine women. And, hey, sometimes even a super-smooth dude like Mickey here can forget his manners, but we forgive him. He can't help it.'

She linked her arms through his and through Angelica's. Angelica was smiling as if her face would split, and for all the world he thought Ms Devine was going to take a bow. He couldn't help but chuckle at her little speech. He'd obviously upset her ego. Always the same—the brash types were the mushiest inside. So he'd give her this one, but he'd also make sure they moved well out of the range of any more cameras or reporters, just in case she got brave again.

'Angelica, I'm having the time of my life trying to keep up with all the highbrow conversation in the room. The car will be here in about five minutes. Does that give you enough time to do whatever it is you're hell-bent on doing?'

Angelica had stopped giggling with her little friend and was scanning the room.

'Yes, Michael. Of course.' She suddenly seemed a little tense. 'I'll just get you and Tara another drink—wait here.'

Another drink? With Whiplash? He moved to cut that right out of the plan but his sister was off, and it struck him, as it suddenly did at times, just how much she was like their mother in the line of her cheek and the fall of her hair down her back. Such regal quality and such ambassadorial skill. She smoothed and shushed where he bulldozed, and they both knew it. And it worked.

So what angle was she working now? Something was up.

'Where's Fern?'

He turned to Tara. She glared at him with those huge blue-black eyes. And then shrugged her shoulders.

'No idea.'

She lifted a glass of champagne from a passing waiter and knocked back a large gulp. Not quite the ladylike sips he was used to seeing in the women he dated.

'Thirsty?'

'Bored.' She pointedly looked away, then knocked back another mouthful.

'You should get out more.'

She turned to face him. Set a scowl across her face and pursed her plump, pouty lips into an even more furious moue. 'If it wasn't for the company I'd be having a wonderful time.'

'You would?' She was so easy to snare. He smiled as her scowl deepened. 'What's wrong with the company, then?'

'Isn't it obvious? I can't be the first person to call you on your appalling manners, surely?'

'Actually, my manners are the least of your problems.'

It wasn't like him to be anything other than courteous to women. His mother had been pretty lax about most things, but charm came cheap—the problem was this one got under his skin like a heat rash, and he didn't want to stop scratching.

'Meaning…?'

'You really have to ask?'

She swilled what was left of the golden liquid in the narrow flute, and then tossed it back in one mouthful. He watched her throat constrict as she swallowed, half expecting her to wipe the back of her hand across her mouth like a saloon whore from a fifties Western. Ms Devine was anything *but* ladylike. And she was getting all fired up—maybe this was going to turn into an interesting party after all.

'The only problem I can see is that you and your ego are still here. I can't be the only one who'd much rather you and your dull suit and boots got yourselves the hell out of here.'

Just as she hissed her little putdown another bunch of lovelies fluttered over. 'Actually, I'm not so sure everyone sees it that way…'

Far too young and, honestly, too far gone, but it was easy to let the charm drip as he kissed and complimented them. Tara stood to the side, pointedly looking away, then whipped out her phone. He watched her face change as her fingers scrolled the screen. She tucked it back in her little cube of a bag and seemed to brace herself. Interesting.

She walked over to him. Slowly. Almost dragging her heels.

'I'm going to get another drink—would you like one?'

He cocked an eyebrow. He hadn't been expecting that.

'What happened there? Did you get a text alert to be more pleasant?'

She smiled the fakest smile, but even though he knew she was forcing it, it was still a great smile. Her perfect mouth split to showcase white teeth that were perfect bar the front two, which sat at an offset angle to one another. Quirky. Cute.

'No, I just thought we should grab a drink to loosen up while we wait. But if you're too busy I quite understand.' She nodded to the girls.

'I'm loose enough, thanks—but don't let me stop you. I'm going to chase up my sister. Time we left the party to those who still feel the need.'

'Oh, come on. Just a little one? I'm sure Angelica will only be another minute.'

'I'm sure she will too. But I think I've indulged her long enough.'

'You see this as indulgence? People sharing some

fun together?' She swung out her arm, indicating the
groups of people chatting, laughing, drinking, dancing.

He'd seen so many similar scenes in so many corners
of the globe. At one time in his life this *was* his life. But
party fatigue had set in some years ago and the whole
scene now left him cold.

'It's all relative. Fun for you and fun for me? Not
compatible.'

'You think? I bet we could find at least one thing
we both enjoy.'

He turned back from the throbbing crowd to face
her. Let his eyes drag slowly over that intriguing face.
Was she coming on to him—after being so hostile? Did
she have a short-term memory problem or a personality disorder to add to the mix?

'What did you have in mind?'

On anyone else the slight colour that crept over her
skin would have suggested a flush of shame, but on her
it was lost in the assault to the senses of hair, make-up,
outfit and attitude. She was like a caricature. But she
had something. He couldn't put his finger on it—yet.
Maybe it *was* just attitude, or energy. Or overt sensuality. But he'd met a lot of women, for sure, and she did
not fit neatly into any of his boxes. That didn't mean
that he wanted to hang out with her at this or any other
party, but it might explain why Angelica had decided
to add her to her Pandora's box of friends.

'What do I have in mind? It's way too early in the
night for me to tie myself down to anything specific.'

He grinned at her. Couldn't help it. 'You've got an
answer for everything, Ms Devine.'

She grinned back, and this time it was natural. Like
the sun coming out. Like there might be a natural beauty

under all that make-up. *That* he'd like to see. But he was not going there. Yep, he was single, and until Fern was sorted—probably after Fern was sorted—single he'd stay. He could see no reason not to be. The only thing to be gained from adding emotion to sex was that it helped women to loosen up.

Even when they knew in triplicate that he'd had elective emotional bypass surgery, they still thought that they'd be The One to reverse the procedure. Shame they couldn't tune in to the notion that he liked himself better that way. No lies. No doubt. No guilt. Just sex. As and when he wanted. But not tonight. There was something about this one that lit up the warning signs in his head. And he was not in the business of ignoring warning signs. Not since he was sixteen.

'Sadly it's too late in the night for me to stay on and find out what you'll tie yourself down to. Or tie yourself up with. I'm going to get the car, and Angelica, and leave you to your fun.'

Though where his sister had got to was another problem. And one that was beginning to annoy him.

'Anyway, I'm sure Angelica will catch up with you later. It's been…interesting.'

He leant a hand on her shoulder and leaned down for the obligatory goodbye cheek-kiss. He could smell product—perfume, hairspray, cosmetics. He touched smooth skin. He felt the swell of her fabulous rack press against him. He let his lips linger for a second too long to be strictly platonic. His fingers closed more tightly over her shoulder and he curled his other arm round her waist, drawing her closer into him. He felt a strong urge to grab her by the bottom and scoop her against him. Her body was soft and nestled perfectly, and he moved his lips to her other cheek. But her lips were in the way, so he placed his kiss there. Just one.

She. Was. So. Hot.

Her eyes, when he stepped back, flew open. They were searching. Almost innocent. And again he got the feeling that she was a better actress than she got credit for. Still, it wasn't his business to stay and find out.

'Yes, it was…lovely to meet you.' She seemed out of breath and hitched back on her heels in a stumble.

He steadied her elbow.

'Don't you think we should wait here? I'm sure she won't be long.'

'No. Much as I'm tempted, I'm beginning to think there's something up. So—as I said—have fun, take care.'

He whipped out his phone and called for the car. Disappeared into the crowd, eyes on the alert. This night had tested his patience long enough.

CHAPTER TWO

IN A FEW seconds the party would begin to reconfigure itself. Blaring noise, pulsing lights, skin, smiles and wild-eyed stares.

What on earth had just happened there?

Tara reached out and gripped the table, her fingers closing round the sticky mess of spilt drinks. Michael's back was just disappearing into the crowd and she needed to go after him. But she was still reeling from that kiss—it hadn't even been a proper kiss, just a lip-press. But man alive, he'd aced it!

'Hey, Tara—you wan' a drink?'

Definitely—but she had work to do first. She needed to lasso Mr Wonderful and keep him occupied until she got the all-clear.

'Be back later, Jonny,' she murmured to her DJ friend, who had just packed up his vinyl. The same friend she had been texting like fury to make sure he hung around after his set—he was the best party animal she knew, but she was going to have to put him on ice for just a little while longer.

She checked her phone as she started the sticky trail through the club. Her foot connected with a shot glass and sent it spinning onto the dance floor—exactly what *she* should be doing.

Her phone buzzed. Another message.

Michael's waiting for you at the car. I've told him I'm on my way separately with a couple of friends. I'll drop Fern at mine first, then meet you at his place. Thanks so much for keeping my brother occupied. Hugs, Angelica.

Hugs? Who needed hugs? Fizz! Party! That was what she really wanted. But they were such nice women and—what the hell?—it wouldn't kill her to miss an hour or so. Actually, it might kill her—walking right into the lion's den without a stun gun. Guys who looked like that, kissed like that and, even worse, acted like that, were not part of her daily grind. She would need two layers of Kevlar at least.

The car would be out front. She'd have to pass another load of snappers—if they were bothering to stay up. She quickened her pace out onto the stairwell and tottered down carefully. The last thing she wanted was a jpeg of her landing in a heap at his feet.

But it was the slap of the pre-dawn grey-blue light and fresh air that hit her skin. That and the now familiar sight of a super-fit guy in a perfectly cut suit, lolling—yes, actually lolling—against a car that was… large and low and sleek. And he was killing the whole look—she had to hand it to him.

Michael looked at her. He raised one eyebrow. Opened the door and gestured her in. Now, that just riled her all over again. What was wrong with a few manners? She wasn't asking for anything more than a hello, or a please and thank you. He just couldn't seem to treat women as anything other than little pets to train and reward. But he was way off if he thought she would roll over like a puppy. After witnessing years of fear and subservience she had honed her bark and her bite to perfection.

'I'm not stalking you. I said I would come along to catch up with Angelica for a little while. OK?'

'You're invited. Happy to escort you.'

He was looking over her head—checking out who was watching.

'Embarrassed to be seen with me?'

He did a perfect mock gasp through his perfect teeth. Smirked. 'Now who's defensive?'

'Not defensive…' she said, bending into the car and knocking the top of her damn hair on the doorframe.

He slung himself inside after her and she scooted further along the seat. The backs of her thighs felt the cool of the leather, but the heat from his left leg where it sat open, relaxed and rock-hard, seeped right across the inch or so of space between them. She couldn't keep her eyes off it.

'Just perceptive.'

He cocked her a look, his arm stretched across the back of the seat and his hand just lying on his other thigh. The car started up and she noted other taxis and cars for a moment. Coming and going. And she was going further away from the club—her home away from home.

'You're perceiving too much, then. There's no sub-text—I'm out tonight to spend time with my sister. We don't see a lot of each other at the moment—she's mainly in London and I'm mainly in Barcelona, for Fern's school and business. So…'

He looked at her for a long moment and she nearly had to look away—his gaze was *that* intense.

'I'm here for them. Always.' Finally he drew his eyes from her and stared out of the window. 'But Angelica has her London circle, so it's all cool. She'll catch us up.'

He turned back round, actually shifted his leg up a bit on the seat until it was pressing against hers. She moved back, crossed her legs, stared straight ahead. He had turned that intense look back on her.

'No, I'm definitely not embarrassed to be seen with you.'

She flicked her eyes and couldn't help but twist him a little smile. She should know better, but he was a work of art. Maybe not her type—but undeniably attractive, and undeniably good at working women. Thank goodness she wasn't stupid enough to fall for him.

'That's such a relief.'

He laughed. 'You don't look relieved. You look uptight and anxious.'

She felt that—and worse. She'd had—what? Three glasses of champagne over three hours? At the party of the season? And now she was in what might as well have been a hearse, heading to a party for two that neither of them wanted to attend.

'I'll cope.'

'Sure you will. You're hard as nails. You can cope with anything.'

She spun round to see him watching her. Baiting her.

'Anything *you* could throw at me, that's for sure.'

His eyes lit up. His smile tilted and as the car sped along and the lights from outside brightened, then dimmed, then brightened, she saw his wicked, wicked mouth mock her. She saw it and she felt it. That same heavy tension she'd sensed twice around him now. She had to get a grip—it was beginning to feel as if her comfort zone was somewhere about two miles back. Where her immunity to men was second nature—normally.

'You're a very interesting person, Tara.'

It felt as if he had put his hand on her jaw, turned her to face him, but his hands were in plain view and it was some deep, feminine instinct that had her moulding herself to his will. Thankfully she was ruled by her head and not by her gut. Fortunately she could remember how to deal with very persuasive men…

She turned away, saw the back of the driver's head. Noted his eyes flick to hers in the mirror. He probably saw scenes like this every night of his life. What a shame she wasn't going to oblige this evening.

'So I'm told.'

'But I get the feeling you don't really know yourself yet.'

She felt her jaw tighten and her teeth clench. How arrogant.

'That patronising comment doesn't even deserve an answer.'

'But I'm pretty sure you'd like to give me one anyway.'

She shifted right round on her seat. He was watching her, smiling softly.

'What would you know about me at all?'

His eyes never left hers. Dark and demanding. She wanted to look away, but she couldn't, and that swell of fog or emotion or awareness bloomed around them again. She felt as if she was breathing in his air. As if something of herself was seeping into his space.

'Just what I say. You're a very interesting person but you don't fully know yourself yet…or you wouldn't be battling the attraction that clearly exists between us.'

'You must have some ego to think that every girl who rides in the back of your car wants to kiss you.'

He shrugged. 'I think *you* do.'

Still he stared, and still she stared back.

'Because you dropped one on me as you were leaving and I didn't slap your face? That doesn't mean I want to repeat it.'

'You *don't* want to repeat it?'

A low, quiet probe.

The car had stopped. She didn't know if they were at lights or at their destination. But nothing could drag her eyes away from his to check. A shadow was cast across his face, lighting only the mocking twist of his mouth. But his eyes flashed like polished coals in the darkness.

She swallowed. 'Not a chance.'

He was utterly still, completely and intensely present. She knew he could read her, but the chance of her admitting that? Zero. Even as she thought it the urge to feel his lips and taste his mouth swept over her. A shocking pleasure pulse throbbed between her legs. The air swirled thicker. She was definitely not in her comfort zone any more.

'Better get the party started, then.'

He broke it. Moved fluidly to the door handle. Stepped outside and held out a hand for her. She ignored it and gripped the doorframe instead. Stepped out and straightened in the lemony light of early dawn. The most sober, most disconcerted she had been at this

time of day since…since she'd started realising that
hedonism and ambition could be neatly packaged together. Since she'd purposely and deliberately burned
every bridge that led her back to small-town, small-
minded Ireland.

So what if her family looked down on her? She knew
the truth. She knew she had a cast-iron marketing campaign that made her unpalatable to them and delicious
to others.

She smoothed down her dress and touched her hand
to the back of her hair. She dreaded to think what her
face was like—lipstick probably smudged all over her
mouth and the panda eyes slipping south. Who knew?
That might be her best form of defence.

He was watching, waiting. Chivalrous, she supposed.
A doorman stood sentry and a plush carpet swept ahead.
The car behind them moved off and she had a sudden
image of walking into this nineteenth-century apartment block with him, black suit, and her, white dress,
as if she had done it a thousand times before.

Boy, she needed a drink.

She couldn't even look at him in the elevator. Didn't
make small talk and didn't let the intense air-sharing
affect her in any way. No way.

When the lift slowed to a stop she watched as the
doors eased open and she stepped out and waited. He
indicated left and she walked at his side as if he was
showing her to a vault. He unlocked the door with a key-
pad and held it open for her. She took one step inside
the room. Not as expected. No cherry floors, leather
and chrome. There was smooth carpet, richly coloured
rugs and silk-covered chaises.

She turned to comment and then she felt his presence behind her, heard the door click softly.

She bolted into the space as if branded, suddenly realising that her whole safety in numbers default was not going to be much cop here. How long were they likely to be here, alone, before Angelica showed up, with or without her little posse? This whole *keep him occupied* plan was all well and good in a nightclub. But claustrophobic empty spaces, even ones as grand as this, suddenly seemed to suck up her bravado.

'Champagne? Or would you like something stronger?'

He was moving into the open-plan lounge, jacket tossed onto the back of a posture-correcting couch. Even the furniture looked down on her. Devine girls sat on sofas with their dinner on trays and their eyes on the television. She could make out a dining alcove, with a huge dining table and artfully mismatched Deco chairs, complete with seat-pads in jewelled satins.

She definitely needed something stronger.

'What have you got?'

He swallowed his knowing chuckle and moved to a bar area. 'I'm sure I'll have what you want.'

'Mount Gay?' *Suck on that, smarty*, she thought, dredging up the name of the most inaccessible rum she could think of.

He produced it. Of course he did.

'With…?'

'Awww…' She breathed out with a slice of defeat. 'Just give me it on the rocks. I'll be gulping it anyway.'

He laughed then. 'You're surely not nervous?'

She laughed back, despite herself. 'What? You think a dragged-up fashion-head like me can't cut it in Luxe

Land? With European aristocracy like you and *les belles* Cruzes? You'd think I feel any self-doubt? No chance. I'll have what you're having, baby. Every time.'

'*Every* time?'

He snared her gaze. Held it. *Again*. Walked towards her with the glass of rum, ice clinking gently off the sides. Soft smile so sexy on that mouth, so sinful.

'Cut it out.'

He held the glass as he passed it to her, still smiling, cocked an eyebrow in question. 'What?'

'You know what.'

He stood almost in her space, with a matching drink, a roguish look.

'Do I?'

'You're freaking me out. You're just freaking me *right* out!'

He laughed properly then—no artifice or charm. Just a belly laugh. And suddenly she felt relaxed.

'No one could accuse you of not speaking your mind, Tara. It's refreshing, I have to say.'

She nudged her glass against his. 'You too. I suppose.' She took a long drink with the cubes bashing off her teeth and shook her head in wonder at her own self and this crazy situation. She could have happily strangled this man a few hours earlier, but now it seemed… it seemed he was maybe human after all.

'You got any music?'

'Sure. Come and choose what you'd like.'

She wandered behind him, watching his fluid, masculine movements. There was a man who worked out. No doubt. His ass was absolutely perfect. If she'd been in the club she might even have grabbed it, given it a little squeeze. She'd done worse!

He passed her his laptop and she flipped through a few lists. Taste was OK. Could do with a little education, but passable. She selected something mainstream, safe, stood back and felt the bass tones fill the space. That was better...

Michael. She turned. He was frowning at his phone. Then he placed it down on the bar and caught her up in another of those stares. What the hell was going on? Demanding dark eyes drilled straight into hers and made her feel exposed, on fire, exhilarated, choked.

'Everything OK?'

He nodded as he walked towards her. 'Fine. Just no word yet from Angelica.' He tipped his glass. 'Refill?'

'Peachy.'

She followed him to the bar. Stood watching. Jiggled her hips in time to the Balearic beats. Felt sort of good. House parties had never been her thing, really. Especially tiny house parties. Big crowds, big music, big hangovers. Absolutely. But there was something sweet and soothing about watching him move about his home, pouring drinks and looking so hot.

'You here a lot?'

He shook his head as he screwed the top back on the rum bottle. 'Once, maybe twice a month. But that's only temporary. I plan to move back once Fern gets a place at university here.'

Tara opened her mouth. Closed it. Things were quiet and calm and maybe, just for once in her life, she should keep her opinion to herself. Not her business after all.

'Cheers,' he said, and tipped his glass against hers.

She tipped hers right back, avoided looking up at him. But it was as if he knew. How weird was that? He laughed.

'I'm not giving you my eyes again, mister. You do strange things with them.'

He laughed again. Put his glass down. Stepped a little closer to her. The atmosphere felt heavy.

He reached for her glass. She held it—held onto the cool, the solid, the known quantity.

'What things?'

'Things…'

Her voice trailed off, quietly. He closed his fingers round hers on the glass. Fire round ice. And then she limply let him put hers down too.

His hand cupped her cheek. His fingers trailed across her skin. She closed her eyes and quivered as if she had been holding back a tide. And then she gave in. The moment when she could have stopped it had passed.

He slipped his hand to the back of her neck and hauled her up to his body. She pushed her hands to his chest and felt the muscle she had imagined. His mouth found hers and she moaned deeply as he took her, moulding her lips and tasting. Taking his fill.

He stepped her backwards with him, his mouth still fixed on hers. The hand that had cupped her head now touched and traced a path across her collarbone.

'Your skin taunts me.'

It was all he said before he resumed his assault on her mouth. He trailed down her bare arm, slow, warm and necessary. She made her own trail up—neck to jaw. A scrape of stubble rubbed at her hands and the scent of woody citrus filled her head. His tongue probed and licked and she fought to keep up. His hands were now on her waist, feeling and learning her shape. She knew he was going to cup her heavy breasts and she longed for it.

'Touch me, please…' she said, his mouth swallowing her plea.

And he did. He filled his hands with the heavy weight of each breast and he gently massaged. His thumbs brushed over her nipples through the satin material of her dress, and then he rolled them into points of utter agony and pleasure.

He didn't ask her what she wanted. He just gave her what she needed.

He scooped her up and strode with her into—it had to be his bedroom. Dropped her to her feet and spun her round.

'Dress. Off.'

He was worse than rude but she sucked it up like nectar and began to push silk-covered buttons through loops, to unzip and shimmy her dress over her hips. Nothing in the world would stop her getting her fill of him—of those warm strong hands smoothing their way over her skin. Even as she stepped out of it he was working magic with his touch—leaving hot trails in the wake of his fingers.

'You are so damn hot.'

All he said as he took his hands and mouth from her for a moment. She grabbed at his shirt, fingers useless on the buttons. But he stilled her. Stepped back from her. Looked at her standing in a pool of cream silk satin, her nipples straining hard through the gauze of her bra and her knickers shielding the last of her secrets. She felt as if his look was licking the flames of hell across her skin.

It was a party she'd never been invited to before. And she wanted some.

Her eyes drank him in now. Nothing but pure, firm,

wide muscle across his chest. She ran her fingers; then her mouth across it, inhaling and tasting and licking. He pulled off his trousers and her mouth opened in wonder. His thick, long erection jutted out and she couldn't stop herself from dropping to her knees, wrapping her hand and then her mouth around him.

But he heaved her up by the arms and lifted her to the bed. Placed her down and pushed her back. Then his hands wrapped around her panties and he tugged them down and tossed them aside. She sat back on her elbows and watched his face. He took her ankles and opened her legs, then dipped his head and licked the hottest trail of fire up and over her.

She jerked up and he put his arm across her chest. His head shook.

'Not yet.'

He dipped his head again and lapped and suckled her mercilessly until she began to feel the fire inside her building and spreading. Burning and blooming through her lower body. She looked down, loving the sight of his dark head nestled between her thighs. His mouth tortured and the spasms built until she lost her mind and her orgasm rolled and crashed. She screamed with the release and then lay still, aftershocks jerking suddenly, gently, quietly.

But his mouth, laced with the taste of her, came down swiftly on her lips, kissing and tonguing and building the fire all over again. He grabbed at her wrists and tugged her up the bed. She followed, unhooked her bra and watched, fascinated, as he sheathed himself with a condom. She longed to feel him inside her— just longed for it.

He wasn't going fast enough and she moved to sit up.

'Just lie back, Tara. On your back.'

And she fell back to the bed to watch him. And his eyes held hers again as she felt him nudge her open and then slide deep, deep inside. She whimpered—like a puppy—and then moved with his rhythm. All the time his dark eyes sparked and held hers.

What had she been doing those other times? With men who'd needed a road map?

He loomed above her, wide strong shoulders and caramel skin melding with the warm waves of pleasure that were rolling with every hard thrust.

'This feel good, Tara?'

Those eyes drilled and held and the intensity built.

'Hmm, honey? Do you feel it now—the attraction?'

She didn't give a damn that he was proving his point. He could prove it to hell and back if it made her feel like this.

And she grabbed his head down to hers and kissed him quiet. He leaned forward and flipped her round so that she rode him. She tilted her hips and shifted her weight and still she stared into those eyes. Something else was building—something huge and powerful in her chest—and she felt a moment of fear or wonder.

Then he reached up and touched her mouth. And rocked her even as she rode him. And she knew nothing could be this good ever again with anyone else. Her next orgasm surged and rolled through her as he jerked and exploded deep inside. And all the time his eyes held hers and she felt the burning squeeze in her chest return. Too intense. Too strong.

She closed her eyes. Hung her head and calmed.

A moment passed—two at most—then he threw his arms back and blew out a breath. That would be the sign to hop off, then. She braced her arms on the bed and slid slowly off. He still felt big and thick inside her, and it felt so damn good. But reality was beginning to dawn along with the early autumn sunrise. They had just had sex. He hadn't looked at her, touched her or soothed her. He hadn't said a single word. She was just a lay.

Silence.

The window she passed was undressed and looked out onto all her favourite London landmarks. She paused for a moment, imprinting the view on her mind—all the shapes and colours of skyscape and roofline—bridges, towers, clocks and wheels. All with the flush of dawn behind.

He blew out another long breath. 'You'd better get dressed.'

'I am.' She cast a look round to where he was still lying. Michael Cruz—beautiful, arrogant, not her type at all.

'Don't sound sore. I only mean that Angelica and her friends are bound to be here in minute, and it would best if we were ready to welcome her to a party rather than a love-in.'

'I know what you meant. I said I'm going to get dressed. You don't mind if I have a little clean-up first, though, do you?'

She knew her tone was bitchy, but he was such a swine. That had to be the worst post-coital talk she'd ever experienced. And she'd walked right into it. What was she even *doing* here? A favour? To a girl she barely knew and her extremely cosmopolitan sister? And, OK, she felt a solidarity with them, was happy to help them get one over on yet another controlling man.

A controlling man with a legendary sexual reputation that she couldn't even begin to conjure up any immunity to.

Why had she let herself in for this? What had made her think that she had the emotional wherewithal to pull it off? She needed rules and boundaries. She couldn't dabble like this! She could flirt. She could most definitely tease. But she knew herself well enough to understand that she invested too much when she took it any further. She couldn't help it that the heart she wore on her sleeve was just really well covered up. And the camouflage of her comments would be all that he would know.

'Go right ahead. There's a bathroom—there.'

He flicked his hand and stood up and she tried hard not to be impressed by that body again, but the man was beyond fit. What a shame his personality was so rank.

She felt around on the cool tiles for the light, but he came up behind her, stretched in and flicked it on. 'Thanks,' she said, aiming to shut him out.

But he stepped inside and reached out for her. Her skin was rapidly cooling, and she craved the warmth of his body, but she held herself rigid in his arms. He draped a heavy golden arm across her chest and the contrast was striking. Her milky Celtic skin was the perfect foil to his smooth caramel body. And even with her full breasts and hips she still fitted neatly within his outline.

In some perverse way it pleased her—but in the way that counted it annoyed her that she had gone and done what every other idiotic woman with a pulse seemed also to want to do with him.

Her eyes fell to her treasured necklace. Her grandmother's ring strung on an old gold chain. The little bit of love she fingered every day. Her little bit of sanctuary and strength. She touched it now, waiting for him to leave her.

'Look, I need privacy if that's OK.'

He took the thick, snaky strands of her hair that had worked free and tucked them behind her ear. Trailed his finger under her chain questioningly. She said nothing.

'Sure,' he said, but he spun her round and cradled her face. Kissed her. Slow and sweet. 'Whatever you want.' He gave her one more kiss and then pulled back. Trailed his finger down her shoulder and her arm. 'Beautiful.'

She watched the door close behind him and made a face. They were all beautiful—every one of the ten thousand women he must have slept with. And she was number ten thousand and one. What kind of fool was she that she couldn't even resist him?

She looked at the mess that stared back from the mirror—everything wiped off or smudged. She looked like her mother—weak and worried. And she felt sick at that.

Michael must have used another shower, because he looked like an aftershave advert when she finally got herself out of the bathroom and along to where coffee seemed to be brewing.

'Still no sign?' she said, thinking that *surely* Angelica would be making an appearance soon.

He shook his head and sipped at the coffee. 'No. Change of plan, apparently. Coffee?'

She shook her head. Who drank caffeine at this time in the morning? She had already filed this night in the 'delete' folder and was going to ditch the party at Jonny's and head right back to her bed.

'So what was the change?'

He had his back to her and again she felt her eyes

drawn to examine the way he moved, the slide of his muscle under fabric.

'Seems like everybody had enough of a good time at the club and by the time she got to her apartment she just decided to stay there. I don't have any missed calls—do you?'

Tara's mind whirred. What the hell was the right thing to say here? Surely something had happened so that Angelica had never made it over? Something with Fern, perhaps?

'Dunno. I'll check in a minute. So…'

'So you can have coffee, but the car's waiting when you're ready.'

He was sitting on a bar stool, the morning paper flicked out and open on the honey wood work surface. He raised the irritatingly small espresso cup to his mouth and she had the overwhelming urge to smack it right out of his self-satisfied hand.

'For the record, Michael, I reckon I misjudged you. I thought you were merely arrogant. But now I see that I was way off. You managed to single-handedly spoil a night that I'd been looking forward to for weeks. You're beyond arrogant. You know that?'

'Interesting. *I* spoiled *your* night.' He spoke to his newspaper. 'So you'll be ready to go? I'll phone down to let the driver know you're on your way.'

Tara scooped up her bag. And what was left of her pride. Could not get out of there fast enough.

Her heels sank into and caught on the thick pile of the carpet as she made her way to the door. Hot sharp tears pushed against her eyes. How could she have let herself down so badly? What on earth had she been thinking, having sex with a guy like that? No amount of

pleasure was worth being made to feel like a hooker—
an unwelcome hooker at that. He had totally wiped out
every post-orgasm happy hormone and nuked her self-
esteem. And, worst of all, she had let him. She should
have acted breezy—even if she didn't feel it. Should
have climbed off and swung her bra over her head in
celebration. She really shouldn't be allowing his dis-
missal of her to hurt her like this. She was Tara Devine.
She didn't give a damn.

Except she did. She so did. And it was so, so sore.

But every day was a school day. After what she'd
been through it had to be. And this was small stuff
compared to some of her other life lessons. She just
wished she'd been better prepared. That she could wear
her heart anywhere other than her sleeve.

CHAPTER THREE

'I'M NOT BUYING it, Angelica. Where is she?'

Michael strode through the hallway of Angelica's chi-chi apartment, his scowl black and irritation bubbling.

'Good morning, Michael. So we're in one of those moods? What happened last night? I hope you weren't this rude to Tara—were you?'

Michael tracked Angelica with his eyes as she glided through the perfectly furnished space. And that wasn't a question he was prepared to answer either—no one's business but his.

He looked for evidence of…anything, but the place was immaculate. Though Angelica did look drawn, which was a pretty unusual occurrence. She busied herself in the kitchen.

'Don't put coffee on for me—I've had too much already.' He'd thrown it down his neck as he'd tried to force out flashbacks of Tara's shock at his comments to her.

It had been the night from hell and he knew he'd been manipulated—he just didn't know why. But one thing was certain: the idea of losing control to a woman did not sit well with him. And he'd come very close to that last night. Hadn't been able to stop himself from taking her. When was the last time he had shown such complete contempt for his own values? He hated that out of control feeling—it was too fresh in his mind, even though it was over twenty years now since he'd truly been in a tailspin.

'Where is our sister?'

'Oh, Michael—for heaven's sake, she's in her bed! She's been working all week and she's only young. Try to remember what it was like and give her a little rope. Hmmm?' Angelica flicked on the coffee-maker and swept about, producing crockery and cream.

The trouble was he remembered only too clearly what it was like to be young. Not the details, but enough to know that night was day, uppers balanced downers and sex was available everywhere. Enough to realise that it was a carefully choreographed disaster, directed by his management and enjoyed by his fans. And had he not had the cold shower of his mother's death it might have ended up for him the way it had for too many others.

So when Angelica suggested 'a little rope' he would be using it to tie Fernanda down until she was mature enough to cope with it. Different story if she'd been like Angelica—but she was too volatile still. And this interest in the fashion scene was a worry. One that had to be carefully watched. Starting now.

'Breakfast? Have you eaten?'

'No, thanks—nothing.'

He walked on into the apartment and up to the spare bedroom, knocked swiftly on the door, cocked an ear and entered. The smell of booze hit him square in the face. He walked to the sleeping mound and stood over her. She was zoned out. Totally. So she had hit a wall last night.

He moved to the window and pulled open the curtains. Then back to the bed.

'Morning, Fernanda.'

'She needs to sleep, Michael—leave her be.'

Angelica had come in and was fussing about, lifting clothes and folding them. The room looked like a thrift shop. There was a huge glass of water at the side of the bed and jewellery and clothes trailed everywhere.

'Is she wasted?'

'Michael, calm down—she's fine.'

Angelica's fluttering was beginning to annoy him. Fernanda was lying in a white trash coma—he had enough experience to know that—so why was anyone trying to tell him otherwise? This was how it started. This was how kids like Fern took the hand they'd been dealt and tossed it up in the air. She was sixteen years old—exactly the same age he had been when he had begun to run with the wrong crowds and then down the wrong roads. Too cocky to listen to any advice that hadn't been about how great he looked or how good he was in bed. And totally too stupid and too naïve to know he couldn't possibly be good in bed. This was how lives careered out of control—when there weren't adults around who really, truly cared.

And Angelica might think she was doing the right thing—like his mother had thought she was—but they were different people. Trusting, kind, good. Not like him. Not at all like him.

And he wasn't going to let history repeat itself. No chance.

'Get her up, Angelica. And then you can tell me what

the hell went on last night. You think I can't see through your scheme? You planted that little sex bomb with me to keep me out of the way, didn't you?'

'Oh, Michael, you weren't horrible to her, were you?'

'You've already asked me that. And it has nothing to do with you what I did or didn't do, or say, to Tara.' He was getting distracted and losing the whole point of why he was here. 'Just get Fern up—I'll be in the kitchen.'

He strode through to the gleaming, glossy kitchen. His head pounded with too much caffeine and too much grief. He'd been played for a fool by three women in one night and for the first time in years he felt that things were spinning off in directions he didn't like.

He took out his phone and stabbed in the code. He had the rest of the weekend and then a trip to Spain on Monday. Things to sort, zero sleep and a crushing series of flashbacks involving Tara Devine.

Tara Devine? What or where or how had that name figured with his? Twenty-four hours ago he'd been given Fern's itinerary and had agreed to accompany Angelica to Tara's show. Had reluctantly agreed. Had sat through an hour of torture, counting his blessings that he had nothing to do with any of this puerile drivel any more.

Eighteen hours later he was banging the same Ms Devine for all he was worth and not getting anything near his fill. Was that his problem? Sexual frustration? It had been a while since his last lover, and maybe Tara had just sparked something.

'You're up.' He watched Fern's cagey steps through the kitchen. She was walking as if she had broken glass in her brain. 'Headache? Or worse?'

She kept her head down. He couldn't see her face for her hair but she sat up on a bar stool with her phone in her hand, ignoring him. Her normally upright posture was folded in on itself and she looked pretty fragile in her short pyjamas and giant socks. That didn't stop her from texting continuously.

'Put the phone down, Fernanda.'

She clicked it off and turned it face-down, but still wouldn't look at him.

'Where were you last night?'

'I was out. At a party.'

'So why say you were going to stay home?'

She looked up at him. Pasty, shadowed. Confrontational. He'd never seen her like that before.

'Why do you think?'

'Answer my question—and not with one of your own.'

She scowled from the depths and muttered, 'Tara's right. You *are* a control freak.'

'I'm glad we've got that ironed out. Tara's opinion is really important to me.' He was that good a control freak that the words were coming out calm and slow.

'Fabulous! We can all have a chat about that in a moment or two. She's on her way over.'

If he'd had coffee in his mouth he would have spurted it. But he was smarter than to give anything more than a bemused look to Angelica, who had just joined them in the kitchen—breezily, as if this was like any regular Saturday morning and Tara Devine was any regular visitor.

'Lunch? I suppose it's time for lunch…we seem to have missed breakfast.'

The ridiculously flippant musings of his sister were interrupted by the doorbell. He looked at the others but they were playing their little game. So he went through to answer it.

If Tara hadn't been expecting to see him she hid it well. The super-bright smile, pink lips today, and a flick of her eyes as if he was so much rubbish on the street and she would sweep it away. She walked straight in.

'Michael.'

On down the hall and his eyes followed the swagger of her ass in a leather skirt that fitted her like a second skin. That skin—her skin—he'd never seen or felt anything like it. Dove-pale and down-soft. His eyes trailed her all the way until she reached the kitchen. He heard a whoop of welcome from his sisters, even from the pathologically hung-over Fernanda.

'So you'll come?'

Come where?

He entered the kitchen. Saw Tara approach Fern. Hugged her and was rewarded with a soft smile.

'I'd love to. But I have a lot on, so maybe best to leave it. Until all the other issues are sorted.'

What issues?

Angelica's performance was award-winning. Little light smile and duchess head-tilt.

'Of course...of course. We could diary some time in for after Paris. I worry about leaving it too long, though. I think these may be the only free days I have between now and next month.'

Tara was handed a cup of coffee and now stood next to Fern.

'It's going to be tough. When would you need to know?'

Need to know what?

'Oh, I just need to know so that I can pick you up before we fly—or if you need to make your own way. I can collect you from the airport.'

What? Had they all been handed a script before he came in?

'What's going on here? Where are you all going?' Michael demanded, barely able to keep a lid on his growing frustration.

They turned to him—two dark heads and one blonde. All big eyes and mouths in perfect Os.

'Barcelona. Tara has agreed to design my wedding dress and she's coming out to stay for... Well, we can sort out the exact details later.'

'Is that right? Tara, maybe you and I should have a talk.'

'About...?'

About the state of Fernanda. About the signals she was sending his impressionable sister. About the mind-blowing sex they'd shared less than six hours ago. Her coming to Barcelona was not an option. He wanted order, not chaos. He wanted Fern calm and back at school. He wanted to be able to think about Tara Devine in the past and not look at her in the present and want to rip her clothes off.

He *needed* control over his head and his body. And Tara Devine seemed to have this insane capacity to reduce him to knee-jerk reactions and bizarre emotions. Who the hell wanted *that* near them? She'd already made him question his self-control, his sense of guilt and his whole value system. This was not an option. *Could* not be an option.

His sisters seemed to have left the room. But it was more the fire in Tara's eyes than the absence of other people that alerted him. As the door clicked shut she turned on him.

'I agree that we should talk. Me first. I came to your

house in good faith, expecting to catch up with the others. I told you clearly in the car that I didn't want to kiss you. I get in the door of the apartment and *you* clearly decide that no means yes.'

'Are you saying you didn't want to do what we did?'

'No.' She couldn't hold his eyes there. 'No, I'm not. All I'm saying is that the way you treated me afterwards was shocking.'

She turned back to face him. Her eyes were huge. The spill of vulnerable tears would have formed in any other woman's eyes but she was white-hot with hurt. And that hit harder.

'You sent out some pretty clear signals yourself. I came after you—in the bathroom, remember? But you wanted privacy.'

'Do you blame me? My pulse hadn't even settled back down and I was told the meter was running.'

'Tara, you're a player. Don't try to fool me that you were hoping for some gallantry. You know how these games work. You're in or you're out. And you were in up to your gorgeous neck.'

He looked right there, right then. Her silver slash-necked knit top showed more expanse of that silken skin. Her collarbone etched out a line that he had run his mouth over. The swell of her cleavage lay just out of eyesight, but the knowledge of it was all he needed to kick his lust awake again. He looked up and she was staring right back at him. Those blue eyes still stored hurt and the pinkest, plumpest lips still formed that tetchy moue. But she couldn't hide it any more than he could. They had a huge thing going on—a thing that he needed to rein in and redirect.

It had happened before—this kind of heat between

two people. OK, maybe not to the extent he was feeling it right now, but close enough that he knew how much havoc it could cause.

'A player? *Who* plays games with rules like the ones you made up? Rule One: act like an arrogant jerk. Rule Two: ignore the other person's clear warning off. Rule Three: muscle in like an uncaged beast…'

'Rule Four: respond like the Miss Whiplash you paint yourself as.'

She gave a little gasp there.

'Well? Did I call it wrong? You're playing with the big boys now, Tara. Better make sure you've thought it all through, because this isn't a rehearsal.'

She put her hands on her hips and squared right up to him. Her chest was heaving and her skin had flushed to the colour she'd bloomed when he'd made love to her. She was magnificent in her rage.

'Just listen to yourself. You absolute ego trip. I wouldn't *play* with you again if my life depended on it.'

'Your life will depend on you staying away from my sisters. So why don't you go and tell Angelica you've changed your mind?'

'Are you *threatening* me? Are you *seriously* threatening me?'

No, of course he wasn't threatening her. It had just come out like that. He needed her away—from them and mostly from him, and *now*. Because the way she looked right now, with her eyes flashing and her mouth open and moist, with her hands on her hips and her breasts pressing their tempting outline against the thin, soft fabric of her sweater, he wanted her as up close and personal as he could possibly get her.

'This isn't going to work, Tara.'

'This is going to work perfectly. And here's how. I won the commission for Angelica's dress fair and square. I need to spend time with her to get her thoughts. We've arranged that for next week. The fact that you and I had sex is irrelevant. The biggest problem is your need to control every aspect of everyone's life—including mine! Well, that just isn't happening. OK?'

She moved toward him to emphasise her little rant and it was all he needed. He reached out and cupped her face, stepped closer and hauled her right up against him. He took that pink mouth and made it his. He tasted her lips, her tongue, and silenced her but for the bone-deep sigh she finally eased out.

He moved her steadily backwards until her back was against the door. He pressed her with his body and ran his hands over her breasts, under her sweater and inside her bra. She yelped into his mouth with pleasure and he swallowed her sounds. Her hands were all over him, clutching at his butt, running over his shoulders, down his pecs and finally cupping his erection. She was hotter than the Mojave and she matched him in every way.

He stepped back, braced his arms on her shoulders, drew breath. She was right, of course. Even if she really was the full-on party girl she painted herself to be, and he was beginning to suspect it was a media myth, he *had* been bang out of line. But that was really beside the point. His first loyalty was to his family; and always would be. And no amount of sexual attraction or the spur of smart-mouthed comments were going to make her the sort of person he wanted hanging around. One week in her company and look what had happened to Fern. One week in her company and who knew what would happen to him?

'I don't need this kind of thing in my life. I don't want Fernanda any more influenced by your world than she already is. You've got your commission with Angelica—fine. But the rest is off-limits.'

The venom was back.

She recovered quickly and stepped to the side. One hand on the door handle, the other patting her hair. She eyed him, shaking her head and breathing her contempt.

'As I said. I make up my own rules. Deal with it.'

CHAPTER FOUR

THE LAST THING she needed was hassle. Of any description. The stress of organising the next show was off the charts and, yes, she was brazening it out in front of her team, but her shoulders were only so broad and her skin was only so thick.

She clicked the phone off and looked at it in her hand. Closed varnish-chipped fingers over it and wondered if it would ever ease up. So Dutch Ronnie was backing out. She should have seen it coming. He was too good to be true. Well, apart from how self-obsessed and downright dull he was. Beautiful, bisexual and boring. And also broke, it now seemed.

She rolled her eyes. This would mean another grovelling interview with the bank to extend her borrowing. And, sure, there were definite advantages to looking bad girl gone worse, but when it came to meetings with the suits that held all the cards she sometimes wished she owned even one thing knee-length in navy. The business side of life just seemed to roll much more easily when you played with a conservative ball.

Still, her media strategy had held her in good stead up until now. They loved that she was a natural at self-promotion. They loved that she 'was her brand'. And she knew most of them could see past her party persona when they focused on what was coming out of her mouth rather than what she was barely wearing.

That was the real irony, of course. That these stuffed shirts knew her better than most of her friends and *all* of her family. Funny that she could feel quite comfortable baring her soul to them, plotting out her five-year plan and being totally overt about how she wanted... okay, *needed* to have achieved a foothold in Europe within the next twelve months. The only thing they didn't know was why.

Why was she so driven? What had turned the quiet, unassuming mousy-haired, Girl Least Likely to Succeed into the competitive, controlling, crazy woman she was today? Did she even know herself?

Sometimes. And it didn't make her heart sing.

Which was why a head full of business was way better than any amount of navel-gazing. She just had to get things back on track.

Still, a week ago she would never have called this one! Angelica Cruz's wedding dress. It wasn't going to save her whole empire, but it could lead to some very lucrative long-term interest. If only she could keep her mouth shut and her gaze away from the eye candy that she seemed to want to gorge on.

She cast her eyes down over Barcelona outfit number one—a little red full-skirted silk-satin shirt-dress, peep-toe nude patent slingback wedges and... She lifted out what jewellery she'd brought, which was a joke: a few hoops of gold... She hated that she'd had to rush to pack like that. She back-combed her hair and then smoothed it into a ponytail. Red matte lips—no trace on her teeth—and…she looked down…yep, flaky nail varnish.

But she'd have to get around to that later. For now it was time to soak up the Cruz family atmosphere and start to tune in to Angelica's muse. A couple of hours of wandering around the house and gardens before lunch and then some time together reviewing the albums of previous Cruz brides that had been left out in her room on arrival.

And what an arrival it had been. Radio silence had been observed since she'd told Michael to 'deal with it' and he'd obviously gone all alpha and cracked his Daddy Cruz whip. Fern's pouting lip was big enough to trip her up and Angelica's almost brittle brightness had taken hold since they'd landed at BCN. Tara knew family dynamics well—Devine style. No words left unsaid, no look left undelivered. Tears, screams and tantrums. Then repeat until exhausted.

Until Grandpa Devine came home. Then everyone scuttled to the shadows. Whispers and eyes cast down. Favourite dinners and nothing a problem.

She picked more polish off, scraping her cuticles, drawing blood, feeling nothing. No, nothing was a problem—even in-your-face bullies like her grandfather. Her problem was that she'd had the front to call him on it. That had made *her* the problem.

So when the time had come to make choices—when some had got jobs, some had chosen college—she'd chosen the fastest train out of town. And never looked back. And, really, Michael Cruz was just a Hollywood version of Grandpa Devine. Smoother edges and whiter teeth, but that arrogance, that expectation that all females would do exactly as they were told…

She looked at the little pile of scarlet shards now lying on the crisp white bedcovers. *Sweep up the damage and get on with it. Get on with life. Because no one was ever going to stand behind you, let alone agree with you that women were created equal! Oh, no. Not your aunts, not your grandfather, and certainly not your mother.*

And that was why it was a far better idea to be completely and utterly independent. In every aspect of life. To stay as far away from people who would control her. And, if she absolutely had to date, she dated carefully—no lies, but no promises. And absolutely no men who judged her or disrespected her. They had to be totally in tune with their feminine sides. Or they didn't even get past first base.

And that did *not* make her a player! Damn Michael Cruz and his insults. Look what happened when she ignored her own rules…

The heat of the day was OK and the light was fresh and clear. Her heels clicked pleasingly on the marble as she walked through the house. The vibe of the place was strange—she couldn't quite tune in to it. There was happiness and love, but there was so much order, even with all the feminine touches that were so obvious—the flowers, the scents, the pretty soft furnishings and drapes. But among all of that was the *maleness* of the place—the presence of Michael. It was enough to suffocate the living daylights out of her.

She looked around. Heard voices. A voice. Followed the sound.

There it was again—just when she had filled her head with all the reasons why Michael Cruz was a flaw in the fabric of life she saw him, and life seemed to be a palette of beautiful colours.

Dark jeans literally hugged the best butt she could remember seeing on a man. *Ever.* The cut was fabulous and suited the length of his legs, easily thirty-four inches of hard muscle The simple white shirt didn't fool her for a moment—exquisite collar and cuffs and perfectly tailored to show off those shoulders—those shoulderblades. Hands should mould them and slide over them to absorb the breadth of bone and muscle. Fingers should feel the bulge of bicep and tricep.

Flashes of those arms holding her hips as she rode him exploded in front of her and she felt her legs almost buckle. She reached out to the edge of a chaise as he turned to face her.

The missile of that brown-eyed gaze hit her hard. But she held it until he flashed a look all over her, still talking in fast, low Catalan, and finally acknowledged her with a nod. She touched her hand to her ponytail—ran the tip of it round her finger and moved into the room, as if it was *her* air to suck and *her* view to savour.

Phone call over. A pause. The tension arced.

'Hi.'

'Hi.' She gave him a little grudging smile—all he deserved. 'Business call? Did I interrupt?'

He made a face that told her nothing. 'You get settled in OK?'

'Yes. Thanks.'

She moved through the corridor of space slowly, dragged the fingers of each hand across the veneer of a table, over the tips of tall cushions poking up from the back of a couch. Settled herself at the high, wide

window, looking out for more life to absorb her than
the all-consuming presence of this man.

'You look lovely. Your dress is very flattering.'

What? A compliment? She curled her lip and waited,
for the *but*…

'You suit the colour too.'

She twirled her ponytail, looked out of the window. You couldn't call this guy. *Really*. She was all
set to deflect and fire back and then out of nowhere a
curve ball. Was that a strategy guys like him used? To
double-disarm by being so unpredictable?

'Do you like what you see?'

She turned. Did he know she'd been checking him
out when she came in to the room? Or was this another
of his little control games? Didn't he know the rules?
He criticised and she responded. Simple. *Compliments?*
After their last little exchange that was just too weird.
That smacked of mind games.

'Look, Michael, I appreciate the compliment, but
I for one am a bit puffed out with the whole split personality thing you've got going on here. I mean, was
it a different Michael Cruz who basically warned me
off coming here? Am I supposed to predict if you're in
a let's party mood or a back-off mood? Am I? 'Cos I
haven't got the time to second-guess you. All I want to
do is my job. And then get back to my world.'

She just couldn't afford to let her head get messed
up by him. It was hard enough keeping the sexual attraction she had for him in some dark corner of her
mind. The last thing she needed was to let him get in
any more of her headspace. That way led to disaster.
She needed total concentration for her business. That
was her lifeline, her safety net—whatever you wanted

to call it. It was the reason, ever since she'd left home, that she hadn't gone mad. So, yes, she *had* let herself go there with him—but she'd tried to set out clear rules. Mutual disrespect and a mutual, though waning, sexual attraction. Then back to business. End of. Surely he understood that?

'That's what we both want, Tara. I'm just being civilised about it. You're here in my home and I'm extending you the same courtesy I would extend to any guest.'

His voice was low. It was calm. It was laced with something she didn't understand.

'Oh.'

'Oh,' he repeated.

He was so sure of himself.

'So I should tell you that lunch is being served on the terrace.'

She cocked her head to look out there. Dishes were being set out and she did feel hungry.

'Shall we?'

She plastered on her best glacial smile and moved towards him. 'We shall.'

She passed him where he stood. She was so aware of him—the energy, the mind, the look of him. He watched her, and then all he did was put his hand out—touch the small of her back—and instantly a huge sexual high pulsed through her.

It was immense, the throb of pleasure unmistakable, and she paused for a moment, stifled a gasp. Stifled it for all she was worth because there was no way she was letting him see how he affected her.

She felt him at her back all the way through the house to the terrace. She moved like clockwork and kept her eye on the table like a homing device. Bowls of salad, meat, bread, olives—all the stuff she liked. Glasses. Thank goodness she could have a glass of white to take the edge off. She was feeling the edges right now— sharp and dangerous.

'Are the others joining us?'

She needed the answer to be a yes. Because couldn't he see that them being together, unsupervised, was going to lead them to the same place? Did he really want a repeat of what they'd started? She knew he wasn't just chipping away at her willpower—he had taken a sledgehammer to it. To the extent that now she was as likely to make a move on him as he was on her. And this was so, *so* not good news. She needed clarity and control. She needed her rules to work!

He was still behind her—tucking her into her seat like an overly attentive waiter. She scraped her chair in and out as soon as he had left it—OK, it was childish, and maybe a bit passive-aggressive, but he would get the point that she could move her own damn chair.

'Fernanda? No. She's going back to school tomorrow, so she's gone to the city and the library to get on with her assignments. Yes. Remarkably, it turns out she had *work* to do.'

'And Angelica?' She ignored his loaded comment and poured herself some sparkling water from a bottle with a spring-loaded cap. Waited for the reply he was forming as he did the same.

'She's popped over to Girona. Didn't she see you before she left?'

He flashed her a look as water splashed near the rim of his glass. Expertly twisted his wrist to stop the flow.

'No.' *So it was just the two of them.* 'When will she be back?'

He took a deliberately long time to answer—eased the cap back onto the bottle, placed it in the centre of the table, flicked out a linen napkin and sat back, glass in his hand, eyes on her face.

'That I don't know. She does her own thing.'

Tara struggled really hard not to get annoyed. 'Was it an emergency?' She could only assume that something important had taken her away without even so much as a *see you later*.

'If you can call a lunch date with girlfriends an emergency. And some might, I suppose.'

He was helping himself to food from the different plates. Sunglasses were removed from his top pocket and put on his face. He looked hot as hell. Mysterious as the devil.

'I'm finding that a bit odd.'

'Don't. Angelica is flighty. Someone will have sold her a line to get her over there—she'll be thinking she's on a mission of mercy. And she won't be worried about you.' He replaced a dish on the table, pushed it towards her in encouragement. 'You're in good hands.'

Which was exactly the problem.

She pulled dishes towards her. Scooped spoonfuls of salad and oily fish onto her plate. Kept her face down.

'So, have you been to this part of Spain before?'

'No.' Where was the wine? *Was* there any wine? She looked about. 'No, I haven't. I hear you have vineyards, though. That true?'

He looked at her. His eyes creased and his mouth split into that brilliant rarely seen smile.

'Wonderful vineyards, yes. I'm assuming that your interest in them means, in your very direct way, that you would like to have some wine? Which would you like to sample? *Tinto, rosado* or *blanco*?'

'Honestly? The way I'm feeling right now? If it's wet—it'll do.' She shook her head, pulled a face.

He laughed again. 'Come on, it's not that bad. You're in a beautiful place, gorgeous food—and the wine... Hey. Let me get you something special.'

'Special...ordinary. Wine is wine. You choose.'

He regarded her. 'Quite the enigma.'

'Yeah, you can explain that while I listen to the restful sound of a cork popping. C'mon, Michael—it's been a long weekend. And I could really do with a glass of your best Chateau Less Stress.'

'Wrong country, Tara. We're in Spain. Catalonia. You'll need to pay homage to the area before I can ease your tension.'

'Ease my tension? You *are* my tension!'

He laughed again. Not a throw-your-head-back belly laugh, but a rich, warm, easy laugh that instantly had her mirroring.

'I don't think you mean that as a compliment.'

He didn't know? He really didn't know that with everybody else she spent her day lining up the guns and then firing them. With him around she wasn't sure if she had even packed her ammo belt. Maybe he *was* oblivious? Maybe he thought she was this jaggy with everyone?

'Take it any way you like.'

He had so many dimensions himself. He never failed to amaze. Right now—when she should be feeling annoyed at being left high and dry in a strange country, while her business was effectively hitting the skids and the money to pay not only the wages of her team but the ongoing costs of the next show was trickling out of a Dutch Ronnie-sized hole in her piggy bank—right now she was smiling at the man who had riled her, stoked her, fired her to a crazy sexual high and then riled her all over again.

And it was, just for this moment, in the late September sunshine, the *best*.

'Tara, I don't want to be or even add to your tension, so why don't I just be your host for the afternoon, until Angelica gets back?'

'Why don't you be my host? Why do you even have to ask?' She picked up the still empty wine glass, looked at it pointedly and then raised it to her lips, sucking noisily on the air it held. 'Still empty. Come on, Michael, pour me a glass of wine and then let's get on with hating each other. At least we know where we are then.'

Hands on the table, he shook his head, still chuckling. Stood up and went to an ice bucket that had been sitting there the whole time. Pulled out a slippery, chilled green bottle and wiped it with a linen cloth.

'Hate is such a wasteful emotion, Tara. And it's miles away from what you and I feel for each other.'

She nudged her glass across the table and held the stem steady while he poured. The lemony golden liquid sloshed and coated the sides of the glass, but instead of instantly lifting it to her lips and downing a large gulp she stilled her hand, and her mind, and wondered what he really, *really* thought of her. She wouldn't give him the satisfaction of a second thought, but her own mind went there.

'I know I'm supposed to play coy at this point and say, *Why, Michael, what is it you and I really feel for each other?* But I'm quite sure I know what I feel for you. And at the end of the day—at the end of *my* day—that's all that matters.'

'Nobly delivered. But I couldn't be the age I am and have seen the things I've seen and not know that people's opinions are supremely important to someone like you, Tara.'

She felt the thin column of glass rotate between her fingers. She still didn't lift it to her lips.

'Maybe. But when I know the answer to the question what's the point in pretending I don't?'

She raised her eyes to him then. *Challenge.*

He sat opposite her again. Well back in his seat in that open-legged, confident way. Those probing dark eyes were trained on her in a way that made her want to lift up a shield. Or a spear.

'It's just a matter of time. As you move through life you'll find you care less and less about the opinions of those people who really don't matter.'

'And yours does?'

'With regard to our relationship? Sure.'

'Relationship? We don't *have* a relationship!'

He gave her an indulgent, absent-minded half-smile. Like an old uncle watching a toddler stumble over their first steps. Patronising, actually.

'Tara, any two people who have any interaction have a relationship. Of sorts. And we most definitely have had an interaction. A very memorable interaction.'

The shimmer of heat transferred from his words to her memory. A memory that was being etched more firmly with each passing moment. She refused to look up at him.

'The sex was OK. I hope the wine's better.'

She lifted her glass finally and took a long inhale, a

gulp, and then swirled it round her mouth. It burst on her tongue with flavours that she couldn't name and slid down her throat. But if he thought she was going to pay him a compliment after the way he'd treated her and spoken to her...

'Well? Is it?'

She put the glass down and lifted her lashes. He sat there like a king on his throne looking at an amusing subject about to subjugate herself. A self-assured smile played on his mouth as he lifted his own glass to his lips, waiting for her reply.

'It's passable. So, yes, better than the sex. Much.'

This time he did throw his head back and laugh. And she crashed out a laugh too. *Swine.*

'You should come with a health warning—an emotional health warning. Heaven help any man who doesn't have intact self-confidence taking you on. You'd annihilate him.'

There was something in that, she supposed. Maybe it came from her gene pool—though it would have had to skip a generation. Maybe it came from years of realising that it was easier to show strength than weakness? On any front. Attack—the best form of defence. Wasn't that what she'd learned that final time? Too many times hiding... So that when that moment had tipped, when she'd reared up and answered back—she would never forget how it had felt. Never forget that when bullies were actually confronted...the shock, the retreat...the world reconfigured.

'Yeah.'

'But I'm pretty secure, so I know you're lying through your cute little offset teeth.'

'That a fact?'

'You know it is. You know that we scaled the heights. And even before then—when we met in the club, in the car, in my lounge. Right here on this terrace. You can feel what I can feel. And I can see it all over you, even though you refuse to look up at me.'

She smiled into her wine glass. Too right. All of it. Every word he said. And then some. There was no mistaking the thrum of arousal in the air. Good to know he was feeling it too.

'Would there be any point?'

'In looking at me? Or in acknowledging it?'

She hazarded a very direct stare right at him. 'You don't hold any fear for me, Cruz.'

'That's interesting.'

She mentally raised her shield higher as he lengthened the look, seared her eyes.

'Though I'm not sure you're right there.'

She allowed him a smile for that. What did he know? What did he care?

'Whatever, Michael. Though, if we're on the subject of being honest with ourselves, maybe you could shed a little self-searching light on the fact that you seem to find me an "enigma" in private and a royal pain in the butt in public? Is that because I hold some kind of fear for *you*? Hmm? Worried that I'll act the way you seem to like me acting in private when your adoring public or, worse, your adoring sisters are around?'

Self-satisfaction. Not her usual tone, but he definitely deserved it. And he didn't like it. His brows knitted and his jaw tightened—which, if anything, made him look even more handsome, accentuated the square masculinity of his face.

'You deliver that as if it's a newsflash. Tara, but it's

obvious. You're… Of course I find you attractive. I also find you intriguing—genuinely intriguing. But the truth remains that what I find intriguing and what Fernanda needs to find in her life right now are two separate things.'

'I'm trying really hard to keep my wine in this glass and not throw it all over you. That's the second time you've insulted me like that. Do you *really* think I matter so little that you can assassinate my character because I'm here in your house on a commission? You think I'm so beholden to you that you can say what you like? Is this how you treat all your guests?'

'What I like is honesty. No games, no artifice or pretence. And I'm surprised that you are continuing to take offence instead of seeing things from Fernanda's point of view.'

She shouldn't be letting him push her buttons like this—she knew that—but she couldn't seem to stop herself while he sat there like the Commander in Chief, sipping his wine, chewing his olives. Just one more overbearing man, making all the rules. And wasn't that just the thing? The way they could twist it round to make you feel like the guilty party!

'Fernanda's point of view? You can't be trying to pretend that you care? What do you think her point of view would be if she found out that you were more than happy to have sex with me as long as no one found out about it? Maybe you should think about the level of hypocrisy you're exposing her to—never mind the fact that she might actually have found a job that excites her rather than a job counting your beans and boring herself to death!'

Maybe an olive had got stuck in his windpipe, be-

cause he sat immobile opposite her and it was as if a
very black cloud had suddenly darkened the midday
sky. She felt a strong urge to run indoors and get away
from the storm that was sure to follow. But she didn't
run away. She was not the type—not really. And—
whatever he was about to launch across the table—it
was only words. Not burglary or bankruptcy or any of
the other things that either had already or potentially
might have an impact on her life.

So she fought the urge to shy away from the intense
mood that had descended and sat back. Lifted the glass
now saved from being a projectile to her mouth and
sipped on her wine, staring at him, challenging him.

'What's wrong? Suddenly realising that maybe you
don't yet know yourself fully? Just like me? But it's OK
for people to hurl words at you across a table or a car
or a kitchen sink?'

'Actually, I think that right now you are more beautiful and sensual than any woman I have ever met.'

She was not expecting that. And even though it made
her head rage it sent a dart of pure lust right to her core
to know he thought of her like that.

She couldn't take her eyes off him. They roamed to
his mouth, with its full, formed lips, and she remembered kissing them—the perfect fit of them round her
own, the way he'd used his tongue and his teeth to stoke
and nibble, the licks and thrusts that had matched how
he filled her and how he'd moved inside her. She looked
back to his eyes and this time the throb was something
deeper, something more frightening than lust itself. It
was openness, exposure, trust and care. And suddenly
the shield was far away—out of reach, useless. And she
was wide, wide open.

'But, whether you see me as a hypocrite or whether I see myself as protective, the issue that matters is that lust is just that. And if there's one thing I am sure about it's that I am more—and hopefully *you* are more—than a wild animal ruled by passion. So…'

She couldn't believe it—she was feeling as if her heart was beating on a plate beside her tapas, and he was talking as if he was giving a traffic update.

'So, regardless of how beautiful or sensual you are, this trip is about Angelica's wedding dress. Nothing more. I'll leave you to your own devices this afternoon. No stress. No tension. And no distraction. I hope you can deal with that.'

His chair was pushed back. He moved up onto his feet. Napkin tossed down. A smile. Little quirk of a smile. A final tug at the wine glass. Placed on the table. And he was off—away.

CHAPTER FIVE

BARCELONA OUTFIT NUMBER three. Two had been a swimming costume and wrap that Tara had shoved herself into when the excruciating silence in the house and the excruciating man of the house had both played mind games with what was left of her sanity. It made her feel almost like the unwanted child she'd once been—when she'd been too small to pick up on the undercurrents that little girls should be seen and not heard.

Well she'd more than made up for that since then.

She pulled out the dress and looked at it critically. A swirl of vibrant print on silk jersey. The obligatory deep-cut V. She held it up. Maybe a touch too deep? Had those words ever been formed into a sentence before? Tara shook her head—never in *her* mouth, they hadn't. But this was dinner with the Cruzes. No doubt in some ten-star restaurant that he'd managed to get a table at without booking a year in advance like lesser mortals.

She looked at her shoes. Great colour match but, again, nothing there was whispering *demure*. Everything was screaming *where's the party at*. Strange that she should be feeling like this tonight. It must be the knowledge that Angelica and Fern would be Princess-Grace-Perfect eating away at her self-confidence. But even that was unusual. She'd spent so long honing her own image—happily honing her own image and then reinventing it—that to question herself now was a bit odd.

She got dressed anyway. Maybe she should do something different with her hair? Less up, more down? Not straightened, but maybe waves? Big waves, of course, and a smoky eye, nude lip. She worked her way through the routine and then stood, faced herself in the antique mirror.

She was unrecognisable. It had to be the lack of eyeliner. She could have coloured in a path to Australia and back with the eyeliner she had used—but even her recent craze for the liquid line had died a sudden death. Must just be time for a new image—maybe something she could capitalise on in the next collection. She pulled a face. If she could capitalise on this she would be working a whole new demographic. Something was definitely off.

Her phone buzzed in her hand.

A text from Angelica.

Sorry, darling. Am caught up with poor Sophia. She has had terrible news and I can't leave her yet. Fernanda is on her way here too. Hope Michael is looking after you and see you very soon. Ax.

Great, just great.

She sat on the bed. Felt a bone-deep weariness. Sighed to her soul.

Another night of defending herself against his charm, his insults, his off-the-charts attractiveness. Another night when she'd have to screen every comment and field every probing, penetrative look. One to one, face to face. This was why she liked parties. To flirt and, yes, to hide. Because sometimes the whole effort involved in being Tara Devine was just too, too much.

She looked down at her nails. Now painted perfectly. Fingers bare of rings—because the only ring she wore was on the chain round her neck. Her grandmother's wedding ring. Her fingers absently found it and rubbed at it. Her grandmother had known what it was like. She'd had the battle scars. But she had protected her girls as best she could. She had put herself in the firing line and kept her flock out of his reach. But she was long gone. Long, long gone but never forgotten.

Tara felt the swell of sadness and crushed it back down. There would be no more tears. Not now. Not when she had come so far—so far away and so far on. So standing one more night with Michael Cruz shouldn't really be too difficult...?

Maybe she could try to make him see a bit more reason about Fernanda. Maybe she could do what her grandmother would have done—she would always do the right thing if it was going to help the underdog. All she had to do was remember she had her Kevlar body suit on under her dress. And not one single word that Michael Cruz fired at her would pierce it.

She snatched up a bullet-deflecting pink patent clutch and headed for the door. Time to dine.

The SkyBar? Or a backstreet Irish pub? Michael Cruz knew women. And he made decisions. So why was he over-thinking this simple decision as if it was a billion-dollar arms deal?

He glanced at Tara, sitting beside him in the car.

It was a deliberate act on his part to drive, and a last-minute decision after seeing her come towards him through the foyer. She literally took his breath away. Total remarketing job. But that didn't fit either. He really didn't see her as that type of game-player—the type that would try to read a guy and act and dress to suit. For one thing, she couldn't seem to hold her tongue in check for long enough to engage her control mechanisms.

She was a heart-on-her-sleeve blurter—a take-me-as-you-find-me or take-a-hike type of girl. If anything, she was a bit less ballsy than she made out—a bit more vulnerable. And he had caught a whiff of that vulnerability again tonight. She was preoccupied. Distracted? Maybe it was the enforced closeness they had again. Of course he could have left her to her own devices in the house—fed her and excused himself—but there was no budging Angelica from her latest project, and it was as clear as the water he was going to be drinking all night that Angelica knew he'd host, and he'd host well.

So where to take her? Yesterday it would have been the Irish pub without question—where she would have fitted in and had a laugh, and he would have relaxed, knowing she was knocking back shots and cracking jokes with the best of them. But tonight that seemed less and less like the right thing to do. She looked…she looked almost demure—if not elegant.

And quite why that was so unsettling him was anybody's guess. She was off-limits. They'd had their fun. And as soon as she had her meeting with Angelica and got the hell back to her world, the easier everyone's life would be.

SkyBar. Without a doubt. She'd love it.

* * *

She looked at him over the edge of the cocktail menu. Then dipped her eyes again. He ignored the city at night view that normally called to him and steadied his eyes on her.

She peeped up again. Then down. He laughed. 'What's wrong?'

Finally she closed the menu. 'How can I choose? I want them all! That's a ridiculous list of booze for a lush like me to cope with.'

'Why do you do that?'

She lifted up her water glass and poked at the lemon. Another of her little quirks. 'Do what?'

'Belittle yourself like that?'

She shrugged. Pouted. 'Depends what you see as belittling. I don't think that calling myself a lush is as bad as being called a bad influence.'

She pointedly looked at him and then sucked water noisily through her straw. A few people turned to look at her. She put the glass down with attitude, snaring a few more looks and responding with a confrontational grin.

'Ever get any paparazzi here?'

'Do you want some publicity?' He nodded to the waiter, who was expertly hovering, and ordered more water, a gin martini and a champagne cocktail. She could have whichever she liked.

'No, I just wondered. I am actually enjoying flying under the radar for a few days.'

She sat back in the seat and she did actually look as if the champagne cork that seemed to be permanently wedged in her solar plexus had finally popped and the fizz was trickling over her.

Now, *that* was a very stupid thing to think. His eyes

lingered where he knew they shouldn't as she twisted to take in more of the view. Her look tonight was all woman—with none of the comic book. She was lush, all right—but not in the way she'd made out.

Her thick, peachy golden hair framed the curves of her cheeks and lips. And her body was killing him. *He*'d been almost painfully sore since he'd seen her at lunch, and it didn't look like there was going to be any relief. Was it just that she had that perfect female ratio that tuned to some prehistoric part of his brain and made him want to throw her to the ground and claim her like a crazy man? Or was there something more complex? He wished he knew. And wished he could do something about it other than the obvious.

'Are you OK?' She was looking at him as if he was about to pass out.

'Sure.' He laughed. She had no idea—he hoped. 'How's your drink?'

She sipped on the cocktail and nodded appreciatively. Sipped again. Then again. Guzzled it. It was half gone.

'You maybe want to slow down. Remember you've got another one.'

'It's *so* good. Mmm.'

He had to look away. Her mouth was wrapped round that straw as if she was sucking up nectar. Her tongue jabbed the froth and his erection hardened. Maybe he should have taken her for a mojito on Passeig de Born. At least there would have been crowds there. And movement. Not the highly charged sex bomb that was about to go off right in front of him.

'So you're taking a break from publicity-seeking while you're here?'

She drained the last of the cocktail and sat back.

Her breasts rolled pleasingly under her dress and she crossed her legs. Was there any chance she was putting on a show for him?

'Not deliberately. I'm not in a place to do that right now—*especially* right now—but I can honestly say it's quite relaxing to think there's no need to choreograph the whole night just so I'll get the column inches I need. Though the way things are looking now I'll be back on the conveyer belt come Monday.'

'I didn't realise you were that dedicated. You must be exhausted. All that partying but one eye on the pay-back…or the fallout—because there has to have been some of that too?'

She ran her tongue over her lip. Chewed it a little. 'Always a risk. But, as I said, I'm not in the clear yet so I take every opportunity and make the most of it.'

'I thought you had things pretty well sewn up. Angelica mentioned your backers.'

She lifted her water glass and attacked the lemon again. 'They let me down. Today, actually. I just heard.'

She shook her head and a look of vulnerability slid over her. And it was striking. Those tiny flashes of the other side of her personality just added to the enigma. She sat quietly, stirring the shards of the lemon she'd massacred in her water. In a little world of her own. It made him realise how lonely she suddenly seemed. Fitted with what Angelica had confirmed on the phone earlier when he'd tried to probe a little more. That she was a master of self-created PR who'd honed the party girl persona—a single party girl. No one there at her elbow or her back. Maybe she had a great family—he didn't know and he didn't really want to know—but right now she looked as if she needed someone to scoop her up and take care of her. There must be someone close who cared? Women like her didn't come along every day. He'd certainly never met one.

'Don't you have other options? Other ways to raise the cash you need?'

Suddenly she brightened. Or at least she tried to brighten. The wide, full mouth split to reveal that unique smile and her eyes flashed. She raised the martini glass and threw the contents—almost the whole glass—down her throat. Wow, she could pull it back to the gutter when she wanted!

'Sure!' She spluttered, choked on the word, the alcohol clearly burning and making her eyes water. He reached over and patted and rubbed her back as she laughed and clutched her chest. 'Wow. That was strong!'

'Is it not a bit early to drink to the success of your new backers? Maybe let's get some food first?'

She was still choking and laughing and then, as he watched, it looked almost as if she was veering on the other side of humour.

'Hey, are you OK?'

Tears had definitely gathered in her eyes and the bursts of laughter were not sounding so funny any more. Was she...*crying*?

'Hey—Tara, *querida,* you're OK.'

He moved right over beside her. Curled her under his arm and tucked her head against his chest. Her hair was soft and he breathed in her scent for all of two seconds until he felt her push back against him and sit right up, her head still turned away.

'I'm fine.'

Her voice was still croaky but she was back in the game—no doubt about it. 'Do Not Touch' radiated off her in waves. Maybe she was one of those types that didn't like to be comforted. Though, thinking back, he couldn't say that he'd met any real resistance to his touch when she'd been naked in his bed. And he was back to *that* again. He really had to get a bit more perspective on this.

He studied the line of her back. No matter how she dressed herself up, Tara Devine was an ambitious, driven woman who just happened to push his sexual buttons like a pinball machine. She was upfront about who she was and what she wanted. Fine. But what she wanted was taking her in a direction he'd already been. And he had no wish to go back there—ever. And every wish to make sure his family didn't go there.

It wasn't a good world. It was shallow. It was dark. It brought out the worst in people. Had brought out the very worst in *him*. It wasn't the first time he had realised that with his mother's horrific death had come a very big silver lining in the form of a crushing sense of responsibility. It hadn't seemed that way at the time. But in a way it had been his saviour. Because he knew that in his day he had been much, much wilder than Tara Devine had *ever* been.

'You sure? Did it just go down the wrong way, or were you overcome with grief at finishing your martini? I can always get you another. You just need to ask. No big deal.'

She turned a blotchy face and gave a little half-smile. 'Thanks. All good. Maybe I'll have another water.'

'So. Backers. You need any help with that? Or you got it covered?'

'Nah, I'm going to be fine. There are plenty more Dutch Ronnies out there.' She settled herself back in her seat—at least she'd got whatever emotions had been rolling through her back under wraps.

'Dutch Ronnies? Is that a type of condom?'

She raised an eyebrow. 'Not one that I remember *you* using.'

He had to admit that his use of condoms that night was nowhere near as maxed out as he would have liked it to be. In fact, had he known then what he knew now, he would have planned a much, much better night. One where she didn't slip off and out of his grasp. One where he had the chance to bend her into the shapes he had spent a lot of time imagining since. Some of which had taken even *him* by surprise.

What was he getting himself into here? It was time to get back on track.

The waiter put down their water and they waited in silence until he left.

'Do you think Angelica will be back tomorrow?'

He had to admit that he was counting on it. 'Honestly? I don't know. I think so—but what you need to know about Angelica is that she manages to make everything fall into her lap. And she sometimes forgets that there are agendas other than hers. Not that she's selfish. Far from it; in fact most of what she's about is helping other people—finding what I call her "projects" and moving them on, like a little ambassadorial conveyor belt.'

She looked directly at him with eyes that were earnest and blue as truth. 'Does she see me as one of her projects?'

He could only answer as honestly as she deserved. 'Truthfully? I think so. But that's no reflection on you and no statement about your independence or capacity. She gets attracted to people for all sorts of reasons, and she gets as much out of helping people as they get from her help.'

She finally let his eyes go and the dip of lashes curled a shadow on her cheek. Golden light from the table candles danced across the planes and hollows of her face. She was bewitching. Too bewitching.

'I know. I'm not that naive. I'm just so used to being the only one batting for Team Devine I suppose I find it hard to understand the motivation of anyone who would want to help just for the sake of it.'

And just when he'd thought he had her all figured out… It wasn't just her words—her tone, just for a moment, had been so soft, vulnerable. And he felt again that sense of responsibility she stirred in him. She really must have had a raw deal somewhere along the line.

'Not everyone in business is cut-throat, Tara.'

'But most are.'

'Is that why you project such a ball-breaker image?'

She shrugged. 'I project who I am. I told you: I don't play games. It's just that some people deserve to have their balls broken. And others…' she slanted a flirty look right at him '…deserve to have their balls…'

He turned right round to face her. 'Are you seriously going to finish that sentence?'

She threw her head back and laughed. A laugh from her soul that washed through him like a fierce warm wave. And then he was really in trouble.

He reached for her. No way he couldn't. Took the back of her neck in his hand and pulled that mocking mouth right down. Crushed it. Over and over and over. He thrust his tongue in so deep that he stilled her and felt her go limp in his arms.

He held her close, then closer still, as he dragged her to him across the leather of the seat and pressed his body into hers, feeling every curved inch of flesh. Took both hands and cupped her jaw, still not letting her up for air, and kissed her more. Skimmed one hand over her collarbone and laid it flat against her chest, his fingers almost circling her throat.

And he felt her respond. Heard her respond. She liked that—oh, yes. He pulled his mouth back and stared deep into glazed eyes that had fluttered open. He searched her, shared the air that she was drawing in and out, and felt like the mad man he knew he was around her. She was so dangerous for him. Dangerous but irresistible. He *had* to have her again. Had to take it to the next level with her. Not intimacy, or love, or any of that romantic stuff. Just pure animal lust—because he recognised it in her.

She was tuned in to him so well that he was going to give her the best time of her life. And maybe then she wouldn't feel quite so all alone.

He stood up, threw some bills on the table and reached for her hand.

'Come on—we're going home.'

But she sat there. OK, she was still in a state—as was he, a very painful state—but she made no move, didn't even look up at him.

'No,' she said. 'No, Michael. It's not happening.'

He trailed his eyes right round the bar. He saw people laughing, people chilling at the aqua-lit pool. Waiters walking past, professionally oblivious. A party next to them of elegant middle-aged women who clearly recognised him. And then his gaze fell down to Tara. She sat there, golden head dipped. Arms stretched, holding on to the edge of the seat. Knees locked together.

'You don't want to do this? You don't think we have explosive chemistry?' Seriously, in his life he had never known such off-the-charts detonations when he'd just kissed someone.

'It doesn't matter about the chemistry. What matters most comes before and after the chemistry.'

He looked down at her. Kissing him like she was pouring her soul into his and then saying *thanks, but no thanks*?

'I didn't figure you for a tease, Tara.'

'But I figured *you* as an everyday player who wants to take a woman to bed—only if the important people don't see, of course—and then, once he's played, he tosses her back. He doesn't give a damn about how that makes her feel. And, Michael…' She looked right up at him and the fire was back. 'I am way better than that.'

She stood up.

'Just because you caught me in a vulnerable moment just now because some other guy let me down… this time over money, but, hey, who's counting? Just because I got a little stressed about it all. It doesn't mean I would ever, *ever* go back there with you. Why would I repeat anything that made me feel dirty and worthless?'

Sometimes he really did not understand women. 'I really hate to think that you felt dirty after what we did, Tara. We *do* have chemistry. You want to call it something else, go right ahead…'

'Chemistry doesn't give you the right to treat me like you did—and probably will again if I let you.'

Her eyes were glazed with tears but they flashed blue fire and her mouth shaped her anger. For the second time nothing could stop him. He took a fistful of her hair, twisted it and drew her fast and close to meet his mouth. One long, silencing kiss and one tug of his wrist to let her know her words were empty nonsense. And she buckled. At the knees.

He held her, turned his mouth to her ear and felt her shiver to her core. 'Say what you want. Act like you don't want it. But we both know this is happening again. And the next time you'll be begging. Screaming for it. And you won't feel dirty or worthless. You won't feel angry. You'll feel more alive than you've ever felt in your life. Understood?'

He scooped her under his arm and walked her to the elevators. She didn't fight him, but he knew he had winded and wounded her. If he'd made her feel any of those things then he'd more than make it up to her. Even though he knew, sure as he knew his own name, that she wasn't going to roll over and let him.

CHAPTER SIX

THERE WAS NO DOUBT that the beauty gene ran deep in the Cruz women. Tara flicked through pages of photographs, each one showcasing yet another even more sultry dark-eyed, dark-haired goddess. Photos from decades past of women—a few even in the traditional dark bridal colours, wearing mantillas and looking in some cases as if they were going to a funeral rather than a wedding. She could pick out clear family traits—the long, graceful neck and the high, wide brow. Open features, easy loveliness—and, more than anything, elegance and intelligence.

She glanced up at Michael, who was pouring coffee for them both and eyeing her carefully. And he had the male version of all of that in spades. *Damn him.*

She still hadn't got over the scene at the SkyBar. Him kissing her so publicly and then dragging her off like a caveman to the elevator. She'd more than put him straight when she'd got her breath back—and he'd more than backed off. Right to the corner of the elevator. And then he'd kept a respectful distance for the rest of the evening. Or at least pretended to. She still wasn't sure of him or his motives...

And she still didn't know how she'd got through it.

Emotions she hadn't felt for years had been on a rolling boil and she'd really struggled to keep a lid on it.
Tears! *Why?* She hadn't even shed a tear in her darkest
moments. She'd got her act together and got out. Never
looked back. So why was it all bubbling up now? Just
when she could see the light at the end of the tunnel—
just when everything was stacking up in her favour. OK,
most things... She could cope with the Dutch Ronnies
of the world letting her down—all she had to do was
hunt hard enough and another couple would roll along
in the next limo.

But the intensity...

She flicked another glance up at Michael—he was
still studying her on the quiet. The cut of his jaw was
serious and he was definitely holding back. The intensity of this man was unravelling layer upon layer of stuff
that she'd thought was buried for ever. It wasn't that he
directly reminded her of her grandfather. It was more
that she hadn't met anyone—not one single person—
who made her stop and question herself, who made her
wonder even for a second if what she was doing was
completely and utterly correct.

Since she'd left home she'd known that what she was
doing was on the money. Getting the courage to leave
had been easy. Keeping the courage going had been
easy. But suddenly, just when she could almost touch
the prize, she felt she didn't even know if she had any
right to claim it. He had unsettled her so much—made
her feel so confused about herself. Had unleashed so
many old ghosts that the urge to run was building higher
and higher.

She was going to give Angelica until the end of the

day and then she was heading home. She had to. For her own sanity.

'See anything inspiring?'

She felt the now familiar rush and whoosh of adrenalin as Michael settled himself beside her on the floor, extending long legs in dark denim out in front of him.

Her knees were tucked to the side, wrapped in cute cropped trousers and low-heeled slingbacks. Between them lay the piles of photos and photo albums. He was a foot away, but still the energy zinged and it was as if his hands were touching her. She budged slightly over...away.

'Yes. So many traditional elements could be incorporated.' She turned more pages. 'It's just a pity Angelica isn't here to give her view.'

He sighed—and did he actually move another inch closer?

'Honestly? She can't be too much longer. I think this is a record. Usually she indulges for a few hours. A day—and a night—is pretty extreme stuff even for Angelica.' He leaned forward and started to sort through some albums. 'Have you got any of my mother?'

She hadn't wanted to say. Yes, her second wedding—to Angelica and Fernanda's father, a respectable Spanish politician—was there, and it was everything she had expected. She'd been a classic Spanish bride of her time. But the wedding album Tara had really wanted to see—the man who had won her nineteen-year-old heart, Michael's father—was missing.

She handed him the album she had and he quickly scanned it.

'You're not in any of them.'

The words were out before she could stop herself.

'No. I'm not. I wasn't there.'

He sounded matter-of-fact again. So she could probe?

'How old were you?'

He continued to flick pages. 'Not sure. Teens. Maybe seventeen. Sixteen?'

'And you weren't invited?'

He half laughed at that and a little tension bubble popped. 'I really don't remember.'

She turned to him and frowned. 'You don't remember? I don't buy that, Cruz.'

He shrugged and paused on a couple of pictures. 'It looks like it went well. Looks like it flowed exactly as my mother would have planned it. Which would have been like a military operation. And genuinely...' He looked right at her with the gaze that captured her every time. 'Genuinely, I don't remember if I was wanted there or not.'

'*Wanted* there? Are you serious? Why not?'

Who wouldn't remember whether they were invited to their own mother's wedding? Unless they were so spaced out at the time... Those were the rumours, of course. The pretty boy, the child star had gone out of control. With a mother who had been more interested in solving other people's problems than her own.

He and his girlfriend had been the sweetest little toxic twosome. He'd been the European face of the biggest soft drinks company in the world, and then he'd hit the skids. Oblivion. At least he'd made it out alive...

'Ah, it wasn't the best of times for me. Truthfully? She may have wanted me there, but I was in no fit state to know that, and if she didn't want me it would have been for the same reasons—that I'd let her down, turn up high or drunk or both. Probably bring some totally

inappropriate girl or even a whole bunch of inappropriate girls. So it was for the best that the most important day of her life was spent *without* the carnage that
I'd have created.'

He was speaking in that matter-of-fact way again.
Tara didn't know if she would have been able to pull
off nonchalance like it—ever. He seemed to major in
it. But she couldn't see it from his mother's point of
view. Surely any mother would want her own son to be
at such an important event? Surely it wasn't all about
appearances?

'Maybe your memory is clouded? Maybe your
mother did want you there but you got caught up in…I
don't know…stuff—the stuff you did?'

He shook his head and smiled at her indulgently. 'I'm
not hurt, if that's what you're getting at. I was out of
control. I was all about me—as selfish and hell-bent on
a crazy cocktail of self-destruction and self-promotion
as it was possible to be. Don't think that my mother
hadn't tried to reach me—of course she had—but I was
out. Out for the count.'

Tara knew the crazy cocktail he was referring to. Her
own life could be said to currently resemble a 'lite' version of that. But only she knew that her self-destruction
was more fiction than fact. His past, from what she had
picked up on, was more of an Armageddon than any
of the little sham-pagne celebrity after-parties that *she*
tripped up at.

'She must have been out of her mind with worry
about you.'

He pulled one of those impenetrable faces. Smiled
at an image of his mother, standing with regal elegance
oozing out of every pore of her perfectly postured body.

He trailed his finger round her face and nodded—a tiny nod.

'I'm not judging her. She had every right to get her life back on track after losing my dad like that. Then all the heartache of coming back to Spain and building bridges, re-establishing herself.'

Tara said nothing. Not sure if he wanted to keep talking. And not sure any more if she wanted to listen. It was all getting a bit too much like a therapy session. And she wasn't prepared to man up and go next.

'Any photos of that wedding—of your mum and dad?' She *desperately* wanted to see those. To see the young Maria Cruz before she became the *grande dame* of Spanish society. To see the man who had won her heart: Michael's father.

A mirthless laugh. 'It wasn't that kind of wedding. No white dress or morning suits. No bridesmaids catching the bouquet. Not a chance. It was an elopement—Spanish wealth and class meets London East End. A match made in heaven—ending in hell.'

Bittersweet desolation. It was there in his voice. His usual black and white, here-are-the-facts tone had darkened and she was sure there was still something very, very raw in there.

Tara fought an urge to reach out and touch him. He was so close. The sinew of his bronzed forearm bunched and stretched as he flicked through more albums—but there was no way he was really looking at the pictures. Still, she didn't probe, or reassure, or offer any kind of solace. But it was getting harder. He was getting easier.

He put down the albums, stretched out his legs, seemed to lean a little closer—but maybe that was just her imagination.

'They were your classic explosive relationship. Fire and passion, uprooted lives and lost friends and family. And all for what? A fantastic sex life and a baby?'

'You?' she asked.

He nodded. 'And then it all fell apart. He'd had enough. Or at least he said he'd had enough. He worked for some very well-connected people—and I don't mean the royal family. So, whether he was trying to protect her, and me, or whether he really had had enough of her...' He shrugged, tipped his head back onto the leather seat, stared into nothing. 'None of that really matters because she was shipped home, back to Papa, and ten days later he was dead.'

Tara felt a stabbing heat in her eyes. She reached for his arm. 'I'm sorry.' Her fingers closed over warm skin and muscle and she kneaded softly. He didn't budge. Didn't notice. Kept his head straight ahead and his eyes on who knew what? It was as if she wasn't even there.

Finally... 'Don't be. It's nothing to do with you. Barely anything to do with *me*. And it's well in the past. So there's no need for analysis or sympathy.' He turned then and his face was almost weary.

Her fingers stilled. He kept his eyes on her. And it came again—that huge swell of strange emotion—as if he could see right inside her and she could see right into him.

'The one thing I did take from it, though, is that no amount of passion is worth ripping your family apart for. Everything fizzles and dies. Family is what holds us together.'

Tara instantly retracted her hand. *Family is what holds us together.* The words rolled round her mind. He really thought that? Then he'd had a totally different experience than she. In her book, family was what drove people apart. Not one single member of the Devines from back home had ever called, written or visited. Not one. For all she knew they could all be dead and buried.

'So what about *your* family? You never really mention them.'

She simply stared. How could she begin to tell him about that lot? Where to even start? *Oh, I had a wonderful grandmother, who was a victim of domestic abuse by her husband until she died. And she bore it like Joan of Arc. And instead of being taken to task for his outrageous behaviour he was left to fester and get worse. Everyone ignored it. Everyone excused him. No one wanted to know. And no one was safe, not even children. And all the while her mother, with her own crucifyingly low self-esteem sat back and let him.*

Heaven help her if she ever asked about her father. That was tantamount to war crime. All in all, they were a perfect family. You couldn't make it up.

'Tara?'

'My family?'

'Yes. Your family? Got any? You know—brothers? Sisters? Skeletons in your closet?'

She just couldn't form the words. Her eyes continued to be held by his but her lips wouldn't shape any words. What words *were* there? No way she was going to start offloading any of *that* drama to anyone. Least of all Michael Cruz.

'You OK?'

He had shifted right round to face her now. His elbow rested on one leg, bent at the knee, his other arm lay along the leather cushions. His inscrutable face was showing interest. And she wished to hell it wasn't.

He reached out for the hand she'd placed on his arm. But she jerked it up and away.

'Fine. Of course I'm fine. Why wouldn't I be fine? I really, *really* need to get some ideas down for Angelica. Can I scan these? On the copier in the office? I think I've got all I need here now.'

She tried to stand. He looked up at her. His interest was getting more piqued. She was stepping on the photos. Low kitten heels pierced an album cover. He looked at them. Back up at her.

'Calm down, Tara, I'm only asking. It's no big deal if you don't want to talk about them.'

'What's there to talk about? No big deal is right.'

She bent to catch up the loose photos that had fallen out of albums. Stood and dropped another load on the floor. He was on his feet in a heartbeat.

'I've got them. It's OK.'

She hated that he was fussing over her. Hated that she was making such a fool of herself. He'd only asked her a simple question and she was behaving like a complete lunatic.

'I'm fine! I'm absolutely fine… Look. Really. This is going to be better if I get these pictures copied and work on them back in London. I think I'll change my flight and leave in the next few hours. No, you don't need to drive, get a driver…I'm cool with it.'

'You're cool with what, exactly?'

He was lifting the photos out of her arms. He laid them down on the table next to the leather couch. Slowly. Carefully. Put his hands on her shoulders and stepped her back, steered her round. Gently pushed her down onto the couch. Eyes on hers the whole time.

'What do you think you're doing? You know I hate that macho act you shove at me.'

Instead of lifting his hands away he massaged her shoulders. Tiny little circles but pretty near perfect touch.

'This isn't macho.' He kept kneading. 'This is what you need right now.'

She opened her mouth and he *actually* put a finger on it, shushing her. And then he laughed at her shock.

'Tara, *querida*, you need to learn to relax. Stop being so defensive. I only want to help you. Live in the moment and go with the flow.'

'What? Are you a Buddhist now?'

He smiled softly. Moved his hands from her shoulders to cup her jaw. Thumbs traced cheekbones. Slowly. And she felt as if she could feel every line of his finger, every pore, as he swept his soothing path. She sat where she'd been placed and drank in his comfort. And for a moment it felt like heaven. Warm and welcoming. Easy and soothing. For that moment she felt she didn't need to keep fighting. That she didn't need to hold up her shield and her sword and run at everything.

She felt her shoulders sag and her heart slow. Felt her breathing deepen and steady.

The thumbs trailed down her cheeks. He dragged one firm pad to her mouth. Round the edge of her top lip and down over the swell of her bottom lip. Velvet brown eyes bored into hers. Her lips opened. Her tongue eased out and tasted his thumb, welcomed it inside her hot, wet mouth. She suckled it as she stared at him—not even knowing herself. Not knowing that she was the kind of girl who would do that. But it felt so special and so simple. Felt so right.

'Tara.'

He said nothing more. Lifted his hands back and placed his mouth to hers. The softest, gentlest kiss she could ever imagine. Barely a kiss. Her eyes flew open and he opened his slowly too. Long moments passed. He cradled her face again, ran thumbs in gentle circles over her cheeks. Looked long and steadily into her eyes.

'Give yourself over to this. Just for now.'

And he dipped his head again and kissed her with such kindness and care. She felt something building inside her and it frightened her. She tried for a moment to pull back but he steadied her.

'No, no, no. Just a kiss. Nothing more. Just a kiss.'

She felt his lips on hers once more, this time firmer, reassuringly firm, and then his tongue opened a path inside her mouth and she knew this was the best kiss she had ever had. His mouth was the perfect foil for hers; his tongue already knew her mouth and stroked the hot, wet corners. His warm breath mingled with her own.

Wave upon wave of pleasure began to wash over her. Her body loved what he did and swelled up, opened like a flower for him. A sound built in her throat. A moan of abandonment and joy. She placed her hands over his and then moved them to his face. Felt the harsh trail of stubble and loved it.

She tried to deepen the kiss, tried to get him to move to a higher gear, but he resisted. He pulled his face back, out of reach, and she saw how greedy she was for him. Her tongue followed in the wake of his mouth and he smiled.

'You feeling better? Calmer?' His hands held her back at arm's length.

She swallowed back her hunger. Gulped down her

craving. Eyes drank in his stepping back—and she felt the distance choking. Why had he stopped? Why pull away like that? Was he regretting what he'd just done? Again?

'Calmer?' *Did* she feel calmer? No. She felt open and vulnerable, and those were two emotions that she hated feeling. 'Thanks, but I think I'd feel more calm if you left me alone.'

He chuckled at her. Shook his head.

'Tara, don't start going all defensive again. You and I are hot together. And you should use that to your advantage—take pleasure from it. That's all.'

'Hot but inappropriate? Just like the girls you never took to your own mother's wedding?'

He took her verbal missile, held it and crushed it right in front of her. He reached out and trailed a finger down her cheek. She flinched. Not because he'd caused her to, but because she wanted to. She would show him rejection right back.

'Tara—you're harder on yourself than anyone I've ever met. Why is that?'

She forced her eyes shut rather than look at him. Couldn't bear the fierce rush of tears that threatened. Could feel the cauldron of emotions bubbling up again and had no energy to quell them this time.

'We've been over this a million times. I'm not up for a bit of fun with you or any other player. I'm here to do a job. I've done what I can and I'm going to copy these right now. And then I'll pack. And then I'll go.'

She didn't even recognise her own voice. A husky crackle. She kept her face turned away from him and began to pick up the photos she wanted.

But he grabbed her wrist and turned her round. 'You

know, you've got a lot of stuff in your head that's really holding you back. You throw out an image of a girl who doesn't give a damn, but the minute you think something threatens you, even if you're way off, you fire back. I just don't get it. You must waste so much energy just battling people. Tara! Look at me. Please.'

He held her wrist up between them like some kind of staff. But still she kept her head twisted away. Just give her a couple of minutes and she would be back under control. Just a little distance and a little quiet. She could still remember the breathing techniques from her self-help books. Just a moment and things would settle.

'Tara.'

He was quieter. His voice was calmer. It was as if he was soothing the angry tiger in her soul. But that made it even more difficult. She couldn't look at him at all. Tried to budge her wrist free.

'Would you please let go of me?' Her voice was still a whisper.

But he didn't. He pulled her close to his chest. He held her head steady. He smoothed her hair and almost rocked her in gentle motions. He murmured. She couldn't make out what he said—but it was soft and sweet. She wanted to give in. She really did. She wanted to recline in the warm waters he was drawing her into. But it was too, too hard. She wasn't used to comfort. Had never been used to comfort. Even before the dark days after her grandmother had died they'd been a family of rockets who shot about, never sat still. Noise, energy and action. Or hiding and fearful.

She breathed out a long, slow breath. Felt moisture on her cheeks and at the corner of her mouth.

Heard movement in the house—heels, doors, a change of air.

She stiffened. He gripped her now. As if he was squeezing strength into her. She could open up, absorb it, or do what she knew and fight it off.

The heels came closer and he would not yield.

'Michael! Tara! There you both are! *Darlings*.'

She pushed him back and he let her. Lifted her chin. Wiped quick fingers under her eyes and squeezed out her best smile. Touched a hand to her hair and tilted her jaw. Big eyes. Ready.

CHAPTER SEVEN

ANGELICA LOOKED AS if she was always walking in on scenes like this. Remarkable. Especially because he'd never offered one up before. She floated through the room, smiling like it was Christmas Day, picking up photos and swooning over this cousin or that aunt. Like she'd popped out to mix a cocktail and come back to the room as if it was littered with confetti instead of emotional carnage.

Yep, she was doing well to gloss over the scene. A natural. He'd never so much as given her cause to worry about him or his private life before. Everything was strictly off-limits. Sure, she'd met some of his past lovers. But he had always maintained a careful distance between his sisters and his personal life. Better that way. He didn't really want them getting to know women who were only passing through anyway—it sent out the wrong signal. Like permanency.

Tara was not coping. She hadn't been coping since the cocktail bar. She was all over the place. Maybe it was spending intense time with just one other person. Maybe it was a come down from the party scene she was so hooked on. Maybe she was struggling with her attraction to him. Hey, he wasn't all ego—it was obvious. Like the permanent erection he was trying to tame.

Still, she wasn't the only one who was reeling after what had just happened. Since when did he talk about his mother...to *anyone*? He had to force himself not to close down conversations when Fernanda wanted to talk about her—to find out what she'd been like. It was so sore. Still.

He watched Tara with Angelica. Her cheeks were scarlet and she couldn't keep her hands off her hair—twirling strands round her fingers and patting it as if it had a life of its own. She never even glanced in his direction, but less than ten minutes earlier she had been running her hands over him like she was trying to catch his cologne.

She gathered up that ridiculous pile of photos and settled onto a couch with Angelica. He had to hand it to his sister: she had a knack of smoothing out some very rough edges. And he knew Tara's edges were rough *and* sore.

She had so much going on in her head. So many issues. She wasn't needy, just prickly. Very, very deep and troubled. And she'd put up such high barriers to climb over. For some guy it would be worth it. She was quality—on so many fronts. Her look—not just the obvious, but her whole look—the lips, the full, thick, lustrous hair that she never had her damn fingers away from, her pure blue eyes and her energy. But most of all, now that he knew her a bit better, she had passion and drive and a very, very soft side that she was totally bent on hiding.

It brought out all sorts of feelings in him that he hadn't even known he had. Yep, no doubt about it: she had pulled a number on the public—even on him, now that he thought about it. She was no more a one-dimensional party girl than he was.

He paced over to another couch and sat with his phone, catching up on emails. Well, sort of catching up on emails. There was a bunch of shows being streamed to him for final edits and he'd need to spend a good few hours absorbed in them. Which worked out well. He could hear Angelica work her magic and Tara begin to respond—as if she *hadn't* been teetering on the edge of an emotional abyss just moments before.

The women homed in on a few pictures and Tara's wrist flew across the pages of her sketchbook. He wondered what the images were like—wanted to see for himself. Then the chat seemed to move to fabrics. Not that he was listening. He was watching the shows from his laptop and making notes.

He'd never really taken in the image of fabulous contrast between them—Angelica all poise and control, Tara all energy and movement. Dark serenity versus blonde vitality. He couldn't take his eyes off her—how natural she was with Angelica. How she lit up the daylight-flooded room. Like a string of fairy lights.

Angelica caught his eye. Got up and left the room. Bestowed one of her serene smiles as she passed him.

He was bent double again over the screen, wondering why the hell one of his best guys had decided that fly on the wall documentaries were a good idea. Still it was clear the public were fascinated with some characters. He looked back over at Tara.

'What about your flight? You still heading home tonight?'

The look that arced across the room to him was telling. Watchful. Wary. But it was a connection, nonetheless. She almost shrugged her shoulders as her vivacity seemed to slip away again

'You should stay—at least one more day. Tara, you look tired.'

The feeling that flew through him as he thought of her getting on a plane he didn't really want to name. It just wouldn't be a good idea for her to travel tonight. She needed to get her full energy back, for sure. And he knew that they needed to revisit the energy between them. They needed to see how far it went. He suspected it would be pretty far. She was the most sensual woman he had ever met, and she still had so much to let loose. He'd love to be the one to help her explore the other side. The connection they could build during sex would be off the charts. He knew it. Didn't need to think about it—just knew it.

'I'm going to stay until the morning. But I have a meeting with the bank in the afternoon. I need to get their approval for another loan extension.'

She looked down at her sketchbook, lifted up a few photos and shuffled them into some sort of order. 'Thank goodness Angelica came back when she did, though. I could have taken the wrong turning entirely on what she liked. She's much less classic than I thought.'

'Really? That surprises me. Maybe you're encouraging her to branch out a bit—walk a bit wilder? To be honest, she's never even been adventurous with her breakfast cereal before. No bad thing as far as I was concerned—you know, as her guardian. Viewing any risk-taking behaviour in my sister was never going to be my favourite hobby.'

'That I can understand.'

'You can?' He found that interesting. She'd accused him of being a control freak where his other sister was concerned. 'What's brought on that change in attitude?'

'Oh, I don't know. Maybe seeing things a bit more from your perspective. I suppose you've got your responsibilities. The only responsibility I have is to myself.'

'That's all most people your age have. You're not unique. It was all *I* had until the accident. If that hadn't happened I still might be in that mind space.'

Which was entirely true. Funny how life could completely switch course within a heartbeat. And, strangely, he was getting that feeling again. He clicked 'pause' on his laptop and walked over to her. Idly lifted and laid some of the photos that now seemed to be in the 'chosen' pile. Glanced at her sketchbook.

'May I?'

She looked a bit tense. In fact she looked crazy tense.

She covered up the sketches with her arms. 'Ah, I'd rather not. I'm a bit…possessive of my work until I'm satisfied with it. It's just a… They're just…'

'They're just parts of you that you'd rather not show the world until you're fully satisfied that you've hidden yourself behind all your walls of hair, make-up, clothes and attitude? You edit your own productions even more than I do, *querida*. Hey, I'm not criticising,' he said, realising that she wasn't exactly looking delighted with his analysis.

He so, *so* wanted to keep her spirits high today. Having seen last night the range of her emotions, he knew that she was so easy to tip into anger and passion. And it was the passion he wanted to see in her again. Those kisses they'd shared before Angelica came home—

sweet and sexy. And she'd been so alive in his arms. Until she'd taken fright again. She was like a little feral cat—defensive, beautiful, hard to catch. But the challenge to tame her was building in him.

He reached out and stroked her hair—the gentlest touch…she could have barely felt it.

'I'm not criticising at all. It's who you are, it's what you are, and only you know the story of you. Which is fine. No one, least of all me, is going to press you for details you don't want to share. But, Tara…' He quietened his voice, watched her soften before his eyes. 'There's something between us. Something—I don't know what. But I don't want to waste any more time battling with you. I want to spend the rest of the time we have here in a whole different place than the war zone we've been in. What do you say? Hmm?'

He tipped up her chin and drank in the blue depths of her eyes. What a face. So honest and open for the briefest of moments. Then she dipped her eyes and hid herself away again.

'I think we've had our chance at that kind of zone, Michael. And I think you know how I feel. You can't lift me and lay me, with *lay* being the operative word.'

She still wasn't looking at him. He let his fingers trail slowly off her jaw. Absorbed the softness, the ridge of her jawbone from the point of her rounded chin to the perfect pink lobe of her ear. She stifled another shudder. He saw it. And it fired him. He was going to be inside her tonight if it was the last thing he did.

'Darlings, are we ready to have some food?'

Sometimes his sister could be a total pain in the butt.

'I've organised some light dishes on the terrace. But I'm afraid I can't join you.'

Or maybe not.

'What's up, Angel? The United Nations been on the phone again? Is there another crisis at a make-up counter?' He deliberately left his hand on Tara's shoulder as he stood behind her. Close. He felt her shift to move away from him—especially, he'd bet, because Angelica was right on it—but he wanted to set her mind at rest.

'Ha-ha, Michael.' Angelica took out her phone and waggled it at him. 'No special envoy missions, but I do have to attend a function with my future husband tonight. Sebastian is feeling sadly neglected. Tara, I hope you don't mind me leaving again so soon, but maybe you have enough to get on with the sketches?'

'That's exactly what I'll do. And I'll see you back in London in maybe two weeks. I'll email you, of course, before then. We can narrow down what you like and then take it from there. I've loved this, Angelica, I really have. It's been so helpful.'

She stood and the girls hugged. Not the usual fashion set kiss-the-air-next-to-the-air nonsense, but proper affectionate hugs. It took him aback. Surely she was just one of Angelica's projects—nothing to get worried about. Nothing to do with the fact that he had been deliberately touching her less than thirty seconds earlier. That had been for Tara's benefit, to keep her on the up. Last thing he wanted was his sister reading anything more into it.

'You want to eat now? Maybe go out later—since it's your last night? Fern is going to be staying at school all week. So there's not a problem if you want to just chill. Work on your sketches? Or I could cook later—another option. Just let me know what suits you, Tara.'

Angelica had gone and the air had settled back down.
It was just the two of them again. No staff, no noise.
She turned where she stood. Her blue eyes so vibrant
in her face. Her cheeks were flushed and her lips were
plump and parted.

The urge to grab her was immense and he walked to
her. 'You've finished sketching, right?'

She looked down at her piles of paper. 'I think I've
done enough for now.'

He could almost feel her wavering. She knew he
was bursting to touch her again. But he also knew that
they needed some kind of honesty before she would go
back there with him. Kissing was one thing. But she
was right. He wanted more of her—much more of her.
But here. Now. End of.

There was no way this could be repeated because it
didn't fit in with his life. And he didn't fit in with her
life either. So maybe the best thing would be to have that
discussion and then get down to exploring the depths of
their chemistry. That way everyone was walking into
this with full disclosure and there could be no hurt on
her part. And no need to revisit anything on his.

'Tara.'

Just her name. But even that brought a crackle of
passion to the air. She looked up sharply. Narrowed her
eyes at him. No doubt she was trowelling bricks into
place even as she stood there. No time to lose.

'I really want us to finish what we started. I need to.
I think you need to, too.'

She touched the chair next to her and he saw her fingers curl round its back. 'I think I need distance from
you, Michael, not closure.'

'I know I hurt you. But that's more because of your

imagination than anything I ever did. Sure, I was off hand when I first met you. You're not my type—on paper you're not my type at all. All I did was try to ignore that. But the minute we were alone in the car, and then in my apartment… Tara, I can't keep my hands off you. Look at you—look at what your body does to me. I'm aching, just standing next to you. Just knowing that we have a last few hours together. You do things to me that I can't ignore any more.'

Her eyes were wide and dark. She was ready for him. He looked over to her, caressed her with his eyes—couldn't stop himself if he tried. The tight silk blouse she wore showed him everything that was going on with her body. Her perfect rosy nipples were fully erect and straining through whatever underwear she was wearing. Her chest was heaving with deep, uneven breaths and he knew as he trailed his eyes further down that she was going to be as ready for him as he was for her.

An electric storm seemed to have filled the room.

She'd stopped building her wall.

One more minute and he'd knock the whole thing down.

'You know how it feels when we're together, Tara. Our mouths fit. I've never kissed anyone the way I kiss you.'

She nodded. There was no way she could deny it. Their kisses were dynamite.

'Your skin is like silk, and when I run my hands over any part of you it makes me want to follow it with my mouth. I want to lick and touch and kiss my way over every inch of you, Tara. And that hasn't happened yet. It needs to happen, Tara. Take your blouse off. Let me see that skin. Please.'

She put her fingers to the sides of her blouse and began to finger the long strands of silk that tied it together. His eyes fell to her chest, to the creamy cups that were now being uncovered. He could not imagine anything he wanted to do more than touch her, hold her, and make her cry with pleasure as he fixed his mouth round each of those firm nipples.

He walked a step closer. 'You look so beautiful.'

But she stopped. Stepped back. 'Michael—this is… it's too much. It frightens me. *You* frighten me with what you do to me. What you can make me do even when I know what you really think of me.'

He had it. Finally. The way in.

He shushed her. Shook his head and lifted her jaw into his hands. Gazed down at those bright blue open eyes. 'Tara—what I *really* think of you? I think that you're an amazing girl. *Amazing.* I respect what you've done in your life. Your bright, quick mind and your unending energy. You know I love your body. I can't believe myself how much. But we have to be open. We're on different life tracks. That's all. And, yes, I've been a fool the way I've tried to put that across, but that's all it is. This body of yours screams to me. I've got to have it, Tara. We've got to explore this while we're together. That's not wrong. Not wrong at all. It's all right. All good.'

And he dipped and tasted her mouth. Let his lips find its form and trace its path. Snaked his tongue inside and trailed it to meet hers. Duelled with it. Absorbed the sensations coursing through her, knowing that she was being washed clean with hot sexual energy and that she wasn't fighting back the tide any more. She

was with him, moaning into his mouth and grinding
her hips into his.

His erection responded, throbbing with pleasure, and
he fought the urge to rip their clothes off right there. He
ran his hands over her bare flesh, unhooked her bra and
filled his palms, watched her head fall back and took
his mouth down that pale column, sliding kisses and
tongue. Eating her.

'Bedroom—now.'

Dark, sensually drugged eyes closed for a moment
when he scooped her up. She was soft and warm in
his arms. Precious. He got through doors and up to his
bedroom. She held on to him and slid down him. And
then she became a wildcat. Her hands were all over him,
tearing at his clothes. He helped her—ripped his shirt
off, tore everything else off.

She dropped to her knees and took him. Mouth
wrapped right round his erection and tugged softly but
expertly. He groaned out loud and ran his hands through
her hair, pulled her up sharply before it was all over.
She looked wanton and wild. Half crazed. Her flesh
was pink and damp with perspiration already. She was
still half clothed and he needed to see all of her. Both
of their hands landed on her waistband and he left her
to tug off her trousers while he filled his mouth and
hands with every other part of her.

Finally she was ready—naked, half lying back on the
bed. Her perfect breasts were bared and the V between
her thighs screamed for his mouth. He opened her legs
and ran a finger to feel her wetness, knowing it would
turn him on even more to see how lost she was in him.
And just that touch, that feeling of her, so swollen and
wet—it undid him.

Where were the condoms? It felt like life or death—
he was so far gone. He fumbled to find them and quickly
sheathed himself.

'Tara, I've got to do this. Can't hold on—you're driving me—'

And he found her and plunged in. Felt her heat close
around him and squeeze him. He rode her, looking
down at her beautiful face, her eyes open, watching
him. And that turned him on even more. She was pulling his orgasm out already. He couldn't stop. She was
the best. She felt so good, so right. He felt the moment
switch—knew there was no going back—and he was
shooting inside her as he'd never done before.

He collapsed onto her, still hard, still breathing as if
his heart was about to burst. But he knew she needed
him and he raised himself up on his elbows. Looked
down on her. Felt he was looking right inside her. And
what he saw was just *right*. Strangest thing, but that
was the only way he could call it. He kissed her long
and slow. Poured that feeling right in there. And it was
as if he was buoying her up.

She took it, and loved it, and it was she who took
charge. She slid out from under him and he rolled over.
Then she climbed above him, rested her knees on either side of his head and dipped herself down on him.
He was instantly hard again. Had never seen or felt
anything more erotic. He pulled her hips just where
he wanted them and tasted her, turned her inside out
with his tongue. He touched himself and knew that
the minute she came he wanted her all over again. She
was heaven. And hearing her scream out her orgasm
made him feel more of a man than anything he could

remember. She was wild. She was beautiful. She was all woman.

He brought her down to him and kissed her exhausted face and chest and stomach and legs, and then he resheathed himself and found the core of her again. They lay together, sliding across one another. Two bodies that somehow seemed to have fused. Two mouths wildly tasting and kissing and two hearts beating the fervour of this passion.

He opened his eyes and knew she had just done the same. Something bigger than sex was happening between them. He would deal with it. He couldn't name it, but he would deal with it. Touching her inside and out right now was all he could do. And he did it until he felt her build to another orgasm, and then he held back, had to feel her clench around him. *Had* to. And the moment came with some sort of primordial power. He burst inside her, throbbing his release over and over again. The wildest, wildest time of his life.

'Tara…' He smoothed her hair and nestled her in his arms. She was molten. And he was going to make sure that she didn't feel anything but cherished right now. They lay panting, flesh cooling. 'That was…'

He laughed. Rolled her under him. Stared at her. She closed her eyes. Laughed back. Empty. He knew then that she was withdrawing. He could feel it.

'You were—you are—so sexy, so beautiful.'

'But still inappropriate.' A hoarse whisper. Hardly heard.

He stilled. 'Tara… Why?' Her face was turned to the side. He grabbed her jaw. 'Why would you sabotage what we've just done?'

She kept her eyes squeezed tight shut and her mouth

formed a tight line. Her body was withdrawing and he saw her rebuilding her defences.

'Tara. You need help. Your mind is so damaged. That was…it was beyond amazing. On so many levels. There was nothing inappropriate about it. It was one hundred per cent special and right.'

She had opened her eyes but they were staring ahead, at nothing. She said nothing.

He was still inside her—he eased off her but held her as close as he could. Didn't matter. She was gone. Away. Curled up against his chest with a thirty-foot wall around her. He stroked her hair, kneaded her arm, murmured how sweet she was.

Nothing. What damage had been done to this girl to make her act like this? Was it his responsibility to find out? He couldn't leave her like this. It was beyond terrible.

But she took the decision away from him. Got up. Spoke into the air.

'Michael, you are a great guy. A great brother to your sisters. And I have had the best of times here. But, really, I think that maybe us doing that was a mistake. As you said, we're on different life tracks. So, thanks. For a good time—a great time. But I'm going to get ready now—if you could get a car sorted? I need to get my plan ready for the bank. I've got those sketches to finish. I have to see what I need to do for Paris. I have so much to organise. Can't believe it—should've made a list.'

He watched, transfixed. She moved around, her beautiful body still naked, picking up clothes, running her hand through her hair. She made it to the door. Opened it, turned to look over one shoulder and drop the most fake smile he could ever remember seeing. Coy, and sexy as Marilyn. And easily as damaged.

Just what had he done? What had he become involved in? And how did he sort it out? She needed someone. His mind was rolling. She needed to talk through what was poisoning her mind. She needed to be looked after—simple as that. She was the most vulnerable creature with the most impenetrable front.

And he was letting her walk right out of his life.

CHAPTER EIGHT

THE BANKERS WERE FREAKS. Worse than she expected. And as for that half-assed so-called business consultant who had drafted the worst business plan... OK, so maybe she should have checked it over herself first. Or used a genuine recommendation rather than a favour from a friend of a friend, when—let's be honest—she didn't really have any of those. Party people were great in the good times. But as soon as your tank ran dry or your credit ran out they vanished faster than champagne at a free bar.

She'd have been better giving the five-hundred-pound fee straight to the Selfridges beauty counter, because she was already planning which totally unnecessary products she was going to have to buy as an upper after this brutal meeting. She closed her eyes and mentally picked her way across the ultra-bright pigmented eyeshadows that she knew already she was going to love—for about two weeks. And maybe some of the winter nail colours...she looked down at her destroyed cuticles, maybe not.

The lecture continued. The terms were being agreed. She should have brought her accountant, but that would have been more money. She could suffer this. She checked her watch. Saw the purple bruise on her arm. A finger-mark. Well, that was what happened when you had wild sex with the hottest man in Europe.

Her heart lurched again.

How many times could she take that sickening feeling that started at her diaphragm and swelled into her chest?

'Are those terms agreeable, Miss Devine?'

'Do I have any choice?'

'Of course. You can walk out of here and see if you can find better terms elsewhere.'

She crossed her legs. Her skirt rode up and she didn't give a damn. Her hold-up stockings were just the thing to make her feel that she had an advantage, because she could predict where their stupid eyes would fall and that gave her some small sense of satisfaction. Even as they looked down their conservative noses at her.

'Yes, I'm sure I could. However, let's not pretend that you've not hiked the rate up because you know my back's against the wall and the clock's ticking.'

She took the paperwork that appeared and signed her name. Stood. Smoothed down her purple silk jersey mini-dress that really didn't need any smoothing. Offered her hand to first one then the other of these sweaty-palmed loan sharks and bolted.

That was one thing ticked off the list. The rest of the list was actually a blur. *Everything* was pretty much a blur. She knew she had some last-minute calls to make, and she wasn't sure about some of next week's details around transportation, and there was a niggle at the back of her head about some deal she'd negotiated with a blogger.

This just wasn't like her. She was usually so on top

of everything. And since she'd got back from Barcelona she'd been on top of nothing. In fact she wasn't even in the middle of things. She felt as if she'd run head-first into a wall and was now lying at the bottom in a pile of rubble. She was physically exhausted, mentally exhausted, and—hold the front page—emotionally exhausted. It didn't even feel like a come down. It felt as if the universe had reordered itself and she was spinning off alone into some other cosmos with no control and no way back.

She tripped down Oxford Street, eyes up, seeing nothing. Heading to offload some cash. Finding solace in crowds. *Again.* When had that started? Heading home from school via every shop or friend's house so that the journey never ended? Staying out of the way when she knew Grandpa Devine would be home before her? Leaving by the back door when he came in the front? Plotting and planning her escape. Dreaming of when *she* would be the one in control, not him. When she didn't need to rely on anyone other than herself for anything.

And she had achieved that. As soon as she'd hit London she'd known that the world was hers now. Maybe one day she would loosen up and share some of the control with someone else, but she was still far too raw for that yet.

So what had she been thinking, getting into bed with Michael Cruz again? Of all the stupid, *stupid* things to do. It wasn't as if he hadn't taken up nearly all of her headspace just by being in the same house as her, and now for her to have placed her holiest of holies back in his possession... She had no one else to blame for this monumental downer.

She shoved open doors and involuntarily offered her wrist to the first perfume girl. She hated flowery perfumes. It was a flowery perfume. She sniffed it. *Yuk.*

Her phone lit up in her bag. Her eyes widened in hope—but, no. It was a message from a publicist friend who sometimes worked with her. There was a party tonight with a lot of key players. There was a hot young Danish boy with plenty of family cash in town, looking to bankroll some 'assets'. Tara should get herself to Shoreditch and see if she couldn't persuade Lars that investing in Devine Designs would provide all the assets he would ever need.

Tara's heart sank. She should be pleased. This was a genuine opportunity. But the thought of it just exhausted her. All over again. What to wear, how to travel, how long to stay, how much to drink, who to chat to—the list went on. And all she wanted to do was soak in a bath and curl up in bed. But even that was a lie. She wanted nothing more on this earth than to lie in the arms of Michael Cruz.

The sex had blown her mind. She knew she'd acted as if it was even more pastel than vanilla. In fact, she'd told him that it was worse than 'passable'. Had she really said that? To the man who had taken so much time over her? Who had relentlessly shown her care and concern, even trusted her with his secrets? Was she that much of a terrible person herself that she had to deliberately hurt him to keep him away from her? And that had worked *so* well!

She walked on through the throng. She was even more of hypocrite than he was. She should be ashamed of herself for her lack of integrity.

Her phone flashed again. She sat on a make-up bar

high chair to read the message. Her heart flew, hoping it was from Michael. Her heart sank when she saw it wasn't. Feared the worst and so it came. There were more capital problems. The transportation costs had been raised. She hadn't nailed that side of the deal and it was coming back to bite her.

There was no more scope at the shark bank. So the party. She sighed from her soul. *Here we go again*.

By the time the fourth glass of actually pretty good-quality fizz had hit the back of her throat Tara had decided that she had nothing left to lose. She was back in her scene. She could mope about. She could play hunt the celebrity—the *real* celebrities. She could flirt with Lars—except she couldn't find him. Or she could just drown her sorrows. Like a sackful of unwanted kittens. Boy, she was feeling sorry for herself!

She checked her phone. A complete waste of time. She had been more than clear with Señor Cruz that he was the last person she wanted to hear from. So why did her sad little heart sink every time she performed this sad little ritual? He was not going to contact her because she'd done everything in her power to push him away. She hated that she could cut people off at the knees. Hated to hurt anyone. *Ever*. But it was who she'd become in this game of hide and seek that she'd started

Another glass. Another scout around the place. A trail to the ladies'. There were so many people offering her things tonight…but nothing that was going to do her any good. The new turquoise eyeshadow was stuck in the creases of her eyes. And it made the whites of her eyes look pink. Or was that the drink? She'd get another. Find Lars. He had to be here.

Stupid shoes. They were too high. She lost her balance and her foot slipped over. Drink spilled on her hand. She licked it.

The glass was taken from her hand. 'Hey!'

'What do you think you're doing?'

It was him. Michael. It was Michael. Her eyes focussed. A little bit. He was so handsome. He was so beautiful. His golden skin over those perfect bones. That smudge of stubble. She put out her fingers to touch his face. He grabbed her wrist.

'Tara. Are you OK? Had enough to drink?'

She just wanted to touch him. 'Hey baby… yes, I'm having a good time! What are you doing here? Have you come to party? You need a drink. Give me mine back and let's go to the bar.'

'I don't think so.'

'Wha…a.. at? Come *on*! There's such lovely fizz, and I spilled mine.'

She reached for her glass but he was being weird and wasn't letting her get it.

'What's wrong?' She pouted.

'Tara—you've had too much to drink.'

She tried so hard to stand straight, but one foot wouldn't find the floor properly. 'I've hardly touched it. Only had two or three…maybe four. Five. Oh, come on, Michael, its a party and I have to find Lars. Give me my drink.' She swung out an arm to get her glass but he was still being such a killjoy.

'Who the hell is Lars?'

Who the hell *was* Lars? 'I don't know. Some guy. With money. For me.'

'What? He owes you money?'

That was funny. She laughed—a bit too hard—and fell against Michael again. It was so nice to fall against him.

She held onto his shirt. 'Cruz…'

But he took her by the arms and held her away from him. 'Tara. Sober up. Tell me again—what's the deal with this guy? Does he owe you money?'

'No.' She did sober up then—for a moment. 'I'm broke. My business is broke. I went to the bank and they gave me some money but not enough. But Lars… wherever he is…he wants some "assets"—ha-ha. And I have assets, Michael. Don't I?'

Oh, that had been the wrong thing to say. Even though it was hard to focus on him completely, she could see and feel that he didn't like that.

'Your assets are not up for debate. And you're not going to stay here drinking—with Lars or anyone else.'

'But it's early. It's…' She tried to focus on her watch. It looked like it was only one a.m. Far too early to go home. Some people wouldn't even have arrived yet. 'It's early, Michael. And I need to stay for just a li'l longer. There might be some good publicity too. And I really need it now.'

'You don't need to get publicity this way, Tara. There are other ways to promote yourself and your business.'

'Yeah, but…' she poked at his chest with her new nails '…this way is free. And it suits who I am. '

What a look he was giving her. Like she was a real disappointment. 'We can talk about that. Let's go.'

His touch was crazy strong. He scooped her close and put his arm round her. That felt good. But then he marched her, and her feet just wouldn't do what she wanted them to do.

'Michael. Slow, baby. I can't keep up.'

She almost went over on her ankle, so he scooped her in harder, until she was plastered right down his side and she didn't need to use her feet at all.

'Wheeeee!' She giggled as she was scooted along. 'You're so strong…' But then they went to the stairs and not the bar, and she realised that he was heading out… 'Michael. Where…? What…? Hey, I can't go. I told you—I need to find Lars!'

'Yeah? Well, we can talk about that too.'

'Michael, put me down.'

This wasn't funny any more. Cold air hit her bare arms and thighs. He still held her clamped to his side. There were paps about and their flashes and catcalls sounded. She started to struggle against him. That feeling of being powerless was taking over. Didn't feel good. *At all*.

A car door opened and he put her inside, then jammed himself in beside her. 'Drive.'

The car moved off. Fast. She jolted to the side. She was really beginning to sharpen up now.

She turned to him, her voice choked with fury, furred with alcohol. 'What the hell is all this about? Just who do you think you are, dragging me about like you own me?'

He stared straight ahead, his jaw clamped and his mouth worked into a tight line. No way was he going to sit there in silence. Not after that disgusting display of machismo.

'I mean it, Michael. What do you think you're doing? Didn't you see the snappers? They were all over the place. I'm going to look like an idiot tomorrow.'

Swift turn of head then. 'You'd have looked like a bigger idiot if you'd stayed on in that club. You're drunk.

You're alone. And you were cruising the place for men with money. What on earth are you playing at, Tara? You're asking for trouble—and who knows how you've managed to escape so far? So you can consider this a favour. No need to repay.'

'I decide what I do and what favours I call. Not you! You're nothing to do with me! What's wrong? Have you run out of sisters to bully?'

He shook his head at her and stared straight ahead again. But there it was again. He actually thought she was just another little girl to order about. He hadn't so much as stopped to ask her if she even wanted his help. Maybe she should lighten up and let him? After all, he could solve her problems in a heartbeat. But really? Had she put all that effort in over all the years just so that she could pimp herself out down his version of Easy Street?

'You can look down your nose at me all you want, but I've managed to survive perfectly well up until now by doing things my way. So you can tell your driver to turn the car around. I've got business to attend to.'

'Business? Dressed like that? Full of drink? Not a chance.'

She was sobering up at lightning speed now. She leaned forward. 'Driver. Can you let me out, please?'

She saw the driver's eyes flick to Michael's in the mirror. The car didn't even slow down.

'You're coming to my apartment. You can have a business meeting there. When you've sobered up.'

'You know, you've got serious control problems. Do you really, *really* think that I'm going to just walk out of this car and up to your apartment? Because you *tell me to*? And dressed like *what*, exactly? What's that supposed to mean?'

He sat there. Didn't move. Didn't even seem to have heard her. It was as if she was insignificant. Irrelevant.

'Are you even *listening* to me?'

He turned his head. Just a bit. Looked at her out of the corner of his superior eyes. As if that was all she merited.

'I'm listening to a woman who isn't capable of rational thought because she's too drunk. So let's keep the sartorial chat until the morning.'

'The morning? *The morning?* You actually think I'm going to spend the night with you?'

'No, I don't, Tara. Not in the way *you* think. I wouldn't take advantage of any woman who was as out of control as you are. It's not my style.'

'Yeah? Well, I wouldn't let you near me tonight if my life depended on it.' She tried to hiss at him, but it came out in a jumble and made her feel even more furious—with herself and with him. 'Oh, you know what I'm trying to say.'

'Just about. But that's fine—it's sorted, then. You can sleep in the guest room and then in the morning we can talk about your business.'

Still he stared straight ahead, as if looking at her was going to make him lose his lunch—or whatever meal he'd last eaten. He was so arrogant. Really, it was all she could do not to slap him. *Hard.*

She looked down at her dress. There was nothing wrong with it. Well, nothing that a ton of accessories better than she could afford could fix. To be honest… it was way past its season. And its sell-by date. In fact a firelighter and a pyromaniac could sort the whole lot out in a heartbeat. She really was looking awful. And that eyeshadow. What had she been thinking?

The car braked and lurched. A crowd of drunken girls had spilled off the pavement onto the road, squealing and laughing. They looked as drunk as her. She was knocked into the door as the driver swerved to avoid them. Michael slid against her and she yelped. He was right there. Warm breath on her cheek.

'Tara! Are you OK?'

His whole weight had smashed against her as the car turned and she felt him jerk back, fold his arms around her, scoop her close to his side, comfort her. There it was again. That feeling of letting herself sink into him. Into the warm tropical waters of his presence. So easy. Would be so easy to let go. But she mustn't. Must never give in. Must keep him back. Never let him get her heart. Or her mind. He'd had her body. Her body loved his body. But he would never have her mind. *Never.*

'Tara…'

He was smoothing her hair, her cheek. Kissing her cheek. Holding her head as if it was a glass egg. She shoved at him.

'Fine. I'm fine.'

The car stopped. She wasn't fine. She was shot. Shattered. Too much stress, too much drink and too much emotion had decked her like sucker punches. The end of the road. Felt like she wanted to sleep in a layby. Just until this next lot of emotional traffic passed by. So tired. So, so tired. She rested her head in her hands, her elbows on her knees.

The door opened. He was there. Arms, body, warmth, strength. She was lifted. Held. Secure.

Her head fell against his chest. Every part of her felt contained. She loosened and let go. Treacle in his arms.

He carried her through the space to his apartment.

She felt the changes in the air, felt his heartbeat against her cheek, felt the solid wall of his chest and the solid wall of *him*. Man. Just pure man. And for the first time in her life she accepted it.

'How do you do this to me?' she whispered into him. Didn't know if he could hear her, but it didn't matter. 'How do you make me melt when I want to stay so strong? I need to *not* melt. I don't want to be soft—and sad. I don't want to be like her, Michael. I wish you could see that.'

He opened the door to a room that was silver. And white. Brittle light from a sparkling chandelier. A large white bed stuffed high with pillows. Gently laid her down. Sank into the softest mattress. Felt it envelop her. Felt a soft, heavy quilt wrap around her. Felt the cloak of sleep steal over her. Darkness.

CHAPTER NINE

TARA AWOKE TO more darkness. A tight, tight band of pain across her head. Pressure from where she had lain all night in the same position. The quilt had fallen away but she was warm. She turned on to her back, pulled the quilt over her and just lay there. What had happened?

A knock on the door and then it swung open. Michael walked in. She squinted at him through the hand that was nursing her head. He looked amazing. Jeans and a shirt. Tall and impossibly handsome. He glanced at her and then made it to the window. With a whoosh the blind went up and daylight seared her vision.

'Wow, the sun's up, then?' Her voice was hoarse and crackly.

'For a good few hours, yes.' He walked to the bed. Placed a glass of water on the table beside her.

She shuffled and leaned up on her elbows, but the pain in her head was immense. Had to flop back down again.

'Feeling less than perfect?'

She kept her hand over her eyes. 'Slightly. Can't you shut the blind again? That's just cruel.'

He sat down on the bed. She felt his weight and sank towards him a bit. 'You've got a strange view of cruelty, Tara. Imagine how you'd be feeling if you'd stayed there even longer.'

'Yeah, but I didn't.' She hadn't wanted to go at all, but she'd forced herself. For... *Lars!* 'Dammit!' She sat straight up in bed and winced at the axe through her eyes. 'What time is it anyway?' Maybe there was an after-party somewhere. 'Where's my phone?'

It was worth a text—she had such little time left to get anything sorted before she had to start shipping clothes to Paris.

He handed her the bag which was sitting at her feet. She scrabbled through it—pulled out her phone. Dead. 'Ah, no! I've got no power!' She looked up at Michael. 'Have you got a charger for this?'

'Tara. Calm down and drink your water.'

'But I could be missing something. That guy—Lars. I never got a chance to meet him. Haven't you got a charger for this? I thought you had the same phone as me?'

He shook his head. Stood up.

'Where are you going?'

He didn't turn round—just walked to the door. 'To get a different perspective on life.'

She looked at his disappearing back. 'What the hell is that supposed to mean?' No response.

What did he mean? What other perspective was there when your business was going down the tubes? Closely followed by your life. If she didn't get this sorted she risked everything she'd gained at London Fashion Week. If she didn't have the cash for Paris she wouldn't have the cash to keep going. Period. And that was way bigger than just expanding her business. That was public humiliation. Bankruptcy.

And where did you go when you had no money?
Home? With your tail between your legs and your ears
full of *I told you sos*? Never! Never, never. Never.

It was all right for him—he had piles of money and
piles of contacts. She had…she had… She had the hangover from hell and in one way he was right—it could
have been much worse. She reached for the water and
took a long, gulping drink. Finished it. And she had
dehydration.

This was not going to plan. She had two days left to
get more cash. If she got on it now she could maybe,
maybe see if she could get a meeting set up. Surely there
had to be someone interested in funding her? Maybe
she'd made some impact last night? She should get online, see what was being reported about the party. There
was still time to cash in.

She got out of the nest of a bed, noticed that the pu-
trid eyeshadow had transferred itself to the snow-white
linen. Then she caught her own reflection in the large
freestanding mirror. Oh, man, she looked like a bouquet
of dead flowers! Her hair was sticking up, her face was
smeared with make-up and her dress—all forty shades
of vibrant neon jungle print—was wrapped around bits
of her. Just bits. With the rest of her poking out at various angles—none of them flattering.

She needed a shower. Maybe Michael would have
some of his sisters' clothes she could borrow until she
got home? Ha-ha—get real. She might just about be able
to squeeze into Fernanda's duvet cover.

She went through to the kitchen. It was like a photo
shoot for Sunday mornings. High windows, lazy light.
Gorgeous guy on a bar stool, papers spread in front of

him, espresso cup and half-eaten pastry at his right-hand side. Place set for her. All you could want.

His laptop was open. He glanced up at her, then back to his paper. But his probing eyes saw everything in the two-second body-scan. She hugged herself. She didn't belong in this photo shoot.

'OK if I have a shower?'

'Of course. Though you may want to see these first.' He touched the laptop towards her, then picked up the corner of his paper and his coffee cup, got on with the business of breakfast.

She looked at the screen. 'What is it?'

At first she couldn't make out what she was seeing, but then it registered. It was herself and various others. A photo-montage of the party, with editorial. There were clips of her arriving in Shoreditch. She brightened. She actually looked OK! The dress was not as bad as it had ended up…having been slept in. Hair was fine. Make-up—not so good, but she'd pulled it off—just.

Ew. A back view—her generous bottom, swaying as she walked into the club. 'Oh, well no need to ask if my bum looks big in this.'

Shoes were fine, but definitely too high for a night on the fizz. Then the clips changed. Others entering and leaving. Michael. He walked in looking—the only word for it was *immense*. Dark suit, white shirt, no tie. Face relaxed but eyes intense. A nod to the cameras and right on inside. Suave. It made her want to plant one on him—he was so edible. Just like now. How could one man hold such a full deck of cards? He had absolutely everything going on. Including being the best lover she had ever had. *Ever.*

A glass of juice was placed in her hand. A stool was

nudged towards her. She hoisted herself up onto it, still watching. He went back to his reading. More video of more people. Her publicist friend. Dutch Ronnie. He damn well didn't *look* broke, that was for sure! Then the real A-list arrived. She hadn't seen any of them. Honestly—how hard was it to get an autograph these days?

'Oh, well. Looks like a good crowd. Glad you went?' She knocked the glass against her wonky teeth, dribbled a little juice and wiped her mouth with her hand.

He glanced up at her, then to the screen. 'Keep watching,' he said.

A head shot of a reporter in front of the entrance. Then the camera zoomed to something over his shoulder. And there it was. At first she thought it was a bouncer, throwing someone out, and then she realised it was Michael, dragging *her* out. She looked ridiculous. Tucked under his arm, her legs almost lifeless, shoes trailing on the ground. But it was her face. To describe it as angry would be a kindness, but it was twisted in an ugly scowl. He looked implacable. Even when he put her in the car like a box of old junk.

'Well, you got your wish.' He took another sip of coffee and read another inch of paper.

'*Sorry*?' She was stunned. The reporter laughed into the camera. Behind her the paps were running after the car, training their lenses on it. 'You think I wanted *that* kind of publicity?'

He tilted his face to her in that annoying way he had. 'You *didn't* want that kind of publicity? You want *any* kind of publicity. You've proved that again and again.'

'You honestly think I want to be shown to the world tucked under your arm like a drunk getting ejected by a bouncer?'

'What I honestly think is that last night you didn't seem to care who or what noticed you, as long as someone did—and preferably someone with money. So, lucky for you that I was there. Not only did I notice you, I also have money. And once you have showered and eaten—if your stomach can cope with that—I'm going to sit you down and show you some options for funding. Options that don't include dressing up, drinking and falling about. OK?'

'No! Not OK!' His tone had imperceptibly risen with every word but she pitched in with an extra fifty per cent volume. Just to emphasise her point. 'What makes you think that I want to hear anything you've got to say?'

He nailed her with a full-on stare. She heard her own words echo between them. She was an idiot. She knew she was an idiot. But they were out of her mouth and suspended in the air like day-glo graffiti. He was trying to help her. She could see that. But did he have to be so dominant? So overbearing? So…so much of a man?'

'You know, Tara, for an astute businesswoman you can be pretty damn stupid. But fine.' He gestured with his hands in a motion of defeat. 'Fine. Do what you want. Or don't. It doesn't matter to me. If you want to take the independent female high ground, that's your shout.'

He picked up his paper again.

'You know where the bathrooms are. Help yourself.'

He picked up his phone, pressed in the code and read a message. Put it back down. Gently. Took a bite of his pastry. Ignored her. Completely and utterly.

She sat there. Two words stuck in her throat like dry toast. She couldn't say them. She looked at the screen again. His screensaver had come on but the image of her being put in a car was imprinted in her mind—very, very clearly.

'Surely you can see how that made me look? To be carried from a club and put in a car? Like you were my dad picking me up from a church disco, or something?'

'I don't know, Tara. Because you don't tell me anything. Do you even *have* a dad? Where were you born? I don't know anything about you other than what you choose for the world to know—that you like to drink, and dance, and flirt. That you're a ball-breaker and a risk-taker.'

'Well, I don't know anything about you either! Oh, sure, I know where you were born, and that you went off the rails, then back on them when you…when you became your sisters' guardian. But what have you really told me? Or shown me? What do *you* let anyone know about you? I could have read all that on the internet.'

That got a double-take. The cup that was halfway to his mouth paused. 'Good try, Tara.'

'What do you mean? I'm telling the truth. You're even more of a closed book than I am.'

He finished his coffee. Walked over to the machine and poured some more. Leaned back on the counter and perused her like she was a museum exhibit. 'I mean, good try because you are an absolute master of subterfuge. But I can see right through you. Distract. Divert. Decoy tactics. That's your speciality.'

She frowned. Truly didn't know what he was getting at. 'I'm only being honest.'

He smiled. 'You don't strike me as anything other than honest. I've worked that part out for myself. But you give nothing away. And when the conversation gets anywhere near the real Tara you switch—go on the attack, change the subject.'

'No, I don't! No… I don't…' Her voice trailed off. He didn't need to come back at her. She suddenly heard herself. Wow. She sounded ridiculous. Absolutely ridiculous.

His smile broadened. He pushed himself off from the counter. Put his coffee cup down and walked over to her. Eyes fixed on her the whole time. 'No, of course you don't! You're more defensive than an armed guard.' He braced his arms on either side of the counter where she sat.

She flashed him a grudging half-smile. 'Can't help it.'

'Maybe you should try.'

He put his arms right round her and hugged her into him. She stiffened. For a moment she stiffened. But he wouldn't let go. And then he began his master stroke— his touch. He drew slow circles on her back. Held her and touched her. And eased the tension right out of her. It was heavenly. She should give in. Her body already had.

He lifted her to her feet, cupped her face. Smiled right into her eyes. 'Do you trust me?'

She nodded.

'Enough to let me into your head?'

He held her so steady, stared straight into her eyes. That feeling swelled to her chest again and she knew right then she would refuse him nothing. 'I'll try.'

'Good. I know you'll try. I don't know what's stuck inside you, or what's caused you to be this way, but opening up will help you through.'

He stroked her hair and she found words coming into her throat.

'What do you want to know? That I left home when I was sixteen? Left town. Left the country to come here. Got a place in college and never looked back.'

He smoothed her and soothed her and more words came.

'I had to get away. My life was not good. Not good at all.'

She tucked her head against him, spoke into his chest. She could feel his strength and patience. He wasn't pressuring her, but it was so much for her to pull up these dark buried memories.

'And no, I don't have a dad—not one I ever knew, anyway. I have a granddad. And a mother who "let herself down" and was never allowed to forget it. And neither was I.'

She couldn't say any more. It was like a rock had been shifted. A tiny chink of light was behind it, but the rock was huge and heavy and she had no more energy to push it. She laid her head against him and felt the wetness from her breath on his shirt. His hands had never stopped stroking her. There were no other sounds. Nothing.

'*Soft and sad*. You said that last night. Is that who you were talking about? Your mother?'

She nodded into him, willing him not to ask any more. She couldn't give up any more to him just now. The soothing touch of his hands was like some kind of balm and she absorbed it easily, thankfully.

'OK, baby. OK.'

Long moments passed and then he eased her off him.

Cupped her jaw, smiled. His eyes were kind. Warm, dark and kind.

'You look like a paint palette.'

She smiled back, found her voice again. 'I can only imagine.'

'Want to shower? Together?'

Just those words sent a quiver of passion right through her. She lifted her face to him, desperate for his mouth. 'Now who's offering up distractions?'

'Oh, I think we could distract each other for quite a few hours this morning.'

He placed a kiss on her cheek. Slipped his hand round to her ribs. Slowly raised it to cup the underside of her breast. Palmed it. Touched her nipple. Her sex thrummed to life. He kissed her other cheek. Circled her nipple over and over. She found his mouth. His perfect mouth. It was a full-blown assault. Defence was futile.

He took her hand and she followed him out through the door. They walked down the long, daylight-flooded hallway to his bathroom.

She caught sight of herself in a console table mirror. 'I look horrific. Like a bomb went off in a flower shop.'

'I'm not going to lie to you, Tara...'

She mock-punched his arm. Tried but failed to run her fingers through her hair. 'And *you* look like your usual fragrance advert. So there's no point in competing.'

'Tara Devine? Not competing? Does your publicist know?'

She smiled and laughed. *Ugh*. That had brought her right back down to earth.

She stalled. 'I really need to get back on to this. I need to find another backer, or at least some short-term cash. Otherwise I'm finished. And just as it's all taking off.'

Michael stopped. Spun her round to face him. Held her face again. 'The offer's there, Tara.' He bent forward, kissed her. Slow. Deep. Long. 'And I don't make it lightly.' Kissed her again.

Her mind was beginning to go fuzzy. She couldn't drag her mouth away. Could not get enough of his tongue. Her hands went to his shirt. His hands went to her dress. He ripped it up and over her head. She clawed at his buttons.

'We need to do this. I need to be inside you before I can make another coherent sentence.'

He was out of his shirt now. Bare-chested. The most fabulous defined bare chest she could ever remember seeing. Golden skin and light dusting of dark hair. Pecs that looked too perfect to be real. Musculature that was not too heavy but radiated strength. She dragged her fingers across him, relishing the sensations.

He stilled her wrists and held her arms open, exposing her in her underwear. But she felt his adoration—wave after wave of it—as he looked her over. Then he dipped his head and tugged at her nipple through the silk of her bra, soaking her.

Even though she felt like yesterday's rubbish, she could no more stop this than stop breathing. She held his head in place while he worshipped her breasts. Her legs went weak. Knees buckled. All her blood rushed south.

He stopped and held her close. 'C'mon, let's get dirty.'

Michael watched her towel her hair. Wrapped in a bathrobe that drowned her, and with one leg crossed over the other, she looked strangely at home. And he wanted her all over again.

He had to move away. Had to get some space. He'd lost count of the different ways they'd made love. She brought out sides of him he hadn't known he had. When he got his hands on her—every time since the first time—he just wanted to possess her. It was almost primal. Then he wanted to play with her. Like his very own private movie. And then he wanted to cherish her.

He walked into the kitchen. At least this time she hadn't bolted the minute they'd finished. This time he'd held her in a grip like a vice, completely wrapped his legs and arms around her, tucked her head under his chin and held on. Even then he'd sensed her struggle with the aftermath. And even now he knew that he had only kept her with him physically. Her mind had drifted away.

He wondered how much her head was wholly with him when they made love? There was always that feeling of distance with her.

He was beginning to feel like Angelica. Like Tara was some sort of project. He could rationalise his offer to help her with her business—anyone would do that, especially if there was a quid pro quo, which there would be. And he was about to outline it to her as soon as she had finished fixing her hair. But why was he so caught up in what was going on in her head? What did he care if she gave him the best sex he'd had in years—OK…ever—and then wanted to retreat back to her shell? Wasn't that every single guy's dream?

He flicked on his laptop again. Found the page he was looking for. Looked at the footage. She looked so vulnerable. Even entering the club, she looked not just alone, but lonely. That fabulous smile with the quirky teeth. He could read every one of those smiles now. And the emotions that shone through that one were watchful, guarded and, yes, defensive. She didn't just have her armed guard—she had a whole battalion behind a fortress.

But there was no doubt she was getting closer to letting him in. Whatever hurt she held from growing up in a family where she was seen as something shameful—if that was what she was getting at—it had scarred her pretty harshly. Of course it had. And of course she would haul that about with her and let it shade her life.

That was a lot for anyone to handle. And, to be honest, the fact that she had chosen him to share it with... that was a responsibility he wasn't even sure he should be handling. She needed—she *deserved* somebody who could help her work things through. Maybe even a professional. Because the thing he'd thought he wanted to know—that she wasn't going to rip the heart out of his family, that she wasn't going to turn Fern's head the way his had been turned at that age—was the thing he still wasn't sure about.

He heard her moving about in his house. It didn't feel wrong.

'Morning again, beautiful.'

She walked into the kitchen looking fresh as spring flowers. Her skin was scrubbed clean and flushed pink. Her eyes, even shaded by lilac hangover shadows, were bright. Her halo of crazy peachy blonde hair was tamed. And her smile—her Tara smile—was as natural as he'd ever seen it.

'Morning again, handsome.'

He couldn't help it; he trailed a finger down her

cheek and cupped her face up to him. Dragged a kiss from that sensual mouth and felt intoxicated all over again.

Drugged.

Obsessed.

Not things he wanted himself to be feeling. He really had to get back on track and stop overthinking her and her issues. She spoke to him sexually. OK, she *screamed* at him sexually. That he could handle. But all this analysis and worry that she was beginning to generate in him…?

He had enough to be getting on with—with the increasingly smart-mouthed Fernanda. He had to remember what his main responsibility was. Yes, he would help Tara, but he really had to get a grip and not lead her into thinking that this was anything more than what it was. Confessions about her mother might be the very thing to help her move on—but they came with flashing blue lights. He had to pause this and work with his own family before he could help anyone else work out theirs.

He was not himself. This was not how he handled his life. Dammit but he had to get a grip.

'You got your business suit on under that robe?'

She beamed up at him. 'Of course. Do you want to check?'

'Ah… I think we'd better leave your outerwear in place for the duration of this meeting.'

He turned his laptop round to her, found the site he was looking for. 'There you are. Have a look at this and then we'll talk.'

She squinted at the screen. Then up at him. 'What is it?'

'It's how you can promote yourself, earn yourself

a truckload of money, and not have to sell so much of yourself in the process.'

He knew he wasn't missing and hitting the wall, but she had to know that her ways were not the wisest.

'It's a new line one of my production companies is moving with. Taking "behind the scenes" web productions forward and doing a more in-depth take on some subjects. Fly on the wall, if you want to use that expression. Very special subjects. And, in your particular field, the links you could develop with other associated businesses could be very, very lucrative. Way beyond product placement.'

She sat still. Super-still.

'What do you think?'

Not a sound. He waited. Filled nobody's silence in business. Ever.

He got up and moved to get some coffee. The silence swelled, broken only by domestic noises—coffee sploshing, fridge door creaking, a swallow sounded loud in his head.

Finally...slowly... 'I think... I'm not sure...but I think I love it.'

He swallowed more coffee, watched her as she scrolled through the site.

'It could be perfect. How long would the cameras be there?'

'That all needs to be discussed. And, remember— it's not me you'd be dealing with.'

She looked up at him. 'Oh? Who, then?'

'This is new for us. And, to be honest, it wasn't my favourite idea. But I think it could work well for you. It's been brought across from a company we've acquired. The producer's an easy guy to work with.'

'I think it could be the perfect vehicle, but I'd need to be really sure how it would all roll. I mean…' She looked up at him, excitement writ large on her face. Her eyes sparkled. 'It's a good offer. A *great* offer. I suppose my only worry would be how much control would I have? You know…you hear of these things. People get sucked in. Start to show themselves. And then the final edit is out of their control. They end up being made to look like a fool, or they totally open up and their whole persona is gone.'

'The persona that you've created that is actually nothing like you? Are you afraid people might see a woman with drive and talent—a real human being? Worried that they might see the real you, Tara? Whoever that is.'

'That's not fair. You're just as much of a two-face as me.'

He absorbed that one. Let it sink in. She had a point in some ways, but so much of his life was an open book. Facts—and fiction—were available, as she'd said, on every internet search engine. He couldn't have lived the life he'd led and expected otherwise. But nobody really knew what had gone on in his head. No one had any notion how bad the carnage had been. Not even Angelica. And certainly not Fern.

'You've tried that before, Tara. This isn't about me. But I don't have anything to hide. I'll tell you whatever you want to know. Ask away.'

For a moment she looked as if she was about to. She looked up from the screen and right into his eyes. Her mouth formed a question but the words didn't come. He cocked his head in a question of his own, but she closed her lips and went back to the screen.

'I think this would be a good chance to let the spotlight shine for just a moment on something other than the hedonism, Tara. Editorial control? I'm not going to promise you would have control, but I will promise that you will not be made out to be anything other than what you are.'

He could feel her internal squirm starting up. It would be a major step forward for her if she could.

'You know that I use the media. That's no secret. But I'm not a big enough name for them to follow me everywhere, so when I do pop up it's exactly how I want it to seem, I suppose...'

'This isn't sensationalist, if that's what you're worried about. It's art. I'm not in the business of offering free advertising. So what you need to ask yourself is if you're comfortable with who you are in the downtime, when your beautiful smile and party antics aren't there to keep everyone at bay. I'm not talking about showing yourself warts and all, I'm just suggesting adding another dimension. And, Tara, if you can, if you're able to show people more of how you get your muse, how you organise your business, then people will warm to you and your profile will rise. All good.'

She nodded. He could see every thought fly over her face as she worked it through.

'It still doesn't solve my cash-flow problems. My immediate need, five-grand-right-now, cash-flow problems.'

'Not in itself. But I'm sure a contract with us would go a major way towards releasing funds. Hell, I don't mind taking a look at your business plan, seeing if I can't make it a bit more appealing.'

He felt so responsible for her on one level—she was

his sisters' friend, a family friend. And she was his lover. For now. For today. Who knew where that would end up? But most of all she was a single girl in a big world with a lot of talent who just needed a little direction. Anyone in his position would help out.

He could give her the cash right now—but if he even suggested that he knew what would happen next. And he definitely wasn't going to force the issue. If she didn't want to bite, he wasn't going to lose sleep over it.

'Ah. I don't know. I really don't.' She sat running her fingers through her hair, twisting it over and over. 'It could be good—it could be great! But you've already said that I wouldn't have editorial control. I mean, what if I come across as a neurotic freak? What if it turns into one of those "how many bugs can the crazy girl eat" shows? I've been marketing myself in a whole different direction. That's not who I am.'

'But that's the whole point, Tara—do you *know* who you are? Does anybody?'

She looked startled for a moment, but then the defensiveness returned. 'Good question, Michael. Do you?'

'I'll tell you right now who I am—I'm a survivor. And a damned lucky one at that. I was born to two parents who loved each other, and but for the world my father was caught up in they might still be together. But they're not.' He paused. Hearing himself speak about this out loud was almost shocking. She was the only woman he had ever spoken to about his parents before. And for some reason he trusted her enough to take the lead.

'I'll tell you it all, Tara—open book. Is that what you want to hear? Will that help you?'

She was wide-eyed, watching him.

'For years my mother and I were a team. Then when she met Carlos I felt abandoned. All over again.'

She reached out an arm to him.

'It's fine. I had hours of therapy—enforced therapy—to help me see that. I was sent to therapy even before I needed it, that's how considerate a mother she was.' He laughed—an almost bitter-sounding laugh. But he wasn't bitter. He was lucky. 'Then I landed big jobs on the teen acting and modelling circuit. The shallow, vacuous world of how good everyone looks and how fake everyone is.'

'Is that why you're so against Fernanda getting involved?'

He knew he was getting near to dangerous territory, but she deserved to know. It wasn't personal, anything against Tara—it was loathing and fear of how that world could corrupt. Because *he* had first-hand knowledge.

'Yes. But more than the pointlessness of that 'industry', for want of a better word, it's the side issues—the drugs, the drink, the parties.'

'And you think that I represent all of that? You think that I'll corrupt Fernanda and lead her into a life of debauchery?'

He shrugged. 'I did. But I was seeing what you wanted me to see—what you want the world to see.' He moved towards her—her and her scrubbed-clean naturalness that no one ever saw. 'You're not that person, Tara, but you're still in that world. And you might be able to stay in control and manipulate the world to suit you, but others can't. I couldn't.'

'Yes, but you were—what?—sixteen?'

'Exactly.'

'And you made your own choices. I made my own choices at sixteen. You're not giving her a chance.'

'I'm giving her the benefit of my experience. Tara, this is way beyond choices—this is about personality types and what can happen. Fern is like I was. We both get hooked into things, obsess about things until we master them, and then move on. Which is fine when the things are positive. But I got hooked into things that I don't want her anywhere near.'

'Oh.'

'Yes—*oh*.'

She would know exactly what he meant. But she still didn't know the extent of it. No one did, really.

'I went down. Crashed. Burned. The lot. Tara, I tried everything—*everything*. Sex, drugs and rock 'n' roll. But I left out the rock 'n' roll.'

She nodded. 'We've all had those offers, Michael. It's part of life. All kids get those offers when they're at any nightclub—it's not just the media kids.'

'Yeah, but when the offers get wilder, and when the people making them are controlling you, supposed to be looking after your interests…'

'Oh.' Again.

The dawning look on her face told him she knew what he meant. And she hadn't been expecting it.

'I lost six months of my life. But I didn't lose myself. That's what I mean about being lucky. No one really knows this, Tara. I had dropped off the face of the earth when I got the news about my mother and Carlos. Their accident. And it came on the front of a newspaper that someone had left lying in a flat I was living in. I think it had been there for two weeks by the time I saw it. I'll never forget the feeling—I thought it was

some kind of trip. I couldn't understand it or rationalise it. And I'd missed it—missed my mother's death.
I realised that my two baby sisters were completely
alone. So somehow I got myself out and I turned myself around. Realised that I had to and, even more, that
I *wanted* to protect those that needed protecting. Like
Fernanda. And…you.'

'Me? But I don't need protecting from that kind of
world—I get offered things, but I know my limits. I
know who and what to avoid—I know my way round
the scene. I take care of myself. And I would never lead
Fern into those situations. *Never.*'

She didn't get it. She just didn't get it.

'I know that. And I'm not saying you need protecting from pimps and pushers. But you need someone at
your back. And you seem to bring out that part of me,
Tara. You call it control freak? I prefer to call it my
sense of responsibility.'

Her eyes were totally wide now.

He smiled at her. 'Yes, *querida.* Whether you like it
or not, I'm that kind of guy. Maybe it was the fact that
my father sacrificed so much for love, or maybe it was
the years with my mother, but it's part of me and, like
I said, you bring it out.'

He had to lay it out for her now. Saying the words out
loud was making sense to him. He hoped it was making sense to her too.

'And I trust you enough to hold this close. Between
us.'

He couldn't stop himself. Did not want to stop himself. So much for keeping it all business. That had
lasted—what?—ten minutes max? She was his drug
of choice right now. No debate.

He closed the gap and cupped her face, just the way he liked to. Drew the pad of his thumb across her still incredulous mouth. 'I am one lucky guy.'

Her big blue honest eyes were staring right back at him. 'You are… You *are*?'

'Sure. You're such a beautiful woman.' He pulled another kiss from her. Opened his eyes and drank in the scrubbed-clean version of her. 'This face. This body.'

He couldn't get enough—could not stop himself dragging kisses from her, running his hands over her skin, under the robe. But he had to step back. She needed to see what was so obvious—that she was way more than image. She was talented, kind. And much, much softer than she ever made out.

'You're a survivor too, Tara. But your path is narrow—maybe this is a chance to open up. See if there are other ways to be Tara Devine.'

She cast her eyes down again. Her hand went to her hair. Twirling strands round and round. 'This is such a tough call, Michael. Taking me so far out of my comfort zone.'

He shrugged. 'We're looking at options just now. You seemed like a natural fit. But not if you're not comfortable.'

'I need to think about it and…and I don't have enough time to do that. I take risks—but every risk is thought through and measured. I don't know. I don't know…'

'Don't do anything you're not sure of. But, Tara, you need to prioritise some things in your life. You're holding yourself back. And what you started to tell me earlier—about your family, your mother.' She opened her mouth but he shook his head, shushed her. 'You need to deal with that. Or start to deal with it.'

'That was just a comment I made, I don't let that get in the way of anything.'

He couldn't stop the double-take, held his hands up. 'OK. Whatever you say. My only advice, for what it's worth, would be that you might want to book some time and talk it through with someone.'

'It's my business that's important to me,—not what some sad old man thinks about me.'

'The sad old man being your grandfather?'

He watched as her face flushed and tightened.

'He has nothing to do with me or my life any more.'

'Clearly.'

He wanted to shake her. Gripped her arms instead and held her there. 'Tara. You're running so fast, but you can't see that you're still tied down. Take some time—think instead of trying to blast your way through life. You'll get there faster in the end.'

She was retreating. Defending. Right in front of his eyes he could see the walls going up again. She was moving back into her safety zone. And the worst of it was how close she had come to taking a really big step out of it.

'Yeah, well, that's time I can't afford right now. Same as I can't afford to stay here and chew the fat. I need to get going—get this show back on the road.'

He nodded. Maybe this was for the best.

'Of course, baby. No problem. The offer still stands—if you want it. We'll be finalising the schedules quite soon, but don't feel under any pressure.' She looked so uncomfortable, so vulnerable, so desperate to get away. It made him ache for her. 'Tara…'

'I'm fine, Michael. Thanks for the offer. It's a great offer. Ehm… I'm going to head off now. Can you call a cab?'

'The car's here—I'll phone down; it'll be ready to go. Take the car.'

She tried a full smile. He wanted to comfort her but she was away, out the room, off down the hall. Tiny and fragile-looking in the big white robe.

He watched her try and fail to pull off a confident stride. Knew without looking that the emotions would be rolling over her face. Maybe there would be tears in her baby blues. But the heavy black weight in her heart was a definite.

CHAPTER TEN

WITH HER PHONE CHARGED, Tara was confronted with a stream of notifications—texts, tweets and posts. Wow! And one call from home. With voicemail. She ignored it. Could not even *think* about going near that right now.

Lars hadn't been at the party after all, but he was still in town and still looking for assets. You had to love a guy who went shopping on that scale—retail therapy for billionaires. Luckily they needed to offload 'pick-me-up' cash too.

Tara started to read through the stuff on her phone. She'd figured she'd be an easy target on social media for her less than elegant exit from the club with Michael, but she'd totally, *totally* underestimated the volume of traffic it had generated.

Even driving out of the underground car park of Michael's apartment building had been a shocker. The driver had warned her there might be a squad and he'd been right—at least half a dozen snappers had stuck their cameras to the window of the car as it had eased over the ramp. Those pictures—flat hair, bare face and hangover—hadn't appeared yet, but it was probably only a matter of time.

But even without them she seemed to have rocked

straight to the top of the 'what's hot' gossip columns. This was easily the most publicity she'd ever had.

Tara Devine—London's newest It Girl?

She warily opened up the link on a tweet from the bitchiest blogger in town.

Answer—no! What's happened to party girl Tara? One week at Camp Cruz and she hits the scene looking like an homage to the Flintstones. Sorry, Tara, but you're def not rockin the It Girl look. Is this what happens when you hook up with a man? Last week you launched a kickass collection to the world. Grown-up Girlpower. This week? The wrong dress, the wrong hair and under the arm of the wrong man. Not sayin' any of us would kick Michael Cruz out of bed, but, girlfriend... what you doin', letting yourself be dragged home like carrion?

Well, she could have predicted that—but it still hurt. As did the dozen or so posts below it. There was no such thing as bad publicity? *Really?* In her position, with another fashion week to go, she couldn't afford to be making mistakes. She might even have made a Worst Dressed list somewhere. Where was her head at? What had she been thinking? So much for her carefully constructed image. Fashion designers just did *not* make bad fashion choices. She needed to get this sorted. And fast.

The wrong man.

Why on earth had that even got a mention? They were reading so much more into this than was real. Michael wasn't her 'man'. She didn't have room in her life for a man. And there was no doubt in her mind that he didn't see it that way either. He was…

Her mind rolled with images: of herself choking on her drink when she saw him that first time at the after-party, watching him walk away after he'd kissed her, him handing her the glass of rum and laughing at her nervousness as she knocked it back. Staring at their reflection in his bathroom mirror as he held her against him. He was…

He'd been vile. He'd been amazing. He'd been offensive and sweet and kind and loving.

His dark intense eyes as he handed her coffee, held her face in his hands, kissed her…

Then, this morning, sitting on the bed with a glass of water. Offering to film her for a documentary. Asking her about her mother. And listening to her answer.

She breathed in and closed her eyes, letting the memories wash over her.

Him leaning up on his elbows, filling her and gazing into her eyes. Complete. Replete.

He was too much. Too intense. Too close.

He was the last thing she needed.

She scanned more posts.

She needed to clear her head.

There was so much fallout after last night. Could she really blame him for it? Maybe not, but he hadn't helped.

So, the documentary—definitely not. And Lars—definitely.

She jumped up. She just needed to come clean—maybe tweet about wardrobe malfunctions. Laugh at herself online and then get back on the couture wagon.

Slip into something from her current collection and stalk Lars.

There was no way the last ten years were going to be ruined by an ill-chosen dress and a moment of weakness. OK, Michael was more than a moment of weakness—he was a seismic shift who had taken her on and trusted her with so much. He was everything—handsome, smart, the most sexually perfect partner she could ever imagine having. He was kind, trusting. But for these last few days she had lost herself in him. Lost who she really was. And she couldn't afford to do that. Couldn't afford to get knocked any further off track. Couldn't afford to fixate on him or dwell on the past the way he was suggesting.

Everybody knew where they were with Party Tara—especially her.

She braved the phone again and messaged her contacts. Someone had to know where Lars was. Time for favours to be called in.

By the time she emerged from the hotel room where Team Lars were holed up she had a sponsorship deal, a cash-flow solution and an invitation to dinner. Not a bad day's work considering she was so not an It Girl.

She made her way past the super-rich, who were accessorising the various corners of the hotel like throws and silk cushions. Sheikhs, thin women in couture, couples in identical cruise wear, and then the bag lady types—usually the richest of them all.

She skipped along, feeling almost fantastic. A couple of hours' downtime and then on to meet Lars in Soho. She wasn't really sure what his MO was in all of this. He had a lot of cash. He was light on fashion in his portfolio. He had a big interest in her assets. It almost made her squirm. But, hey-ho, she could cope with that and then some.

She took out her phone.

Her breath caught in her throat.

A missed call from Michael. And another call from home. She screwed up her eyes. *Not yet. Please not yet.* She wasn't ready. Just not ready.

An eight-course, wine-matched dining marathon was not quite what she'd had in mind. Her heart sank after the wasabi sorbet, and she was counting the hours until the white chocolate mousse with truffle-roasted hazelnut and blueberry coulis. She could hardly say it, never mind eat it. And by the time she rolled out of here she would have gone up another dress size.

Lars was a sweet kid. That was all she could describe him as. Well, cute. He could be described as cute too. But he was way better suited to someone like Fernanda than to a woman like Tara, who'd lived through two editors of French *Vogue*. When she spent time with a man she wanted it to be someone who'd lived, who was intelligent, who could have a conversation that ran further than television stars and where to park your yacht. But that was way off in the future. Right now she wanted this night to end and her life to settle back down.

She turned her phone over to check for a message. Or a call. Nothing. Good—that was good. She could not cope with anything else right now. Once Paris was in the bag, maybe then she could stop and think. She could maybe meet Michael for lunch?.

Maybe not. *The wrong dress, the wrong hair and under the arm of the wrong man.* She couldn't get that

out of her mind. How could something that had felt
so right be so wrong? No, better to put distance between them—miles and miles of distance. Focus on the
show next week. Get the media focused on that side of
Devine Design again. A few photos with Lars would
be a good start.

It was when he put his hand on the small of her back
that she really began to get annoyed. Getting out of the
car to go to yet another function. Walking in and seeing Michael. And wanting to turn and run right back
out through the door.

It was a retrospective photography exhibition being
held in a cavernous nightclub, and she should have
known he would be there. He was with Angelica. He
was the most handsome man she had ever seen. He was
staring right at her. Even among the giant canvasses
of iconic images, huge portraits that seemed to have
stunned everyone else, he was like a beacon and she
couldn't take her eyes off him.

Lars dragged his hand across her back and looped
it over her shoulders. His fingers rested on the top of
her breast. Michael's eyes were like missiles. She was
pinned to the spot. His jaw was tense and almost totally square. His fabulous, loving mouth was set in an
angry line. She could feel the energy from across the
room. Angelica placed a hand on his arm, but it was
like a blade of grass on a tsunami.

Who the hell did he think he was?

OK, so maybe he'd been expecting her to return his
call…but she'd been busy! And agreeing to go to dinner and an exhibition with Lars was actually not a big
deal. It was the polite thing to do. It gave her that little
bit of distance she needed. And she'd been more than

up-front with Michael that she was not going to change who she was and how she did things just because *he* thought she should.

But he'd turned his head and was talking to a group of *his* type of people—all money, class and effortless charm. Wow. She was *so* not part of that scene. Thank god. She was so different from him. Even though there had been times when she'd felt absorbed by him, part of him—as if no one else in the world understood her like him. But that had just been the heat of the moment. No big deal.

She needed a drink. Even with his back to her she could still feel his presence. He was still making her feel that she needed her shield. And her sword. Or her running shoes.

She checked that there was no press. There was no press. But there might be some opportunists. She shrugged her shoulders out of Lars's octopus arm and made her way to…to anywhere other than this public arena.

A few people stopped her, complimented her on her clothes—the red version of the cream satin dress she'd been wearing that first night she'd met Michael. In-laid with darts of rubber and more than a nod to the fetish scene.

'Wrap that round ya, Cruz,' she muttered to herself.

She moved through the crowd. Fielded a few questions about Lars. Laughed off a few bitchy comments about last night's exit. Tried to bluff out her media thrashing.

The eight matched wines had been small measures, drunk slowly, but there was no doubt that her senses

were a bit dulled. She ordered a shot to give her an edge.
Lifted the glass to her mouth.

'Tara.'

She let the glass hover, then downed it. Slapped it
down on the bar. 'What?'

'You tell *me* what.'

'I'll tell you what, all right.' She knew she was making a mistake taking him on. In public. And after the
day that she'd had. But he wasn't her keeper and she
had every right to sink a few. 'Thanks to you I've had
a fantastic time explaining your caveman tactics from
yesterday. *Oh, how we laughed. Oh, how I loved Michael grabbing me up and stuffing me in his car*—said
no one—ever.' She nodded to the barman. 'Same again.'

'You don't need another, Tara. You need to go
home—preferably with me. You've had a lot to drink
and it's been a tough day for you. I've seen the media.
I know how you'll be feeling.'

His voice was low, totally uncompromising. Utter
control and no room for manoeuvre. But he was dealing with her. Not his sisters. Not his idealised version
of a woman who did as she was told.

'Wrong, Michael. You don't know how I'm feeling—
you *think* you do, because you think you know everything. But you don't know me. And don't even *think*
about laying a finger on me to drag me out of here.'

He was right beside her now. Looking down with
that intense dark stare. She turned right round to face
him—body to body. And what a body it was. She knew
it. She felt drawn in to the energy he radiated. It would
be so easy—so gloriously easy to wrap her arms around
him and let her mouth tug out those divine kisses. She

was right inside his arc of strength. He was everything. No touch but he could twist her to his will.

'I'm not taking you anywhere you don't want to be. But you were in too deep last night and you're heading that way again tonight. And the worst of it is you don't even want to be here—it's obvious. You put on your smile and you put up your hair and the Tara Show comes to town.'

'The Tara Show? Is that what you think I am? A pantomime?'

'I think right now that you're spoiling for a fight. And I don't know why.'

She turned back to the barman, who had lined up her next shot. Truly, the thought of it was making her feel slightly sick.

'I don't want to fight. I just want to be me. And that's not a pantomime—or a show. Until I met you I didn't have any self-doubt. None. I knew where I was going and I knew how to get there. But now? Now I'm questioning every move that I make—every dress that I wear. And I'm getting it all wrong!'

She heard her voice getting more and more high-pitched. Picked up the shot glass. Held it between them. 'I don't even know if I want to sink *this*. That's how you've got me! All over the place. I missed a call with a really high-end fashion editor. I forgot...*forgot*...to get my transport sorted until it was nearly too late! I'm losing control.'

She threw the liquor down her throat and winced as it burned. Slammed the glass down.

'Feel better after that?'

She hiccoughed. 'Much.'

He trailed his finger down her cheek. Warm, soft, tender.

'It doesn't always have to be the hard path, Tara.'

She felt the pull of him. Oh, he was so tempting—she could so easily reach out and touch his chest. Feel his heat and wrap herself up in it. But that wasn't going to help. She needed space and distance—not more closeness.

'I'll be leaving shortly. Angelica is meeting Sebastian and I want you to come with me. Let me look after you, *querida*.'

She rolled her eyes. 'Stop trying to order me about, Michael. Don't you know me by now? That just gets my back up.'

She turned back to the barman. 'Spring me another. Please.'

'Wow, Tara—you're determined to wreck this, aren't you? You're really set on another night like last night—and you know I'm not going to be here to pick up the pieces.'

'I've never needed anyone to pick up after me. I sort things for myself, Michael. No interference necessary. Thanks all the same.'

He held his hands up and stepped back. 'You know where I am and you know what I want. But I'll not bother you again—not while you're working through whatever it is that's eating you alive like this.'

She grasped the shot glass that had been placed before her. Closed fingers round the glass that was already sticky with liquor. Threw it down her throat. Closed her eyes and felt it burn. Coughed. And when she looked round he was gone.

For a moment she wanted to run, to chase after him. She actually felt him withdrawing, leaving, and the force of it hit her hard like another sucker punch. She braced two arms on the bar. Dipped her head. Felt a huge, harsh sob swell from her soul and bit down hard. She couldn't lose it here. She *couldn't*.

She stifled it and swallowed and kept her head low, until she was sure she could walk without her legs buckling. But the tears had gathered—a thick film that swelled over her eyes. She couldn't see where she was going. Two slim arms reached for her, steered her to a corner. Angelica. Hugging her and holding her and shushing her.

'Tara. Go after him. He only wants to do the right thing for you. I know it. I can see it. He loves you. I'm sure he does.'

But Tara shook her head as the tears began to fall. Even if it was true she couldn't let herself open up any more. She had so much riding on these next few days. Her success. Her sanity. What good would it do to go after him? To say sorry? To tell him she loved him? How could she be sure she even knew what love was?

'I can't, Angelica. He's not right for me. He's too much. I can't take that amount of control in my life. I'm the boss of me—not any man. And Michael is more than any man I've ever met—it's who he is. It defines him. I need to be defined by me and me alone. He would swallow me up. I already feel I've lost my way and things are falling apart.'

She squeezed her friend's hand and then slipped out of her grasp. She needed to go now. At least she had figured one thing out—at least she knew now for sure that she was better off alone permanently. All those feelings of leaning on Michael, being absorbed by him and enjoying his strength—so tempting, but so wrong.

She walked to the doors. Squared her shoulders. Wiped her eyes and fixed her smile.

CHAPTER ELEVEN

IT WAS A day like any other. Michael told himself that over and over. If he viewed it as anything else he would risk getting caught up in the hysteria that seemed to have settled like an electric storm over this corner of Catalonia. Thankfully he'd left the house to the girls, so the frenzy was only an imprint rather than the real deal.

He drained his third coffee of the day and looked over at Angelica's fiancé, Sebastian. Pacing. He'd been up for hours and the strain was already beginning to tell. Crazy that people put themselves through this. Actually volunteered to tie themselves in knots—not only in the preparation, but then on the day.

Even the most cool and collected of them all—Angelica—had been showing signs of stress in the past forty-eight hours. And he'd never, ever witnessed that before. Fern, of course, was playing the sulky teenager to perfection. Like a military strategist. Withdrawn, one-word answers, and then without warning she'd flare up and fire a couple of missiles that took everyone by surprise. Maybe he'd been like that at one point. Who knew?

There was so much going on at work too. His phone was permanently in his grasp but he'd cleared everything for what he was determined was going to be a turning point in his life. That seemed to have taken his assistant by surprise, because in the past few months he had agreed to almost everything to do with business.

Nothing better for getting a sense of perspective than to immerse yourself in a new project and bring it home. He wasn't stupid. He knew that his ventures were his way of dissociation from the events that had happened six months earlier. With Tara.

Leaving that photography exhibition without throwing her over his shoulder had been one of the hardest things he'd ever done—he who prided himself on his self-control and on the unflinching compliance of others. But she had to *want* to come. She had to control herself. And he had to let her. Though it had almost killed him.

He could still see her so vividly—standing at that bar, in that red satin dress, looking like every man's fantasy. But only truly totally his. And the way she'd been knocking back those shots, as if every one was underlining more and more the Tara she wanted the world to see.

He had ached to take her in his arms, to show her with his body that she was so much more. To tell her that it was her courage that he loved, her wit, her passion. Her heart. But she might never have forgiven him if he'd acted the caveman again. He hadn't been able to risk that. He'd had to give her the space she needed. So there had been no alternative—he'd had to walk away. And that had really, truly taught him a lesson.

It had taken some solid hours of his life. Alone. Working through who he thought he was and who he thought *she* was. Coming to terms with the fact that she wasn't going to roll up at his door and beg him to let her in. Battling with himself to stay away—because he really couldn't trust himself not to use his body, their red-hot sexual chemistry, to get her to submit to what he wanted—which was her in his life for ever.

He'd had to come to terms also with the fact that the issues that were in her mind might never be fixed. There was a lot buried inside that beautiful head of hers. Maybe too deeply buried. He'd had time to piece together the little she'd told him. Growing up as an unwanted baby, her mother's guilty secret, in a house ruled by fear. If that was what she had suffered throughout her childhood it was going to take an awful lot of love to put right. All he could hope was that she had left the door open wide enough for that still to happen. And that it was him she was going to let in. The part he had to master was his almost pathological need to break it down and force her to see that.

She could not and would not let anyone do anything to help. Unless she decided it for herself.

So it was a question of timing. She would work this stuff out. One day. But life moved on. She might meet someone else—someone who would be there when she finally crossed the emotional rivers she swam in to reach the other side. But how long until she was ready for that? He had seen enough of life to know that you couldn't force that kind of personal growth. Would she still be single when it all fell into place for her? Would she wait for him?

But he had faith. And he believed in luck. Believed you made your own, and Tara seemed to be doing just that.

He flicked through the apps on his phone. His guilty

secret. After the small successes of her shows over the last few months things had really begun to take off. She had a blog now, for fashion TV, and he sometimes—OK often—read it. It was his way of keeping an eye on her while still keeping his distance. Giving her space. And she was good. She was developing her profile appropriately, in a way that suited her and that she clearly had control over. Her fan base had swelled and she seemed to be getting more credibility as a designer.

And that was what she needed. She needed approval and validation from people she respected. Fair enough. That was a natural reaction. One day she would realise that it was approval and validation from herself that would show she really had moved on. He hoped for her sake that that day wasn't too far ahead.

He scanned the blog. It said it all.

Summed up the craziness of what he was about to walk into.

Wedding of the Season: Angelica Cruz and Sebastian Frietze. In less than twenty-four hours the legendary Catalonian beauty and heiress will marry her long-time sweetheart Seb Frietze.

You've all been waiting to see why a goddess like Angelica would choose to ask a demonia-devotee such as myself to design the dress for her very, very special day, and all I can say is... wait and see! I'm not gonna lie and say that she's going to shimmy her way down the aisle in rubber or latex, and the wedding favours are not going to be handcuffs, but she's pushed some very important boundaries, girls!

And as for her bridesmaid, Fernanda? Let's

say you'd better clear your diaries for the whole
of next week as you check out the online frenzy
that's going to follow this teenage idol. Oh, and
finally, there's no truth in the rumour that the men
will be wearing gimp masks.

She was a little witch. He had no doubt that that was
a prod at him rather than Sebastian. A dig at his 'ultra-
conservative' image that she had taken great delight in
ripping him for. He smiled. Flicked the photo on the
screen larger. Seeing her winking by-line photo grin
up at him, he smiled even more broadly. How he loved
that face. He loved the mocking intelligence in her eyes.
He loved her quirky teeth and the way her face tilted so
happily with her smile. He loved those lips, those kisses.
Man, how he missed her kisses. Missed her. Ached for
her. Loved her.

When had he known? He'd asked himself that over
and over. So many flashbacks of so many treasured
moments. But it had been when she was least 'Tara'—
when she had been stripped of everything she thought
made her who she was—no super-styled hair, no make-
up, no crazy clothes. When she had been in his kitchen
dressed in that huge white robe. Just a person. The most
adorable person in the world.

Well, Ms Devine—I'll be seeing you soon enough,
he thought. And he knew he had everything riding on
getting this just right. He'd stayed out of the way while
she was scooping up the rewards of Fashion Week. He'd
given her all the space she needed to forge more success
with her business. And he'd stayed well away from all
the talk about her carefully orchestrated by Angelica.

He'd even withstood the temptation to catch her at

the house before she made last-minute adjustments to the dresses, but in less than two hours he was going to be face to face with her. And he was determined. This would be nailed. Finally.

Tara's fingers were sausages. Her head was soup—and not consommé. Angelica stood before her, Fernanda and her phone sat at the side of her—and if she was on social media she was going to be toast.

She knew that this was the design of her life. And she couldn't have dreamed up a better model to showcase it. Angelica's classical beauty was the perfect foil for the slightly *outré* but totally feminine dress that she had designed. On anyone else it would be too corseted, too burlesque, too much. On Tara herself it would look like she was auditioning for the lead as *Bride of Frankenstein*, but on Angelica it looked truly divine.

She should be content. Excited, but content. It was the culmination of weeks of collaboration and fittings. But it was excitement at seeing the other Cruz sibling that was eating her alive. She couldn't believe Michael had walked out of her life like that. She'd been so sure that he'd come over all caveman and drag her off later that night, or at least in the days that followed. She'd begun to prime herself to accept that that was just his way, and that she should swallow her horror and maybe come to terms with it.

But he hadn't come back. Hadn't called, texted or in any way made contact. Had left her with a massive gap that came from the immense physical and emotional contact that had been withdrawn, turned off, extinguished. And she had hurt. So badly. Not even the amount of business her sales agent had managed to generate with stores all round Europe had completely erased the bleakness she felt. Just putting one foot in front of the other and breathing had become harder than she'd ever have thought possible.

Still, she had taken the time to really work herself out. And that hadn't been pretty. At all…

The make-up artist and hairdressers were finishing off. She had declined to let them near herself—she'd already lived through one of those disasters, when Angelica's hairdresser had thought he understood her look and she'd had to pull the whole lot out and fix it herself later. No, the last thing she could afford to look today was anything other than lovely.

Her own dress was also new. Showcasing a new mood, a new muse. A new understanding of her own femininity and personality. And she'd be lying if she said she hadn't designed it knowing Michael's eyes were going to fall on it.

In approximately two hours.

Sebastian's anxiety was viral. Michael had contracted a severe case of pacing and hand-wringing himself now. And even standing at the foot of the stairs, waiting for Angelica to descend with her one bridesmaid and her one dress designer, he could only be grateful that he was hidden from the sight of the two hundred or so of Angelica's 'close' friends—aka projects—who had gathered in their garden to watch this wedding.

And of course she was going to be late—more hand-wringing—and it would be hours before he got a chance to speak to Tara alone. To see where they were going. And to make sure it was together.

He heard a noise from upstairs. Felt tension and excitement waft down to him like heavy perfume. Top notes of high-pitched voices and hints of hysteria. He began to feel—actually, was it flu coming on? This was so, *so* not like him.

And there they were. His sister looked stunning. Truly he'd never seen Angelica look so beautiful. And even Fernanda was more breathtaking than usual. But it was the small strawberry blonde behind them that his eyes searched for. And as his sisters moved downstairs and Tara finally came into view it was her blue eyes that found his. And the world felt better

With every step that she took he locked her with his eyes. He told her he loved her. He'd missed her. He told her she was not going to get away from him again without a fight. He never let his gaze falter for a second until he had to stretch out his arms to his sister. And then he looked at Angelica with pride. Because this was her day. And he was her brother. And he would do everything he could to make sure she got the best start to her married life.

Angelica beamed. A tear was in her eye. She stood at the foot of the stairs and let Tara reassemble her train. She looked voluptuous, like a goddess, a screen siren—he'd never seen her that way.

And as Tara stood, finally content with the way each layer of dove-white satin and antique lace was lying, Angelica, ambassadorial as ever, took their hands. 'I'm so, so happy you're both here for this day.'

Tara looked at him. Strong, but fragile—sure, yet open. Her perfect porcelain skin was lush with health and he wanted her more than life itself. She nodded the truth of her heart into his eyes and he braced himself to do this duty for Angelica. They would have their time to sort out the words that needed to be said soon enough.

Tara was basking in the comments from the guests. She was basking in Angelica's joy and Fernanda's happiness. And she was absolutely luxuriating in the attention she was getting from Michael. He hadn't taken his eyes off her all day—since she'd seen him at the foot of the stairs, looking as if he'd been cast from the most enchanted spell. He was more than handsome, more powerful, stronger, more solid, cleverer, kinder than anyone she had ever known. And she knew that just by breathing the same air as him.

He walked towards her now and she knew that their moment was coming.

'Tara.'

She put down her champagne flute carefully, untouched, not even a lipstick stain on it.

'I've missed you.'

He stepped up close and placed first one slow kiss, then another on each of her cheeks. He circled her waist with his hand and he made her feel simply cherished.

'I've missed you too.'

She allowed herself to be led to a corner. There were guests milling all over the house. A buffet was on offer and the joy of the day was still in its infancy. Her duties were done but his were stretching out ahead. This moment was going to be short, but she would know how his heart lay.

'You look…simply beautiful.'

She sat down beside him, still not taking her eyes off him. His skin was paler without its summer tan, but his lips were dark as red wine and his eyes were a warm, rich brown. She scanned his face and saw fine laughter lines, involuntarily trailed her fingers there.

'It's so…so good to see you, Michael.'

He took her hand from his face, held it to his mouth, turned it round and kissed her open palm. All the hot, physical love she had missed rose and bubbled immediately, shocking her with its intensity. And he read that and smiled at the gasp she had released.

'It's been too long, *querida*. But we both needed the space.'

'Did we?'

It didn't feel like that to her. It had felt like she was incomplete. Especially since she had waited and waited for him to contact her. And that just hadn't happened.

'I was sure you were going to get in touch. In fact I was sure you were going to haul me off to your cave.'

She laughed and he smiled, turning her hand over in his, enclosing her fingers, trailing his thumb across the veins of her wrist.

'It's not that I didn't think about it. Maybe daily— maybe every hour on the hour.'

He smiled into her eyes and she had to know—had to wonder if their intoxicating kisses were going to be as good as in her dreams. She bent forward into his space, closed her eyes and felt the firm seal of his lips. She moulded her mouth and slipped her tongue to taste him. It was better than good. It was hot. It was perfect. She pushed her chest forward and reached out to touch him. Felt the firm ridge of his biceps where her hands landed lightly on his arms.

'I wish you had. How I wish you had.'

She felt him cup her face, holding her just out of reach as he looked at her. He'd done this before and then she'd taken it as a sign that he was withdrawing. This time she knew that he was only savouring, reading her, learning,

'Tara, if I had done that you might have come, but you would have resented me for it.'

'It would have put me out of my misery.'

'I know—and it would have ended mine. But you're not a trophy, and I'm not looking for that in my woman. I need someone strong, independent. I need a match, Tara, not a princess.'

Really? She smiled. Then that was a total turn-around. It sounded like the right words, but she couldn't see the Michael Cruz she knew really meaning them.

'Michael. You're the most dominant man I've ever known—just think back to the very first time we met. At the after-party. Fernanda was hiding from you and Angelica was using me as a decoy. And you seduced me—swept me off my feet so much that I was happy to jump into bed with you. That's not the behaviour of an equal rights activist in touch with his feminine side.'

He chuckled briefly. 'Well, let's not labour the "in touch with my feminine side" part too much—let's call that an objective rather than an actuality. But you're right. OK. In some ways, yes, you're right.'

Well, this was progress. She'd never expected to hear those sentiments coming out of his mouth.

'But you've also got to remember that I was, and still am, responsible for a girl who has diva potential in every pore of her being. If I hadn't taken a hard line with Fernanda who knows what kind of nonsense she'd be up to? It's hard enough, Tara. But she takes a lot of work—as you know.'

'Like her big brother.'

He leaned in for a gorgeous, long, sensual kiss and she melted right there.

'I'm a pussycat where you're concerned.'

'Now you're just being ridiculous. And you know that I no more want a pussycat than you want a hard-ass bitch.'

'Sounds like we might be learning to compromise, then.'

He kissed her again. Melted what was left. Someone approached them—Sebastian.

'Michael, I'm sorry to interrupt, but Angelica is asking for you?'

For a moment he looked as if he wasn't going to move, or he hadn't heard. Then his face softened. 'I'll be right there.' He ran his hands up and down her arms. 'I have to finish this for Angelica and Seb. But I want us to have time to talk. Properly talk. Without our lust for each other getting in the way. I mean that, Tara. I think it's really important for us to clear up the stuff that's plagued us up until now. Hmm?'

She nodded. Really, the last thing she wanted to do was talk if there was even half a chance of getting naked any time soon. She'd never thought she had a high sex drive before, but sitting here without ripping his clothes off was a real test of character.

'I'm not going anywhere. I'll be here when you're ready. We've got a lovely day ahead with Angel and Seb, and I'm just so glad to be here to share it with them.'

'Good, baby. That's good. We'll have plenty of time later.' He gave her another drugging kiss and then stood up.

She watched him walk away, so tall, so erect, so in control of the whole room, of his whole world.

She felt the back of her hair. A couple of pins had fallen out of her loose French roll. Why was she such a slave to fashion? If Mario and the guys she used for her shows had said *tight* French rolls were in she would have backcombed, pinned and sprayed like a fiend. And then she wouldn't have had to worry about her hair all day. Loose French rolls? One of fashion's more stupid ideas.

She stood up and went upstairs to her room. She could check her messages, maybe even have a glass of iced tea and change her shoes. The day couldn't be going any better.

She closed the door of the guest bedroom and headed to the dressing table. Started to undo the remaining couple of pins from her hair and kicked off her heels. They were beautiful. They were a quid pro quo promotion by a colleague she was in partnership with, and they'd served their purpose, but no way was she going to last the day in them.

Her phone sounded. She glanced at it. She would get it in a minute.

She moved to the mirror, looked at herself. Although he hadn't commented, Michael couldn't have failed to notice the change in her. Everyone else had. She was still Tara Devine, but she was just a bit less full-on, a bit softer. Her designs this season were still super-flattering for curves, and still oozed sex appeal, but she liked to think she'd found dignity and an air of mystery…even if it was just an inch lower on the hem and higher on the cleavage. It was something to keep the critics in column inches anyway.

Her phone sounded again. She picked it up. The screen was covered in messages. She held it in her hand and looked at them all. There was no ignoring it this time. Missed calls. Texts. And she knew without even opening them up what they were about.

She sank onto the bed. The last contact had been to tell her that he was ill and ask if she wanted to come home. Were they out of their minds? she had said. Another couple of attempts had been made.

Maybe it was the way she had been feeling about Michael, although she doubted it, but she had almost, *almost* spoken about it. Had wondered if it was time and had actually looked up a therapist's phone number. Maybe she should now. Maybe she would. There was no doubt it was all going to come to the surface now. No doubt that something serious had happened. And no doubt she would have to deal with it…

It was only when the door opened that she realised how long she had been sitting there. It was Michael. He walked to her. There was no need to discuss anything. He just knew. Just his being in the room consoled her. And she felt another part of the dark shadow within her fade and die.

'Tara? What's wrong?'

He scooped her into his arms and she sat there numbly. Just being held. Words were in her heart somewhere, but she couldn't feel them or properly form them yet. He soothed her and held her close. Maybe it was the beat of his heart—slow, steady, reassuring. Maybe it was how far she'd come already herself on her journey. But she knew that she was going to get past this.

She swallowed. Tried to sit up. 'Just some news from home.'

He looked at her closely. She felt such a wave of love from him. Returned it. She didn't even need to say the words—she just knew how he treasured her. There were so many more important things for them to fix than any old skeletons in her closet. They needed to talk about practical things—like how he was going to cope with her moods when she had one of her catastrophising fits when stylists totally misinterpreted her fifties fetish in a Thunderbird vision in her latest ad campaign, or when make-up artists put far too much smudge into her 'slept in my mascara' catwalk look. What was wrong with people that they didn't get that? These were the kinds of things that could really bring her down.

'Tara, any news from home, or anything else you want to share with me, I'm here for you, *querida*.'

He looked so concerned. And it was like drinking an elixir. She reached out and cupped his cheek, kissed his lips.

'I know, Michael. I know. And truly, truly, I will tell you everything. We'll fix this together. Just not today. Not on Angelica's special day.' She had to have his mouth then. Had to feel the force of his love around her. 'Do you think anyone would miss you for ten minutes?'

'Tara, I think they're surprised I've not disappeared before now. But we promised we would talk. We *should* talk.' He gripped her face and took her mouth. 'But I can't get enough of you. I'll never have enough of you.'

She felt almost overwhelmed by the force of his kiss. But she gave it right back.

'Tara, I love you. I haven't told you yet.'

'You didn't need to. I can see it. I can feel it. You've wrapped me up in it. I love you too, by the way.'

He laughed and showered her face with more kisses. 'Yeah?'

'Yeah. But we still need to agree who's the boss.'

'No contest. You are.'

She grinned. 'Really? *Really?*'

He grinned back. 'Well, unless you step out of line. Then I might have to get physical.'

He kissed her in between each word. Pushed her back down on the bed.

'This kind of physical I can deal with. As long as you know that I'm still going to be the boss.'

The pull of their mutual desire was huge. It had been building for all these months and she had to let it take over. Had to be imprinted on him, had to breathe his air and learn his body all over again.

She flipped round, lifted her skirts past her thighs and straddled him. He lay back on the bed, undid his trousers and pulled out his hot, heavy erection. She shifted her tiny pants to the side as it stiffened in her hand. Looked at him. He reached up to her face, cupped it the way she liked him to. She turned her head and kissed his palm—and then they could wait no longer. He filled her. She filled him. Love and passion in balance.

'I only want this. Only this. You and me. For ever.'

He touched her, made love to her, and she knew then that every last demon was exorcised. She had no need to defend herself. No need to fight. No need to fear. He turned her round, slipped his arms under her and held her close while he rocked them both to their peak. And when they finally lay together, entwined in hot limbs and breath and happiness, she whispered her love to him over and over.

A total connection. A total partnership. Totally true.

EPILOGUE

BY THE TIME the last of the models had done her final turn Tara was ready to make the trek herself. She linked arms with Fernanda, and Angelica, her most special guest. Angelica's agreement to model some of her new bridal collection had been the total icing on the wedding cake after the media furore generated by her first bridal design. The plans she had begun to sketch for her own dress were still strictly private, and even though she now shared everything with Michael this was one design he would only see on the day itself—in six months' time.

She smiled at her girlfriends. What a team.

Fernanda was easily the most marketable model she'd ever known: a darling with the press and muse of one of the most famous French fashion houses. And all of that fitted in with her studies, just to be sensible. Angelica's new role with UNICEF was keeping her very busy, but Tara was sure there would be other more personal news she would be sharing soon. There was no way her waist had thickened like that by itself.

Some terrifying people had attended today, but the immediate reaction had been positive and the knot in her stomach had loosened and shifted. She squeezed her *amigas*, stepped forward and paused.

Polite applause and raucous cheers. And there in the front row was her darling, her Michael. Easily the most handsome man in the room, and putting his charm to good use sitting beside one of the most formidable fashionistas, who looked actually—happy!

She stepped out, keeping pace as best she could with the long-limbed beauties. And as Michael's eyes caught hers, as they always did and always would, the euphoria she felt at her success was redoubled by the knowledge of his pride and their love. She winked at him and he beamed right back.

She toured past him, down and back up. He was with her every step of the way, showing the world and, more importantly, showing her that even though he still preferred to dress like a boring banker, as she called it, he could appreciate her art and her creativity.

Which was just as well because, oh, yes, she thought, *she* was the boss. But later she hoped he would get as physical as possible—just to keep her guessing.

* * * * *